HARLAND'S HALF ACRE

David Malouf is internationally recognised as one of Australia's finest writers. His novels include *Johnno*, *An Imaginary Life*, *Harland's Half Acre*, *The Great World*, which won the Commonwealth Writers' Prize and the Prix Femina Etranger in 1991, and *Remembering Babylon*, which was shortlisted for the 1993 Booker Prize and won the inaugural IMPAC Dublin Literary Award in 1996. He has also written five collections of poetry and three opera libretti. He lives in Sydney.

ALSO BY DAVID MALOUF

Fiction

Johnno
An Imaginary Life
Fly Away Peter
Child's Play
Antipodes
The Great World
Remembering Babylon
The Conversations at Curlow Creek

Autobiography

12 Edmondstone Street

Poetry

'Interiors' (in Four Poets)
Bicycle and Other Poems
Neighbours in a Thicket
Poems 1976-7
The Year of the Foxes and Other Poems
First Things Last
Wild Lemons
Selected Poems

Plays

Blood Relations

Libretti

Baa Baa Black Sheep

David Malouf

HARLAND'S
HALF ACRE

VINTAGE

Published by Vintage 1999

6 8 10 9 7 5

First published in Great Britain in 1984 by
Chatto & Windus

Vintage
Random House, 20 Vauxhall Bridge Road,
London SW1V 2SA

Random House Australia (Pty) Limited
20 Alfred Street, Milsons Point, Sydney
New South Wales 2061, Australia

Random House New Zealand Limited
18 Poland Road, Glenfield, Auckland 10,
New Zealand

Random House South Africa (Pty) Limited
Isle of Houghton, Corner of Boundary Road & Carse O'Gowrie,
Houghton 2198, South Africa

Random House UK Limited Reg. No. 954009

A CIP catalogue record for this book
is available from the British Library

ISBN 9780099273837

HARLAND'S HALF ACRE

KILLARNEY

[1]

Named like so much else in Australia for a place on the far side of the globe
that its finders meant to honour and were piously homesick for, Killarney
bears no resemblance to its Irish original.

It is lush country but of the green, subtropical kind, with sawmills in
untidy paddocks, peak-roofed weatherboard farms, and on the skyline of
low hills, bunyah pines, hoop pines and Scotch firs of a forbidding
blackness. Tin roofs flare out of an acre of stumps. Iron windmills churn.
On all sides in the wet months there is the flash of water. These are the
so-called lakes. Rising abruptly around fence-posts to turn good pasture
for a time into a chain of weed-choked lily-ponds, they are remnants of a
sea that feeds one of the great river systems of the continent – fugitive, not
always visible above ground, but attracting at all times of the year a variety of
waterfowl and real enough to have had, when the native peoples were here,
an equally poetic name that no one has bothered to record.

Harlands are brought up on the story of how they won and then lost the
land.

First the overland trek from somewhere beyond Tamworth into an
unsettled area that was immediately, to the three brothers, so much like
home (so much that is like a place they had never laid eyes on but whose
lakes and greenness were original in their minds) that their breaking out of
a gap to see it laid mistily before them was like a recovery and return.
'Killarney,' they breathed and were there.

Possession was easy. One brief bloody encounter established the white
man's power and it was soon made official with white man's law. Subse-
quent occasions, if less glorious, are still recounted with Irish pride in the
extravagance of their folly. Within a generation the Harlands had squan-
dered most of what they owned and were reduced to day-labouring for
others; or, like young Clem Harland, to grubbing a livelihood from odd
patches of what was once a princely estate.

A dreamy, fresh-faced, talkative youth, not keen on hard work, he had been spoiled by his mother, half-educated at a boarding school at Toowoomba and had his twelve acres in a direct line from the eldest of the Harland brothers, Jack. He married early a woman several years older than himself, a draper's daughter from Harrisville, a passionate girl whose awkward intensity put stolid men off – but not Clem.

Lying in bed together in the spare, clean one-roomed house that was full of the moonlit reflection of chairbacks, they would have time for talk. While she filled the chairs with figures whose names she did not know – or not yet – he would be laying out for her his boyish notions of the life they were to share.

He was full of notions, all cloudily unreal. She was waiting for him to grow out of them. For them to be drained out of him by the seven days a week of milking and feeding and sluicing out the bails, of driving the cattle to pasture and hefting the cans full of frothy saltish milk to the bench beside the road. She was attracted by his dreams but her own life was grounded in what she could touch. She could do no more for the moment than help him over his time of useless yearning and believe that the routine of daily existence, as it toughened and refined him, would bring him home at last to the actuality of things.

She would lie awake feeling the weight of his arm across her and listening in the dark to the drawing of his breath, to the slow mysterious power of life in him. Sometimes when he was out of the house she would take up a shirt she was about to scrub at the washboard and be overwhelmed by his hot presence, or weighing in her palm the little mouth organ he played after tea, would put her lips to it.

She sought no tunes of her own. The touch of wood and metal was enough, and the echo of his breath. Then there were her chairs, and the rose bushes she was determined to bring back from the wild, the eggs she had to get down on her knees to find, following the chooks into their brooding-places in the grass, the set of stepped canisters on the top shelf of the dresser, her satin-lined sewing basket with its darning-egg and thimble, and the quilt that covered their sleep.

She had made that herself while she was waiting for her stale maidenhood to be over, out of some old calico tablecloths and a set of green velvet curtains from her mother's lounge, and given time she thought she could make something of Clem as well. She was very determined. She had refused to be left on the shelf or to accept that the feeling she had for the world, and all its visible touchable objects, had no life beyond her.

What she failed to see was that talk for Clem was its own reality. It was to him what drink had been to others of the Harlands, or cattle, or land. He made himself up out of it. He made the world up out of it. His cloudy speculations, the odd questions he put, the tales he told of experiences that had come to him at different times and places, were flesh and spirit to him because they touched on what he was most deeply moved by, the mystery of *himself*.

'Listen,' he would begin, his voice low with excitement, 'there was this time – I was sixteen or seventeen, about that age – anyway a youngster – you know, full of the first urge of things. Everything, I don't just mean women,' and he would grin and look shyly away, especially if it was a woman he had begun to charm. 'Well, I was comin' back after a dance, barefoot, with my boots over my shoulder – I didn' wear boots much in those days, except f' dancin' – and as I come down past Mackays – you know the place, there's that old pepper-tree just at the turn of the road – well, I was a bit tired, from the dancin' an' that, and from yarning outside with the boys, an' I thought I saw somethin'. There was this mob in the horse-paddock, all shiftin' about in the moonlight with the moon playin' on 'em, and what do I see suddenly but this girl? Right in among the horses and sort of rolling over their backs like an acrobat. She was naked of course.' He swallowed. His adam's apple went up and down and his eyes were wide above the tanned cheeks. 'White she was, in the moonlight, and naked like a mermaid slipping in and out of the waves. So I jumped up into the tree to get a better look. Only the moment I took my eyes off of 'er she was gone.' The disappointment hit him as if it were new. He shook his head. 'I just sat there, looking, waitin' t' catch another sight of 'er, and must of dozed off, 'cause next thing I knew it was light, a lovely sunrise like streaky bacon, and I realized I was hungry. I got down pretty smart then in case someone saw me and thought I was cracked.'

He stopped, grinned, his adam's apple climbed and fell.

All his stories were like this. Evocative. Inconclusive.

'Well,' he would enquire after a pause, 'what do you make of it?' But the real question was 'What do you make of *me*?'

He was deeply puzzled by himself and went in hope that one of his listeners might see a point in what he had to tell that would turn him, in his own eyes, from a vague and shadowy figure to a clear one.

His wife found these stories distressing.

'Clem,' she would complain, 'that's all rot.'

'Is it, love?'

He wasn't at all abashed. His eyes were clear, round, bright with anticipation. He was waiting, shyly submissive, for her to enlighten him with her doubts.

'Anyway, you already told it to me.'

'Did I?'

'Yes you did. An' it was *different*.'

She would turn away in the lumpy bed. They already had one child, just eighteen months, blowing wet bubbles beside them, and she was expecting another.

'Madge? Madge? You aren't mad at me, are you?'

He would reach his hand out then to comfort or assuage her, or to follow a line of excitement in his story of which this had, all along, been the real object. What stirred him was what his telling most vividly created, that image of an earlier self standing barefoot with his boots over his shoulder, and his passionate yearning given the shape, in moonlight, of a naked girl among horses, a mermaid in the waves of an ocean he had not yet seen. When she softened and turned he had proof of himself. It was all real.

'Oh Clem Harland, you're impossible,' she moaned. 'What am I going to do with you!'

He laughed softly and appeared to make amends but was delighted with himself.

There were no wolves here, except in the stories they had brought with them into this half of the world, but she thought of the night as a grey wolf prowling beyond the house, and of the stars as its teeth. They were children, and she the stronger, holding each other hard against the dark.

The second child was again a boy. They called him Frank after her father as they had called the first one Jim after his. Six months later, with the two little boys on his hands, he was a widower. He was twenty-three.

It was all so sudden. He couldn't believe it. In the first days he was dumb with grief. He stumbled about the empty house with the children in his arms, or sat on the bed while they slept, like an older child who has wakened, found himself alone and is too numb with fear to weep. Often he would snatch the children up so that they too woke and cried. He would occupy himself then with comforting them. Sometimes, even at night, he would go out and confront the rose-bushes.

A rose thorn it had been. Blood poisoning. So sudden. He couldn't believe it.

He clung to his boys, nursing them as well as he could and refusing all help. There was a feminine side to him that made tending the children, bathing and changing them, feeding them, walking them up and down, feeling them nuzzle and squirm against him while he mouthed lonely baby-talk, a pleasure he would have been shy of admitting. He let the farm go.

But the cows suffered if they were not milked and he had to attend to them as well, to their feed and to the filling and hefting of the cans – every morning and afternoon the same cans with the day's milk swinging as he took its weight and walked three times back and forth to the road. He lost himself in the routine.

There was in him, after all, a recognition of the priority of these things. They were fixed, they demanded submission. He accepted the work now and let his grief be subsumed in it.

The two little boys, for ever trotting at his heels, plucking at the seat of his pants and murmuring, were a joy but also a hindrance. They were an odd sight, the father, not much more than a boy himself, and the two ragged children. Women took pity on him. They swept the little boys up in an ecstasy of cries and hugs and offers of motherly affection that included the young father, and the third of them, after a few months trial, he married.

By this time the older boy, Jim, was five and a bit; he could fend for himself. But Frank, once the new wife was pregnant, was a problem, and though he had never considered it when he had the two children to manage alone, Clem agreed now, after many nights of shame and self-accusation, to send the younger boy away. He had a sister, several years older than himself, who was married to a fruit farmer at Glen Alpin near Stanthorpe; they had just lost a son in France. She would look after Frank for a year or two and see that he was clothed and fed. The child would be well cared for

7

and Clem promised himself that he would ride across every couple of weeks to see him.

[2]

Frank Harland grew up with only the vaguest recollection of his other home.

What he remembered was a special quality of warmth, and outside, a vivid greenness and an expanse of blue where they had sometimes gone for a dip. There was only a muddy dam on his uncle's farm and rows of orderly trees, with knobbly twigs that developed swellings with a touch of pink in them that were flowers at first and later fruit – so round and luminous they looked as if they had never grown at all but had been hung for decoration under the leaves.

The ground between the trees was uneven, baked to a hard grey. It crumbled in his fist. The earth he had known before was black. Where the land was not fenced and planted, it was all dry slopes broken by great round boulders of a grey-brown colour. They thrust up out of the earth and were tilted, or they littered the slope like giant eggs rolled playfully downhill. Sometimes, as a joke, a big one had another smaller one balanced neatly on top. There was a time, you felt, when this place must have been less quiet than it was now. Frank would lie still and imagine all those great stones being shifted, or rolling about and crashing in the dark.

It was colder here, there were frosts. On winter mornings the trough in the yard would have a sheet of ice floating on it as thin as glass, and once, when a pipe to the sprinklers leaked, a crystal bud appeared and grew each day till there was a flower with huge ice-petals, on a stem nearly a foot thick.

His aunt's house had seven rooms instead of just one. There was a fireplace for which he carried wood, a carriage clock, the twin of one in his father's house, and a gramophone that had been his cousin Ned's. He was allowed to wind music out of it in a long long trail. It made his aunt cry. The carriage clock, last relic of a vanished grandeur, he stared at and puzzled over.

It soon became his favourite object here and the source, as he grew older, of his deepest musings. His aunt taught him to tell the time by it and he liked, at night, to hear it beat out the hours and halves, recalling how he had listened to the same sound in his father's bed and telling himself that the same hour was being struck now at home. It wasn't the same clock as the other, he understood that, but it kept the same time.

The twin clocks in their different pozzies – his aunt's on a table in the hall, his father's on a shelf among mouse droppings and dead matches and brown apple cores – became the poles of his world. He kept them both in mind.

In his other house he had slept with his father and Jim. He had his own bed here, in Ned's room, and got lost in it.

Those first nights, waking to a strange darkness, he had felt panic. Reaching out for Jim or for his father in the big cool spaces he had found nothing but sheet; though it would have been scarier of course if he had found the body of the cousin he had never seen, who was dead on the far side of the world, but whose shirts, all mended and ironed, hung in the wardrobe against the wall, and whose spirit haunted so much here. In particular a galleon made of glazed matchsticks that stood on the table beside his bed, and the blue kelpie Max, who was always waiting at the gate for Ned's familiar whistle. And the mind of his Aunt Else.

He saw sometimes, when she came in to get him up, that she was surprised to find him there, so little and sandy-headed; as if he had got into his cousin's bed by stealth.

It was a long time before he was used to the empty shirts in the wardrobe and the lonely bed.

The house too seemed lonely and big. His aunt liked swept spaces but grieved over them. There was no closeness. There were no cows either. Only trees that changed throughout the year, were fed with powder, and did not stray, whereas the cows back home had breathed and wandered and then come lumbering in like clouds out of the grass. They ate fodder and salt-cake and would feed, the littlest ones, the poddies, from your palm. Their tongues were rough and warm, their noses moist, and they had a sweet-smelling breath. You could get right in among them, and it was shitty but warm, and the sharp smell, which he never forgot, was the smell of where he came from. He thought he could smell it on his father, when he came each month to visit; but it might have been no more than the warmth he felt, and associated with the old byre smell, when he was picked up and carried inside his father's coat.

His two worlds were quite clear to him. They looked different, they smelled different, they had a different quality of warmth and cold. One was original, it was the place he came from. The other was the one he was in.

His aunt Else was a kind, strict, orderly woman, who disapproved of his father for some reason. That is, she listened to everything he said with a closed look on her face and a hard straight mouth. Uncle Jack said his father talked too much. 'Blarney' is what he called it.

Talk was not thought much of in his aunt's house and the boy grew up silent, learning to keep his thoughts to himself.

He went to school and in the afternoons and on holidays helped his uncle with the farm. It was a neat, well set-up orchard; his uncle was as particular about the running of it as his aunt was about the house. When the fruit was ready and the pickers came, he ran back and forth on messages between the kitchen and the pickers' shed, which was a noisy sort of place with everyone in shorts and singlets. He helped carry plates to where they ate at trestle tables under the trees, counted boxes as they were packed and nailed down, and watched while they were loaded on to the trucks that would take them to the markets in Brisbane. In the evenings his Uncle Fred showed him how to make things with matchsticks. The man had big hands, very cracked and hard from work, but was marvellously delicate when it came to rolling the little logs, and full of fantasy in the creating of stockades and castles. They worked at the kitchen table while Aunt Else did the ironing, and built together a cabin, an open boat with paddles and a bridge that lifted up for ships to go through.

It didn't interest Frank all that much – he did it to please his uncle – and the galleon Ned had made when he was only thirteen remained a reproach to the younger boy's lack of skill. He preferred drawing.

Uncle Fred began by showing him how to make a picture of a horse with high-stepping feet and a cart with a stiff little driver, and he quickly learned to make a livelier picture of his own. His horse had more fire; there was more detail in the eye, the nostrils, the mane. He went on from that to copying illustrations out of the newspaper, automobiles with curved mud-guards and spoked wheels, houses from the land agents' advertisements with wonderful trees and clouds. His hands, though small compared with his uncle's, were too clumsy for the matches but felt easy with a pencil. He loved the precision it took to recreate, detail by detail, and with delicate strokes for shading, the professionalism of the newspaper ads, and was delighted when his aunt accused him of tracing.

'But you must have,' she insisted. 'You did, didn't you, Frank? It's silly to tell a fib about such a *little* thing.'

He heard from his father of new brothers, and from Jim, who stayed overnight once on his way to a bush-children's holiday by the sea, of their stepmother, Sally.

'She's oright,' Jim admitted. 'A bit scotty but. She doesn' just go crook on yer, she flies f' the hair-brush, then feels sorry afterwards and cooks golden-syrup pudding, 'cause it's me fav'rit.' He gave a big-toothed grin. 'She's oright. She's got three small little kids to manage.'

When asked what he remembered of their real mother he looked embarrassed and had nothing to tell.

It was, perhaps, Jim decided, because he had never known Sally that Frank thought of their mother's place in the house as empty. It was not. Sally filled it with her flaring temper, her shouting and swearing at them all, her clattering about with pans, her preoccupation with nappies in a tub and with babies who were always tugging at her nipple or hauling at your knees under the chair.

Sally was only half grown-up. She had a scar above one cheek where a pebble had flicked up in the school playground. She went barefoot. And once, to Jim's astonishment, when she was fed up with them all, she had shinnied up the trunk of a pine-tree in the yard and refused to come down. She had just gone on climbing right to the top, swinging on the springy top boughs and shouting out all she could see. His father had come out of the cowshed in his boots, laughing at first, then anxiously pleading with her. But Sally, unwilling to give up her moment of tomboyish elation and high freedom, had told him to piss off. She had to be coaxed down like a cat.

When she did come at last, in a bit of a huff, her legs were all scratched and pricked with blood and his father that night had bathed them tenderly in warm water and Solyptol.

The wonder of all this Jim could not have conveyed. He would have had to admit how he too clung to Sally and accepted even her tongue-lashings and cuffs, and the attacks of tickling that left him helplessly squealing, as the effects of a female presence he could not have done without. She was mother and woman enough, Sally, to have replaced their real mother. He found Frank's attempt to revive that shadowy being and restore old loyalties disturbing.

But for Frank the question had had another point altogether. He was not surprised by his brother's blankness of memory.

The more he thought about it the more it seemed to him that he had had no mother at all but had been born out of some aspect of his father that was itself feminine; not in being soft or yielding, but in being, quite simply, powerful, and so full of animal warmth that it must inevitably give birth to something other than itself.

He had begun to think of himself as existing in a unique relationship to his father that ought not to be spoken of, and guessed that it was for this reason, as a kind of diversionary tactic, that his father had sent him away. They shared a secret, perhaps even a crime. How else explain the shyness his father showed before him – which he took to be of the same kind as that awe, that sense of being in the presence of the powerfully sacred, that he himself felt when, outside the influence of his aunt's house and her sceptical eye, he was swept up into the folds of his father's coat and carried out on to the slope.

There, seated together on a round boulder and gazing out beyond a landscape of cataclysmic upheaval towards the lush green valley that was Killarney, they would be in utter communion. His father would have a suffering look, as if their being together like this, and for such a short spell, evoked pain as well as love, or as if those emotions were insolubly linked or were the same emotion in different forms; like the two forces, male and female, out of which his father, by a process that was not to be referred to and which obeyed other laws than the ones he had observed among animals and learned from the brute facts of the school yard, had brought him to birth.

Breath – that was the sacred thing. Even the Bible said it. Hence the clear silences and bare swept spaces of his aunt's house, which was entirely secular, and on the other hand his father's *talk*, the endless flow of words on that caressing breath that must itself, Frank decided, be the creative medium. He could only have been breathed forth in a great bubble or spat bodily from his father's mouth.

His father's talk of his youth at Killarney, and the odd bits and pieces of family history he liked to retell, all mixed in as they were with myths, legends, jokes, facts, fables – these things explained to the boy's satisfaction, and more convincingly than anything he had been told either at church or at school, both what he was and where he had come from, and gave him such a vision of Killarney itself that he knew just how it would look when he returned there.

Every grass blade and bush, the many waterholes and their names, and the little round hills and farmhouses and timbermills and barns, were utterly familiar to him. Killarney was the realest place he knew. It had been created for him entirely out of his father's mouth.

[3]

All this was secret in the boy and would remain so. It belonged to a religiously preserved silence.

In the meantime he lived with the ordinary facts of school on five days of the week, farmwork on the others, and with such scraps of information as his aunt, who was a close and lonely woman, might impart to him on stormy afternoons when they had draped all the mirrors in the house against lightning, put away all the knives, and in rivalry with the rain that was drumming on the roof, sat knee to knee tumbling peas into a pot.

It took a good thunderstorm to shake words out of his Aunt Else.

'When me and your father were young,' she told, 'we were very poor. Poorer even than your father is now.'

She frowned, and might already after twenty syllables have felt piqued with herself for having said too much.

'He was younger than me, your father. Twelve years. And a fascinator. He got away with it. With everyone, including my mother. But not with me.' She looked for a moment at the peas lying side by side in the transparent shell and then pushed them out with her thumbnail. They clattered. 'I reckon he'll get away with it all his life. I used to think, people will see through him. In the long run, truth is truth. Only it isn't. He used to fascinate people because he was just a boy. Now he fascinates 'em with the same trick because he isn't. People never learn. He's always looking for sympathy, he makes use of everyone. He'll never change.'

He recognized in this some confession or complaint on his aunt's part that might be the nearest he would ever come to hearing her view, not just of his father but of life itself. Perhaps she intended it as a warning. In so far as it appeared to warn him against his father, he could not accept it.

He was just eleven.

Later, when he tried to establish in his mind the order of events, he would place this conversation in the midst of a storm whose beginnings he had seen from the top of a granite bluff; which means that it must have followed immediately on the announcement that he was to leave his aunt's house and go back. But he could never be sure of this. Storms were frequent in that part of the country, and he might simply have made this last storm the most violent he could remember, and then, conflating two passions – the one recklessly breaking, the other tightly held in – have transposed his aunt's words to the eve of his departure.

He had seen the storm's approach and had clambered up, using his bare feet and knees, to a viewpoint high above the farm, in a stillness, once he had reached the top, that seemed ultimate.

The birds had fallen quiet. They had gone in out of sight. Only a chicken-hawk, high up, sailed and propped, then stood perfectly still in the air as if it had been stopped by an invisible hand. The leaves around him were glowingly still. They seemed to have passed out of any reality in which they might be touched by rain or wind. They were transparent, you could see right through them.

It was the light. The granite outcrops and enormous stone eggs were also changed by it. They showed their fault lines going back into the earth.

The light was inside things. He thought of the stained-glass window of St. Michael's when there was a night service and all the colour and glory of the figures, afloat above clumps of darkness, existed for those outside – animals or tramps or ordinary passers-by on the road – for whom they had a brightness and clarity of line and form that was denied the kneeling congregation. It was as if he had got to the other side of things. It was the quality of his seeing that was changed. Every tree now started out of the earth as a separate object newly made; not a peach tree, one of a row, but *this* tree and no other, all the trees in their rows utterly separate one from another and casting shadows of individual shape on the sloping earth, which was all rough clods, each one golden brown and also lighted from within, and so real that it came to you as if it had been flung clean at your head.

On the horizon to the south-west a great stack of cloud was building and spreading, so fast that time might have been speeded up. Invisible pitchforks were at it. It tumbled within itself. It whirled and spiralled in wisps of blue, purple, black. It began to tease out and topple towards him.

It was the activities of this cloud that made the light so strange.

He looked at his hand. Even that was different. It had never before had quite this shape or colour.

Was he responsible? Had he brought this cloud into being as, through some power of wishing or working that he only half believed in, he had brought about the event that would take him away?

He took one last breathless look, which he would retain as his final view of the place – that was why he had climbed so high – and sliding down the smooth curve of the rock began to race the cloud home, controlling its tumbling power of growth and motion as he ran, watching it roll, within his will, right across the sky towards the town: an immense stack of water, tons and tons of it, suspended there, swirling and darkening everything its shadow touched, but at the same time catching it in a new light from within.

He ran fast.

Old Mr Koenig, whom he was fond of and would never see again, was out among his bee-boxes, covered with a gauze helmet like Ned Kelly and working quick spells with his hands. The bee-boxes were a brilliant blue. You could see the bees dancing in miniature storm clouds above them while Mr Koenig conducted.

The O'Deas were at the clothes props, shouting and hauling down sheets: Mrs O'Dea with the clothes basket, the two skinny girls, Francie and Rena, even Leo, who would be ashamed to be caught like this. Leo was his best friend at school. Or had been.

'It'll be a humdinger!' Jake Shoals called down to him, standing still a moment, halfway up a slope strewn with bits and pieces of machinery, car engines, the cabin of a truck, stacked oil drums, the ribs of a dismantled harvester. His wife Milly – they were their closest neighbours – was driving chickens into a shed, whose rusty blood-redness in the new light hurt.

High up on the roof of the house an iron sheet had risen and begun to flap. Jake Shoals had never got round to nailing it down – too busy always with the machines at his feet, which alone stayed anchored as the grass suddenly flattened and flowed uphill, and dry leaves, twigs and feathers ascended and whirled.

He ran as fast as he could. His breath was holding out, he didn't have a stitch, and the cloud was still growing.

His Aunt Else was terrified of thunder and would be alone in the house. There would be things to do, windows to fasten. And in a storm she liked to shut out the noise with talk. He was sharply aware as he ran that he would never see any of these things again, was taking leave of them and of a whole phase of life. He hadn't expected to have to do it on the run, or to find himself seeing them for the first time as well.

Milly Shoals turned and waved to him. Her luminous old dress was the colour of soft butter, and the chooks, leaping up and flapping their wings as she drove them in a dusty rabble, crowding, trampling one another, were of an angelic whiteness.

He turned up the long drive, still running under the cloud.

The first drops came, so big they splashed.

When he left next morning his aunt was upset and would have liked to cry over him but would not allow herself. He was fond of her and did not know what to say. She too had known that his father would take him back one day. She had insured herself against a second grief by never really giving herself to him. 'Be a good boy,' was all she said now. She embraced him briefly then locked her arms over her flat chest.

It was his uncle, who was simpler and had fewer defences, who said: 'We'll miss you lad. Won't know what to do without you. It'll be like losing Ned all over again.'

He promised himself that some day he would say what he felt for them, these two quiet people who had fostered him for so long. Or show them. But for the moment he was too full of his own passionate exultation.

The talking was done by his father.

'No, no, Clem,' his uncle insisted, shaking his head. 'It isn't necessary. We on'y done what anyone would. What's family for?'

His aunt made a line with her mouth. She had baked an early Christmas cake with holly and a frill and made a tin of pink-and-white coconut-ice.

No one would ever know the triumph he felt in having made all this happen. He was going back to his father, to his real family, and to the *place*. Killarney. His father's wife, that Sally, had died of the Spanish 'flu and his father had decided they should be together again. His will to return had been stronger than the woman's will to survive.

'He wants a cheap nursemaid,' he had heard his aunt whisper in bed after the letter came.

'Ssh! The boy will hear! There's no point in carrying on at this stage –'

'It's always the same. He never thinks of anyone but himself. It's the unfairness of it!'

They were whispering in bed with the door open, and he was standing barefoot at the sink, having come out in his pyjamas to get a drink. He wouldn't dare now. The gulping and sudden rush of the tap would give him away. He stood eavesdropping while they whispered over his life, smiling to himself that his fate was, after all, in his own hands, and aware, with the same physical sense as of the cold that came up through the flags and made his teeth chatter, of a turning-point in his life, of his being set in a new direction.

[4]

The house he moved back to was in every way unlike the one he had known for the past eight years. It was immediately familiar to him, not as a place of particular walls or objects but as a quality of warmth and proximity that his body had clung to and agonized over in the clear swept spaces of his aunt's house and in his single bed.

It was one big room with two beds: a double bed where his father and Jim slept, and where he now rejoined them under a patchwork quilt, and another for the smaller kids, who were seven, four and three years old and all had a dazed, dark-eyed look that he guessed was their mother's, and flat, straw-coloured hair.

He loved them at once for their difference. They were all three alike but of another family – it might have been another planet. They hung together and had signs and even a language of their own that was all sing-song vowels. Muddled together like puppies in their own bed, which was set at right angles to the other, in a communal warmth and breath, and murmuring secret syllables to one another in a tangle of arms and legs and almost indistinguishable blond heads, they made the strangest possible link between him and this old yet changed world he had come back to.

Half brothers. He found the concept magical, especially since they came to him complete. He would stare at the one photograph of their mother, who seemed more like a cheeky boy, and trace their strangeness back to a likeness there of snub-nosed, dark-eyed blondness that was a new element of his life. He felt guilty before them, and this too determined the quality of his passion: he had, by the power of wishing, driven their mother from the house. Though unrepentant he was consumed with guilt.

But physical closeness in his father's bed made up for any chill he might have felt on his soul, and the three little boys were innocently forgiving, delighted to have a new adult in the house to pester and perform for, and especially one who needed to be shown and told so much that they already knew: like how many scoops went into their father's morning pot, the half-dozen places a lost tea-strainer might get to, and in which of the stepped canisters you would find cinnamon or rice or sago (since whoever had first established a kind of order here hadn't stuck to the worn and unreadable labels); how to flake Sunlight Soap for washing, where to keep butter from ants and bread from the eternally scampering mice, and a hundred other details of their rough house-keeping.

Then too there was the fuggy warmth and rich, earth-animal smell of the cowshed, which he had never forgotten and was delighted to rediscover. He was gathered back into a daily routine that was the ground of his father's life and the source of that essential smell of the man that had come with him on all his visits, reminding the boy always of the different life they lived here, among animals rather than trees, and lingering afterwards to torment him with homesickness and a passionate longing. He burrowed back into it. It became his own.

The work however was harder than fruit farming. It had different hours and used other muscles.

He and Jim got up with their father, just before five, and all three did the milking; he half-asleep at times with his head against rough hide and only his fingers working the regular, dreamy routine. Later they helped with the separating, and while their father lugged the cans out and he hosed down the bails, Jim made breakfast – puftaloons – in a big black pan that filled the house with the smell of fat and added each day, along with woodsmoke and resin, to the deepening colour of the walls and roof-beams and to the stickiness of things, so that whatever you touched here showed your prints. (Frank's were soon laid down over the rest, as his height-mark, with name and date, joined the others on the jamb of the door; but it appeared as from nowhere, four foot three, whereas the others, all mixed in together as they passed their old selves or one another, were traceable through months and years that he deeply brooded over and regretted.)

The littlies would be up by then, and he learned to dress them while the seven-year-old set the table, laying out treacle, jam, a slab of honeycomb.

He was called Clyde, and the others were Tam, short for Tamworth, and Pearsall. Even their names were of a different kind from his own and Jim's and belonged to a different family.

Then he, Jim and Clyde walked three miles to a one-teacher school that sat all alone in a paddock among blazing pebbles. Clyde without the others seemed diminished. He had nothing to say and his hair was too pale. The dog Jellybean, an old kelpie bitch who had her own litter of half-grown pups, waddled out and sat in the shade of the bench where the milk-cans waited, to watch them out of sight.

After school he and Jim drove the cows in to be milked a second time, and afterwards they sat at the kitchen table and did their homework while the younger ones climbed on their knees and mumbled, and had to have snot wiped or their braces undone so that they could run outside to the dunny; and a minute later, one of them, usually Frank, would be called out to wipe an arse.

They seemed to believe, Tam and Pearsall, that Frank had replaced their mother. They came to him for all their needs and were forever tugging at his sleeve or whispering into his ear or trying to snuggle up to him. He found he could push his pen quite easily through a copybook exercise while Pearsall, with a wet tongue at his ear, 'told him things'. Pearsall, he thought, already resembled their father. He too told stories – most of them made up – of things that had happened to him, and was only content when he was burrowing into your shirt, or snuffling at your neck, or sucking the warmth from under your collar.

It was a cosy world, and in its easy disorderly way quite orderly and safe. Frank liked nothing better than to see their six places set on the oil-cloth under the lamp which he himself had climbed on a chair to pump, and to have them, all six, seated there with food before them, and afterwards, still in their places, to have their father tuck one bare foot up under him (it was a way he liked to sit) and play softly on the mouth organ or tell one of his stories.

In this closed world, the boy felt, there was permanency. It was only when they went together into the little township to buy provisions or to shop for new pants or shorts or woolly jumpers that he would see, as they all trooped past, a look on people's faces that made them in some way outlandish, and would catch in the men's voices as they addressed his father a note of humorous scorn.

'Hey Clem! How's that fence comin'?' someone might call, as if it could only be coming badly (it was, but that was bad luck), and some galumphing fool would snigger. His father took it good-naturedly but shooed them quickly on.

'What about ice blocks,' he'd coax, 'from old Mrs French? Coconut and raspberry. What about it, eh?'

He was easier with women, their father. Frank saw it and was surprised, then no longer surprised. Women were good to them, always. They got free barleysugar from French's, to carry off after the ice blocks, and from Wilson's, often enough, an orange to share or a stick of hard sugarcane. But only if May Wilson was in the shop, who had been in their father's class at school.

'We're doing all right, eh?' the father would say, leading them off with their purchases and the free gifts. 'You happy there, Pearse?'

But these trips into town were rare and Frank was glad of it. He liked the idea of their being outlandish, of their having only themselves.

Sitting on after tea, with the plates cleared away and scraped of their fat, and the mouth organ restored to its box, their father would begin on one of his stories. The man's dreamy manner and low resonant voice soon put them, one after the other, to sleep.

The little ones dropped off almost at once. Then Jim, who could never hear any story out, sitting bolt upright and with his eyes open, would begin to tilt and sway. His eyelids would droop, flutter, close; then suddenly jerk up again with a wild look in them, as if he were miles from where he should have been. Then he too would give in. Laying his head down on a lean arm he would descend into sleep.

Frank listened and drew. While his father went romancing he let his hand move over the pages of a fat little pad, catching to his own satisfaction the roundness of Tam's cheek where it dented a plump forearm, or the angle at which Jim's head, rolled back as if supported on a cushion of air, exposed all the bare throat and the prominence, below the fine and slightly crooked chin, of his adam's apple. Mouth half-open, eyes showing just a gleam under the lids, the dozen strokes and shadows of a chestnut fringe – this was Jim dozing, Jim abstracted and removed to a distance, but for a moment most touchingly vulnerable, and closer, because less defensive, than when he was awake.

Frank drew, exploring the differences and odd resemblance between them all that so attracted and moved him, while the vibrancy of his father's voice, a melodious sing-song, cast its spell upon him. He idled upon it. And this was easy since the voice was no longer directed at their little group under the lamp (which is why it didn't matter that four of them were already asleep) but like Frank's doodling, moved off on a line of its own. You could tune in or not as you pleased.

'Once,' it told, 'I saw a ghost – you know, up there at the homestead. A lady in a yellow frock. Very beautiful but sad-looking. She was walkin' up and down in the long grass as if it was still a clipped lawn – I mean she was walkin' right through the grass as if it didn't hold her back, her long skirt, any more than water would – or not even that much. I was sittin' on the edge of what was the verandah. Just sittin', n' thinking I ought to start back, it was getting dark. And she kept lookin' towards the house as if she expected someone to come out of it. As if the house was still there, all solid walls – you know, weatherboard, n' glass in the windows, the way it must have been – like she 'ad just stepped out of it upset or angry or somethin', or hopin' some man would follow, an' didn't realize the years had passed and it was a ruin.

'It was weird, I can't explain it. She didn't *seem* like a ghost. That's the odd thing. I mean I didn't *feel* her as a ghost, she looked so real. The yellow of her dress, and her shoes with dust on them where she'd just stepped out into a cleared space. And 'er shoulders. You could feel the droop of them. That was 'er sadness. And she gave such a sharp look backward when she turned that you knew the house must be just the way she thought it was. It made *me* feel like the ghost. I mean, I was sitting right where the verandah rails should've passed through me, and I wasn't aware of it any more than she was of the long grass. Do you reckon there can be ghosts of the future as well as the past?

'There must have been a time, you know, when it was all so solid and settled, their life up there. Well-to-do-people with aristocratic connections, silver on the table, n' big vases n' marble statues and that. And in my time it was all gone, and I was grubbin' away at a few acres of what was left, milkin' seven days a week and always dog-tired with never a spare penny to buy a bit of luxury, and no real knowledge of anything except a few Latin verbs they taught me at Toowoomba, and *algebra*! The prospect of it was enough t' make you cut yer throat.

'An' maybe I already have, I thought, and that's what she's lookin' at. A bloke who's taken a razor, set a basin in front of him and slashed. I don't know.

'Well, I didn' do it, of course. I married your mother instead. I don't know how I thought that would help. It only made things worse. I wasn' cut out to be a dairy farmer, that's the real truth, but I wasn' educated for anything else, so there I was. I used to look at pictures we had of my grandmother, all dolled up in satin – even in this climate! – with pearls n' stuff – God knows where it all went! – and then I'd think of the life we were tied to. Me up at four t' milk the bloody cows, yer mother scrubbin' clothes on a washboard, an' not even a proper dunny to the house or any ceiling or coverin' to the floor. It's a hard life if you're at the bottom. Once –' And his complaints, or musings, or odd moments of wonder at his own experience, would soon come up with another story, more wonderful, more inconsequential than the last.

These tales, woven out of his life, out of the countryside and the past of their family, went down into the boy's imagination, and as his hand moved on now from the heads of his sleeping brothers to freer landscapes of grass and cloud, answered yet again, when he put it, the question of how he came to be Frank Harland and how he had got into the world – at what point in time and place and through what bright hole in reality.

Two or three times with his father and many times alone or with one or other of his brothers, he climbed the long road from the township, out past logging-camps and the shacks of loners to the plateau, site of the family's real and legendary beginnings.

You moved out of the rich green of Killarney, where the air seemed half composed of water, into blue-grey scrub. The trees were stunted at first with trunks thrusting at all angles out of yellowish rock, some of them burnt black below and bursting into new leaf above, others a skeletal white from ring-barking. But on the plateau itself the timber grew straight and tall, you were in forest. Cool even at midday in winter, and in summer a glittering, sighing, shimmering ocean, it was its own deep blue this gum-forest, with a whiteish foam on the surface, and on still days it was glassy. Where a breath, high up, caught the furthest crest of it, turning single leaves, or a bird pushed off and a twig vibrated, ripples flushed through it that were felt below as a trembling of light over the steady earth.

Their father's stories had made this a haunted place. Or it really was haunted.

Not far before the ruins there was a platform of rock. Aborigines had foregathered here, all the local tribes in their wanderings, and left crude rock carvings. Though far from the sea, turtles, starfish, even a giant whale, lay stranded by time and the sun in spare outline on the scored rock-surface, recalling a time when all this country really had been covered by the sea. With their knees drawn up they would sit on warm stone in the very midst of it, among the sea-creatures and the flights of wallabies and paddymelons and every sort of bird; that other world would be all about them, abstracted into enduring lines that crossed and criss-crossed in an endless puzzle. The outline of a whale might be broken by that of a bounding kangaroo, the separate orders of creation, sea-beast and land-beast, interpenetrating in an element outside nature – the mind of whoever it was, decades back, who had squatted here and with bits of flint or a sharpened stone made the clearing a meeting-place for separate lines of existence.

Stepping back into the lives of those first creators, they would crawl about, retracing the lines with a forefinger, clearing out leaf-grist, pollen, fragments of bark, the husks of dead insects; or would themselves take a knife and scrape, so that figures only vaguely discernable would, as they shifted about on their footsoles, climb back to the surface and surprise them.

'Look,' one of them might exclaim, standing up to see what they had made. 'It's another whale!'

Tired at last, they would lie spreadeagled on the sunlit surface, where old fissures in the rock made their own pattern, and doze off. In the midst of that still menagerie.

Further on lay the ruins of the homestead. There was a single chimney-stack of crumbling brick, but the foundations of rooms could be made out if you cleared away the rubble with a bare foot: the original ground-plan of the house as it might have appeared when the elder of the three Harland brothers first sketched it on a sheet of notepaper or scratched it on the earth with a stick – the first rough vision of an empire – and someone with a bit of science in these matters had measured and drawn it all, with arrows and neatly printed specifications, on a builder's plan.

It had returned to that; on a larger scale and in broken stone. It was that plan in the elder Harland's mind, drawn roughly on the earth, that you could lay bare by crawling about and removing the layer of windblown dust and leaves; revealing the flat elevation first, then raising it, out of Father's talk, as an elegant and spacious homestead with windows and verandahs, quiet by day – while the men were out with cattle and the women sat inside in the cool, reading or sewing or preparing huge meals – but filled at night with voices, snatches of music from a little organ, then later with the beating in the dark of twin carriage-clocks and the odd, indecipherable murmur-ings of family sleep.

Noble forebears.

In fact it was the ruins of a folly. This had never been cattle country. And the three brothers, though tough enough, and filled with the heroic spirit of the times, and a vision out of their reading (and out of other fellows' talk) of what was possible here to men of pride and limb, had been poor managers and no sort of cattlemen at all – dreamers too easily defeated. Within a decade the high place was deserted. Only a crazy sister was left to watch the verandahs rot and sag, then blow away as dust. She had taken up residence at last in a tin shed. The rusty-red sheets of it were piled up now under sprays of briar-roses in a thicket ten feet high, from which, at the expense of scratched arms and blood drops, you could pluck chipped enamel basins, half-plates and cups without handles, steel knitting-needles – inglorious relics.

On one occasion, three of them, Frank, Clyde and Pearsall, eager to confirm a belief in spirits or to assure themselves that there were no such

24

things, had camped there overnight. They ate their supper of bread and dripping, boiled a billy of tea, watched the sun sink down into the plain, where it was damped out smokily by a dozen lakes, then lay out their blankets and fell quiet.

They were waiting for mad Maud Harland to appear and splash her face with moonlight from the basin they had set out, between the cindery remains of the house and her alive but ghostly rose bush.

There was a moon. It was nearly full. Cicadas drummed in long waves, then faltered, then burst out again. They waited and no one came. But Pearsall after a time began to whimper. Behind them the forest was in motion: all the tree tops had begun to sigh and fret and the night insects were stilled.

'What is it?' Clyde asked, putting his arms round the child and crouching to bring their heads close. 'What are you scared of, Pearse?'

'Abos,' the boy told them, sniffling, and the transparent white spooks they had been expecting were there in negative. Black ghosts. Black.

They reassured him and sat stiffly for a time watching the enamel basin but giving glances over their shoulders as well. In hollow trees back there, wrapped up in bark that must long since have rotted, were the bones of abos. They imagined skeletal feet dangling or a bony arm, and before too long, declaring disappointment and renewed scepticism, decided to pack up and go down.

It hadn't occurred to them till Pearsall saw it that the spirits of the place, born out of rocks and tree trunks and returned in their rough bark envelopes to the forks of trees, from which they would descend through tap-roots and rocks into the earth, might be more enduring in time, and in their numbers going back to the days of the first rock-scratching, than mad Maud Harland – who had lived with all this night after night half a century ago, and in trembling or not, become part of it.

On Saturday nights now their father went to a dance. He took a bath in the round washing-tub in front of the stove, ironed a shirt – usually all their clothes went unironed, it was Frank or Jim who did the washing – cleaned a pair of old dancing pumps, did his hair carefully in front of a mirror over the sink, and went off whistling.

'There's no harm in a bit of a dance,' he'd tell them over the last of their tea, as excited as a boy at the prospect of his night out, but shy of disapproval. Of Jim's disapproval that is, which he feared the others might catch.

There had begun to be a kind of hostility between Jim, who was fifteen, and the boyish father. Jim's face during his stories had a hard line about the mouth in which Frank recognized a likeness to his Aunt Else. He would shift uncomfortably. Rage grew in him. He would be on the point of bursting out.

'Well,' the man would say, 'maybe that's silly. Jim thinks it's silly, don't you Jim? He thinks your old dad's a dill!' He was wounded, but hoped by getting in early and making a joke of it to forestall whatever bitter, contemptuous thing the boy was preparing to say that would shame him before the rest. He preferred to wound himself. They recognized the ploy and were embarrassed for him.

Jim declined at first to take the bait. He put his head down, gripped his cutlery in hard fists and chewed. But after a time his fury could not be kept in.

'Bullshit!' he would say fiercely. 'Bloody bullshit! Can't you shut up and let us eat our meal in peace? Just eat for once? I'm sick of hearin' you go on. All that – bullshit!'

The father blushed. 'Jim,' he said mildly, guardedly, 'you oughtn' to speak to your father like that.' Then with an anger that was feigned to hide a more painful emotion: 'I won't stand for it!'

Jim sniggered and made a gesture of contempt. He went on eating. And while the others sat stilled with their knives in the air, the man made an attempt at conciliation. He reached out to set his hand on the boy's shoulder.

Jim ducked. 'Keep yer hands offa me, I'm sick of it! Don't try that stuff with me!'

Out of some newly-discovered distaste for the man, and his own sense of being no longer a child, Jim refused now to sleep in the same bed with him. He made a rough sleeping place for himself on a bench near the stove, and Clyde, breaking up at last the threesome of younger brothers, climbed into the space he left between the father and Frank.

'Jim's growing up,' the father crooned. 'He's got an eye for the girls. Well, that's on'y natural. Nothing wrong with that, Jimbo. I've got an eye for the girls myself. It's another influence.' He glanced about the big untidy room with its heaps of dirty washing, its unmade beds, the sink full of pans and dishes and the litter of the table with his five boys around it, all chins and elbows and scarred and grimy knees. He groaned a little. 'Look at us! Look at this mess! Snips and snails! We're too many men in this house, that's it, eh Jim? Some other influence. It's missing. That a woman could provide.'

Frank could make nothing of this. He wondered if his father wasn't preparing to marry again and had been using his quarrel with Jim as a way of breaking it to them.

Meanwhile Jim sulked and stormed in genuine anguish. There was always tension among them now. It came out in every way. Their father found fault with everything Jim did: with how slow he was to get up in the morning, his sleepiness at the bails, the slovenliness with which he hosed out the stalls and did all his duties, the way he sat at the table, the look on his face. Everything about the boy's change into something other than the child he had been (and Frank too saw this) affronted the man, put him out of sorts or enraged him. The dancing was a compensation.

'There's no harm in it, you know,' he'd tell them as he tied the laces of his glossy shoes, 'a bit of a waltz with a nice woman on yer arm an' a bit of talk. It relaxes you, the dancin', takes you out of yerself. It's an innocent enough pleasure, God knows, for a widower with a hard life like mine n' five boys to think of – one of them almost a man. The albertina. That's a nice dance, now. Needs a good straight back, a firm arm and lightness in the feet. A lovely dance with the right couple.'

So he would go on till he was ready; then standing up, all dressed and polished, with his hair slick and his cheeks smooth and burning, he would look apologetic for a moment, with all their eyes upon him, and slip away.

But the changes that came with Jim's growing to manhood and the increasing hostility between the boy and his father could not be contained. The house began to have unsettled areas where conflict brewed. One of them was the bench by the stove, where Jim, in a huddle of sheets and blankets, spent his unruly nights. But there were others. Any of those places in the room where the boy sulked apart, or hunched against a wall with his hands in his pockets and what their father called a 'look' about his mouth, could become the site of a disturbance that translated itself first to the father, whose voice would lose its easy softness, then to Frank as a kind of sickness at heart for what might be slipping away from them, then to the others, who all took it in different ways. Pearsall sucked his thumb and wanted to snuggle. Tam, in his first days at school, was alternately beaten up or accused of being a bully. Clyde, who appeared after all to be the least steady of them, began to pinch things: a penknife from a fellow in the Cubs, pencils from the classroom cupboard, and from French's on the way home, lollies to bribe his mates at school. Frank worried and took it all upon his own shoulders. Having lost his place once he had a horror of losing it a second time.

Things could only get worse. From standing hunched in the open door, neither in nor out, Jim took to locking himself in the dunny or bursting away to sit alone by the water-tank chucking stones.

'Let him,' the father said, 'if he'd rather be out there with the toads than in here with his brothers. It's his nature. He can't help it.'

Soon he was no longer out there in the yard but on the road to town and was free, more or less, to come and go as he pleased. He had a girl at Tannymorel. He would eat, do his share of cleaning up, then slouch off without explanation.

'Jim's after the girls,' the father sneered. 'He's a ladies man.'

But the boy let the challenge drop. He despised his father too deeply to argue with him. It was Frank who was left, after the others had fallen asleep over the table, to listen to his father's complaints and sentimental effusions and apologies for himself; and this was much as it had always been, except that Jim now was away at his girl's place or at the pictures rather than sleeping like the rest.

They were beginning to fall apart, that is what Frank saw; and it was not in their father's power – it was not in his nature – to keep them together. He had taken it for granted till now that some special grace hovered over them, which was inherent in his father, even in his father's voice, and that the qualities it suggested, of love, warmth, a feeling for continuity in the remembrance and recording of things, would hold them against all shocks. But these qualities had no substance. With regret, and without at all qualifying his affection for the man, Frank admitted it: his father was all self-indulgence and wistfulness, there was no strength in him; when the storm came he would run to some woman, hide his head in her lap and demand, like a child, to be smooged and mothered.

Even as he thought this, and recognized the danger, his father would be weaving around them the warm, silk-soft enchantments that Frank loved to hear and still felt the power of but could no longer believe. He listened, half spellbound, half in fear for himself and the others, but with the first stirring in him of a sense of his own power, and a fearful belief that it might after all be his fate, or his duty, to shield them all.

He still brooded, as he listened, over the pages of a pad, and his father's voice might have been an essential condition of the dreamy state in which he worked or played, for his notion of what he was doing swung from one to the other but was in all ways serious. It was a state in which mind was suspended and his hand did the thinking for him.

Each night he drew what was in front of him: a child's head heavy with sleep, a plate of scraps, a cheese dish and cover, a petrol lamp and the shadows it threw up to bare rafters, the light as it fell on his father's hair or on the man's knee where it was drawn up under him, and fell differently on the rucked material of his trousers and on the bare foot – always the same objects, familiar but different.

It wasn't the objects themselves he was concerned with, though they too had their burden of feeling for him and their own dense reality; or the play of light and shadow; or even the weight and volume of each thing as it exerted a visible pressure on the air about it and could suggest, to the feeling eye, a space shared with the viewer that the viewer also displaced. His mind, in its play-work, had got beyond that.

He smoothed the sheet of paper in his hand (it was clean enough) and considered.

Whiteness.

That alone was enough to take your breath away. It was the source of all possibility, an infinity of objects and occasions.

Unsteadily, but with a steady hand, he intervened, he acted; and with his eye on the real object he was about to capture, made a line – one clear stroke, slightly curved.

The page was transformed. Where the soft lead bit into the paper, the paper resisted at first, then yielded, enough for the pressure-point to make a dent, and for the dent to fill with minute crumblings. It looked like a full stop, but was in fact an opening from which the lovely grey-black graphite flowed out.

He let his mind flow with it, and as his eye perceived two dimensions then three and shifted between them, so he uncovered a further dimension. The page was his mind and contained everything that was in his mind and which waited there to be brought forth. Hidden beneath it was the world. He had only to let things emerge, to let his hand free them: on this occasion a head, a specific one, his brother Tam's, on the next . . . But the occasions were without end. The page and his mind could become one, and what they contained was the infinite plentitude of things that was Creation, in which all things were equal; their equality, and the possibility of their springing into immediate existence, guaranteed by his recognition of them and by the space he had prepared and would let them fill.

He sat very still and contemplated what was before him. It seemed to him that he had understood something important; that his hand, almost without him, had made a great discovery.

He had a box of water-colours as well and in moments when he was free from work would try to catch in line, he loved that, and in thin wash, the long undulations of the land under a sky that was filled with happenings. They were so large – such lyrical, slow tumblings and transformings in ice-blue or in opening mushrooms of black all ablaze at the edge – that the earth seemed a sphere where nothing happened at all unless the slope of a hill was made active with running shadows or the stale surface of a lake, broken only by lily-pads, was touched at a distance by a storm that might have been blowing up below its hand-span of real depth out of aeons of mud.

Compared with events in the cloud-theatre above – the towers of falling cities, the rising with a dagger in their fist of ragged pedlars, great galleons, camel-trains, shaggy lions – compared with that, the passage of an old Clydesdale across a paddock that was half grey topsoil and half turned loam, or one of his brothers making a bare-arsed dive from a boat-ramp, or a mob of cows, all black-and-white patches, moving in dust clouds past a slip-rail fence, was as nothing at all – an occasion so deep in the picture as barely to be noticed, until ignoring the real scale of things you framed only that, and made the drama overhead the merest play of light on a mare's flanks or the crests of furrows, or on a boy's shoulderblades as he jack-knifed into it.

But beyond this fascination with mere event, and the challenge offered by light and weather, there was another purpose to his recording on sheet after sheet all the details of a particular countryside, and a pattern in his choice of this or that wooded hill or stretch of pasture.

He was setting down all the places, as he knew from his father's stories, that had once been Jack Harland's share of the triple empire, before it was lost in a card game by that Gem Harland, his great grandfather's eldest, and drunk away by Gem's brother Sam, and schemed or stolen out of the hands of others by sly cousins, envious brothers-in-law, fly neighbours, or given over to storekeepers who had to foreclosure on credit, or to banks run by men who were understanding enough (and shyly sorry) but accountable at last to a head office in London or Sydney; or thrown up in despair by men who were sick, as his father was, of being tied to a shitty herd, and taking the plunge as his father never would, had tied themselves to a conveyor-belt in a canning factory.

The pattern involved a plan. It was, quite simply, to win all this back some day and restore it, acre by acre, to its true possessors. That was the gift he was preparing. It was for them. For his father and brothers.

It was, he knew, a large ambition, which is why he hoarded it up till all was done. He might easily look foolish if it were known. But he was not foolish. The power he had, as he more and more felt it, was a practical thing. His pictures were a reminder and inventory. They were also a first act of repossession, which made them charms of a sort and their creating an act of magic. The idea scared him a little but he was stubborn. He had chosen a course and would stick to it. For life – if that is what it came to.

One afternoon of drizzling rain, when it was hot and stuffy in the closed house with its smell of mattresses and steamy socks on a line by the fire, and the closeness of them all packed into a single room (their father was in bed with 'flu), they had a kind of celebration. It was for its own sake; there was no birthday or particular date.

Half sprawling or seated cross-legged on their father's bed, they had been playing grab with an old pack of cards, and it was Frank who thought of it. Together, he and the smaller kids cooked a bread pudding, while their father, sitting up in his shirt out of a heap of bedclothes, gave directions; though in fact they had made it often before, and knew without his telling how to soak the bread, mix in the suet – plenty, so that it would cut in wet slabs – and the cinnamon, raisins, sultanas. When the dish came out of the oven it was perfect. They could hardly wait for it to cool. Tam and Pearsall kept poking it to see how cool it had got and it was Clyde who dealt with them. Frank was busy doling out mugs and warming the pot for tea. At last Clyde declared it ready to be cut, and with the biggest of their carving-knives, which he held upright in his fist, he cut thick slices and passed them around.

Father had his on a plate. The others, leaning over the worn oilcloth that covered the kitchen table, had theirs in their fingers, slurping tea between mouthfuls and noisily sucking their fingers.

'This is delicious bread pudding,' the man announced from the bed behind them. 'It's a bit on the wet side, but Frank likes it on the wet side, don't you Frank? So do I.'

'So do I!' Pearsall echoed, like Amen.

Jim was there. He ate his slice along with the rest, wearing a cap to show that he was already on the way somewhere and had been caught at the last moment by the familiar smell of the pudding, and by the love they all had of it from the days when their father used to make it with the last of the week's bread.

They gorged themselves, finishing the whole dish and prolonging the feast by arguing over who could be relied upon to cut fair second helpings. They drank the whole pot of tea. Then Jim, a bit unwilling, but too deeply committed by the cap to pull back, hunched his shoulders at the door, buttoned his jacket and turned his collar up against the rain. His face in profile had a bony, painful look that Frank never forgot.

'There he goes! He's got a girl,' the father taunted, sitting up out of the moil of sheets and blankets to shout it. 'Jim's off to his girl!' Teasing, the way none of the other kids would.

Then the boy was gone, leaving the door open on dribbles of rain.

Frank remembered both these scenes as marking the end of something: their celebration at the kitchen table, the last time they were all together, and Jim's isolation there in the open door while the rest looked gravely towards him. Jim went off soon afterwards to be an apprentice printer, in Glen Innes over the border, and Frank inherited the bench by the stove, that staging-place – as he knew, even as he crawled for the first time into the envelope of blankets and his shoulders adjusted to hard planks after the big soft bed – to the world outside. Turning on his side he was right up against the timber wall.

A first step away – the longest that could be taken inside the house itself. One more and he too would be gone.

Clyde, without explanation, went back to his old bed, and it was Pearsall now who crawled in and snuggled up to the father.

These adjustments in their sleeping arrangements, in their lives, occurred naturally, without thought perhaps, certainly without speech; but were statements just the same. Of intention, of alliance, of rupture. Lying awake in the dark, aware of their disposition now in space, Jim at Glen Innes, he on the bench by the stove with the rain drizzling at his ear, Clyde and Tam rolled together in the dip of one bed, Pearsall and his father in the other, Frank thought of their lives as being restated in a new form, like the words in a sentence being shifted about to make a new meaning. He felt dizzy. As if the centre had fallen out of things and he was spinning off now on his own trajectory.

[5]

In the August of that year (he was turned sixteen), Frank went up to Brisbane for the Exhibition, where the farmer he worked for, one of the Mackays, had a bull to show. He took a batch of drawings with him and most of the watercolours tied up in a clean singlet.

They slept in a stall with the cattle like all the rest and he had only his work clothes, but on the second day he asked for time off to see the town and to buy presents for his brothers, and making himself as presentable as he could, set off for a gallery he had read about in the *Courier Mail*.

The woman at the gallery, which was in a basement, looked cool, unapproachable, and the pictures on the wall seemed silly – even to him. They were incompetent, garish. He took one look and decided to go away. But seeing him slinking off, a clumsy kid with a countryman's hat in his hand, rough boots that were not quite clean and with a bundle under his arm, the woman left her desk and called 'Hey!', suspecting him, he thought, of running off with something. But she was smiling, and seemed, on second glance, rather brassy.

'What were you after, love? No need to be shy here, you know.'

She had seven or eight inches of coloured bangles up her arm that clattered when she drew on her cigarette, painted nails, a lot of makeup; and though she must have been well over fifty had preserved her shape. She might, in her smart little suit with the lapels, have been an usherette in a theatre.

'Here, let's see what you've got. Drawings, is it? And what's this? A singlet?'

Before he knew quite what was happening she had taken the folio of drawings and was removing the singlet – he couldn't have been more embarrassed if it was his own, the one he was wearing. In fact it was an old singlet of Jim's.

She was making little clucking sounds. 'Well,' she said, 'that's nice. It's an arm, isn't it.' She regarded it as if she had never seen one.

'Listen, I'll tell you what, love, I'll give you the name of someone you should show them to – they're not our sort of thing. You can see that.' Without apology she indicated the faces round the wall. 'This friend of mine is an art teacher. At a college. Will you go there if I give 'im a tinkle and say you're on the way? It's not far and he'd be intrigued, I know he would.'

Frank agreed. Anything to get away. He bundled the drawings up, still blushing, and tied them with the singlet, while the woman jollied someone, a man, you could tell that, on the telephone. And since he had steeled himself once, and because he knew that in what he had long been preparing for himself it was a moment of great importance, he walked the three streets, past warehouses and open pubs where men were drinking at windowsills, to where the art teacher had his studio at the top of a narrow brownstone building beside the river.

He wasn't used to lifts, and this one was an elaborate cage, so he climbed the stairs and arrived at a landing with three wooden doors, all exactly alike.

He knocked lightly at one, and guessed from the sound and the lack of response that it was a cupboard. He felt foolish. It wasn't a lucky sign. But the second, after a distant cry that sounded like a man falling down a well, was opened by a tall, severe figure with gold-rimmed glasses, a walrus moustache and a loop of watch-chain under the belly of his three-piece suit. He was drying his hands on a bit of towel.

Frank was disappointed. He wasn't romantic – he had grown out of that during long years of his father's talk – but to his eyes Hopkins, no more than the woman, looked like one of those figures he had expected, here in Brisbane, to have charge of the antechambers to life.

'Well then, let's see what we've got,' the man said, leading the way.

The studio too was not what he had expected, or not at first glance, but he recognized and respected almost immediately a place of work: benches stacked with old paint-tins, brushes in dirty bottles, stiff bunched rags. Stuck to the walls at eye level were snapshots that had curled at the edge round a rusty drawing pin and many illustrations from magazines. A low sink. A kerosene heater where a kettle boiled. And in the corner of the room where the best light fell, the easel, with a stool before it on which you could have sat to milk a cow, and a wheeled tea trolley on whose surface Hopkins mixed his paints.

Hopkins, quite unsurprised by the singlet, had unwrapped the bundle and was examining the drawings, some quickly, some with his chin drawn down into his stiff collar. Once or twice he glanced up at Frank over the rim of his glasses, and huffed.

'Well, son,' he said at last, pushing the drawings away and folding his hands over his belly, 'what is it you want?'

'I want to learn how to draw.'

'You know how to draw. What else?'

The boy blushed. He couldn't have said it.

'All right then, here's what I have to say. You know how to draw, but there's a lot of other things you don't know. I'd be willing to teach you. How does it sound?'

'I haven' got any money,' Frank told him. He had no idea how things worked in this place. 'I'm up for the show.'

'The what?'

'The Exhibition. I'm with Mister Mackay, my boss. We're showing a bull.'

The art teacher thought this a joke. He kept his mouth shut but his jaw wobbled and his eyes were screwed up with mirth. 'Well, boy, my proposition is this. I can get you a job – nothing grand, but good enough to

35

start with – advertising art work. You can do it standing on your head. Probably best done that way. Can you stand on your head? – No, no, boy, don't worry – it's a joke, I can't help it, might go barmy otherwise. What do you say, then? If I arrange it, can you start Monday? The classes will be free. You won't charge me, I hope! – No, no, boy, joke!' He was tying up the bundle. He drew out the singlet and made a good knot. 'I'm glad to see,' he said, 'Harland – Frank, isn't it? – that you're not short of undies. It's a good start.'

He wrote:

My dear father,

I am settled in to my work now and can handle it pretty well, so am taking this opportunity to write to you and my dear brothers. I trust you will understand why I have decided to make a start on my own. I think of you all and am very lonely at times, especially for Pearse and Tam, but must stick to what I have chosen, it's the only way. Mr Hopkins is very good to me. He is a funny sort of bloke, but kind, and gives me a lot of help. He is an Englishman and has studied at a famous art school in London. He knows all the tricks. I have a good room now but moved a few times because I wasn't too shook on the other boarders. This room is good but, only two others and all clean. No more for a bit as I am dead beat after work. Please write, and ask the kids to, I want to hear all their news. I hope you got the bit of cash I sent. I wish you could come down here, or would send Tam or Pearse. Hoping this finds you in good health and happy as ever.

Your loving son etc.

He lived in a cheap boarding-house at Red Hill or Dutton Park with other lone men, young and old, who worked as motor-mechanics or factory hands or clerks in insurance offices. He grew the thin reddish moustache he would have for the rest of his life, and developed the self-sufficient ways, the capacity to clear a space around him in a crowded room, of men who live in boarding-houses, often sharing, for whom privacy is a thing to be insisted on. He wasn't unsociable but he had no friends. It was a lonely life. He worked day and night at his painting and was never satisfied, but when Hopkins sent half a dozen canvasses to a gallery in Sydney three of them were sold. He posted the money home. Each week or fortnight at least, he

sent part of what he earned to his father, writing with a stiffness of
expression that came partly from the books he was reading to improve
himself but more deeply from the effects of life and hard times on a nature
that was already serious to the point of severity. He agonized over these
letters, but they never expressed even a shadow of what he felt: his
loneliness, his love, the deep longing he felt for his brothers and for their
old life.

He wrote:

My dear father,
Your letter this morning. It has upset me more than I can say. This is a
terrible blow! I am fond of Clyde and have been afraid for him. He was
always the weak one amongst us – I don't blame him for that – unwilling to
accept the world as it is and expecting always to get things easy, and as far as
work is concerned, with no staying power. But as I say, I don't blame him. It
is hard to be the underdog and he is so full of energy. That's the trouble,
really, he's burning up with it. He wants so much out of life and
circumstances have always been against him. I would have done anything to
save him from this, but what could anyone do? Maybe this time on the boys'
farm will do him good – at least it is in the open, and with animals and a life
that he knows, not a real prison. But I hate to think of him there. Didn't any
of those people see what he is like, how easily led, and how soft if you treat
him the right way? I will try to visit him one weekend but it is a fair stretch. I
have no spare cash, and the work I am doing knocks me out. Anyway, will do
what I can. I can't bear to think of him *boxed in*. My love to you all –
especially to Tam and Pearsall. Write to me, Pearse!
    Your loving son, etc.

He wrote:

Dear Father,
I have been to visit Clyde on what they call a farm. He looks well enough,
from the exercise and from being out in the sun, but his frame of mind is
another matter. It scares me.
    Farm sounds as if it was a place you would recognize. Well, I didn't. In
spite of the animals and machinery. I had no idea there could be such a
place! Not that I saw anything direct. It was more like a smell – the guards

37

and men in charge! And the boys! It would break your heart to see poor Clyde among them. He looks so young and so much like his dear self, and the others are already so hardened and brutal looking – but maybe I could not see them with a brother's eyes.

It is Clyde's attitude that scares me. He blames everyone except himself, and is still skiting and trying to impress people with *talk*. Only when I got him alone did he seem as soft and affectionate as I know he is underneath. What is happening to him? I know he has always been weak. Always trying to win others to him some easy way – by toughness, or by bribing them with presents and things. We did nothing because we said he was young and would grow out of it. I worry now that it is too late. I felt I could not *speak* to him. Everything I had to say seemed weak and old womanish – I know that is what he was thinking. He looks down on me for having no fight, but it isn't true.

I spent the whole time on the train back to Brisbane – it is three hours – going over and over it, sometimes out loud, trying to make him hear. This is real torture to me, not to be able to reach him! I spent the whole journey mumbling to myself and shivering with fright.

What has happened to us? There is more than one sort of courage, surely. But it is a terrible thing to *love* someone and feel held off and unable to –

This letter he tore up. It was never sent.

His evenings in the various boarding-houses (he moved frequently, sometimes before he had discovered a pattern in the worn linoleum or solved the smells from the kitchen) were spent on the steps down from the front verandah waiting for the sea breeze to arrive, chatting with others as lonely as himself, or watching, in those suburbs of unpainted weatherboard and rusty downpipes, the figures of women in floral house-frocks as they gossiped over a fence behind which the sun was setting in a melt of gold; or leggy girls playing hopscotch, or a fellow lovingly at work on his image in the bonnet of a car, polishing and repolishing it till the dullness shone.

He wrote:

38

Dear Pearse,

Thank you for writing such a *clean* letter. It made me laugh a lot, especially
the bit about Jellybean and the toads. I don't think I got such a good letter or
such a good laugh for ages. I miss you all. Am finding good use for the
pen-wipers as I have a lot to do with ink at the agency and you know how
messy I am – ink all over my fingers, up my nose, round the back of my ears
– people must think I dip my nose in the inkwell to see how deep it is! – paint
all over my clothes. Not like Mr Hopkins who is a real artist, always
clean-looking in a suit and vest and with a kind of blue apron he pulls over
his head, you'd laugh to see him. He makes good jokes but, and you would
love some of the things he has! Big plaster noses and eyes – separate – that I
have to sit down and draw. Can you imagine? An eye plonked there on the
table and staring up at you, or an ear as big as a foot? It gives me the creeps
sometimes. Anyway, as I said, the wipers have come in handy. Most of the
ink is on *them* now instead of on me.

Love to Clyde and Tam. Tell them they should be able to write to me if
you can. I want to hear their news. I am sending you all a little present,
nothing much but just so you will think of your brother now and then. Love
to Jellybean. Water my little bit of garden, Pearse, and don't forget the
sweet-peas at St Patrick's. Love to Puss and Boots – I think they are *very
clever* names for kitties! Write soon.

Your loving brother etc.

He got used to Hopkins's jokes. He spent five years in the poky little office
of the advertising agency, doing drawings of models in cheap clothes and
ugly lounge-room furniture, and learning from Hopkins the rudiments of a
craft that had a long history of skills discovered with difficulty and passed
on from master to pupil. It delighted him that what he had vaguely
apprehended, and hit upon by accident or luck, was also a system with
rules. He was freed into discipline, then freed again into his old happy state
of dreamlike self-discovery, but with a new sureness of touch in which the
adventuring mind moved out now into uncharted spaces, over horizons that
were merely notional and had to be passed with no conscious knowledge of
what latitude you were in and with nothing to guide you at last but a firm
hand, and the assured, all-risking, ever-watchful and untiring spirit.

More precisely, he learned to draw with charcoal on coloured canvas and to seal what he had done with a fog of turps and resin mixed up in a milkbottle. He worked with oils on burnt sienna, using white to indicate the lights and black for shadows, till a form emerged, background and figure coming to life in the same instant but in different planes; then when all was dry and had been oiled for fluency he spread his glazes – translucent gold ochre, a touch of rose madder for cheeks, ears, lips where blood flows close to the surface, a trace of *terre verte* under the chin. It was pure sorcery. It had something of unholy deception in it, of alchemy and dangerous play with essences. These were the tricks of the trade. But even as he used them and worked the changes he could never quite catch the moment when magic took over. It was as if he had dozed off for an instant and some other power had intervened.

One day, without telling him what they were to do, Hopkins took him out into the country. They went on the train to Dayboro. Hopkins was bubbling with some little joke at Frank's expense that the boy at first resented, though you couldn't be resentful of Hopkins for long.

It was a new game the man wanted to show him. Nothing much. Just a cardboard square with black felt laid over it.

'All right boy, prepare yourself. Card up to the eye like Lord Nelson, that's it! Now focus on that clump of trees back there.'

He did as directed and the effect was stunning. He thought Hopkins had pulled some stunt while he wasn't looking – the black square was a diversion. But it was all real. The card and his own eye had done it.

So now he knew how to pull the trick on others: darkening yellow by using its complement, giving green a red shadow and orange a blue one, presenting things as they never looked so that you would see them as they *were*. He learned all the dodges and deceptions; then at last, without contempt either for the rules or for moments of magic and carefully-staged illusion, to make his own way in the dark.

People thought him odd, a tall, spare cove, not old enough to be so old-looking, with a gingery moustache and mild, milk-blue eyes. Little girls in faded frocks skipping rope beside a fence would stop with the rope in a limp arc, puzzled by what it might be in them or in the stopped game that had caught his eye; and were not convinced when he smiled weakly, shoved his hands in his pockets and sloped off. He spoke to cats that rubbed his ankles in back alleys, and on Sunday afternoons sat on a seat in the park to hear band music from an iron rotunda. It wasn't much of a life.

Occasionally, parting the half-doors on noise and sawdust, he would push his way into one of the Valley wineshops. In engraved and bevelled mirrors under a ceiling of moulded lead, among lightbursts out of the depths of bottles, black women and men not yet derelict but on a greasy slope made a company whose harsh laughter was softened by the breath of fellowship, and their mouths bunched round obscenities by a haze of smoke. This was the pit, but he thought of its creatures as his own. There was nothing degrading in it. Passages of darkness under smeared table-tops, legs wetly parted; occasions of knuckle and bone; other, bloodier encounters in which a passing insult might develop an edge of bottle-glass. He took things as they came, preferring places where he was a stranger like the rest.

Hopkins, who lived at the end of a tramline where bush ran down to an abandoned quarry, could have shown him another sort of life. He had a wife and three clever, half-grown daughters. But he didn't want that. Though not much more than twenty, he had begun to develop, in the cramped proximity of boarding-houses and in low pubs and wineshops where he never drank more than a lone glass of port, the habits of singularity and a lifelong solitude.

He wrote:

Dear Clyde,
I am sorry you sent me that letter. I know things are bad for you, they're not too good at this juncture for any of us, but we've got to battle through. You must let go the belief that there is some easy way. There isn't any. I have found out *that* at least.

I know it is hard to look about and see so much you want is always out of reach – flash clothes, if that is what appeals to you – cash, a car etc. I have no desire to play the nag, or the old man wise and superior, which I am not! – but am in despair about the way you are going, being so fond of you and of all my brothers, and willing to do anything in my power for you.

But you must not take advantage of me with threats. To hint and threaten as you do is a child's way. It is an old weakness. You ought to have given it up by now. You must know what desperation it puts me in.

The fact is, we are all too close. We find it hard to stand on our own two feet – I'm no different, only determined not to be beaten down.

Clyde, this time I am sending what you ask for. Not the lot, because I can't manage it, but what I can spare. I don't grudge it, but I have to think of Tam – he is a hard worker and wants to make good – and of Pearse, who must be kept at school. I know things have been hard for you and that you get discouraged, but you must not always put the blame on others or on 'the unfairness of things'. I can't write more now but will scribble a few lines soon and send you another pound or so, if I can, at the end of the month.

Your affect. brother etc.

He wrote:

Dear Tam,

I am sending straight away what I have by me at the moment. The doctor's got to be paid and Pearsall looked after as well as poss. I do not want this to make a gap in his schooling. A broken leg is not the end of the world. The rest of us have had to do without education at a time when I see it is the only way of getting on in the world. I want Pearse to finish school and get out of this mire of working always so hard and in such misery as the rest of us. It is that more than anything that has affected Clyde. It is my one hope that he will have some sort of profession. He is a clever kid, I know, and not sulky or rebellious. My only fear is that he may turn out to be a dreamer like Clyde, who can't seem to face up to any sort of reality. He writes me terrible letters from Cairns, where he is doing an animal's work cutting cane, but I am in no position. My own plight just now is desperate . . .

The times had grown rapidly worse. The advertising agency where he worked went out of business and Frank, after a month or two of hanging miserably about the city, looking for any sort of work, took to the road. He joined others out there, moving on daily from one settlement to the next all up and down the state, in a changing company that was sometimes three or four strong and sometimes a mob, but keeping always to himself.

The villages and larger townships where they appeared were never happy to have bands of homeless men in the vicinity and they were often hunted. They slept in ruined homesteads and barns, or on farms deserted by men much like themselves, or in camps that sprang up overnight in clay-pans, along a creek-bed or in the showgrounds of country towns, and if they developed the threat of permanency would be broken up by citizens armed with the law.

He shared a fire or a good sleeping-pozzie and talk with many different sorts of men and heard their stories: drought stories, mortgage stories, wife stories; stories of the war that had been raging during his years in his aunt's house and which some men were still fighting, deep to the eyeballs in mud; stories of prickly-pear, of rust in wheat, of dyptheria and whooping-cough epidemics, of prison terms – the ordinary miseries of the poor. Though it wasn't always misery. Sometimes there were tunes on a mouth organ or on the button accordion some man had saved out of the ruins of his settled life, or old jokes made new with a turn of phrase or a different situation; even, on occasion, snatches of philosophy, since it wasn't only the unskilled who were driven to this nomadic existence, and he began to wonder if even education and the profession he wanted for the last of his brothers was a fence against disaster. The open air did him good when it didn't reduce him to bone-shaking fever, and he saw something of the land he had been born to: cane fields waving their plumes under the moon, and so sweet-smelling you could get drunk on them (that was rum country); greyish plains where ant hills taller than a man were stacked all the way to the horizon – buried cathedrals showing only the tops of their blood-red spires; sea inlets fringed with glossy-leafed mangroves, thunderous surf.

These scenes fed his senses. They were of a grandeur that caught all his blood up in a display of cloud and colour that could transfigure the most ordinary day. They were a drama that had never been expressed. Well he would find forms for it. Great eloquent evenings as solemn and still as the brows of women – that sort of grandeur. Whiplike dawns: a crack of sunlight from sinewy arms. It made up a little for the shame he felt at being ragged, and dependent always on the charity or pity or wary suspicion of women at whose back verandahs he sought the chance to clear up a bit of untidy yard or to clean out gutters or chop wood, and for the hostility he saw in the eyes of men who were still settled and safe but might not be.

He found a companionship in misery that he had never known when he was in work, or which in those days he had not needed. He discovered that he belonged. But with those who were outside.

He might at any moment have gone home. It would have been most natural to him to burrow back into the warmth of his father's house, since he was, of them all, the one best fitted by temperament and inclination to settle and become in time their father's companion and keeper; to do otherwise was to go against himself. But it was the way he went. He had some obscure sense that his life was meant to go crosswise and be led in defiance of his nature rather than in the easy expression of it.

But the choice was not easy. It wasn't only his fate that he was deciding. Among those subtle pressures this way and that in which they still lived, all of them, even those who had moved away, he was delivering up Tam – who would stick to their father now out of duty, then habit, then inertia, and would never get free. That had been determined years back among the shifts from bed to bed, when he had moved to the bench by the stove that Jim had vacated, making it possible for Clyde to move back to his old place and Pearsall in with their father, and leaving Tam, in his innocence, the only one of them who had never come close enough to their father's soft power to throw it off.

He wrote:

My dear father and brothers,
Like you I am knocked out and in deep sorrow over this news. Poor Clyde. I can't believe a young man with so much in front of him could do such a thing, but know well enough from all I have seen out here how much despair and suffering is in the world, and how a man can be beaten down by it. The thought of another spell in gaol – real prison this time – made him desperate, and he did what he did to escape. But he was young. It was only time. And the number of months or years wasn't even decided. I feel bitter, but what can any of us do?

I cannot bear to think of your grief, father, because I know my own. I think of our old times together, and all the while this terrible thing up ahead. I blame myself, as well as all circumstances, that Clyde has not been saved – though I did what I could. I am desperate myself sometimes, both for money and in spirit, but ought to have done more.

Tam, I will do what I can in the other matter. I've asked friends in Sydney to give me an advance on some work I sent them, but don't get a real lot done these days, what with the need to be always on the move. As you see, this news has arrived only now. My best love to you all.

Your loving son and brother etc.

Two or three times a year a bundle of paintings, done on paper or cardboard and crudely packaged, would arrive at the Sydney dealers. The money when it found him went home.

Occasionally, in one of the bigger towns, he would make his way to a library, and under the gaze of students, librarians and odd citizens who had slipped in to while away an hour between appointments (settled people to whom his laceless boots and thin jacket, carefully buttoned to disguise a temporary absence of shirt, proclaimed 'tramp' or 'swaggie') would tremblingly take down from a shelf one of the folio-sized art-books he craved but could not afford.

They gave only the barest indication, the flat prints. But by fixing his attention on them and creating, re-creating the rest, he glimpsed what was possible, understanding best for his own purpose when his state of excited imagination got between him and the mere image so that he fiercely, ecstatically misunderstood. When he crept away these pictures went with him. He stored them in his head, lighting the corner of a shed where he slept on bags with his own version of what he had seen, till the dark grew vivid and his fingers twitched.

Later, when a stranger's generosity allowed him for a time the use of a back verandah, or a boat shed or a greenkeeper's hut haunted by mice, he would lay out his brushes and feverishly, but with cool assurance, begin.

Faces, figures, occasions – some tender, some brutal as blood. He had carried them so far that they had gone already through a dozen transformations, and as his hand gave them form they revealed another and yet another, so that he too was amazed. What appeared, though long planned for, had the effect even for him of something never dreamed of breaking new into the world.

He worked with small means and the difficulty they imposed became his triumph. He worked in paint when he could find it, thick ochres and greys with just a touch of scarlet and expensive, ordinary blue. Mostly he used line, crimson or blue ink with a thin wash, in which he recorded the presence and particularities of men whose names he never knew, sleeping by a fire or playing cards or posing for him briefly after a meal.

He had been adrift so long now that he thought he might never get back. Cross-currents and storms became the normal conditions of his existence; the paintings were flimsy rafts, then islands with their own weather and their own crowded history, then messages scribbled in what was sometimes a cool clear happiness like floating but more often a maddened despair. When he was washed up somewhere it was because he was too sick or too tired to go on.

One night of low cloud under an intermittent moon, wearing a stained felt hat and looking for all the world like a scarecrow that had just climbed down from a stake among rattling husks, he entered a township that spread all along a river-mouth. He had to walk the whole length of it, past tin fences where dogs leapt barking and windows threw their light across stony yards, past one-storeyed stone banks, stores with corrugated-iron awnings, a brightly-lit picture-theatre where a crowd of slick youths and girls with Alice Faye hair-dos stood about eating chocolate hearts under a streetlamp blackened with moths.

He was looking for a place where he could doss down for a day or two and let the fever he had picked up in the mosquito swamps further north run its forty-eight or seventy-two hour course. He was already some hours into it. He sweated, shivered, his bones grated in their sockets; they jarred.

The township was scattered. He thought he would never reach the last streetlamp and the welcome dark.

It was nearly midnight when on the outskirts, beyond the yelping of the last farm dog, he came to a kind of car dump, a place of infested water puddles and coarse grass, evil-looking in the half-dark and worse under the moon, where the bodies of cars, many of them without wheels – square-bodied limousines, sedans, trucks, roadsters with a hood and dickey-seat, their iron paintless and showing lines of rust – sat on their chassis in the swamp as if they were already half-sunken earthwards and the least weight, a night-cricket or a fingertip, might take them down.

Masses of thin cloud rolled overhead. The moon came and went. The land sweltered in tropical heat. In moments when the moon was hidden it was pitch black, a darkness so dense that you might have stepped back into a time before creation, before any of this – grass, mud, rocks – had been thought of. You could turn your head into it and lose all track of east or west or inland or oceanward, and might wonder if there was anything under you at all, and what it was you were on the edge of, what not-yet-formed or created continent. Then the pallid moon showed the tip of a horn; sickly light came flooding back, and there you were again in a familiar century, with piles of highway junk laid out before you like a forgotten car-park.

In one of these shells, he thought, in this graveyard of journeys, I can curl up for a time, a day or two, till the fever shakes loose.

He staggered into one of the lanes between the derelict bodies and had only to make his choice.

It was like standing in a stream of traffic, in the path of a coming pile-up that had already occurred, with your hand out, waiting for one of the stopped vehicles to stop. He set his hand on the handle of a once-green Buick. It refused to budge. Inside, he saw, it was filled with a kind of mould that had grown all over the leather seats with their burst springs, a malignant cloud. He started away.

Sometimes the doors were off and the insides burnt out. They smelled of ash. Approaching one, a limousine with a high hood, he tried the handle, turned it, and was hurled back by a blood-curdling cry. Crouched there on the seat was a black devil, all blue-black hair and breathing fire. Its look of prior right and of fierce dark ownership went right through him. He began to shake, and thought it might be best if he simply lay flat on his back in the spiky grass and closed his eyes. He had no wish to dispute possession with the spirits of the place or with the ghosts of previous owners.

He lay still. After the sound of his own footsteps on the pavements of the town, and then heart-beats, the silence was wide enough to get lost in. He might escape.

But it was not that easy.

A blue shadow approached that seemed to be cast upward out of the earth. Clouds moved behind it. He closed his eyes. Now he was being lifted up, heaved violently aloft and rattled, he heard his bones shake, and smelled the creature's closeness, a smell of char. He felt its fiery warmth as his ribs were crushed and he was clawed at. So that was it! He was being tossed about at the centre of an accident he had hoped to step out of the way of, and when, in the prolonged crashing of metal on metal, the moon appeared through cloud-wrack, he saw by its sick flare that behind the webbed and frosted glass of every car there were watchers: stately figures, also black, who looked on but did not move, their eyes unblinking under the moon.

The place was haunted by spirits older than the ghosts of cars and their owners. He had disturbed a rite, or interrupted an assembly of the dispossessed.

He was shaken. Then the black angel or blue-black devil had its victory or acknowledged defeat – anyway, withdrew its forces and spat him out. When he came to his senses it was daylight. Damp red soil was at his eyeball with blades of blunted, razor-sharp grass sprouting from it, so coarse you could see the crystals that would cut. A host of ants was going about its business all around him, intent and scrambling, as if he were just another element in the landscape they had to negotiate and had been lying here from the beginning, or had dropped from the sky overnight. He lay watching them, their furious, fiercely organized life.

His back, he discovered when he tried to move, was sun-burned right through the shirt, but when he staggered to his feet at last it was into a feeling of wholeness, of renewed power and strength, though he could never be sure afterwards which side he had come out on, or what pact he had made with his native earth.

AN ONLY CHILD

[1]

In the big bedroom off the front verandah of what I thought of as
Grandma's house, with a view, beyond scraggy bunyah pines where
sparrows squalled, to the still pale light of the Broadwater, my grandfather
was dying. He had been doing it for more than a year, and since my mother
alone was tolerable to him as a day or night nurse (my Aunt Ollie was
already occupied in the kitchen and his younger daughters he thought too
incompetent, too silly or too young at forty to be faced with anything so
serious as dying) we had moved from our house in Brisbane and were
settled, not uncomfortably, in the spare room off my grandmother's porch.
My father had the journey up to town each day and I was sent for a term or
two, or for however long this period out of our regular lives should last, to
the local school.

Southport with its pier and beaches was a place I associated with holidays
and our whole time there had for me an unreal air, as if we were all marking
time – my grandfather's time – and even the hard business of parsing and
analysis and mental arithmetic were in that place mere pretend.

It was a heightened unreality. I was just twelve, and freer than I had been
in town to make the sort of discoveries that a freshly awakened sense of
myself demanded. Of myself, but also of the world and the way my body
suddenly fitted into it.

The school had looser rules than I was used to. The pupils, boys and girls
both, went barefoot and we spent a good many of our lessons drowsing
peacefully in the shadow of gums. I slept out of doors on a verandah. It was
not at all like my room at home, with its built-in cupboards and the
collection of old service-medals, inkwells and little celluloid boxes (treasures from the junkshops in Melbourne Street) that had kept me tied to my
previous self and created a continuity, I might have thought, in which I
could only develop along fixed lines. At Southport I had scope. There was
nothing on that sleepout but an iron bed, and moonlight when there was a

49

moon, and at moments the crouched outline of a cat. The air was cool, even on the closest summer nights, and since the sleepout had no walls, this air, in which leaves rustled, night insects twiddled and the sea lapped or lashed according to the weather on the roughstone promenade, was the real medium in which I slept. Faintly silvered with moonlight and smelling of salt, it changed everything it touched, so that even my belly out there belonged to a different creature; I too was changed. My body seemed all on its own to have hit upon a new mode of apprehension and I couldn't tell whether it was time or place that had done it, or some leap I had taken into a new and more passionate form.

Since there was so little traffic on the roads, I was allowed at last to have a bicycle and could sprint off wherever I pleased. In the late afternoon, when the waters of the Broadwater turned mauvish-pink and the dunes that closed in it developed shadowy dents, I could follow the front all the way to Labrador, exploring inlets along the shore and paths leading down to the river, putting speed on to see how fast I could go or stopping, in the free and easy way of seaside places, to talk to strangers. I made friends of a different sort: boys whose fathers were professional fishermen. They taught me to trawl the sandbanks with a gunny-sack full of fish-heads to attract 'pippies', how to lay a crab-pot, and what time of day or month of the year was best for prawning or fishing the still-water for whiting, or when the trevelly were running with tailor amongst them for setting a rod beside the surf. My father, aware of what a rupture all this had made in our lives, and how little time my mother now had for me, took me on the excursions he made – sometimes on business but mostly to satisfy his own curiosity about things and people – into the odd, hidden life of the town. We became friends. He was returning to the world of his youth, and was happy to see me discover, thirty years later, what had once been his.

He had about him, my father, something of the small-town dandy. He had inherited that from his own father. He didn't carry a stick as Grandpa had or wear cutaway collars or a soft hat, but he did on all occasions wear a suit, and that was unusual in those days, and especially at Southport; some wheat-coloured or dove-grey material in summer, with a knitted tie, and in winter a three-piece herring-bone.

He knew almost everyone we passed on our walks, and was greeted, I thought, by some of the queerest characters I had ever seen. They called him 'Boss', or 'Mister', or simply 'Bob', and many of them stopped to yarn, expressing surprise at my existence or the extent to which I had sprung up since last time, or would recall with a moist eye my father's own promising youth, and depart the richer, usually, by a shilling piece.

These were the old-timers of the place. They had been old-timers, most of them, in my father's day, and had names like Snow, Nudger and The Champ. Some of them were returned soldiers from one of the wars. Others had been boxers or footballers, and one was a politician who had suffered a fall. He wore a good dark suit with a watch-chain, and looked, from a distance, every bit as dandified as my father. He was walking, as we approached on the front, with what I took to be a portly swagger, but when we got close I saw him hesitate and prepare to cross, then dither, then determine to come on; but with a pretence that he was deep in thought and had not seen us. I was surprised when my father, who was usually sensitive, quickened his step and with his hand already extended, called 'Dick, Dick Allan! How have you been?'

The man caught my father in a bearhug. He seemed about to burst into tears.

I saw then that he was quite drunk, that his clothes, though well brushed, were worn and shabby, and that his stately progress along the pavement had been not so much swagger as instability. He had a Digger's badge in his lapel, a wet quivering lip, and the same sly, ingratiating look and smell of seediness and booze as all the rest. I was afraid for a moment that my father would produce the shilling. I thought the man might take it and it was something I did not want to see.

'Poor chappie, he's in a bad way,' my father muttered as we moved off. 'Did you see that, Phil? You'd better not mention we met him – or not to your grandma anyway, she wouldn't like it. And not to Aunt Ollie either. She used to be rather fond of him. He's not such a bad fellow as they make out, but he got into trouble, and you know – people are –'

He shook his head and I waited, but the word did not come. I wondered for a long time what it might be, how it was that he saw people. But either he could find no word, no single word, that was the right one or he was ashamed to utter it. Or perhaps he thought I was too young to hear the truth.

In all ways magnanimous, he had the style, I used to think later, of the born patron, that spirit of generosity that asks nothing for itself, feels no threat in the presence of greatness, takes joy in every form of excellence or superior art or skill, and cares only that what has come into the world as a large possibility should not for the world's sake go unfulfilled. In another place and time he might have endowed colleges or commissioned altars or become an entrepreneur of all that was bizarre and marvellous. His restriction, so far as everyday employment went, to the mundane world of fruit and vegetables left his real gifts undeclared, and one caught a glimpse of what they might be only when the fruit-growers and distributors, each year in August, mounted their display-stands at the Brisbane Show. Then at last he could show his hand. Those ordinary objects, Granny Smiths and Jonathans polished to a waxy brightness, William pears, Valencias, paw-paws, mangoes, bananas, were freed into a new dimension. Transcending their edible selves, and leaving behind the world of orchards at Stanthorpe or plantations at Bowen, and the suburban dining tables for which they were intended, they became the merest abstract shapes and colours to be deployed as imagination decreed: in maps of the seven states of the Commonwealth, as the kangaroo, emu and shield in the national emblem, as a star-burst of ten-foot poinsettias, in diamond-shapes, lozenges and zig-zags like the markings on a serpent, or as letters that spelled out the name of the firm in an elaborate scroll flanked by cornucopias spilling giant apples and pears, that when looked at closer were made up of dozens of real-life apples and pears.

These displays were a prodigy of invention. Each year my father was photographed beside his exhibit, along with my grandmother (his partner in the business) and the girls from the office. Beautifully inscribed in copperplate and insipidly tinted, these photographs covered a whole wall of his noisy cubbyhole above the open hall of the markets, where trucks loaded and unloaded at concrete bays and men in shorts and leather aprons hauled sacks about, tossed fruit cases, shouldered great hands of bananas, and the floor was littered with cabbage leaves and a mash of pumpkins and tomatoes.

He had an eye, my father, for the way nature might outdo itself – and not only in the matter of apples and pears. He liked to believe that the world was blessed with men, rare though they might be, of outrageous ambition and uncanny gifts. People knew his weakness and brought him news of wonders. Or as my grandmother put it, pestered him on behalf of every sort of scoundrel, no-hoper and lame duck.

So for several weeks that year we went each Friday to see a boxer train, a young halfcaste, the son of a thin, impossible man, himself a former boxer, who had approached my father in a pub. Punchdrunk, and with one puffy ear, he was convinced that with a little encouragement – good training, that is, and a few pounds to back it up – his boy could be a champion welterweight.

The boy was seventeen: tough, darkly resentful, but good. He trained with a punching bag under their house and we sat on packing cases under a naked globe and watched him hiss and dance barefoot in the dirt, aiming swift hard punches at the bag as if it had done him a deep hurt, while the father, in shorts and dirty singlet, put his shoulder to it and took the blows, cursing, crowing, spitting fierce directives.

They were an odd pair. There was something abject in the man's eagerness to win my father's approval, and a kind of desperation in the way he displayed the boy, pinching his muscles, punching him hard to show his toughness, singing lyrics, all filled out with set phrases from the sports columns, to his 'potentialities'.

For him, after so many defeats, it must have been a last chance at glory and a grab at the big money. The boy was his insurance policy. He talked and talked out of the corner of his mouth, where spit flowed, and sang his wheedling song. The boy said nothing. He just stood, panting, glowing with sweat, his gloved fists loose at his side. He glared, said nothing, and his intensity now that it was no longer directed at the bag which hung at his shoulder, a slack square shadow beside our finer ones, seemed all the more powerful for being unspent. For him this was a way – perhaps the only one – of saving himself for a time from the inevitable round of drink, then jail, then more drink; of keeping off, while he was still strong-winded and fast on his feet, the shadow and sour stink, and angry sick despair, of fellows three or four years older than himself whom he remembered from school as clean-cut youths with a future and whose mouths were clamped now on a metho bottle. He danced a little, and his father crowed and called him a killer. He looked like one. I thought it was his father – that nearest of all white men – he might decide to kill.

The place, their dusty under-the-house, with its cage of enclosing lattice, its twelve-foot stumps, its stacks of half-broken chairs and bed-frames and empty oil-drums, disturbed me. It evoked so many darker potentialities than the ones we had come to judge.

'Well then,' the man urged, breathlessly running on the spot. 'Waddya reckon? Will ya help us git up?'

It was only one of the places my father took me. There was also an old man, retired and half-blind with cataracts, who 'invented things'. He too was eager to have his chance at the big money that was about. He showed us a device for picking up leaves that could be made out of the frames of old umbrellas, and an unwieldy contraption, iron-jawed and sprung, for cracking Queensland nuts.

'You see,' my father explained, 'things are beginning to pick up again, now that the war's over. That man must be eighty, but he wants to be in it along with the rest. Things will get going again. It will be big.'

Another fellow, a barman, had a whole house full of bottles of every imaginable size, shape and colour – earthenware ginger-beer bottles with pebble stoppers, blue, green and gold medicine bottles, beer bottles, bottles for linseed oil, olive oil, calamine lotion, lye. Whole rooms were stacked with them, on shelves that went from floor to ceiling making wonderful lights. He assured us they would be worth a fortune one day and wanted my father to buy the collection or lend him money on it, I forgot which, or talk some Minister into making a museum.

'You see, everyone suddenly is full of ideas,' my father exulted. 'This country' – he drew a big breath and sucked in deeply the spirit of the new era – 'is on the brink of being discovered. For the *second* time. It's all there, three-million square miles of it, just waiting to be grasped and hauled up by its boot-straps into – '

But as usual, the word he wanted that would have fixed its destination was not there. He lost sight of it. It was too blinding or too far off.

It was at this time and in this spirit that he met Frank Harland, another pub acquaintance; or heard from a fellow-drinker that some sort of weird artist-bloke had set himself up in the Pier Pictures, and had gone along in eternal hope of the extraordinary to introduce himself and take a look. The time I went with him was not his first visit. By then he and the artist bloke were in their own way friends.

It was a windy afternoon in late August and we were going to invite

Harland to Sunday lunch. Rain was pitting the grey of the Broadwater, flicking up light like shrapnel; it would ease off, swing out to sea, then blow back again in violent gusts that threw salt into the municipal beds, where cannas grew among clumps of blood-red salvia. The few people who were about struggled with umbrellas that threatened to whip inside out, or went barefoot in capes. The Pier Pictures, out in the wash of dirty water, looked like the hulk of a stranded coral-barge or dredger that might at any moment break up and founder, saving the civic authorities, since it had been condemned for several months now and boarded up for even longer, a fortune in wrecker's fees.

I had known the place for as long as I could remember. A vast wooden structure with a mansard roof and pepper-pot towers, it stood at the end of the pier about sixty yards out in the waters of the bay and was approached by a latticed gallery that extended all along the southern end of it like a closed verandah – a great convenience on days of summer drizzle, and on afternoons when, just as the matinée was out, great storm-clouds came rolling in off the Pacific and all hell let loose, or on wintry occasions like the present when the westerly blew and spray dashed at the lattice, puddling all one side of the gallery with standing water.

Set apart from the rest of the town in the shallow waters of the bay, and dedicated to familiar mysteries, the Pier Pictures was an ambiguous area like my verandah sleepout, neither inside nor out. Daylight flowed in through latticed openings high up under the roof. On hot afternoons around Christmas a line of doors could be opened into the gallery and a warm breeze would puff in under the heavy drapes, in which the smell of the sea, sharp and salty at low tide, would be mixed with the mustiness of velvet and dust. It is a smell I have encountered nowhere else. It evokes for me the peculiar sensuousness and sticky charm of those long Saturday afternoons of late childhood and adolescence, and goes with wet heat, fingers tacky from Have-a-Hearts or Jaffas sucked in the dark, and a kaleidescope of images, in lurid colour or in sharp black and white, that are not only episodes in some external drama of Tarzan or cattle-ranchers or comic chases through trains, but belong as well to the private drama that was unfolding simultaneously with the other in whatever part of us – mind or body – is the seat of our first strong apprehension of the world, of that point in it where we and the multiplicity of things are in touch; an apprehension for which the artificial darkness of three o'clock on a Saturday afternoon, our awareness of the close presence of others in a still but not quite passive crowd, and the excited unreality of the events unfolding before us – sensual, violent, apocalyptic – may be the necessary conditions.

The sea, invisibly out of sight, still touched the air with salt. If a storm had blown up while some encounter in the endless war between cowboys and Indians was being decided, there might be added to our presence in the Nevada desert a sensation, obscurely felt, of our being also at sea, of real waves lashing at the seaweed-hung and barnacle-encrusted piles on which the old structure rested, and of spray, all heady ozone, about to come hissing up between us and the heat-haze of the screen.

It was a magic box, the old Pier Pictures. But it was also close to nature. Too close. It had in the end to be condemned, and even on its better days there were kids who couldn't face it because they got seasick.

It was here, braving all threat of being stranded or washed out to sea, that Frank Harland had set up his makeshift studio. Not in the open auditorium, which had been stripped of its seats and of all its lamps and decorations, but in the sanctum itself. Up where the screen had once floated and a transparent but convincingly solid Tarzan had swung from trees, where Ann Miller had tapped on air and Boris Karloff's iron boot had had just weight enough to crush a skull, Frank Harland had suspended three hurricane lamps from a length of rope, pinned his bits of paper and cardboard to the remains of a hemp curtain, and was at work when we entered on his own view of the world.

'G'day Frank,' my father called across the dripping theatre.

The man left the table where he was working and came, brush in hand, to the edge of the stage. He stood there in the boxlike space with his canvases about him and called back:

'Who is it?'

I had the weirdest feeling. As if, in a sudden reversal of things, someone up there on the screen had stolen the initiative and it was we, at the other end, who were the shadows here.

My father named himself. I think he also named me, but I don't remember the painter paying me any attention. He seemed distant, preoccupied, eager perhaps to get back to his work.

He was very thin, with a drooping moustache and watery, slate-blue eyes. When he moved, as he did very often in a jerky, loose-limbed, dancing way, his feet shuffled, and I thought of him at first as being old. In fact he was younger than my father, and sometimes, when I used to watch him in my Aunt Ollie's kitchen, his manner was even younger than that. With his thin shoulders and lost, blue look, he could seem slight and boyish.

He puzzled me. His clothes, an old army shirt and sweater and boots without socks, were those of a tramp; but he wore them with a natural elegance, as if he had some notion, like my father, of what it was to be a dandy, and for all the mess with which he was surrounded he was himself very contained and formal – almost, I thought, soldierly. His gaze was indirect and kept drifting back to the picture he was at work on. It was spread out on a low, rickety table knocked up out of fruit-cases. He couldn't keep away from it. He kept dancing back to take a quick, shy look as if it were a child he was minding. There was a kitchen chair in front of the table that had once been green, and a little wheeled trolley with a shelf where he mixed his colours in a messy arc and where brushes of all sizes stood in peanut-paste bottles. Away to the left a camp-bed with a heap of grey army blankets, a primus stove and some blackened pots.

It felt strange to be high up on the lighted stage, with the empty theatre out front and the rain dripping into it from three or four holes in the roof, making lakes where only a year ago we had slumped in our canvas chairs and been transported to strange places. I was more impressed at that moment, I think, by what had happened to the Pier Pictures than by the spare, shy figure with the lines in his cheeks – and if by him, by the way his boots flopped because he had no socks and the army boots no laces.

He and my father, after a good deal of embarrassed shifting about and shuffling from foot to foot, had come to the table where the painter's work was spread. There seemed nothing to do but look at it. My father looked and hummed, and I came up under his arm and looked as well. Frank Harland hugged himself, moaned, shook his head, darted off to the left and right, but always came back to face it.

It was a big picture, mostly red, but splashed all over with feathery blue. There were figures in it, two of them, and they appeared to be dancing or swimming or supporting one another against a fall – there was no clear indication and they were hard to disentangle, you couldn't tell where one figure ended and the other picked up. Leaving my father and Harland to scratch their heads over it, each in his own way, and to mumble the formulas of men who cannot find words for what they might have to say to one another, I went off to explore.

The wings of the theatre were shallow and uninteresting, their whitewashed walls all patched with grey where the switchboards had been pulled out. There were no relics. The entire mystery of the Pier Pictures had been in those illusions on the screen and in whatever excitement we ourselves had created in the dark of the stalls. I pocketed a coil of rusty fuse-wire as a kind of souvenir – there was nothing else – and was drawn back to the stage.

The artist-bloke, Frank Harland, was in a state of extreme agitation. He was ripping sketches and smaller paintings from the curtain they were pinned to and tossing them in a pile on the floor. My father, who was deeply embarrassed by every form of emotion, was simply standing there, helpless and appalled.

Harland had dealt with most of the sketches, calling them a dead loss, all botched work, and was dancing in his army boots on the fragments, when my father decided to intervene. He caught up one of the pictures (it was a landscape) and said how much he liked it.

Harland's hand was arrested. He took the picture, looked at it, looked again, and suddenly made a crowing sound, at the same time slapping his brow with an open hand.

'By golly, you know, you're right!'

He scrabbled on the floor and snatched up two or three of the dismembered sketches, holding the pieces together, and considered, then shook his head. 'No, this *is* the one. I'm staggered. You realized it straight off. I don't know what got into me.' He stood holding the scrap of paper before him as if he were seeing it for the first time.

He passed it back to my father, who cleared his throat now and offered in a low voice to buy the painting. If Harland would name his price.

Later, when the little picture had come to have a particular meaning for me, I would spend long hours trying to solve its mysteries; and later again, when Harland was famous, I would understand that it was a masterpiece. But at the moment of first laying eyes on it, it said nothing to me. I was used to seeing pictures in a frame. Seen as my father now held it, slightly buckled and with raw edges that the paint did not always cover, it had no more weight than the painter himself, who was too close to being a tramp for me to see him as an artist.

It was all green trees or bluish-green clouds – it was difficult to tell which – with a chink of brilliant light under them that was the horizon, and another stroke of light, in a jagged diagonal, that might have been a thunderbolt, but could also have been a figure diving. I couldn't see what had caught my father's eye in it, and guessed he had pulled it out of the series at random and was as surprised as Harland was at his achievement.

Frank Harland shuffled. He considered the thing. He wondered if two pounds would be all right; then shook his head as if he had taken advantage of my father's generosity.

'No, no,' he said, pushing the picture away, 'I can't take anything for it. It was your eye picked it out. Let me give it to you.'

But my father was already taking the notes from his wallet. He set them down on the trolley, and I could see that he was disappointed. He had expected to pay more; either because he wanted to give Harland money and buying the picture was a way of saving the man's dignity, or because he genuinely wished to believe that the work was good and expected the painter, in naming a price, to make his own high claims for it. Two pounds was neither here nor there.

'Oright then, you win,' Frank Harland said to cover his embarrassment, since he was clearly in need, 'I'll sign it for you.'

He set the picture down, and with great care now that it was my father's, composed his initials into a curious and beautiful monogram, working the pen very slowly, like a boy doing a copybook exercise, and pushing his tongue out at the corner of his mouth. He retouched and blotted it, then lay it aside.

I was more impressed by all this than by anything the painting itself had revealed to me. It was the hand linking the quite ordinary initials into a complex pattern that struck me; the two letters, beautifully entwined, of the artist's signature, marking so clearly the claim of self. I immediately accorded him, as an artist, my whole-hearted belief. I had thought him odd before, though likeable (he was shy enough to make me feel at ease) but was convinced now that my father, for once in his life, as in the case of the little painting itself, had discovered the real thing.

I wandered off to look at the other things he had discarded, rather as I might have gone through a pile of cast-offs and old junk that my mother, in one of her cleaning fits, had thrown out of our spare room. I had an eye in those days for what I thought of as 'treasures', objects, that is, that I found evocative and which others had no use for. It had led me, on Saturday mornings in Brisbane, to take my shilling pocket money and go off early to the two junkshops in Melbourne Street. And it was in the mood now in which I might have pushed open the door of Old Ned's in the expectation of a cut-glass scent bottle, or a silver button-hook or a postcard of a lady with real hair, that I drew from a pile of sheets against the wall the portrait of a woman and turned it casually to the light.

What I saw drew a gasp from me, perhaps even a little cry, and I wondered at first if it wasn't the spirit in which I had picked the thing up – that mood of going off to the junk shops, first Old Ned's and then Old Knack's – that made me believe I knew the woman. It was her attitude I recognized rather than the face, which was barely suggested by two or three pen strokes under a stack of wispy straw – the way she was settled in the striped deckchair. I saw immediately now what the picture was that Frank Harland had been at work on and what those figures were engaged on in their wash of red.

My cry must have been real. Frank Harland and my father had turned, and Harland was frowning. He had seen at once that I knew the woman. He coloured, gave my father a quick glance, then stared at me with his innocent eyes wide open, waiting for me to tell.

What he had seen in my eyes was shock, but there was no shock in his. Only a pained sadness.

My father stepped forward and took the picture from me. He looked at it with approval, then passed it back. It meant nothing to him.

We left soon after, and if I was more silent than usual, my father, with the little landscape tucked away under his buttoned coat, might have put it down to the driving rain.

It wasn't that. It was the woman, so largely and beautifully and warmly alive again in the striped deckchair.

I had seen her often. She was the woman who lived with Knack, the second of my two junk shop-keepers; so that I had, as it were, been on the way to her, first Old Ned's, then Old Knack's, when I lifted the sheet off the pile. She was a big, lazy, sad-looking blonde, very white, with painted nails and hair piled high on her head that was never quite tidy, and which she kept patting with a plump and rather grubby hand. She sat with her legs crossed, in a frock without sleeves in summer and the same frock with a cardigan in winter, in a passageway between shelves stacked deep with books, and did not move. If you wanted to know the price of something, a silver-plated egg cup, a spoon and pusher, a china sugar basin with a transfer picture of Rockhampton on it, or a miniature Toby jug or a little bakelite stud-case with an initialled shield, you had to take it up to her and she would enquire how much you had. 'Well then, love,' she'd say, 'that'll be sixpence to you.' Or ninepence or fourpence ha'penny or whatever saved her from having to move and get change. I liked her, and couldn't imagine why she had chosen to live with Knack.

Difficult to think of Knack, with his immense stoop, and his accent, and a skull that looked as if it had never had hair at all but had always been polished and bald, as anything but a monster. He had a habit of standing in the doorway to his shop with a little zebra-striped love-bird on his shoulder or perched very prettily on the back of his hand, or (but I don't believe I ever saw this, I only imagined it) on the bald crown of his head, as on a monstrous egg it was trying to hatch. I used to watch him from the tram or from the other side of the street, and would go into the shop at last only when the woman was lolling in the deckchair and he was clearly away. He scared me; and when he smiled, showing all his teeth and adopting a pose that was meant to make him, in the eyes of a small boy, a kind of clown on stilts, I lost all power of speech and was more fascinated and frightened than ever.

So it was no surprise to hear one morning, that in the little flat behind the shop, whose lilac and green wallpaper I had glimpsed behind the woman's head, he had first killed the woman with two shots from a Luger pistol, then turned it on himself.

It was the merest chance that Frank Harland's experience and mine should have crossed in this way, and that I should have come upon his drawing of the woman in a place where I was accustomed, week after week, to make the jump from reality to some other more abstract dimension. Anywhere else I might have missed the connection; and even now there was something in the larger painting that I failed to catch. I saw clearly enough what those linked figures were *doing*, what the red was, and the madness and pathos of those streaks of blue, but I could not understand why the thing was so joyfully undismayed. It was as if all that red – as Frank Harland conceived it – were something other than blood.

None of this could I have put into words that day. I put it into silence. It was a silence, along with other things, that I felt I shared now with Frank Harland.

My father walked beside me, hugging under his coat the painting he had bought, which was all innocent green play; confident, in the way of fathers, that I knew no more than I revealed, and was just what I seemed to be.

[2]

My grandfather was dying, but he was doing it in his own time, and that was the time, day by day that we all lived in. So long as Grandpa is still dying, I told myself, we will go on living here. So that when I think now of my changed life and all the ways in which its old patterns were disturbed – of my father no longer being head of his own house, my mother no longer cooking for us, of our no longer being a family of three but a minor branch of a larger and more complex household, of my having no room of my own and being cut off from all my old school-friends, the one child in a house of aunts and uncles, and of the intense sensations and discoveries of that year, the way my body fitted into the real air, or penetrated or rubbed against or pounded or brushed the objects of the ordinary world – then I think of this too as being part of Grandpa's dying, which was not at all a negative activity but something positive and engrossing.

Grandpa's day, which had previously been idle, given over to walks and conversations on the front with people he never brought home, or to slow games of dominoes and the re-reading of his favourite authors, was pinned down now in real time to hours as regular and unbreakable as business appointments. He was, for the first time since I had known him, fully employed.

There was the hour of his early bottle, which my mother brought in at six and which the old man turned aside to use while she fussed over his tray.

There followed the hour of his wash and shave, his pills, his first feeding with a mush that had to be spooned into him as one feeds a baby, then the hour of his morning visits. First my Aunt Ollie, just risen on her way down to prepare breakfast, then my father on his way to the train and me on my way to school; then my other aunts – last, as usual, Aunt Connie – followed by the hour when my mother read to him. At ten my grandmother made her appearance, bringing an air of brisk impatience and a scent of musk from the little pastilles she sucked to cover her breath, and with the rather haughty demeanour before my mother of a grand lady making an inspection and finding nothing to fault. Then lunch, the bedpan, the thermometer, his afternoon nap. Then in the late afternoon, after my return from school, an hour in which I sat at the end of his bed, high up on the lace cover, and read a book, while my mother slipped away to rest. Rigorously organized and filling every available hour of the day, his dying gave form to the household.

He had made no impression at all in the old days. Nobody had consulted him. His younger daughters' practice at meal-times had been to treat his every word with tolerant amusement – they had learned that from their mother; to interrupt, sigh, giggle, as if everything he said was nonsense or comically out-of-date. Taunting him had become such an established habit that the taunters barely noticed what they were doing. Their assaults lacked all cruelty save the power to wound, and originated most often with Grandpa's favourite, Aunt Roo.

'I feel awful,' she might announce, 'it's this *heat*! I'm sticking everywhere. I could throw every stitch off and just go bare. I don't know why we don't, in a climate like this. Like the abos! It'd make more sense.'

Aunt Roo was strident and fearless of proprieties. She protested with every jerk of her angular shoulders and slewed expression of mouth against the aridity of things. Her protests were useless. They were ascribed not to her view of other possibilities but to her character: her weak grip on reality, her preference for 'scenes'.

'That's enough, thank you,' my grandmother would say quietly. She did not look at me but I was plainly in her mind.

'Well I'm *melting*! Doesn't anyone else feel it? Well, *don't* you?'

'I feel it,' Grandpa said.

'Oh you, of course you'd feel it, all dolled up in a suit. It's ridiculous.

63

You're not *going* anywhere.' Grandpa looked startled, then hurt. 'Where do you think we are anyway? It's eighty-five in the shade.'

'Gloucestershire,' Aunt Connie suggested. Being herself on most occasions the family butt she would say these things out of cowardice, to ingratiate and protect herself. She blushed for her own boldness now and was ashamed.

'Ollie,' said my grandmother, observing that Grandpa had put his spoon down and pushed away his plate, 'I think this pudding could do with more sugar. I don't mind, but your father has a sweet tooth. So does Phil.'

Aunt Ollie agreed: she had been distracted by the postman.

'I'm sorry,' she said.

Grandpa shook his head. It was only Aunt Roo who could hurt him.

We had taken him for granted in those days; he was barely present. Now, when he was permanently upstairs, he was never out of our thoughts. With his papery skin all covered with blotches, the worry about bed-sores, the warmish enamel bottles I had to carry out under a white cloth, he was entirely, unavoidably real.

But if his dying made him actual in a physical sense, then the process of his abstraction (for it was also that) could only, I thought, be a matter of spirit. I saw it as a withdrawal to England, where he had originally come from, a place whose manners and habits of speech had always cut him off from us. Each day, with his extreme whiteness and fragility, and the precision with which he now shaped even the simplest words, he was getting further towards it; he was being refined of everything local and ordinary; he was being 'taken back', and had begun to resemble, with his fine white hair and clipped moustache, old English gentlemen as I had seen them illustrated in books. Colonels. Though Grandpa in fact – and even this was long ago – had never been anything more than a dandified and unsuccessful insurance-salesman.

Dying, it seemed to me, was a process of becoming your essential self, of moving into some realm of a lighter, clearer identity, that would cut you off at last even from those who were closest to you, your children and grandchildren, while at the same time imposing upon them the fullest possible awareness of your presence as it involved a weight to be lifted aside while the bed was made, and the most intimate, but after all unavoidable and in no way shameful excretions. I felt closer to Grandpa now than when he had taken me on walks and gruffly pushed lollies into my palm, or insisted that I face up to dogs; or when, a weak and formal presence at the head of his own table, I had seen him shamed and humiliated.

Often, when I had to lean close to attend to one of his wishes (his voice in my ear came as from a great distance, as if he had slipped back into some remote time, his own childhood perhaps, or to some lost place in England) I would feel his skin against my own as no longer quite human, as having the scratchiness of bark or the papery quality of an insect's wing. This too seemed part of the process. As the body began to change for death it would naturally reveal, it seemed to me, what it shared with other creatures or with the earth. I saw nothing frightening in it. Touching my grandfather's skin and thinking, *he is close to death*, seemed much like bringing my fingertips into contact with the scribbles on a tree trunk. It was uncanny, that was all. Mysterious.

It was from my mother that I had inherited this easy matter-of-factness. I was often her assistant in that room, and it was me she had chosen to replace her when she slipped away each afternoon to snatch an hour's rest. I liked nothing better than to curl up at the end of Granpa's bed, my back against the brass rail with its row of china balusters, and with my feet tucked up under me and my head in a book, to watch over him while my mother slept.

Grandpa dozed and snored, propped upright with pillows. I went splashing through the Canadian marshlands or swashbuckled my way through the moonlit alleys of d'Artagnan's Paris. Occasionally he would speak, odd words or phrases that were not always addressed to me. Sometimes it was my father or my Uncle Gil he had in mind, back when they were my age; or two Gloucestershire lads, Jim Hodge and Will Burnley, who had been the companions of his youth; or Felix Pickup, his first partner at Lightning Ridge, who was a 'decent cove' and never appeared in Grandpa's stories under any other rubric.

Grandpa did not always live in the present. Or rather, his present was a layer of several decades that could replace one another with startling rapidity and in no sort of chronological order. A shouted warning out of his sleep might be intended for the Decent Cove, Felix. The beginning of a reminiscence, a 'Say lad, do you remember?' might be meant to call up Jim Hodge. Or it might indeed be my presence he was anxious to be assured of when he whispered 'You still there, boy?', and reached out his hand to be touched. I replied anyway, for myself or for the others, and he seemed content. He would settle back into his slow breathing, his gentle snores, or he would suddenly be quite awake and ready to talk. I was happy then to lay Dumas or *North-West Passage* aside and hear what he had to tell.

His stories, which were all of his own life, had a deep attraction for me. His odd, old-fashioned manner of narration gave them the quality of folk or fairy tale, so that he, as chief character, seemed already to belong to a time that could be thought of as 'the olden days' and to a place that was unreal and far off, even when it was as familiar from the map as Gloucester or Lightning Ridge.

Jim Hodge and Will Burnley were his Gloucestershire cronies. They were all three great drinkers of cider, great cross-country night-walkers. They might tramp all night sometimes and then seek out a farm kept by some lone woman where they could wash up at a pump and get a good breakfast of porridge and eggs. They knew all the history of places going back under doomsday fields to the Romans and beyond, and Grandpa especially, who had a taste for the weird, was an expert on tales of murder and other dark doings on local farms, of which he knew all the names and believed all the hauntings: how on this one a cord from which a sailor had hanged himself could be heard creaking from a beam, and on another a ghostly hammer, all wet with blood, would turn up on the sill of an upstairs window, its handle pointing to the village, miles away on an opposite hill, where the suspected murderer lived, though nothing could be proved against him.

Will Burnley, with Grandpa to work the shovel, had dug up a whole sackful of arrowheads from the mounds on Crickley Hill, as well as sherds from the Roman villa at Witcombe and a Saxon earring. He had an eye, Grandpa said, that could see through six inches of turf. He went off at nearly forty to the Boer war and died there, just making it into the new century, and he had sent Grandpa a letter, after nearly twenty years, from a place called Walling Koep. Grandpa still had it – he had read it to me. It was full of savage facts about the fighting but had romantic descriptions as well of the southern skies. They had reminded him, he wrote, that his old pal, Jeff Vernon, was down there somewhere in the bottom half of the world. The letter came the same week Grandpa was married and gave him deep pause, recalling as it did all his youth, and drawing so to speak a clear line under it.

Jim Hodge he had lost all track of. He would, Grandpa assured me, be an old fellow of more than eighty now, sitting over a jug of cider somewhere up Leckhampton way, talking sheep with a young farmer or reminiscing over his own younger days and wondering what ever had become of his old mate Jeff Vernon, who fifty years ago had packed up and gone to New South Wales.

The Lightning Ridge stories, all hardship and misfortune, were of another kind altogether. Grandpa's earliest partner there, Felix Pickup, the Decent Cove, had been followed by several others; among them the Real Lout (he was sometimes Ben Thingammy and sometimes Jake Whatsit) and most important of all the Two Devils, Rilington and Hobbes, who had cheated Grandpa of everything he had and whom he suspected of a local murder. The Two Devils had trailed him to Sydney, he couldn't shake them off. They turned up wherever he went, they haunted him. It was, at last, to give them the slip that he had ducked over the border into Queensland, set himself up as an insurance salesman, met my grandmother, married her, and as he wryly put it, lived happily ever after.

He was the second son of a retired army officer from Hucclecote near Gloucester. 'A decent little place – you can hear St. Peter's bells on a clear day and see Crickley Hill and all the road up to Birdlip on t'other side.' He had left school early, and after a wild youth, in which he distinguished himself in no other way than as a game rider at fences and a presentable partner at hunt balls, he decided to cut his losses, break free of his mother and seek his fortune in the Empire.

One of his uncles had gone out to Alberta and been killed in a hunting accident. But the son of a local publican had done well in Australia, and fired by the example of this Twigmore lad who was just his age and already owned a sheep station in New South Wales, he packed his bags, and with his father's blessing, a little string bag of arrowheads and an initialled silver shaving-mug in which I was allowed on Sundays to whip up the lather for his shave, he set out for Bristol and the new life.

He was well-spoken when he cared to be, wrote a good hand, and out of his great love of the place, and from sitting about in farmhouse kitchens and over the bar at cattle fairs and grain markets, had acquired a vast knowledge of local lore, but was unqualified – this was his mother's view – for any life but the one he was leading. He was too much a man of those particular hills, and fitted too well into the heavy tweed jackets he liked to wear (which gave off when they were soaked with rain or dew a peculiar odour of local wool) to be at home in any other place. His mother saw that. He would be a man without roots. She opposed his going and refused to bless him, and when his fortunés did fail as she predicted he laid the blame on her refusal of a goodbye kiss. It put a chill upon him that had lasted the whole of his life.

More than once, in going over some larky adventure he had started out on with Will Burnley and Jim Hodge he would stop dead and look thoughtful, then grim; brought up hard against his mother's silence and the unyielding severity with which she had set her face against Australia and all that it stood for.

So many of his stories, even those that already had him settled at the Ridge, would lead back to the dead cold of that morning as he tramped away and to a series of signs, beginning with the denied blessing, that had foreshadowed, even before he saw the ship that was to take him, all that would occur in the new land. He was, for all his reading among men of truth like Lord Macaulay and Herman Melville, a Gloucestershire country-boy at heart, full of superstitions he had never outgrown: mangles that turned of their own accord, sheep children seen in bottles at county fairs, gipsy curses, sheeps' hearts with needles in them, bound six times with a hazel switch.

'I'll tell you something, Phil. It's something I thought I'd forgotten. It's funny what you remember. When I was just a wee thing, four or five years old, I had an illness. They thought I would die of it. They tried everything, called all the doctors, but I got no better. My mother cried over me, they sent the other children away.

'We had a girl in those days helping cook in the kitchen. She was a bit like Della, only younger, a country girl with only half her wits, that my mother had taken in to please the vicar. Her father was a wagoner who'd been crushed in a spill with his cart. Well, this girl was fond of me, she used to take me for walks. She knew all the best walks around there – the ones with wild orchids or places where you might see a rabbit or a pair of stoats. So she crept out one night to an old woman who lived up Crickley way and she got this woman to brew up some sort of remedy, a lot of wild herbs wrapped in a plaster, and she carried it into the house without my mother knowing and she wrapped me up in it.

'Well, I got better. Overnight. They thought it was a miracle, they never knew. But later, when that girl – Ellen she was called – when she took me out walking one day, she took me Crickley way, down along a gully that was all overgrown with bracken – a dingle we called it – to the dirtiest little shack you've ever seen, with two rooms and a lot of chooks in one and the floor all trodden dirt, and a dirty grey-haired old woman in the other. She had warts all over her face and woollen mitts to her hands with the fingers poking through.

'She made us tea and spread a newspaper, and brought stools for us to sit. And when we were leaving she put her hand with the woollen mitt on my head, and said: "You be one o' mine," and grinned at me. I was terrified, I didn't know what it meant. I suppose she meant I was a child she had saved with her cures, but I thought she had put something in that poultice that had spelled it and changed me, and that she would come one night and take me back. After that, for about three years, I was afraid of going to bed in the dark. Then I forgot all about it – oh, for ages, and only remembered it the other day. Ellen! But most of all those dirty fingers sticking out of the mitts . . .'

He scared me sometimes with his tales of Gloucestershire. It seems such a gloomy place, all smuts from coal fires and storms in old black kettles, and curses that could cross water from Hucclecote to Lightning Ridge.

But they were happy hours, those times in Grandpa's room. The mahogany wardrobe and dressing table with their wing-shaped projections and cornices and bevelled glass stood solid against the drifting of the curtains. From the trays of the wardrobe, where Grandpa's shirts were stacked, came a whiff of camphor or moth-balls that added itself to the smell of the spirit lamp beside his bed, the disinfectant from the bed-pan that was kept out of sight behind a screen, and a peculiar smell, as of sweet-spice or nutmeg, that belonged to the timbers of the house itself, especially where the boards had gone soft under the paintwork so that you could press with your thumb, feel the layer of enamel crack and produce a fine reddish dust. And beyond all this, as the long curtains stirred and lifted with the springing up at last of the sea-breeze, the salty, ever-present, clean but sourish smell of the Broadwater.

My grandfather would wake with the sea breeze and I would have to settle the spread about him. It was the sign that my mother would soon be back, that another afternoon had passed and he was still alive in the high room above the bunyahs, and that we were all, once again, in sight of tea.

When I pulled up the spread, fussing a little in imitation of my mother, he would set his hand on the crown of my head, so light and dry that you barely felt it, and say, 'Thank you, boy,' a kind of blessing, and I would lean forward and kiss him on the forehead. The skin was paper thin. You were aware of bone. But there was nothing frightening in it, and I wasn't in any way disgusted by the odour of decay.

Children, my mother thought, were quite capable of facing reality. It was my father's younger sisters, Aunt Connie and Aunt Roo, who had to be spared. They came only in the morning, when he had already been brought back and restored from the ravages of the night: or in the evening, when with his hair combed wet like a schoolboy, all freshened up and buttoned into his flannel pyjamas, and with the blue night light showing its flame, he had the air of a sick and spoiled child.

My aunts were not callous. In fact they might have claimed an excess of feeling. But they fled from the truth. My grandfather had always known what they were and forgave them.

'Don't let the girls see,' he would tell my mother when some physical accident of a particularly repugnant kind had overtaken him or when he was in pain.

As for my grandmother, she treated him as she always had, and would have been ashamed, I think, to let his dying make a change in the cool proximity that was their established way with one another.

She came in twice a day, always immaculately dressed, and sat a moment on one of the cane chairs beside his bed. She asked how he was, informed him about household matters, settled the sheet with a fold here or a smoothing gesture there, then rose, set her lips to his brow, frowned a moment, and went back to her accounts: back to what she had been occupied with for the best part of forty years; to what his fecklessness had forced upon her – the holding together, with her strict, uncompromising style, of a family, and the running of a large and profitable business.

'Weren't Grandma and Grandpa happy?' I asked my father once.

He looked embarrassed. It was an effect of our new closeness to one another that I could speak to him like this, and he wanted to be frank with me; but his whole life was built on the assumption that such questions were never put, because they were irrelevant, or because they were too difficult to answer. He was sufficiently like his father to feel threatened by my grandfather's failings, and had spent many years proving to his mother that natural affinities could be transcended by force of character. His loyalty was to her.

'Your grandmother's had a lot to put up with,' was all he said now. 'She's been very – brave.'

'Grandpa's brave,' I asserted, thinking of how patient he was in all his trials. 'Mumma says so. He makes so little trouble.'

'Well, there's different sorts – of bravery, I mean. Your grandmother's is the moral sort.'

I chewed hard on that. I thought my grandmother might, in time, come to have the same opinion of me as she had of Grandpa. I didn't have my father's resistence to natural weakness, which was his own form of bravery and which my grandmother approved of because it was modelled so closely on her own.

She was, at this time, a woman of sixty-seven, still imposingly beautiful in her way and still empowered with an energy that had never, one felt, found its proper outlet. The business was large but it was not large enough. Given some other place than our modest backwater – given Chicago or New York – she might have led a different life altogether. She belonged, I thought, to the world of big deals, of big desks, with a window full of skyscrapers at her back and a sense of real power under her fist. Utterly modern in her tastes, she loathed this big old-fashioned house and its Victorian clutter. Her marriage to my grandfather had been a misalliance, not only of temperaments and styles but of epochs. Everything about him, his stance, his pace, the stories he told, even the silver-topped sticks he carried, belonged to the century he was born in, which had passed with his first manhood. My grandmother had rejected all that as she had rejected him.

Married at sixteen, before she could have had any notion of what the coming world was to be, or of her own part in it, she had subdued her energy, her angers, her passionate sense that she had the ability to move at a faster tempo and *achieve* things, and produced, as any girl was expected to do, five children in almost as many years; my Aunt Ollie first, then my father, then Connie, then Roo, then Gil. Her husband, meanwhile, the Englishman whose accent and good manners had so impressed her parents, had drifted from one position to another, and then into a style of living where he had no position at all.

i She was alarmed at first, then cast down, then glowingly resentful of how little lay behind his fine exterior, how little, that is, beyond kindness and charm; but soon saw in it her own good fortune. With money inherited from an aunt and the advice of a clever lawyer – the first of several male supporters – she set her husband up in the wholesale fruit and vegetable business, then ordered him to stay out of sight. She kept him in well-cut suits and the best imported hats, used his presence as a defence against scandal, and devoted herself to the creating of one of the biggest marketing firms in the state.

Full of energy and imagination, utterly ruthless, and ever ready in her proud way for a fight, she was a born businesswoman. Men were admiring but wary. She used their own weapons against them, and when that failed she fell back on her charms. They resented it as they resented having to deal with her as an equal, but she was cleverer than they were, had good luck, and soon won their regard. As for the opinion of women, she thought no more of that than the men did. She had never cared for women. She lived in style again and her children were well kept – that is what she cared about. If my grandfather suffered he was too proud to show it. She left the *amour propre* of that soft, well-meaning man, who loved his children and was astonished at what his child bride had become, to look after itself. What she had become in fact was a beauty; having discovered that beauty, in her case, was a natural consequence of the exercise of power.

All this lay deep in the past. I knew of it only what my father told: how his mother had started the section and how as soon as he was old enough he had gone in with her, and had largely, in latter years, taken over, though my grandmother still managed the book-keeping side of things from a bare, neat little office at home. Here she lived her own life, drinking vast quantities of tea, which she made for herself at a galley, arguing long-distance on the telephone and emerging only for meals. The rest of us never went there. She had no time for me – I don't think she liked children, even her own – and she must have known anyway that I had gone over to

Grandpa. I felt that I barely knew her. I went in terror, as everyone did, of getting in her way.

One day, passing her little office, I was surprised to see through the half-open door that she was in tears. The sight was shocking. I had never seen her weep or give way to passion. She had always been, for me, the strict figure, impeccably groomed, always in control, whose ironic eye kept watch over our ordinary follies, which she did not openly condemn but for which she had a superior and silent contempt. Standing back now where I was hidden by the turn of the stairs I watched her shoulders heave, and heard sounds that even in her, when she stifled them with a handkerchief held hard over her mouth, could not help being raw and ugly and suggesting real pain.

My own emotions surprised me. I had no sort of pity for her such as I would have felt immediately for Aunt Connie or Aunt Roo because I could not imagine her accepting it. What I felt was curiosity, and of a kind that seems to me now to have been distinctly erotic. I was shocked, fascinated, but also felt, on Grandpa's behalf, a degree of satisfaction in perceiving that she too could suffer.

I have no idea what had upset her. Something to do with Uncle Gil perhaps, or some sense of her own weakness before the fates and all that she was accountable for. I saw things too simply to believe that it might have to do with my grandfather.

She looked up suddenly and caught me observing her.

'Oh Phil, it's you.'

Turning her head aside she blew violently into the handkerchief and was immediately herself again. 'Come in a moment. I want to talk to you.'

I stood awkwardly where I was. I had never crossed the threshold of her little office and didn't care to. She had never asked me to go there on a message; if she needed something from one of its cupboards or drawers she always went herself. I hovered now, and she turned in her office chair and faced me.

Her interest was aroused, and I wondered what it was I might have revealed, as with one hand resting on the rolltop desk with its files and ledgers, and the other tight round the balled handkerchief, she observed me over the rim of her glasses. Behind her, in an old-fashioned gothic bookcase, were photographs of the section and its displays.

73

'Come in, Phil. Sit with me a minute.'

I sat on the edge of the chair she offered.

She seemed uneasy now that she actually had me there. She was always so formal. I had some sort of advantage – and not simply because I had seen her in a moment of weakness. She reached out, took my hand and looked at it sadly, as if she read my life there; then turned it over and began, almost absentmindedly, to stroke the back of it.

'You've got your father's hands – your grandfather's. I've noticed that before. He was like you at your age.'

I didn't know what to say. She was telling me something but I couldn't guess what. That she was fonder of me than I thought, and could show it at this moment because she too felt the need for affection?

'You judge people too harshly, Phil. It's easy to judge people when you're young. But people make mistakes – you'll learn that. We have to be –'

Like my father she did not finish the sentence, perhaps, in her case because she was so seldom what she was asking me to be – forgiving. She cast about, wanting I think to make something more of the occasion that would constitute a bond between us. She was still holding my hand but as if she had forgotten what it was. I wanted to take it back but couldn't. It had ceased to be mine. At last she lay it back in my lap, and opening the little silver box she carried, said 'Here, have one of these musks.'

She put one in her mouth, and after a moment's hesitation I reached out and took one too. I hated musk. I tasted it and she smiled. She looked at me sharply, still smiling, and a moment later I got up and left.

It was only outside, as I began to climb the stairs to Grandpa that it struck me. When I kissed him now he would smell it. He would know I had been with her and accepted a favour. I tried, when I leaned over him, to keep my mouth closed so that he would not notice, and immediately retreated to the foot of the bed, but the betrayal was clear. Listening to him tell one of his stories – it was one I had heard a dozen times before – I saw something in his face, an expression, very characteristic, that struck me now as silly. Grandpa! How could I? I had never doubted him before. I wanted to rush and hug him and make amends, but the smell of musk would only have made it worse.

Something in the little pink sweet had bewitched me – that is how I saw it, and that, I knew, was how Grandpa would understand it. My perceiving it may even have come through him.

I recalled what my grandmother had said. How easy it was to make a mistake and be in need of – forgiveness, was it? Grandpa had been weakened by my betrayal. What I saw in him as silliness was a lack of sureness that had come with my doubt.

My Grandmother's beauty was a powerful legend that continued to convince people of the present fact. All three of my aunts saw themselves in the light of it. As an ugly duckling in the case of my Aunt Ollie, who had always thought of herself as her mother's shame, and in the case of the younger ones, 'the girls' as they were called, as timid but not always passive rivals. Their mother, in the early days, had quite simply stolen their men.

Aunt Ollie in fact was not an ugly duckling and never had been, but she had no confidence in her beauty, and I suspect my grandmother from the beginning may have implanted the notion of plainness in her as a way of making certain, once the other children began to arrive, that she would always be there to nurse them. Aunt Ollie had taken this as being the point of her lack of charm. She was to devote herself to the family. That, rather than marriage or children of her own, was to be her fate. She accepted it cheerfully, and so far as one could tell, entirely without question. She had mothered each of her brothers and sisters, and was, when it came to my turn to be mothered, a large, pale, fair creature, as soft as a cloud and with arms that were always powdered with flour.

Her province was the kitchen. With its big central table of scrubbed pine, its marble slab for pastry, its chopping-blocks, knife-drawers, canisters, and the rack on the wall where all Aunt Ollie's saucepans and frying-pans were hung, it was a place of continuous messy activity and perfect order. Sacks of potatoes and onions were stacked in an alcove; jars of melon and lemon jam, marmalade, mango chutney, tomato relish, all carefully dated and labelled, glowed on pantry shelves. The salt-box was of wood and had a thistle motif. There were two stoves. One was modern and enamelled, its legs set in tins of dessicated ants. The other was a range for baking. Very low and black, it was housed in a corrugated-iron recess and fed from a pile of stove-lengths that Uncle Gil would cut – if he was in the mood for it and could be trusted with an axe.

Aunt Ollie's kitchen had its own routine, to which only the privileged were admitted. I spent long hours there on Sunday mornings and in the afternoons after school, watching the miracles Aunt Ollie could whip up in her theatre of sieves and whisks and earthenware bowls of eight different sizes; licking the sugared white off egg-beaters, scraping out bowls, and being told, when I enquired what went into some favourite dish, 'Oh, a little bit of this and a little bit of that,' which was Aunt Ollie's only recipe for a dozen kinds of biscuits, and for wholemeal, pumpkin and marmite scones, treacle tarts, sago plum-puddings boiled in a basin with a clip-over lid, and the two kinds of dumpling that went into the various soups and stews for which Della, wielding a little bone-handled knife or an ancient cleaver, did the donkey-work of peeling and dicing vegetables.

Della was a shapeless girl of Aunt Ollie's age – that is, over forty – with hair so wispy that she might have been balding and odd stumps of teeth. She came from a farm across the border and had been part of my grandmother's household for nearly thirty years.

She and Aunt Ollie were a pair. Aunt Ollie, in her modest view of herself, saw Della as a kind of twin, closer and more like her than her flashy sisters. Della cut up vegetables, washed pots, pans and dishes, which gave her nails in the puffy fingers a horn-like texture, dealt with butcher-boys, bottle-os, ice men and grocers' assistants, fed the fowls that were kept at the bottom of the yard with soaked bread and scraps, and with her skirt hiked up and a pail of sloshy water before her, scrubbed each morning, before the rest of us were up, the worn tiles of the kitchen, the back steps and all the boards of the verandah. She spoke only to her chooks and in a toothless, incomprehensible gabble to the iceman.

She had an understanding with this wiry, red-headed fellow that allowed her to be rough with him.

'Gawn yew!' she would say in a burst of sudden hilarity, and give him a shove that might have overbalanced him altogether, he was so stringy-looking in his shorts and singlet, if there hadn't been the compensatory weight of the ice.

The occasion would leave them both chuckling and shaking their heads as they moved off in opposite directions; the block having been lowered by then into its chest, and beginning to melt, and the iceman, the lighter for the encounter, bouncing a little on his toes.

It was the iceblock that occupied the centre of this daily drama. Glittering there at the end of hooked claws and leaving a wet trail all the way from the gate, with a puddle where the two figures had crossed beside the mint patch halfway up, it gathered to itself whatever heat these meetings contained, so that it might have been the iceman's foxy attempts to catch her hand, or Della's feelings when she turned things over in her little cubbyhole by the stairs, that reduced the great block to liquid, and some understanding between them that the relationship would continue, but not necessarily develop, that created that void in the ice-chest that had each morning to be filled.

Communications between Della and Aunt Ollie were also silent. Words did crop up in them, as monosyllabic requests or directives, but they were not essential. The real dialogue was that set of exchanges by which vegetables, the same ones each day, and chuck-chops and steak, became stews, broths and thick winter soups, and whisks, sieves, bowls, ladels passed from Della's hands to Aunt Ollie's and so on through a complicated process of beating and churning and patting and pricking till the dishes were produced that we would later consume at my grandmother's table; after which, they went back into Della's hands to be washed, dried, restored to brightness and hung again on the kitchen wall.

These utensils, clean and in place by eight o'clock in the evening, when Della closed the kitchen door and retired to her room to listen to the serials on the mantle radio we had given her, were the elements of a lifelong discourse that could for the moment be dropped but would be taken up again in the morning when all these things would come down from their hooks and be gathered back again into the world of use. Even Della and Aunt Ollie's quarrels had no words. They could be guessed at only by the higher level of noise they produced when Della went to work with her hacker, or by the banging down harder than usual of an iron pot.

In the afternoon sometimes, when I came in from school, Della would be plucking and drawing a couple of chooks at the tap in the yard, one foot on the coping round the drain. From inside the house came the heavy chords of the piano where Aunt Roo, in one of her 'moods', was playing gloomy things like Handel's 'Largo' or Chopin's 'Funeral March' – 'them dirges', as Della called them. 'We had a feller at Mullimbimby once used to play like that, but he 'ad an excuse – 'e'd come back from the war – the first war –

with only one arm. But you should of 'eard 'im, you'd never of guessed. 'E 'ad one sleeve tucked up with a safety-pin and bandages all round his face – 'e couldn' talk except through them – an' he used to sit in 'is room and play, just like that. Dirges. Classical. And sort of *moan*. It gave me the creeps. I left in the end, I couldn' stand it. Still, 'e 'ad an excuse, poor devil.' Aunt Roo, she implied, had none.

'Is it true,' I asked, 'that she ran off once and played with a dance band?'

Della looked astonished.

'Who?'

She jerked her head towards the music. She seldom referred to Aunt Roo by name.

'Lady Muck?'

'That's what she told me.'

Della considered. 'Well I never heard of it.' She returned to feeling about in the chook and pulling out innards. 'Could be one of her – stories.'

She refused to meet my eye. She had great loyalty to 'the family' and feared perhaps that what she had said was already a betrayal. 'Still,' she said, 'there's plenty goes on here I don't hear about. Not interested. Got too much work.'

It was understood that when I entered Aunt Ollie's kitchen I too would accept the rules of the place. 'A little bit of this and a little bit of that' might be the longest sentence uttered on those close afternoons, with the steam hissing out under saucepan lids, Della's discoloured chopper making its *rat-a-tat-a-tat* and a late storm brewing in the window-panes, though I was never aware of a gap. The passing of a bowl into my hands to be licked clean and transferred to the sink, or the offer of a long spiral of apple-peel, so perfectly removed that it could be held a moment in the round shape of the uncut apple – these were clear statements, in a fullness of communication that was affectionate on all sides: Aunt Ollie and Della for one another, both of them for me, and I for the two heavy silent women, so different, so much alike.

Later, when we were assembled at the dinner-table, I would continued to feel the strong order that Aunt Ollie and Della had established during our kitchen hours. Since few words were passed at my grandmother's table once grace had been said – conversation was dangerous in that tense, unstable household – we were entirely occupied with Aunt Ollie's soups, stews and puddings. No wonder Frank Harland when he did come to lunch at last, in the same worn army shirt but with a bit of blue cloth tucked into the collar and yellow socks to his boots, was so awkward and boiled-looking – not at all the artist my aunts had hoped for. My father insisted on his going up to see Grandpa, who surprised us all by talking for three full minutes about the National Gallery in London. Frank Harland nodded a few times and said 'Aha' but without much conviction – he seemed out of his depth. But was delighted to see his picture on the wall of my parents' bedroom. It might, on this occasion, have been the frame that impressed him.

My aunts giggled, and my grandmother, deciding in her cut-and-dried way that this streaky fellow with the lines in his cheeks, the dirty fingernails and the apology for a cravat, was another of father's lame ducks, a bohemian sponger, simply pretended he was not there and left it to Aunt Ollie to offer him second servings of peas and sweet-potato or a spoonful of mint sauce.

Frank Harland was never the only guest at dinner. One of our regular visitors was a retired doctor, 'Uncle' Haro, who had been a friend of my grandmother's since the early days and whom she still consulted – in the professional sense, that is, though she also consulted him once or twice a week by telephone. I would hear her laughter from the office. It sounded odd. So light and girlish.

They had jokes together, my grandmother and Uncle Haro, that were not explained. I would catch them laughing silently to one another across the table, in the sure knowledge that they were the cleverest people present, but often as if they were also the youngest and had just shared a pre-dinner prank. In the afternoon they retired to my grandmother's office and played honeymoon bridge.

Uncle Haro smelled of tobacco and was shaggy, all shoulders and big hands, and gruffly, deliberately uncouth. It surprised me that my grandmother, with her fine ways, put up with him. He scattered tobacco when he filled his pipe; he disturbed all the knives and forks when he sat down to eat, pushing them off to the side to make a space for himself; and all through grace he huffed, and his chair, on its thin bentwood legs, would scrape and creak. Sometimes, in the evening, he would bring out his violin case and slip from its yellowing sleeve (which was made of an old swami silk petticoat) a half-sized fiddle that was meant for a child. Removing his jacket and pushing up his expanding silver armbands, he would tuck the little instrument under his chin, where it rested on a ruby velvet pad, and play Irish jigs or romantic pieces like Mendelssohn's 'Spring Song' or 'Träumerei' or, in defiance of our other regular guest, Miss Minchin, a lady whose brother was a Lutheran minister, a few frenzied bars of the 'Devil's Trill'.

Uncle Haro had privileges in the house. They derived from my grandmother, and I saw that Aunt Roo, at least, resented them. She treated Uncle Haro in an off-hand manner, or she ignored him altogether, but I guessed there was a time, years back, when she might have climbed on his knee and played up to him. It was from Uncle Haro that I got this sense of a past when things had been different between them. He spoke to Aunt Roo with unusual softness, and when he arrived once with a big bunch of gardenias – 'For the house, for the house!' – he gave her one, and she crinkled her nose and immediately gave it back. He made a clown's face of exaggerated grief.

He was a joker, Uncle Haro. On one occasion he brought a little plaster turd that he lay on the bottom step of the verandah and had everyone running about in circles looking for the dog and wondering how it had ever got in. Della was scandalized. It upset her strict notion of things. He was supposed to be a gentleman. But what surprised me was that everyone else, including my grandmother, thought it hilarious.

In Uncle Haro's presence my grandmother was a different person. She unbent and became easy, not only in herself but also towards the rest of us; which was why everyone had laughed so much, had felt free to, at Uncle Haro's turd. She softened and glowed, as if she had drunk wine or been made sleepy by an invisible fire. I wondered that the others did not notice. I guessed they were used to it.

The first day Frank Harland came Uncle Haro asked him about angels. He claimed, as a medical man, to have seen several of them. They were all declared crazy by their families of course, and were kept locked up, or had been hidden away in institutions, and they did nothing but scream the moment you came near them; but you could tell they were angels by their extreme sensitivity to touch, in fact to all the senses, and by the extreme beauty of their expressions when they were calm. By their muteness too and the fact that they had no sex (my grandmother did not protest but was not quite pleased at this turn in the description) or shared the characteristics of both.

Frank Harland was disconcerted. Yes, he did believe such things could be. He had never seen an angel of any kind himself but his father had seen a ghost once, of a lady in a yellow frock.

Uncle Haro was not interested in ghosts. Only angels. And in big green mud-crabs, one of which, I recall, he set loose under the table from a gunny-sack.

I felt sorry for Frank Harland when Uncle Haro questioned him about the angels. He had set his eyebrows at me once – they were thick and black like Mr Menzies, in contrast to his snow-white hair – and in the same gruff, insistent voice fired off a whole series of questions about 'sexual matters'. Something in the way he pressed Frank Harland reminded me of the occasion and I blushed, but it was Aunt Ollie who spoke up.

'Don't worry, Frank,' she explained, 'he doesn't mean any of this. He's a joker. He likes teasing people. Now stop it, Haro! Mister Harland isn't used to it.' For all her softness she could be fierce in the defence of her chicks.

'You're wrong there, Ollie, quite wrong, I mean every word of it. Frank knows that, don't you Frank? We are talking about life. Not your tidy bits of it but the whole thing. Is that right, Frank? And I tell you, I saw a little girl once, about twelve years old' – I felt that Uncle Haro was looking right at me – 'who had been tied to a bed for as long as anyone could remember and had never done anything but butt her head at the bars of her cot and moan and scream and throw things. Her parents were distracted – I was treating the mother, there was nothing I could do for the child. One day when I was there the noise suddenly stopped and when I came to her the little thing was as calm as could be. Still with one eye set lower than the other and a warped lip and blackened teeth, but so calm that she was – well, I could see immediately what it was and would have given anything to know what her silence was trying to tell us, what tidings, what *gospel* she had. I say a little girl but that is only in a manner of speaking. Because her mother called her that. Claire she was called. At that point she was beginning to mature, she was getting a beard, and it was clear that she was a male – or rather both, it hardly matters really, one way or the other.'

Uncle Haro pushed his lower lip out and defied scepticism. His heavy tweed jacket with its leather buttons and the big hand with its solid gold signet ring gave such substance to his story, and to the subject of it, that I longed to ask where the little girl lived and would have gone any distance to see her. Frank Harland too believed. I saw it. Were they making fools of us?

'Don't listen,' Aunt Ollie insisted. 'He's always talking nonsense – he makes it up just to embarrass people. And pretending all the time to be a man of science! Have another piece of pudding, Frank, and you too, Phil. Help yourself to custard.'

When Uncle Haro wasn't teasing Frank Harland his favourite victim was Miss Minchin. She had done missionary work with the aborigines and had seen a child taken by a crocodile once off a tartan blanket, while they were having tea on a lawn. She recounted this tragedy, and others, in a small flat rather mannish voice and with so little emotion that she might have had a little machine tucked away under the scarf at her throat to save her the trouble of telling her stories herself, they were so unremarkable. One of her former colleagues had been decapitated by the Japanese. That was in Borneo. Another was eaten by headhunters in the Sepik.

My aunts listened to these wonders without blinking, they had been hearing them for years; and Aunt Roo must have wondered at times if Miss Minchin wasn't trying to out-do her in the creation of woppers. But Miss Minchin was incapable of untruth. Life, thank you very much, was quite enough. You didn't need imagination.

But life, mere life as he called it, was too little for Uncle Haro, and Miss Minchin's version of it enraged him. Miss Minchin drew the line at his demented angels and he drew his at her suffering saints.

'What about you, Frank?' Uncle Haro demanded. 'Are you another of Miss Minchin's headless martyrs?'

Frank Harland shook his head but looked uncomfortable.

'Good,' said Uncle Haro, 'I'm glad to hear it. I'd begun to think you were another of these creeping Jesuses. We've got enough of those to stretch from here to Burke. Iron Knob couldn't keep up with the demand for nails –'

'I don't mean,' Harland said abruptly, and seemed surprised to hear his own voice, 'that that isn't part of it. Suffering, I mean. People do suffer, it's terrible. Only it's not all.'

'And who is responsible for it?' Uncle Haro insisted.

'Responsible?'

'That's what I asked.'

Harland shuffled and turned red. 'Well, we must be, mustn't we?'

Uncle Haro's eyebrows went up.

'And our *creator*?'

He put a good deal of spit into the word.

'Oh, well, he's moved on,' said Frank Harland simply. He seemed relieved that the question had taken so easy a turn. 'I mean, the creator doesn't go on brooding over one work forever. He does what he can and moves on. To the next thing. He lets it go. Find its own way.'

'New works you mean, new *worlds*? Funny idea of a creator. Is that your idea then? Of some sort of – excuse me – irresponsible artist?'

'The creator is responsible for what he makes, not for what others make of it. We can't rely on the one who created us' – Frank Harland swallowed hard and seemed to be speaking of something deeply painful – 'but we can't blame him neither. We make our own lives. We're the ones who have made the world.'

'You let God off pretty lightly,' Uncle Haro said, 'and put all the blame on us. That's a nice bit of theology. I don't let him off so lightly.' You could see that Uncle Haro's magisterial eye was on something beyond Frank Harland, and that the angels he spoke of, ambiguous in sex, deeply tormented, all howls and hollering, would be the only kind possible for the creator he had in mind.

'Well you see,' said Frank Harland, 'whatever the realities – of what we see around us I mean – the cruelties, the horrors – I think we were meant to be happy.'

He offered this as some sort of answer, it seemed, to Uncle Haro and Miss Minchin both. Having got it out he blushed and observed his plate. There was a long pause. There had been, at the end, a fire in his voice that commanded respect.

'Good on you, Frank!' my father said too loud. He looked round for congratulations. His man had finally justified him.

Uncle Haro glared.

'Do you really mean it? Just – *happy?*'

Frank Harland's whole face was contorted. He must have hoped it was over. He was torn now between a wish to say no more and a painful desire not to be misunderstood. 'Not *just*,' he said low. 'Because it's so difficult, you know. What's asked of us would have to be hard, wouldn't it? And that's the hardest thing of all, to be happy. The strongest. Suffering couldn't be it. Suffering's too – easy.'

'Huh!' Uncle Haro looked at Frank Harland as if he had said something astonishing, and disappointing, but it flummoxed him just the same.

'Huh!' he said again, and Aunt Ollie laughed outright.

'Here Haro,' she said, 'have some more pudding,' and she piled his plate with it before he could wave his hand in the air to ward her off.

[3]

Frank Harland was often at the house after that first time. He liked to sit with Aunt Ollie and Della in the kitchen and was there sometimes when I came in from school. He made no difference in what I thought. He knew the language because it was his own and was included in the patterns that unfolded out of Della's hands, or Aunt Ollie's, as I had been. We sat round the table, drank tea, ate buttered scones or biscuits, said nothing, and everything was as before.

To my other aunts these occasions were incomprehensible. They found Frank Harland comic and could not imagine what anyone saw in him. In the way they had of giving nicknames to people they wanted to mock in open company they called him Ollie's Iceman, a phrase that never failed to send them into fits of laughter and raised a tight smile even from my grandmother. Ollie's Iceman. Like Della's – because he was such a block of ice.

Sometimes he brought his work-things, paper, charcoal, inks, and while Della and Aunt Ollie banged about in their usual way he did sketches or made quick studies in line and wash.

It was an odd business. He muttered to himself as he worked, let out sudden chuckles that might have been approval of a line or a row of dots, or hissed with disgust, or cried out, or crowed or snarled, and if he glanced up and caught my eye would look apologetic. He was ashamed before such a young person to reveal his own childishness.

As for the works themselves, they were so little what I expected that he might have been engaged with quite different events in another room. It made me uncomfortable. I felt I had missed something – and that the most important thing of all.

'Well,' he would say, observing my disappointment, 'it's just a sketch really, an idea. There's a lot more I could do. What I wanted to catch, you see, was –' But he stopped there, looked miserably at what he had done and gave up. I felt sorry for him. He was surprised when people were puzzled by his work. He expected them to see just what he saw.

Della also looked. She was fond of the fellow and hated to see him made a fool of; but one glance at the sort of stuff he did and you knew right off, there was nothing to be done; he could not be saved.

Aunt Ollie refused to look at all. 'You finished for a bit, Frank? These scones aren't worth tuppence if you don't eat 'em warm.'

When he did complete his portrait of Aunt Ollie, and it was produced at last and seen, the consensus was that it was awful. Even my father hummed and looked embarrassed. 'It's very good, Frank,' was all he could find to say. 'You've made Ollie very – strong.' ('Like a wrestler,' Aunt Roo whispered.)

It was an opinion that appeared to please the man. 'Yairs,' he said very slowly, and grinned.

'Well it is *different*,' said Aunt Connie.

It was Uncle Haro who surprised us all. He asked for a special showing and was in such a bad temper afterwards that we all knew he had been struck. He thought enough of Harland's talent, it seemed, to feel threatened. It made even my grandmother give the thing a second look.

'Oh, it's me all right,' Aunt Ollie admitted when pressed, though she had barely looked at the portrait. 'It's the *real* me,' and she laughed for her own awkwardness and rocklike solidity. 'He's caught me to a T. I never said I was a beauty.'

My opinion, which no one asked for, was that the painting spoke for some special understanding between Frank and Aunt Ollie, and I wondered what it could be.

'Do you reckon Frank's in love?' I asked Aunt Roo in one of our moments together. She was usually receptive to notions of romance.

'That Frank Harland? For heaven's sake, sweetie, he's so wrapped up in himself he wouldn't know a chair leg if he fell right over it, let 'lone a woman. You're not much of a matchmaker, love, if you think there's anything in *that*.'

It would have surprised them to hear it, but my further view was that my younger aunts were jealous. They had reason to be. Compared with Aunt Ollie, whose presence was monumental, they were lightweights. They did nothing in the house that was of use. Their sole contribution was to its weather.

A kind of friction would disturb the air, electrical vibrations that set everyone's nerves on edge. A plate might get broken in the kitchen, or I would knock over a bottle of ink while I was doing my homework at the dining-room table and ruin a good velvet cloth. Or my grandmother, who had a temper but kept it under control, would suddenly snap back at my Aunt Connie and there would be streams of tears. On days like that, of pent-up tension, when everything you touched gave off sparks, the atmosphere could usually be traced back to one or other of 'the aunts'.

Aunt Roo was stagestruck. She had in her room, with its Spanish shawl across the window and its vase stuck with peacock feathers, all open eyes, a stack of leather hat-boxes, more than a dozen in all, and two vast travelling-trunks of solid hide that were crammed with costumes – relics, you might have thought, of a long life on the boards: straight, low-crossed evening gowns from a twenties comedy, many of them beaded or with bursts of pin-holed sequins at the waist; gypsy skirts with ruffles; Ruritanian coronation gowns in scarlet or prussian blue, all trimmed with ermine; crinolines, riding habits, Edwardian morning-gowns with leg-o'-mutton sleeves, ivory fans, fur muffs, boas, rhinestone tiaras, ropes of pearls; floppy panamas trimmed with a velvet ribbon and flat or peaked or Dogelike saddle-shaped toques.

They were all make-believe. My Aunt Roo had never uttered a word on the public stage. Her mother wouldn't have allowed it – or anyway, that was the easy answer she gave herself. Instead, she had made her real life theatrical, and had, for the past twenty-five years, played out in spirit, and in costume if she felt she could risk it, the various characters she might have excelled at but whose lines had never passed her lips. Clothes were her passion. She was forever running up something new for herself that would create a 'brilliant effect'. She would call me out to the closed-in verandah that was her sewing-room to give an opinion, or tackle me at the gate as I came in from school, before I could change and slip off, as I usually did, to the kitchen.

'Look kitten, I want to show you something I've just made. It's pretty, Phil, you'll like it, and I need you to advise me. I need a *man's* opinion. You've got an eye, pet. You've inherited that from our side. Come and look. It won't take a minute.'

Or she would hang about on the landing while I was still on my second cup in the kitchen, singing to herself and waiting to trap me as I came out. I thought of it as a trap.

'Here, love, a surprise,' she would offer, 'I found them in a drawer.' It was a little bag of shiny buttons, some of them regimental, others from firemen's uniforms. 'I could sew them on to a jacket for you, you'd look smart. Come on, kitten, and we'll see what we can do. Honestly, I don't know how you can *sit* so long in that gloomy old kitchen. Your aunt Ollie and poor Della haven't got a word to say between them. I suppose it's the cakes, is that it? The best way to a man's heart, they say. But what about your old Aunt Roo? I've been stuck up here all day without a living soul to breathe a word to. You're a tonic, pet – no, really, you are! You understand things.'

I shrank from something, some view of myself that I couldn't accept, but was fascinated just the same.

She was never still.

'When I was little,' she said, 'your Grandpa used to say I had ants in my pants. Poor pet, he's so innocent! But it's true, I've got to be *doing* something. I can't stand all these strong, silent types we've got around here – always leaning on bloody invisible axe-handles, even when they're supposed to be bank managers or dentists, and with no talk and no imagination and no wish to *get anywhere*.'

She herself was full of talk, and between bursts of the machine in which she guided the needle expertly between middle-finger and index, would give me good evidence of what it was to have an imagination. Her own was as vivid as the colours she preferred, 'to wake them all up – those axe-men!'

She sewed at all times of the day, and sometimes late at night, and the whine of her treadle-machine, whirring, stopping, whirring off again at a panicky breakneck speed, is one of the sounds I associate still with the wide, silent spaces of that house. I thought of it as a kind of demonic bicycle that was screwed into the ground and never 'got anywhere', and saw her in the same light when on Sunday evenings after tea she seated herself at the pianola in the downstairs sitting-room, and with her dark hair blazing, pounded her feet, worked her shoulders, and produced waves of mechanical sound that shook all the glasses in the cabinet and the drops of my grandmother's lustres. Her feet pedalled, her knees rose, her hands gripped the edge of the ebony seat, and music came welling and cascading out of the solid furniture as from an object possessed.

She was not quite forty in the year my grandfather died and still had one or two suitors. She dressed young, affecting a whole series of *ingénue* roles and voices that she had picked up from the pictures, and was fiercely jealous of my grandmother, whom she blamed not only for her failure to have a career but for having drawn away, with her assured and sensual beauty, the young men she had brought home; if not deliberately – and she knew her mother well enough to believe it was deliberate – then at least unconsciously, out of habit, since she could not bear to have a man in the room, if he was in any way attractive, who was not morally in her power.

Aunt Roo had developed her style because it was one her mother could no longer pretend to. It was essentially girlish. But the promise of youthful lightness, and an empty-headed appeal to male vanity, impressed less in the end than what her mother offered – offered, that is, in the slight lassitude she suggested by the lowering of her lids and the placing of a hand, palm outward, in an elegant yawn; both gestures emphasising her best points, eyes and mouth, and evoking an image of her body's easy inclination to the horizontal. All this was second-nature in my grandmother, but Aunt Roo saw malice – a cruel demonstration that mere youth, even when it was the real thing, had no weight where men were concerned, and in the rivalry between them gave the younger woman no advantage.

It was a lesson she had failed to learn. Having adopted a younger style she had been unable to give it up, and since she was all style, no other version of herself had emerged to replace it. She failed with the very men she wanted to attract, and gathered around her a crowd of 'interesting fellers' who were much too young for her and were themselves theatrical. With these young men she went on picnics to Terranora Lakes or the Natural Arch, and on rainy days they gathered in Grandma's sitting room and sang (the young men) with their arms round one another's shoulders, while Aunt Roo worked the pianola. But as well as the interesting fellers there was always, in a corner, some other dull fellow who was being kept in reserve, one of the axe-men, and it was clear that he, or someone like him, was the one she would eventually accept.

My grandfather was fond of his 'little girl' (it was perhaps to please him that she had first developed her style, and for him that she kept it up) and it was Aunt Roo he had in mind when he told my mother in some moment of shameful incontinence: 'Don't let the girls see.' He wanted, in her eyes, to be what he had been when she was a child and he had taken her to dancing lessons: the most handsome man she had ever known.

It was, I thought later, from my grandfather that Aunt Roo had inherited her theatricality. He was certainly the only one who accepted it in all its forms.

For it had its shameful side. Aunt Roo was an inveterate liar. Nothing about her, not even the drawers full of odd treasures like the firemen's buttons, not even her 'costumes', was quite so fascinating to me as the woppers she told – always with her eyes wide open in the utter frankness of their china blue.

What astonished me was the boldness with which she challenged disbelief. Her lies didn't make sense. They were so calculated, so outrageous in the freedoms they claimed from the actual, as to create a dimension of their own in which mere questions of accuracy and all moral questions of right and wrong were of no significance. Aunt Roo in full flight – possessed by one of her fantastic untruths – was her real self at last, the self that narrow notions of respectability, or her mother's jealousy or powerful proximity, had denied.

She paid for it of course, this attempt to turn the facts of her life into gaudy fiction. She suffered from hysteria, she made scenes. The simplest of them were mere temper tantrums; the worst were fits of passionate and helpless weeping. I was impressed by both, but the weeping fits scared me. In that house of established forms and silence they were brutal speakings-out that broke all the rules, named all the unnameables, gathered into their storm of sobbing so much real pain and anger and hopelessness that I was terrified, as I never had been by the merely physical manifestations of my grandfather's illness.

The first of these fits occurred on a still, close night soon after we arrived.

We had gone to bed early, but no one I think was asleep. I lay out in the moonlight with even the top sheet cast off and sweated; waiting for the breeze that would not come and listening for the first stirrings of the sea that lay flat and oily under the moon. My body was evacuated of all energy. My blood had stopped beating. I turned and turned, trying new places on the pillow for my head and new, cool places on the sheet for my limbs. Finally I took the pillow, and as small children do, settled it between my thighs. I began to drop off.

It was then, out of the first drowsiness of sleep, that I heard it: a regular sobbing. I connected it at first with sounds I had heard from my parents' room, which could still disturb me though I knew by now that they were safe. But this was different. It seemed to come from under the floorboards of the house itself, as if some animal had crawled in there, woken after long months and found itself trapped. The sound rose and accelerated. I heard the swishing of bare feet in the corridor – Aunt Ollie. Then another, slippered pair – my grandmother. I began to get out of bed. There were lights. Then the screaming began.

These occasions affected each member of the household in a different way.

My Aunt Ollie was full of compassion, and my vision of her, when I too went at last to see what it was about, is of a motherly figure, herself in tears, embracing and protecting a child. She rocked Aunt Roo, and murmured and soothed and tried to stop the ugly mouth from letting out the ugly, accusing sounds.

'She's so unhappy,' she told the rest of us as we crowded at the doorway, 'she really suffers. It's not just playing up.'

Aunt Connie, herself too highly strung, looked on terrified, as if the words once spoken might demand to be taken up and repeated, or as if Aunt Roo's attacks could create a cloud or miasma in which she too would be caught up, whirled about and turned head over heels. For Aunt Roo's manifestations, for all Aunt Ollie's efforts, did not fall short of a certain amount of rolling about and kicking. 'I can't stand it,' Aunt Connie would scream, 'I can't, I can't, I can't!' and with her hands over her ears she would rush off down the hallway and lock herself in her room.

My father, to whom all this was deeply painful, would slump on the bed beside Aunt Ollie and shake his head. He looked miserably at my mother, who seeing now that there was nothing to be done, and understanding how ashamed my father was, even before her, of his family's weakness, would go off quickly to Grandpa's room.

Only my grandmother remained calm.

'It's nothing,' she would say. 'You're doing just what she wants. She's been putting on turns like this since she was three years old. You know that, Ollie! It's all play-acting. She knows just how far she means to go – certainly not far enough to *break* anything.'

With this scornful judgment she would turn on her heel and go back to bed, ignoring the fact that in Aunt Roo's accusations, which largely involved herself, something had already been broken, and deliberately, that would not heal.

My grandfather, who had been woken by the commotion and was suffering in his own way, would be given an account of all this by my grandmother in the course of her morning visit. He would listen with his face to the wall, recognizing in my grandmother's tones her unspoken accusation.

Aunt Roo's unhappiness, her weakness, and all its degrading exhibitions deeply wounded him. She was his responsibility. My grandmother's favourite, the one who pained her in the same way but about whom she was never wimperingly sentimental and for whom she made no excuse, was Uncle Gil. They must always have played favourites like this; making their choices early and drawing out of the two children, their youngest, those qualities they missed in one another and could best make use of as an indictment of betrayal.

Aunt Roo and Uncle Gil were substitute children. My father and Aunt Ollie, born when their parents were still close, had been left to themselves; they needed no one's special love. And Aunt Connie, lost in the middle of the five, was simply there. Tolerated, ignored, she was one of those whom life treats badly. She had come to accept it as her fate.

Aunt Connie had been married, and the man, out of tolerance for her feelings, was never mentioned; but my grandmother, who had a soft spot for Jack Cassidy, still got letters from him which she answered on my grandfather's behalf.

'Jack Cassidy's a fine fellow,' my father assured me when we met him out walking once, 'but he was spoiled and weak when your Aunt Connie married him and she made him worse. He needed a strong woman. Not a – well, not your Aunt Connie.'

Among all these evocations of strength and weakness, of pulls, ties, repulsions that made a family, a household, a moral field, and to which I as the lone child of my generation was the only heir, it was my father and his one brother, Uncle Gil, standing in positions at opposite ends of the family, my father next to eldest, he next to youngest, who embodied the poles of steadiness and random, nihilistic violence.

'Oh, this family!' I would hear my mother complain to herself when my grandfather had been most trying or my grandmother too coldly insistent on some small but tyrannical point of form; or when our cramped quarters left her with a sense of having, outside the round of the sickroom, no place of her own.

She had much to resent. My parents' late marriage had largely to do with the responsibility my father had undertaken, at barely fifteen, of sharing with his mother the management of the firm. My grandmother tended to think of them as having, as well, a shared guardianship of the others; of my father's being, to this extent, a second husband. My mother could never forget this. Not only the long years in which she had been held back from marriage and the having of her own children, but what she saw as the stealing of my father's youth. She had, moreover, to accept daily now my grandmother's priority in the house and some need she had to prove that my father's loyalty, and their deep partnership, could not be shaken. My father was often torn. He loved my mother, but he had memories as well of the lonely, defiant and beautiful young woman his mother had been in the days when she was managing alone, and of the many anxious times they had been through together. He saw too, how much of her life and power she had given to keeping them all afloat. Her beauty mesmerized him because it had to do with her energy, which was quite undiminished and worked on everything it touched. There was something sacred in that. He must have thought at times, even after he was married, that he could not do without it.

As for my grandmother, I don't believe she ever asked herself what sort of affection she might have for him, or if, in fact, she had any at all. I thought I saw my father, a little wearily sometimes, trying to please her and to win some sign of approval. He seemed oddly boyish on these occasions, as if we were brothers rather than father and son and he the younger of the two. But my grandmother held back. To praise him would have been an admission that what he gave was freely given and could be withdrawn; whereas her power over him lay in the notion of a sacred duty of which she was the sole embodiment. And this too my mother resented.

The truth is that my grandmother cared for only one of her five children. For the rest she had only duties or an amused and unspoken contempt.

'I wouldn't mind,' I heard my mother whisper, in the low voice in which they were forced to conduct all discussions, all quarrels in that house, 'if it wasn't so unfair! Why can't Gil do it? What does he ever do except moon about down there and fill the boy's head with craziness? The war's been over for eighteen months! I don't see why he couldn't take some of this awful *pressure* off you.'

'I'm not complaining.'

'No, you never do. And as long as you don't nothing will change.'

'Gil's all right. He needs a bit more time, that's all. He's had –'

'Don't you dare tell me he's had a lot to put up with. So have we all! We're still putting up with it. Your mother could do something but she won't. She *likes* him the way he is!'

'No, you shouldn't say that. It upsets her too. She just doesn't show it.'

'You're like all the rest of this family. You all make the same excuses, over and over, and things stay just as they were.'

'Yes,' my father said sadly, 'I know that. But Gil is –'

'Crazy. Gil is *crazy*.'

'No, he's shell-shocked, and he was always – difficult. But he's all right. He just needs time to get himself into shape.'

Uncle Gil did not live in the house. My parents were occupying what had been his room, but even before we arrived he had preferred to sleep in the rough wooden shack at the end of the yard that had once housed sacks of corn for the chooks, garden tools and a lawn mower and roller and which now made room as well for a stretcher-bed and the unpainted bathroom cupboard with half a door where he kept his clothes, his shaving equip-

93

ment, a leather sling-shot, an old French horn on which he occasionally blew a garbled fanfare, and a collection of marbles in a chamois bag from which he let me choose, every now and then, a glassie or a glazed taw.

I was still, myself, at that stage of half-boyhood where the highest form of independence is a cubby-house in a tree. There was something of the cubby about Uncle Gil's shack. Its planks, which came only to waist level, were so grey and weather-beaten, and its nails so bent and brittle, that it provided only the flimsiest shelter. Sacking had been nailed to the roof and could be lowered in winter to keep out the winds. Otherwise it was open on all sides and had its own fuggy climate and smell; especially when the cloud-bursts of late summer left the yard soaked but brilliant and everything gave off the essence of itself – leaves, leafmould, bark, dust, clothes – and the sacking, as it steamed and dripped, a cloudy exhalation of hemp, grain-dust and rich old mould. If the chooks got out, as often happened when the prop of the wire gate was not settled, the fowls came flapping in and roosted on Uncle Gil's cupboard or in the rafters, which did resemble somewhat the branches of a tree, and left their soft grey-and-white spatterings to harden on the bed, the beams, the beaten dirt floor: an impossible, rock-hard snow. Against one wall of the shack was a clump of bamboo. Its dry sticks rattled in every breeze.

But for all its air of improvisation and its suggestion of the tree-house or cubby-hole, this was an adult's refuge not a boy's place of escape. Uncle Gil had set himself apart.

He had always been wild for adventure, and when war broke out he immediately joined the Air Force and was sent overseas. Shot down over the North Sea, he had suffered a concussion that jarred his brains, or had 'seen something' as a prisoner in Germany that defied imagination and for that very reason kept us in awe. Della's opinion was that he had gone too fast. Our local pace was that of the bicycle, however many cars were on the road, and Uncle Gil, in one of his dives, had 'got ahead of himself, poor boy, and left his brains behind'. Or exposure to another hemisphere had done it, where the times of day and seasons of the year were upside down – a place so heavy with history, with crowns, swords, Catholic churches, big names, massacres and other forms of injustice, that our own simpler world, when he got back, was too light to hold him. He swung between poles, each with its different pace and its different light or dark.

For long weeks he would be as mild as a lamb. I liked then to go down and help him with his tasks: the hoeing and staking of plants, the filling of bag after bag with beans, the gathering (slipping your hand carefully under the nervous hens) of eggs. He seldom spoke more than a few syllables then, as he directed me in the crosswise setting of a stake or the knotting of the string that tied it. Grasshoppers rose up as we approached, heavy-bodied, lifting themselves awkwardly out of reach. He would grab and catch one, snapping its head off with a flick of the wrist. 'There,' he'd say mildly, 'that's one more of the buggers done for.' I might have felt then that I understood him completely, that of all the adults in that household he was the one whose nature came nearest my own.

Such quiet spells did not last. One day, suddenly, he would be in a talking mood. The next day he couldn't stop, and the talk was terrible. The sounds as they tumbled over one another and flashed and bubbled and exploded in what would soon be a rage, were terrifying to me because they made no sense. Ordinary words such as we all shared and used without question had become parts of another language, and Uncle Gil was possessed by them and became another person. His fingers jerked, his body was clenched or flung about like a puppet's, spit flew from his lips; he would clasp me by the shoulders and shake me bodily with the effort of getting the sense of what he was saying out of his head into mine. I understood only the emotion and struggled to get free of it.

When the words did occasionally cluster, or collide in comprehensible fragments, it was in obscene attacks on his sisters and all women, in savage resentment of my father (who judged him, he felt, and had never made allowance for the difference between them and the fact that two men might see things from opposite angles) or as a deep rage against life itself, which was a stinking muckheap of injustice and hypocrisy and petty torments and an evil that was irredeemable. There was nothing to do but blast the lot of it out of the eye of God, the politicians and the fucking small-minded butchers and their wives, with their *moralities* and their little fingers crooked and lifted as they drank blood.

Only Aunt Ollie, the mildest of all that family, could make contact with the man when these blood-moods were upon him. Undeterred by knives or rages, and deaf to obscenities, she would go down and sit quietly till he had shouted himself out, or had run aground on the rocklike solidity of her calm. They would lean together, not talking, while the bamboo fretted and sighed and shifted its light behind them and the wet sacking dripped.

At last he would be drawn back to one of his tasks, and leaving the kitchen to Della, Aunt Ollie would stay, seated on an up-turned packing case, with her legs apart and her elbows propped upon them, in the same pose in which she was painted by Frank Harland – I recall the pose now because of the painting; it suggested all the weight and stability, all the permanence with which, forgetting the number of things that had to be done elsewhere, she could settle for a few minutes as if they were, in some other method of computing time, whole years or centuries. It was this, I think, that led Uncle Gil back again to his own slower rhythms, and inevitably then to the tasks in which they were fixed.

After a time, without speaking, she would simply push herself to her feet and go.

For Aunt Ollie, Uncle Gil like the others was infinitely forgiveable. As a tiny thing she had nursed, fed, washed him and learned all his tricks and moods. Nothing he did surprised her. When he was a boy he had played the French horn. Beautifully. She often spoke of the lovely sound of it as if it were, for her, the true note of his youth. Later, when he would creep home drunk, it was she who watched and listened for him. Laughing softly and leaning into the warmth of his big sister, as heavy as a bear, he would pretend to be drunker than he was and she would struggle with him in the hallway and guide him barefoot to his room while he laughed and chanted: 'Sorry Ol, Ol, Ol, Ol,' his warm beery breath in her ear, her mouth, against her bare neck and shoulders.

'Sorry, Ol,' he would say now, standing shame-faced among the beans, barefoot still in an old singlet and dungarees. Till the next time, it was over.

He had gone too fast and too far. But Uncle Gil's view of things, however irrational, did not entirely lack reason. The cruelties he raged against were real – so was the evil. I saw that, even in the ordinary rituals of our lives; but we kept them contained, or we averted our eyes and pretended they had been dealt with.

Uncle Gil's outbursts were also contained: in the care with which he lifted hens' eggs and showed them in the palm of his hand – smooth, white, often pasted with shit – and in the regular rhythm with which he threaded wire or staked and tied young plants. If he did break out some day, and taking the axe from the woodpile, laid bare the chicken-brains as he called them of Aunt Roo and Aunt Connie, or set fire to the house, or went out and grabbed the first old woman he saw and tossed her off Southport bridge, or in a reign of terror bloody-well did for the fucking politicians – if he did any of that, I thought, it would be no less part of him than the rest, and continuous with the most orderly things in him, with knotted strings and green young transparent beans in sunlight, his whole world and view.

My own view, as I began that year to stake out the limits of it, seemed increasingly complex. There was my grandfather's dying, both the process of it – a physical process no more alien or alarming as it took him out of the world than the one, felt in every sense and nerve at times, that was drawing me into it – and the particular occasion, still to come, that would put an end to our stay here and change yet again all the details of our lives. Then there was the family, that close, disorderly unit, threatened by conflicts that might at any moment make it fly apart but held always by lines of affection and dependence and by habits that could not be broken: by my father's concern for all members of it, my grandmother's power, sustained over long years and taking many forms, and the ministrations with pots, pans, cleavers of my Aunt Ollie and Della that three times a day, winter and summer, called us all together, sometimes in unity, sometimes in a formal play of irritations and hostilities, round the big scrubbed table outside or the narrower one in the dining-room; and also tied, though separate, like an island held in uneasy federation with a continent, my Uncle Gil, whose notions, given scope, could shatter whole areas of what I had staked out, leaving a charred stump – though even that, I thought, would be part of it and inevitably connected.

[4]

It ended as we might have expected. That is, unexpectedly.

One afternoon, much like every other over the past year and a half, I was sitting curled up in my usual position at the bottom of grandfather's bed, reading I remember the Cymbeline story from Lamb's *Tales from Shakespeare*, and must have been lost for a time in the wild and distant landscape of it, because when I glanced up, as I did every few minutes or so 'to see what Grandpa was doing', he had slipped sideways in the bed, at the very edge of his great bulwark of pillows, and had what I knew immediately, though I had no experience of it, was a look beyond sleep.

His mouth was open. One hand hung over the side of the mattress, the other lay open on the sheet. But the sheet there was rucked and creased as if in the moment before the fingers relaxed he had been grasping at it in an attempt, against terrible odds, to climb back or hang on. Whatever struggle he had been engaged in I had missed. It had taken place while I was far off in another country.

It was unusually quiet. A bank of dull cloudless heat hung over the Broadwater. The sky was glaring but grey. On such still days the only sound was of gulls, their shrill, far-off loops and whimperings.

I got down from the bed as quietly as possible – I do not know why I felt I should creep rather than walk in a normal barefoot manner – went out into the hallway, and pushed at the door of my parents' room.

It was another large, high-ceilinged room, of pale blue tongue-and-groove, with a picture-rail from which Frank Harland's landscape hung. The gauze curtains were drawn. My mother, fully dressed but with her shoes off, lay on her half of the double bed, on a blue spread embroidered with ox-eyed daisies and green clover-leafs. One arm was folded over her eyes, the other lay loosely across her breast.

'Mumma,' I whispered; and though she was often difficult to wake from these late-afternoon naps, she immediately sat up and swung her stockinged feet over the edge of the bed.

Downstairs, in the big closed sitting-room, a clock with gilded lead weights the size of sledge-hammers, that my grandmother wound up every Sunday before lunch, began to chime the hour. It had never, to my ears, sounded so round and solemn. Though I had often lain awake and heard it dividing off the quarters, the halves, the full hours in its companionable way, dealing with the spaces of dark, I had not thought of it till now, as I followed my mother down the hallway, as dealing also in finalities, as mechanically, irrevocably, pushing us out of one moment into the next and closing off forever what lay behind.

The room was even quieter than when I had left it. My mother sat on the edge of the cane-bottomed chair, very grave and pale, with her hands on her knees.

'When did it happen?' she asked. And suddenly the tears leapt out of my eyes in the most alarming way. They didn't well and trickle, they leapt right out as if on springs.

'I don't know!' I gasped between sobs, and she pressed me to her, shushing and patting the back of my head, 'I don't know!'

'Be quiet now,' she whispered, 'it isn't your fault, you couldn't have done anything.' I had climbed on to her knee and was sobbing into her neck. 'Just be quiet, darling, while I think. We mustn't say anything' – her voice was barely audible – 'till your father comes. He should be the one to break the news to your grandmother. I can't do it.'

I had fallen still at last and she eased me off her knee.

'I'll just settle him a little, poor sweet, and we'll wait for your father to come.'

So I sat on the cane-bottomed chair while she took the pillows from under Grandpa's head, straightening him, laying his hands crosswise on his chest, and drew the sheet up to his chin – all the time weeping. Then, not speaking, we both sat.

The light began to deepen. There was the sound from below of Della and Aunt Ollie preparing tea, and my Aunt Roo called once from the top of the stairs and we heard her going down. The sea-breeze sprang up, bringing its smell of salt, quickening all the leaves below and lifting the curtains in drifts. I had had time by now to take the whole thing in. Not just the fact that my grandfather was dead at last, had crossed some physical barrier that was real and ultimate – though sitting in the same room with him I had not perceived it – but that the activities I associated with this room, and which made it, and my grandfather, most real to me, were done with now, and all its objects – bed-pan, bottles, sponges – had become in a single moment as remote and useless as if a decade's dust had settled on them.

My mother must have felt it even more. She had, now that Grandpa was gone, no purpose in this room. Tomorrow or the next day or the day after we could pack up and go back to Brisbane. I felt a pang of anxiety. I hadn't realized till now how completely, over these months, I had come to think of my life here as the only one possible, and could not guess how much of it might be translatable; how much was my own and how much might belong to the household and to Southport itself. I did not want, for the moment, to change, when change was just what I had discovered here.

My mother stirred and shooed a fly from the counterpane. She drew the sheet up over Grandpa's face, then sat again. It was almost dark. It was the hour when she would normally have lighted the little night-lamp. I had been sent down earlier for metholated spirits and it was full. It would not be needed.

It was that more than anything else I think that brought home to me the reality of the thing. Grandpa had been afraid of the dark. Suddenly, startling my mother in the silence, I broke down again and began to weep.

But it was nearly six. Time for me to go down and look for my father on his way up from the station. I blew my nose on a clean handkerchief, assured my mother I was all right, and went out; for the last time leaving her alone with him.

She was not a trained nurse but a school-teacher, who in the early days of the war, when the threat of air raids was pressing, had joined the VADs and been given the usual lessons in first aid and general care of the wounded. My grandfather, it seems, had always been fond of her, but she was too timid in the days when he walked around with a stick and swaggered in public to believe it. Over the long months of his illness they had grown close, bound together in an intimacy that was founded on the regular physical duties she had to perform for him and which he had come at last, through touch, and murmured soothings and easings, to accept at her hands. She alone was witness to the worst indignities imposed upon him by his incontinence, and the agonies in which, for long moments, he became the merest racked meat and bone; and to the fierce wordless hissing that gave way at times to obscenities he would have been mortified to have her think him capable of on saner occasions, and which she would have been ashamed to hear.

Their life together in that sickroom had been a life apart. I came only to the edge of it, pushed out of sight and earshot of what she felt I should not bear. In their quiet times together all they had endured in extreme and barely tolerable passages of mere nerve, made an electricity between them that was like the flow of energy between lovers. I might have been jealous if Grandpa and I had not had our own relationship, and if my mother had not made me her only assistant. Grandpa's body, now that it was laid out under the sheet, seemed barely substantial enough to have been the centre of so much passion. It scarcely broke the line of the bed.

Such stillness could not last. Downstairs the news was broken to my grandmother; my father took her into the darkened sitting-room. My aunts were told. The house was filled with their weeping. Then my grandmother, stony-faced and showing her years, appeared with my father beside her at the bedroom door.

My mother still sat by the high white bed. I stood between the curtains at my mother's shoulder, with the gauzy white blowing over me in the late breeze; beyond the verandah rails, between spiky branches, the flat dark waters of the bay.

I see us all in our positions, utterly still, as my grandmother, rather small and stooped in the doorway, speaks the words that will close this whole period more completely even than my grandfather's death.

'I won't go in till that woman is out of the room. I don't want her to lay a hand on my poor Jeffers, ever again!' She reverted to a pet-name no one had heard her use in more than twenty years, and I wondered for a moment who it was that she meant. 'My husband. *Mine*! Get that woman out of here!'

My mother's face had swung into ashen profile as if she'd been struck.

'Mamma!' my father said agonizingly, seeing the whole of the next ten years open before him, with their divided loyalties and recriminations and the repetition of this moment over and over in the retelling on both sides, with the same words savagely spat out.

'He's suffered enough from her shamelessness, poor darling. He was too sick to complain. And too modest to tell me how she touched and tormented him. But *I* knew. I'm not blind. It was shameful! That woman has no shame!'

'Mamma, for God's sake!' my father moaned. But he must have known, as my mother did, who had risen and was standing dead white with her hand on the back of the chair, that he was the real source of contention between them, that it was him my grandmother had in mind.

'I won't go into the room till she's left it. I want her *out of my house*!'

My mother had already rushed past me, with the white gauze sweeping over her shoulder, and I heard her wrestle with the verandah door, then give an enraged howl from the hallway. My father turned and went after her. My grandmother, her face set, stepped into the room at last. She stood for a moment in the stillness, and then, with her fists clenched, began to beat on the brass rail of the bed so that the whole structure bounced and the body under the sheet began to fly about in terrible convulsions under the hammering of her ringed fists. No sound came out of her mouth. It was my mother's voice I could hear from the other end of the hallway. Then it too was drowned by the combined voices of the aunts.

So the whole thing ended disgracefully, in ugly brawling and insults. Within an hour my mother had packed our things and would listen to no kind of reason: if my father wouldn't take her home immediately she would spend the night in a hotel.

Aunt Ollie tried to pacify her mother, but she too was unyielding. Downstairs, in the kitchen, Della sat in the corner by the range and moaned; partly for my grandfather but also for the meal that would never be eaten, which sat in pots on the stove, getting cold, and would have to be scraped out and fed to the chooks.

Uncle Gil, deeply shaken by a kind of violence for which he had no terms, had fled to the bottom of the yard, but came back later, shamefaced and pale, along with Aunt Ollie, to kiss us goodbye. The others did not dare take sides against their mother; who now, from an upstairs window, began to scream new accusations, and my father, having settled us in the cab, left Aunt Ollie to weep over me and whisper consolations to my mother while he went back upstairs to try for the last time to make his mother retract a little of what, in the shock of grief, and only for that reason, she had said. She refused to take back a word. Not a syllable! Not a breath! My father was a broken man.

'In a few days –' he began, but didn't have the heart to go on. It would be years and he knew it.

'Do what you can, Ollie,' he said miserably. 'I can't believe it can be ending like this.'

'Look after Jess and the boy,' Aunt Ollie advised him, 'there's nothing you can do here. God bless you, dear,' she said into the dark of the cab, and stood large and solid on the pavement with Uncle Gil at the gate behind her. My father gave a nod to the driver and we pulled away.

The silence that descended was of a different kind from the one that for so long had preceded that violent outpouring of breath.

KNACK

[1]

Moonlit dew on the peaked roofs of Spring Hill gave the sprawling suburb, where it ran up and downhill so steeply, the look of turned ground in a bit of cobwebbed garden rather than the rackety, run-down shambles it was, all gapped verandahs and lopsided paling fences; an eyesore, right there where the toastrack trams rattled up from Edward Street in the heart of the city.

It was at once a crossroads and cul-de-sac, a packed settlement of working-class families, older people of good standing who had got stranded when the place declined from the better days at the start of the century, and loose establishments of girls too smart to work eight hours a day in a munitions factory, who were serving the war effort in an alternative, a horizontal position. They sat about in the morning in gaudy kimonos – Japanese, but allowing nothing to the enemy – painting their toe-nails, spreading their hair to dry, and pampering thighs and shoulders with cold cream in the early heat.

Cats melted over fences, or sidled through a gap between palings and were stroked or cuddled or driven off with kicks. Small children in grubby singlets and nothing else waddled about in weed-grown yards, while their mothers, hanging out overalls or bluish-white shirts, wrestled with ten-foot props. In the afternoons after school barefoot boys spat, swore, knuckled and chinese-burned one another, or choosing sides, played cricket on the least steep of the up-and-down sidestreets with a couple of fruit cases for wickets and a bald tennis-ball. At night there were shouting matches, drunken brawls, the soft crash of bottles on warm bitumen, and sometimes piano music in one of the song-hits, 'Paper Doll'. American sailors arrived in taxis, five at a time, ordinary youths released into a new life in an unknown continent, their uniforms and little round caps a startling white. Some of them were black – though the blacks, by army regulation and civic compliance, were restricted to the south side of the river. Occasionally there were irruptions of military police to break up, on the limits of the real war, a skirmish between Southern Comfort allies and locals who were resentful of being kept behind the lines to load ships and service vehicles for their heroic defenders, and took it upon themselves to show now that it was cowardly government policy and arse-licking that kept them out of the fray, not their own unwillingness to have a go, or any lack of talent in the delivery of lead visiting cards or the aiming of boots.

There was a busy traffic here in sly grog, especially port, and a black market in nylon stockings, tinned asparagus, tinned salmon and off-coupon sugar, butter and meat. It had an economy of its own, Spring Hill, that recreated in little the larger one of which it was a distorted reflection. Frank Harland had, for ten shillings a week, a workman's cottage with a double-gabled roof. It had been partly burnt out and was condemned. From the two attic rooms, which were the only part of the house he could live in, he had a view of dew-lit corrugated-iron, electric wires with clusters of cupped white insulators, a maze of rickety fences and narrow back lanes between cross-streets, then, almost without a break, the five- or six-storeyed office blocks and department stores of the city.

He painted while there was light, and when the light was gone went to bed, or if he could get in, to a pub or wineshop, for a single glass of something and an hour or two of feeling at one with the crowd.

It was a time of crowds, and more than ever now he knew what it was to be alone. Everyone else had been recruited into a company of one sort or another; they were living in events he was barely touched by. To settle among them for a while, to smell the powder, scent, lipstick excitement of it all, to be at the edge of brawls or tremendous bouts of drunkenness, made him feel cut off and out of his own times but gave him at least a glimpse of things. The headlong rush into nothingness caught him up and quickened his blood. It was general enough, all that, to ask for no more than your presence as a dispensable unit in an ever-changing and anonymous crowd that was hurtling on into the dark.

He first saw the antique-dealer Knack, and his friend Edna, in a wine-shop in Wharf Street. They too, at their corner table, seemed not quite part of the rout; he in his black suit and soft wide-brimmed hat, she with her straw and feathers; which is why, the second or third time they found themselves at neighbouring tables, squashed in among the half-caste women and thin long-faced drunks, they had exchanged looks, then nods, and had struck up at last a kind of acquaintance that led to his being invited to the rooms behind the shop in Melbourne Street, South Brisbane, where Knack and Edna had their flat.

This Knack as he called himself, or Walter as the woman called him, was a bald fellow of nearly sixty, a giant of a man with a shiny skull and big knuckles to his hands, who wore a sober, three-piece suit in a cloth from the days before coupons, and boots that he mended himself on a last he had in the backyard.

Unlocking the door of the shop with a thin key, he would lead them through a kind of maze – between stacks of old books, past the solid but shadowy presence of dining-tables, sofas, sideboards crowded with little cut-glass or china objects that glittered in the dark, smokers' stands in chrome and polished wood, the silhouette of a harp or piano-frame whose strings turned red and green with the traffic-lights, under rows of hanging lamps of an old fashioned moulded variety on dusty chains.

These fragments of broken households were the stuff of Knack's business. All the elements of several rooms, from different periods and levels of society, had been thrown together, so that a Jacobean table with barley-sugar legs, that had seen half a century of regular mealtimes and still spoke up for solid middle-class respectability, might be no more now than the pedestal for a chipped enamel bath of the poorest quality and most doubtful provenance, while its chairs, including two heavy carvers, swung ten foot overhead; a whole dinner party at one of those mealtimes might have abruptly levitated. There was a buttoned-leather lovers' seat that recalled a century of whispers and tentative, exploratory hands. Open upon it now was a surgeon's case with its nest of blades. A grandfather clock stood among meat-safes; a grand piano with no strings supported a chest of drawers and the chest of drawers an old-fashioned sewing-machine. Everything was higgledy-piggledy, a parody of settled existence that suggested some final break in the logic of things or a general disruption in which every stick had worked loose or floated free of its old use and meaning and would acquire a new one only when it was resurrected into a second (or was it a third?) life. Frank found the place disturbing, especially in the half dark under the intermittent red, yellow and green of the traffic-lights.

But you passed through it, and the room beyond, Knack's flat, was neat and comfortable.

The moment they entered and put on the light a bundle of feathers, a little zebra-striped lovebird flew out. It came to rest on Knack's shoulder. The addition of the bird to his presence, or the flash of colour, or the demonstration of immediate natural affection, lit the man up from within. He cracked his knuckles and showed his teeth in a brilliant grin.

'Allegra,' the woman explained as the bird worked up and down at Knack's ear.

She removed the pink straw, which dipped down to cover one side of her face, and held out her hand to it but the bird did not come.

'Make yerself at home,' she invited, indicating the chairs. 'I'll make a cuppa Horlicks. Horlicks oright?'

'Splendid,' Knack said in his precise but thickened accent. 'Only first, I think, a drop of something – stronger.' He snapped his knuckles again, and stooped – lean-shanked, dark-suited, with the bird on his shoulder and the hat with its turned-up brim still settled on his skull – to the diamond-paned lead-light door of the sideboard. 'Hennessy,' he pronounced, 'Four Star.'

Before long he had established the habit of going two or three nights each week to sit in the room behind the junk shop, sipping illicit brandy, listening to Knack talk or play the piano, and drinking Horlicks made by the blonded Edna. They had come to be the nearest thing he had, in this sprawling transit-camp, to a family, and the room with its lilac and green wallpaper was closer than his own two rooms in the boarded-up and partly burnt-out cottage to being home. He reckoned, on the basis that two thirds of the place was given over to darkness, that about seven-and-six of his weekly ten shillings was paid for the accommodation of spiders, rats and the occasional cat that crawled in through the floorboards to have a litter of kittens, whose mewling he heard but which were too quick to take refuge in old cartons, or under piles of newspaper, to be caught.

Knack's place on the other hand was cosy. There were big Genoa-velvet lounge chairs, smokers' stands in embossed silver and gold (though neither he nor Edna smoked) and a good upright piano with candle sconces that was kept perfectly tuned. Once when he dropped in there in the afternoon, the piano-tuner was at work, a blind man. He went on striking notes and tightening up keys while Frank, working quickly with line and wash, made a sketch of Edna Byrne in her striped deckchair, her plump arms folded, the blonded hair in a wispy pompadour, the eyes round and dark like the beads you stick in a snowman on a cake.

He worked in the dark. There was a golden languor and deep warmth to her that he would have to catch some other way; the pure quality of being curled up in itself, in its own life, of a tortoiseshell cat in sunlight. Her flesh purred. It was that he would have to catch.

The piano-tuner, screwing and tapping out single notes was an accompaniment to the sketch he made and would later amplify, as Knack, with his huge hands, which he often snapped and clasped together above the keys, would improve on the tuner's work by developing single notes into the most extraordinary sounds Frank Harland had ever heard.

But for long periods on these afternoon visits he and Edna would sit in silence. He liked that. They had no need to speak. They would sip tea while shadows gathered in the shop – lamps, wardrobe-tops, chairs, all up in the air; or he held skeins of wool while she wound them dreamily into balls. He liked that too, the bright wools and her hands making over and over the same spell-like gestures as they shared the task – women's work, out of the repetitive lives of women; he had forgotten that, having barely known it. The activity was soothing, it put the spirit to sleep. It encouraged, with the repeated tumbling motion of her wrists and the unwinding and winding of strands, a kind of drowsy intercourse between them in which it was easy at last to talk.

'I come from up Childers way – you know? – sugarcane country. Lovely! The soil's red but. I don't think I ever saw a white shirt or had a pair of real white undies till I come to Brisbane. Gets into everything, that red soil. The dirt under your nails is red, and kids have red ingrained into the soles of their feet, you never get it out. The bottom half of the bath is always pink. But the smell's lovely, nothing like it, and the cane-tops when they're in flower. Oh, an' the fires when they're burning-off, with all the snakes running out of the flames n' the men's faces n' shoulders sweaty n' black with smuts. I miss that, I really do. S' funny how a place you hate can be a place you miss. Most of all the smell. Once you've smelt that sweetness everything else smells grey – you know what I mean? Dusty!'

He did know, because he had been on the road through all that part of the state: rolling canefields under a ceiling of cloud, a wash of blue between caneflowers of a cloudy white-pink and the feathery bloom of clouds, with red-dirt tracks, often greasy, and banks of coarse green grass. Off in the distance a verandahed farmhouse on stilts with a scatter of corrugated-iron sheds and a lone windmill. Little trains loaded with cane on a narrow-gauge line. And the whole landscape glittering, steaming. He could imagine her as a child with pigtails and bare legs red to the knee, sitting on the back seat of a sulky in one of those stunned towns chewing a stick of cane.

He let the knowledge of it work under the image of the over-blown woman in the striped deck-chair, as the blind man, feeling for the rightness of a note, repeatedly plonked and the taut string whined and was screwed into place: one clear stroke of colour in a rainbow (as Knack would create it) of chromatic chords.

'I worked as a housemaid when I first came down. Atcherly Private Hotel, d'you know it? Petrie Bight. I was a housemaid. Made beds for rich country people that were down for the Show, or to see Gladys Moncrieff or the lights for the Coronation. Got sick of it but. Turning down all them damn beds at four o'clock in the afternoon. Embarrassing sometimes too. There's people find four o'clock on a rainy afternoon a good time t' be in the cot, y' know? Get worked up by a good storm and dive into the sheets and don't wanna know if you come hammerin' at the door. So I left and went to work for this photographer, Mr Margolis. He was a sort of hunchback. Well, I suppose he *was* a hunchback, but he was a real nice little bloke, polite. Very dark, with the most beautiful eyes – soft black, a proper gentleman. The kiddies weren't the least bit scared of him. I mean, they could of been – that black cloth over the camera, y'know, and the hump under it that was Mr Margolis, and then him stepping out, not much taller than a kiddie himself, and the hump on *his* back, like there was another little photographer under that one as well. On'y he'd be smiling and holding the switch at the end of the cord, and saying 'Big smile now!', and the kiddies, when they come out, looked like they'd been smiling at an angel. You'd never of guessed it was Mr Margolis in a nicely cut black suit. He had it made specially of course.

'I really loved that place – the Studio. I used t' have to dust it, and set up, and of course I took the orders and that, at a proper desk. There were these two big black umbrellas in the corner – always open, he didn't seem worried about bad luck – and the place where you stood, or sat, was like a lovely little stage. When it was lit up it was really lovely. A white column, a big glossy palm – I used to have to dust the leaves and paint them with oil – an' behind, three painted screens that you could roll up and down for a bit of a change, with the prettiest landscape you ever seen. One was a kind of lake, with mountains. Another was a garden with all flowering vines in the trees. Y'know, people would look quite ordinary, brides and that – dumpy, or pale, or scared, or a bit scraggy, even in their satin, and the men – you know, all hands and ears. But the moment they stepped up into the scene, with the column and the view and the way Mr Margolis spoke to them – charmed them like, put them at their ease and *composed* them – well, it was a miracle, they were different people. They looked as if they belonged to – I don't know – anyway, as if they hadn' just stepped in off the street in a hired suit and a shop-bought wedding-dress, but belonged to some – I don't know. You couldn't of guessed from their faces, or the way they sat, that it was all set up – that the column and palm were on a platform that only went two feet either side of 'em.

'Sometimes, when I felt crook or down in the dumps, I'd go in, turn all the lights on till I was dazzled and sit there myself – rest me elbow on the column and sort of daydream. It did me good.

'It was a lovely job, that, it really was. Especially the kiddies. Mr Margolis used to have jelly beans for 'em, on'y he'd eat all the black ones himself and some of the bolder kiddies used to say it straight out: 'Someone's eaten all the *black* ones!'

'Black jelly beans and tangos on the gramophone, that's what 'e liked. But then Mr Margolis's sister took a dislike to me – said I was common – she was an art of speech teacher – so that was that! Mr Margolis was very upset, but he had no guts poor little bloke. Said he'd never had anyone who was so good with the kiddies, or with jittery brides!' She laughed, a full-throated laugh. 'I used t' give 'em a Bex in Coke if they was too bad, and they'd come out looking so – you know – as if life couldn' touch 'em now that they'd seen what they had – which was just a coupla black umbrellas' (she laughed again) 'and Mr Margolis under a cloth. Anyway, to make a long story short, I become a barmaid. Big places – the Criterion, the Grand Central – and that's where I met Knack.'

She softened and smiled, almost the shy girl. She was fond of the man with the bald head.

'I reckon it was the music. I never learned, but when he plays – well, you've *heard* it – I get all goose-pimply, I can't speak, it takes me breath away, it's another world. And then Knack, you know – Walt – is a very clever man. Educated. Back there, it's not the same is it? As here I mean. They're more cultured. In spite of the concentration-camps. But you know without me saying it. You've *heard*.'

He had, many times. Difficult to say which was the more impressive, Knack's music or his talk.

There were occasions when the music seemed too big for the room with its lilac and green wallpaper and its one sash window looking on to the yard; but not too big for Knack's head, which shone with a gleam of sweat on the crown and was monumental, and made up for the absence of columned and gilded halls. Blood bunched at the temple; there were strange depressions on either side, as if while the skull was still soft two huge thumbs had been pushed down, permanently denting the jelly-like bone.

Knack left them behind when he moved into the music, though they too were transported. Frank had never glimpsed such power in the addressing of thunderbolts, or felt such after-sweetness of sorrow as when the voice – no one's voice in particular, only the linking together of notes the piano-tuner had made way for – went singing through all the agonies, the unstillnesses and doubts and conciliations, the risings over and above the actual pain of snapped limbs and pinched and torn flesh as you might apprehend it in the white of Knack's knuckles or in the raddled veins and greasy roundness of his skull as skin worked over bone.

Frank knew nothing about music. He had no idea whether Knack played well or badly or how many wrong notes he struck among the right ones. It was mere noise at first, in which he recognized a kind of power – the Furies. What held him was the contortions Knack endured; either through the physical demand upon arms, wrists, shoulders as he belted it out or made single notes hang on and grieve, or through the convulsive passions the music excited in the man. Frank couldn't have decided between them, the physical and the moral rackings, but it was a rack he thought of. While Knack, in his sober, straight-backed jacket sat upright before it, his spirit was stretched out horizontal and an invisible tuner screwed the strings. You could hear the whining vibrations, feel the tightening of nerves and sinews as the bones approached their point of departure. Frank himself felt it. He broke into a sweat.

As for the woman, she shrank deeper and deeper into her own flesh. Occasionally she shuddered. At other times she leaned back with her eyes shut, blissfully adrift.

In those early days, though he was happy to eavesdrop and touched that they made a place for him, he understood nothing. The music was a landscape of storms and stretches of wide shining weather where Knack walked with Edna Byrne under a solemn sky. But over the weeks it declared its lines to him, then its volumes, there was ground under his feet. He entered a weather of changing light and shade, and occasionally, when he came out of himself, it was he and Edna who had been walking alone together. He felt the music within him, as if he were listening to the coursing thunder or the beat at walking-pace (the world's pace) of his blood.

He still did not know the names and Knack did not announce them. It was music or talk, never both at the one time.

Knack's talk:

'My name, for example, is not really Knack. I call myself that because of the shop. Knacks for fine ladies – a kind of joke,' and he showed his big teeth in a grin. 'Besides, in this place, the real name hardly matters. It is Nestorius – a mouthful, eh? And who cares now that it goes back a thousand years in the one district, with a lake, forests, a kind of castle, even a crest. See?' He showed Frank a ring with a porcupine on it, in a raised shield. 'Might as well be Knack! When I got up out of that ditch and found I had all my limbs, it was near dusk and everyone around me, under me, had stopped moving. Just a little warmth was still coming up, making a sort of fog. Body-warmth. Ah, well I thought, so this is the afterlife, is it hell then? It wasn't of course but it might be. So, I got a new life, a new country, why not a new name? Knack has the right sort of sound, eh? – short and sweet. It fits me better than the other long one, with so much family history, you know, and all the honours to be kept up. A bit on the comic side – the afterlife does turn out to be on the comic side. It is difficult not to appear a clown sometimes, when your head is in one place and your tongue in another. The accent!'

He made a face, solemn clown-like. 'It does not permit you, from many people's point of view, to be quite serious.'

He had an odd way of speaking. It wasn't just the accent. Frank strained to listen but could not always catch the meaning, only the oddness of what was said, its obliqueness, and the man's wry cynicism. Edna understood better, he thought, and he might catch the full sense, later, from her.

He was Polish, from a land of forests along the Baltic.

'Hard little tears that sea throws up,' he told them. 'Amber. Ancient forests have wept. It is cast up on the beach, sometimes in lumps as big as a fist, and often with insects trapped in it from thousands of years ago, little golden flies or bees or a grasshopper, perfectly preserved. Very rrromantic, eh?' He rolled the *r* deliberately and gave a laugh. 'Well, no place is romantic if you live there and know the stink. The stink of that place is fishbones. Herrings! Pooh, you can't imagine! The fog stinks of it, and the shirts off the line. Slimy fishguts on all the planks, a fishbone always in your throat. And then later, as if the stink of fish wasn't enough, ideas. Beautiful, savage, fatal ideas – oh you'd die holding your nose! Then many, many bodies. And there is not amber enough in all the Baltic to hide them – not if the forests were to weep now for a million years. I am one of the fortunate bodies. I got up again and walked right across Russia. With a little assistance from the railway, of course!

'My life,' he mused, 'is strange to me, this new one. I do not know why I was given it *back*.' He produced the last word between his teeth like a bullet, and spat it out. It hung in the air as if it were magical or had no terrestrial weight. 'I think sometimes that I got up too quickly, and left in that ditch my soul or is it my manhood? Well, it is the same thing.'

'Walt dear,' the woman remonstrated, and took his hand.

This sort of talk was unreal to her. It might have belonged to a childish nightmare. When she caught at times a whiff of the reality he spoke of, it was not from his talk but from episodes in the music, when she would glimpse through a break in the forest, and through clearing mist, some corner of an experience that was not her own and could only be his. Or it came to her when the hard ridge of his back, so strictly upright in its dealings with Liszt or Beethoven, would soften, and the great furnace of his breath grew ghostly. Her own existence could not account then for all that she understood.

He was the son of rich timber merchants, minor nobility, and had been the citizen, successively, of three powers. A student of philosophy in his youth and a modest black sheep, he had been a soldier in the civil wars, a black marketeer afterwards, then a playboy, a fugitive, a refugee, and was now a dealer in second-hand books, china, glassware and household effects.

'Did you know,' he told them once, 'that we can determine the exact date, down to the hour, when our Dark Ages began? June the 8th, 1783. On that day the entrance to hell blew open and all the devils broke loose. It is quite scientific, you can read about it, I can show the place on the map. It is in Iceland. A great hot cloud spread out, all over the world. It was full of sulphurous notions that men breathed in with it – not germs but sulphurous *notions*. They got into the bloodstream and were carried in bubbles to the brain. They made men mad – dizzy – sent them whirling off to be demons themselves, organizing revolutions and wars and councils and model prisons, and new kinds of dances to get themselves more worked up, and poems and proclamations against this and that, and a terrible itch to know everything and be everything and cast off limitations. We've been breathing that new air ever since. We've got used to it. If we had a real sense of history we'd be measuring time by it, before and after: BH and AH. We've adapted. We've become new creatures and have stopped noticing that the breath is not out of heaven any more but thick, sulphurous, out of – what do you say? – the bowels is it? Is that right? We are under a new dispensation. This is the year one hundred and sixty-two, AH, After Hekla.' His smile now was on the lugubrious rather than the comic side.

Frank caught the woman's eye. A quick glance passed between them. She was proud of Knack as of a clever child, but there was indulgence in her look as well, as for some sort of clever foolishness that she would deal with later on.

Did she really understand it all, Frank wondered. He didn't. But then Knack had a headstart coming from Europe, which must be an education all in itself – a bitter one; Australians couldn't compete. You had to start from scratch here. From a bit of a yard or paddock, or a room even, and build it up slowly yourself, out of grass seeds and scribbles on bark, or out of the knob on a dressing table, or a door jamb with height-marks on it, or a teapot that had passed down through all the afternoons of a family, or a hive full of bees.

Edna smiled. Ssssh, she appeared to say on these occasions. We got to be patient with him. He's seen too much. He's ashamed to be content.

She was content, so long as Knack didn't unnerve her; serene, indolent, quite comfortable in her flesh.

'But you don't know what I am talking about, you lucky children! Here, listen!' and Knack would swing back to the piano and lead them hand in hand like a wicked uncle; deep in along the gloomiest paths they followed the cloth of his back.

The music scared him, but was easier to follow, Frank found, than the talk. Under clouds of an impossible eloquence, all bannered flame, poisonous berries hung in clusters over a pool, great dolls rolled their heads, their eyeballs clicked. Letting go of the other child's hand, Edna's, who was too entranced to notice, he fell back. It was too dark, all that. It was of a gloom he had never encountered in all his travels up and down the state, and might not exist on this continent or on this side of the globe. The mists here were not thick enough – not enough people. You needed centuries of breath; or maybe the sulphur-cloud Knack spoke of. Had the cloud got as far as this? Had a few puffs of it got in – when was it? – in 1788? Their whole commonwealth according to Knack should have been founded under it. But somehow he couldn't believe that. Knack must be wrong. He hoped, some day, to convert the man to another point of view. A picture might do it. He held in his mind, against Knack's talk and the enfolding music, one of his landscapes, and wondered if that would do it.

When it was time for Horlicks, the drink that kept off night starvation, Edna was in charge again and the mists dispersed.

'What about a bit of bread pudding,' she suggested once. 'If you don't mind it wet.' She showed a half baking dish of the grey glutinous stuff, solid with lard and bruised purple where sultanas, of which there were many, had bled in cooling into the surrounding grey. 'Walt won't eat it, so I make it the way I like it myself. Real wet. Me mum used to make it of a Sunday mornin', with the leftovers.'

'This,' Knack was muttering as over a philosophical problem, 'I have never understood. Bread pudding!'

'Well we do, don't we Frank?'

'Sometimes,' he said, looking at the slices of sweet grey pudding they were stuffing into their mouths, 'this place disgusts me. Worse even than the other. Blood isn't the worst of it.'

'Oh come on, Walt,' she jollied, 'it's not that bad.'

'How would you know?'

'Well I wouldn't!' she said, immediately on her dignity. 'Too ignorant. Too – Australian!'

He narrowed his eyes and said wearily: 'Yes. That too.'

'Well, Frank and I are *enjoying* our bread pudding, aren't we, Frank? *Ummmm!*' She sucked her fingers like a child, and like a child went on teasing just a moment too long. 'I reckon I'll have another piece.'

Knack got up abruptly and she stopped sucking her fingers. Large-eyed and pale she followed his movements across the room. He stooped to the leadlight doors of the sideboard, found the bottle of brandy, and when he turned, holding it up like a counterweight to the slice of pudding she had not yet bitten into, his mood had changed; whatever there was of savagery in him had abated.

'Well, enough!' she said, putting her slice of pudding down and pushing the dish aside. She waited for Knack to say something that would restore relations between them, all three.

'I find, Frank,' Knack said, 'that a drop of – cognac, even after the Horlicks, is a great –'

He did not finish the sentence, being engaged in filling, with intense concentration, the three little glasses he had placed in a row on the velvet cloth.

They watched him in silence, and when he had passed the glasses to them with his long chalky fingers, they drank, very solemnly, as at a feast.

Frank was grateful for their affection, and having nothing to give the household that could compete with the vast jumble of stuff that was stacked outside as in an ante-room, waiting to be moved in, he brought one of his paintings.

He had framed it himself. It was hung above the Genoa-velvet lounge, on the wall opposite the window, its pine frame making a clean break between lilac-and-green and the predominate grey-blue of the landscape he had opened up in the wall: as an alternative, he liked to believe, to the concrete yard and to Knack's own gloomy views. It pleased him to have his painting in that particular spot, and to think that he had, for his friends' sake, changed the room and its perspective in the same way that Knack's music could change it, opening the walls, even at night, on to a new sort of weather.

Knack approved. He would stand before the picture with his hands clasped behind as before a window, his long, cloth-covered back making an impressively solid downstroke, black, against the pale rectangle of the frame and the flickering light within. He took a deep breath.

'I like this country you have painted, Frank. This *bit* of it. It is splendid. A place, I think, for whole men and women, or so I see it – for the full man, even if there are no inhabitants as yet. Perhaps it is there I should have migrated.'

He gave a dark chuckle. It was one of his jests.

'But it is *this* country,' Frank said.

'You think so?'

Knack looked.

'No, Frank, I don't think it is. Not yet, anyway. It has not been discovered, this place. The people for it have not yet come into existence, I think, or seen they could go there – that there is space and light enough – in *themselves*. And darkness. Only you have been there. You are the first.'

Edna was less enthusiastic. Unlike Knack, who hated the countryside itself – too glarey, too many flies! – she would have preferred the real thing, if only on an outing to Dayboro, but was touched by the gift and proud as a sister might have been of the achievement.

'Well, you could of bowled me over,' she said. 'I knew you painted, love, but I didn't know you were an artist. Knack says you're an artist. I feel quite out of it.'

The public had a great hunger at this time for actualities. Each day after ten-thirty there were long queues outside the Carlton Newsreel Theatrette, which showed an hour – interspersed with cartoons in which Bugs Bunny or Tom and Jerry cavorted in vivid colour through a world of aggressive vegetables and vengeful tables and doors – of stark, black-and-white horrors, the happenings of three days or a week ago on the other side of the earth.

As the weeks passed and the horrors mounted the queues grew longer.

Waves of grey figures moving forward under a shaken sky; tall buildings collapsing amid thunder to show all the rooms in section like a grey doll's house; then quieter, remoter events for which there was no sound at all.

Frank Harland went along with the rest to see what sort of world he was living in and what had been going on in it while he was at work in his attic or listening to the music at Knack's. What he saw did not immediately explain itself.

Skeletal figures with all the ribs showing, huge genitals the only sign of flesh about them, were ranged along a cyclone-wire fence. Their eyes were a cavernous black in the smudged, poor-quality film, their bodies a cheesey white. It was difficult to understand what they could be doing. Normal life gave no clue. But others, wearing striped pyjamas, stood in groups in the grey churned-up mud behind, and had strayed, it appeared, out of their safe beds into an area of general nightmare where they had been caught by the arrival of daylight, and had woken and could not get back. A bulldozer, itself a new sort of machine, was turning over a pile of soft rubbish in a yard, out of which arms and legs were flung or whole figures rose up and slowly turned over, showing a withered rump and fishlike backbone, dangling a bony foot. All this had, in the stilled theatre, which smelled of cigarette-smoke and disinfectant, a peculiar unreality – this event out of your own time, of ten days or a month ago, which you sat watching from an armchair, in a set row, while others lounged against the walls. It was so sharply discontinuous with the three o'clock tropical simmer of the streets outside. A grainy, grey-and-white, black-and-white world in which the areas of light were too luminous and the blacks too dull, it was already ghostly. Flesh was not solid enough in this dimension to dissolve or be violated. Impossible to believe that food might go into the open mouths, or that breath or vomit or cries could come out of them. Film took the shadows and made them more shadowy still. It set them, for the viewer, at the same distance of believing unbelief as fade-out kisses, or the picking off in flickering thousands of red-skins on far plains.

An alsatian leapt up. A boy in uniform turned to the camera, gave a wide grin, and set his gloved hand on a holster. The bleached-out film ran smoothly through the projector. Every object within the frame, the boy's teeth, the fur on the alsatian's neck, the leather of the holster and of the suitcase carried by an old man who was being hauled with difficulty into an open truck, had the same quality here, and seemed inevitably linked as the unreal light fell upon them.

These events were actual but unreal. They belonged to the history of another planet that had its own weather and its own range of colours, grey-black-white. It was recognizable but remote, or seemed so. Till in one of the images a figure in the same grey-striped pyjamas as the rest, shaven-skulled and with a shovel in his hand, appeared beside a sunflower. It was taller than himself and in full bloom. The great round head of the sunflower, with its circlet of grey flames, dropped, and was turned towards what must, you saw with a little shock, be a blazing sun. So it could be hot there! Vivid yellow flowed out of the sun into the flamey petals, and as it did so the grey flesh too was touched with light and smeared with earth, blood, shit colours, and along with the colour, sound, smells – it was intolerable!

Frank began to sweat. At last, when he could take no more of it, he got up and began to push out past the real knees, and back, almost choking, into Brisbane, into the airlessness and banked heat of Queen Street.

He was shamefaced now before Walter Knack. What he had glimpsed in those images of a place that was contemporary with last week's muggy weather – with kids, cats, clothes-lines, taxis full of American sailors, and the smashing of bottles on back fences in what passed here for violence – was the gap that existed between Knack's world and anything he himself had known. It invested the man with a quality – history it might be – that he and the rest here, including Edna, had escaped. He couldn't imagine how, in her dealings with Knack, she got over that. It accounted, in Frank's eyes, not only for Knack's views but for his long back as well and the way the cloth rucked across it when he knelt to the diamond-paned doors of the sideboard or leaned to the upright with its empty sconces. It set the man apart, physically as well as in experience, but as one of millions. It was as if he bore on his shoulder an invisible weight that was the shovel to dig his own grave, for which the budgerigar Allegra, wearing the blue-green of the native bush, was no more than a bit of local mockery, or on Knack's part the spirit of wishful thinking, a trick to mislead the gods.

The man had a visible fate. He had sucked it up with the fog that drifted in off his native lakes, or from exhalations out of flooded chalkpits where the dead would not lie still but breathed and gave off gases. It was in the dirt, of whatever colour, that had got in under his nails, and that no scrubbing could flush out; into the pores of his skin, into his footsoles, and was the thickness on his tongue, which would only imperfectly accommodate itself to local vowels.

In other places, Frank saw, men's lives might take other forms and be subject to forces that were inconceivable here. Did that make their suffering different? It must. Did it make it more real? And what of strength and happiness?

These questions were a torment to Frank Harland. What he had suffered himself, and the suffering he had seen and heard of from others, out there on the road but also here in the city, behind crooked grey fences and in bursts of quarrelling and screams of rage or terror out of neighbours' windows – did it lose some quality of the human before those stripped and skeletal figures, to whom Knack, even in a black suit rather than pyjamas, was related by fifty years of breathing the same air, of putting his foot down on the same infected soil? Whereas he and Edna and all the rest here, in their real innocence, were related only by the accident of existing in the same *time* – which was not at all the same thing – and had been let off. Lightly, was it? Is anyone let off lightly? Is anyone let off?

It was Knack's smooth bald skull, that impenetrable hemisphere with the thin membrane that shone, sweated, occasionally drew back in painful corrugations, that fascinated and appalled him.

A monstrous egg. He would have liked to clasp it in his hands and feel what was hatching there, the warmth and the beat of the blood, since there was no way of getting to what it knew, or had seen and walked away from. He wondered – and shocked himself – if Edna, in their intimate moments, sometimes cradled the big stone egg between her breasts. How much did she know from Knack that she could never have grasped in any other way? How much had entered her – and entered her understanding – of what Knack knew?

He understood that this was the real question between them when on long hot mornings, with Knack off at an auction, they sat in a corner of the junkshop while trams rattled past and the women in hats and shopping-baskets pressed their noses against the plateglass windows.

'I've had a letter from me sister,' she told him, 'she's in the WRAACS.

Wants t' come 'n stay.' She turned her hand and examined the lacquered nails. 'I'm gunna put 'er off. I don't think she and Knack 'd get on.' She gave a rough laugh. 'That's putting it mildly!'

Their eyes met. She was, he saw, in glimpsing Knack through her sister's eyes, expressing astonishment at herself and how far she had wandered into some more complex world than her beginnings at Childers.

'I c'n pretend,' she said slowly, 'that the letter never got here. Wartime 'n that. What d'y' reckon? Does it seem awful?'

He swallowed, non-committal. They came from people for whom family loyalties mattered, but Knack's call upon her was greater, and different.

'I'm sorry,' she said, 'it don't seem right. I'm fond of me sister, she's a good sort, and sometimes you know it'd be nice to have a good chinwag with someone who knows all about you. That's the thing about families, they know all there is to know, even the worst, no surprises! We used t' be so alike, me and Bet, peopl'd take us for twins. We've gone different ways. But I've got t' think of Knack. I wouldn' want 'im hurt. They just wouldn't get on, that's all. Better not risk it.'

She glanced up again, shy of what he might think of her; then sighed, having made her decision, and he was drawn, as often before, to something in her through which he glimpsed, as through a half-open door into an unfamiliar room, that corner of her being in which Knack stood tall, dark, dressed in a power that arose for both of them out of stories they had scared themselves with as children and whose fascination they had never thrown off – a gentle, mocking, ugly, clever, tormented *stranger*, who spoke their own language with pedantic correctness but belonged to another world.

He recognized this romantic and rather touching view of Knack because he shared it. But one day, in the course of their easy dealings with one another, she gave him another view of things.

'I can't explain it,' she was saying, 'it's beyond anything I could of expected. Just think! He's come from so far away, Knack; from such a *foreign* place, those forests 'n all. An' you know he was a kind of aristocrat there, he's told you the sort of life they lived, *his* people. Not like us, Frank, not in the least. Fur coats in winter, servants – even a special maid to dress him and put on his little hand-sewn shirts. An' it took all those circum-stances – you know what I mean – civil wars, revolutions and then *this* war and all he's suffered, poor dear, to bring him to a place where we could just meet. I mean, all the chances were against it, but the wars and that happened as if they were just for that. I'll tell you this, Frank, without Knack I'd never – I'd never of known even the half of what I *am*, I'd have missed myself – walked right past myself in the dark. It was like being turned round and seeing yourself for the first time, what he could show me. Like there were things in me – not all good things even – I mean not *nice* – but me; and the same things in him as well, and when we came together they could flow out of me and I could stop being – I don't know – all loaded down with what I was scared of and ashamed of. People think I'm sunny. I'm not. Not always. Not deep down. There's a lot of darkness in us.'

Frank looked at her and wondered. She was no longer talking only of herself and Knack.

She lay her fingertips very gently on his arm. He raised his eyes, having lowered them; questioningly, as to an oracle. The light of the shop, with its free-floating chairs and other debris of ruined households, was strange at this hour just before sunset, with the traffic streaming home.

'You're not to be scared, Frank,' she said softly. 'I've seen that you're scared sometimes. Of what's in you I mean. You're not to be.'

She might have been very old, for all the softness of her fingerpads in the palm of his hand. He felt strongly the beating of his own blood, very dark and loud, and really was scared for a moment, then not. He felt light-headed, free, happy, and younger perhaps than he had ever been.

He was concerned once again at this time with his difficult family. He wrote:

My dear brother Tam,

I am sorry you have had such troubles. You say you have no luck – well, good luck seems hard to come by these days. I know you are a worker and have been a good son to our father – none better, sticking to him all these years and with so much to put up with. I will do what I can but could never raise nearly that much cash. The war makes things hard, even if it is nearly over. I will ask the people in Sydney who have my paintings to advance me a little bit and send it direct. If the worst comes to the worst the five acres must be sold, but it will break my heart just the same that we have not been able to keep it. The best of what we have!

You are a good fellow, Tam, and a kind and affectionate son and brother. I have, by the way, heard from our sister-in-law, Jim's wife. She doesn't say so direct, but seems to have reconciled herself to the fact that poor Jim has perished – no news for sure, but it is more than a year since she had word of him and all those in the hands of the Japanese have had terrible things to bear. We were very close once, Jim and me – as we all were. He has a son, aged ten, I will do what I can for him. Our sister-in-law asks for help and has no one else to turn to, no family of her own. What news of Pearsall? Since I was let out of the army myself I have been a bit crook – chest. Worked for a while in an aeroplane factory, but it was too much for me at that stage. I'm better now and have a bit of a house in Brisbane. Am painting again. Let me know when you get the money, and about the five acres. Do what you can. My love to our father and to Pearsall when you hear from him.

Your affect. brother
Frank

He liked to walk to Knack's through the noisy, wartime city. Down Edward Street, past the steep little triangular park where drunks lay about under the fig-trees and the steps beside the Trades Hall, then down by the Town Hall and along the Quay to the Bridge.

The river was wide, a breathing space in the hot city nights, with its gleam of tropical moonlight and the play on its surface of what lights were allowed under the restrictions. There were concrete pill-boxes along the Quay with sandbags round the entrance. Inside, more drunks, and on the slatted seats the occasional couple who had nowhere else to go. The stench of such places was terrible. Piss mostly, the smell of wet sacking, and the mustiness where summer rains had soaked through the concrete and made a film of slime.

He liked to stand on the bridge, on the footway beside the iron spans, with the trams rattling and sparking behind, and have the city on either hand. In a wide band below, the mysterious moonlit skin of the water, darkness transparent making a sweep between mangroves and the roofs of factories to the arch of the next bridge further on. You could breathe there. The river came down from farmlands off in the hills and went on widening in its slow, snake-like curves to the mouth of the Bay.

The river wound back and forth through the city, and was, in his mind, its real life-line: animal, blue, a thinking and feeling presence with its skin of moonlit or sunlit scales, and its depths. If you saw it from high up – higher than where he was standing – it was a kind of serpent with the sun or the moon on its back, on a shield of earth; throwing off houses and fat public buildings, and warehouses, woolsheds, factories, as it moved in its ancient coils. His mind touched a power under the moonlit skin. Some of it entered him.

Across the bridge, Melbourne Street was a garish thoroughfare with tramlines down the middle and busy traffic on the pavements, especially after dark. Light spilled from doorsteps where crowds gathered: the Blue Moon Skating Rink, with its hurdy-gurdy music and the dull thunder of rollerskates over boards, and round the corner an old-style vaudeville theatre, the Cremorne; on the corner opposite, a two-storeyed pub with verandahs.

Once, walking home late, he had slipped into a laneway here to take a leak and had come upon two figures fucking in the rain. A soldier in a long army greatcoat had a woman against the wall, with her feet in the greatcoat pockets and her bare thighs damp with moonlight. They moved slowly like figures in a dream, making a single creature with two locked and moaning heads, a mythological beast to which he couldn't have given a name, born out of the times, the war, as evidenced by the rough woollen material of the greatcoat with raindrops on its hairs.

It was a street of intense casual encounters and farewells. The high wall down one side, with its giant billboards, was the Interstate station – you could hear the crashing and clashing of carriages, and later, in the city stillness, the shunting of engines. The other side of the street, after the Trocadero dance-hall, was terraced houses approached by steep stone steps with railings: all brothels. Beyond, in a newer building on a corner, the junk shop.

He followed the same route each time, delayed only on occasion by a convoy of shrouded trucks. He might have to stand several minutes then before he could scuttle across: a lean figure who only a few months before had been in uniform like the rest, but had fallen back, as solitude remade him or rediscovered old lines that the rough army material had disguised, into his scraggier self. Sometimes a figure would call out of one of the wagons, 'Look, a swaggie! Hey! Swaggie!' and others would take up the cry till there was a regular hullabaloo of whistling and shouting and chucking off.

He was a leftover from another decade – or maybe he was a few months before his time in the one that was still to come, when all these soldiers, freshly demobbed, with their deferred pay gone and their new suits torn and soiled, after a season of paid boredom, would be scrabbling for a foot-hold again in a sliding world. Poor buggers, they didn't know it yet, but when they leaned out of the wagons and catcalled or chiacked, it was themselves they were jeering at.

He made his way through the greasy streets after a lick of a storm. It had been hot earlier. Now it was cool. The crowds in Melbourne Street were massed round the entrance to the Troc. Taxis were pulled up at the kerb. Red mouthed girls, chewing gum, were stepping out of them in gaudy sandals. They clung to the arms of officers in pink drabs, their caps immaculately straight on their cropped heads or tilted back over a youthful grin. As they passed, enlisted men leaning in groups against the wall sprang smartly to attention, then went back to lounging with their caps off and their hands in their pockets, chewing stale obscenities. Younger girls with skirts too short to hide their pudgy knees giggled and yoked arms, their hair piled so high in an unsteady pompadour they should have staggered. The lounging men offered up a medley of high and low wolf-whistles. From the mouth of the hall came the sounds of a band.

He went on, tripping lightly on his feet, made happy by the music, which he continued to hum, and by the comfort of having behind him a whole day's work in the hot attic under the roof, where he had sweated and produced – well, something, *something* – who knows what? The thought of it spread out there on the low table he had knocked together from fruit-cases made him childishly happy. He thought of the colours up there in the dark. He chuckled. It was like milk in cans. He had briefly in mind three dented milkcans on a slatted bench above sand, set down in the cool of a bunyah pine, the lovely necks of them – blueish metal – and the flat, clip-over lids. Heavy. The milk sloshing from side to side as you walked, and the steel handle cutting, not unpleasantly, into the soft of your hand.

He was astonished to see, at Knack's corner, a crowd bigger even than the one round the entrance to the dance-hall, a few curious GI's, some of them black, but mostly barefoot men in singlets and shorts and women in housecoats or dirndls and felt slippers.

The shop was lit up. All the sideboards and wardrobes and three-mirrored dressing tables with their load of china and cut glass, and the dining chairs hanging lopsided from the ceiling among unlighted lamps, made a clear night-picture.

'What is it?' he asked someone.

'A murder,' the woman told him. 'That German bloke killed his missus or whatever she was – then shot 'imself.'

He threw himself into the crowd round the door and came up hard against the arm of a policeman.

'Oright, fella, what's the rush? Where you think you're goin'?'

He babbled, he made no sense. The policeman, who was young, looked alarmed. It was a woman in the crowd who identified him. 'He's sort of an artist. I seen him in the shop – oh, lots of times. With *her*.'

The policeman called a superior. He was let through to where the detective in charge was sitting in one half of the lovers' seat under the shadowy dining chairs. Beyond, the door to the flat was ajar. He saw the shoulder of a fellow in a felt hat who was half-squatting and moving his arms about in a very regular manner from side to side.

The man in the lovers' seat was suspicious. He fired off a whole series of questions that Frank could not answer – his lips were too wooden. But what he did get out at last must have been convincing. With a policeman at his back he was allowed through into the flat.

Edna Byrne, her dress rucked up a little over her thighs, was sitting in the lounge with her head on one side and a strand of blonde hair hanging. He had seen her sit this way often in their evenings together. She might have been listening, a little puzzled, but quite calm, to Knack's thunderous left hand. He looked, and expected her at any moment to raise her arm and absent-mindedly restore the strand of hair or give him one of her shy collusive looks.

She had been shot twice in the breast. Her skirt, so oddly rumpled, was filled with blood.

Knack, who must have been kneeling at her feet, had slumped forward with the gun between his teeth. He had shot the back of his head off. The bald dome was gone, it was all jagged bone. Frank stared. On the lilac and green wallpaper an area about the same size as his own painting was covered now with a mess of grey and red that was still sliding in wet trails to the floor. There were splashes of red on the walls and in the white space over the picture-rail, and feathery red explosions all over the window-pane and in smears and dabs and swashes across his landscape, changing forever its blue-and-grey.

Frank looked and was stunned. He sank down and covered his eyes. The room was still rocking with wave after wave that beat out from the shock centre, the three shots, and was still breaking in red against the walls. He tried not to see, not to think of the forms of Edna and Knack and what that volley of darkness had done to them, as if by excluding them from what he saw he could save them and take all the shock into himself.

He looked on with incomprehension as one of the men in felt hats picked up the body of the little bird and held it to his ear to see if it was still ticking, and another, with a sudden pinging sound, sent a tape-measure flying back into its shell.

The whole room shook with changes. His picture for instance – the one thing that was near enough to his own experience to offer him access. Changed! Extraordinary. Such reds! What painter would have dared? He was frighteningly dazzled by the possibilities, as if, without his knowing it, his own hand had broken through to something that was searingly alive, savage, triumphant, and stood witness at last to all terror and beauty.

That was what shook him: the sense of triumph, over and above what he would let himself feel, in a moment, as sickening loss. He might be blinded for the rest of his life by the boldness of it.

I could sit here, he thought, for the rest of my life and I still wouldn't come to the end of it.

The police questioned him but it was clear that the odd artist bloke had nothing to tell. An ambulance man, not unkindly, treated him for shock and he was allowed to go home.

The shock, in the non-medical sense, lasted for many days, in which he lay flat on his back on a camp-stretcher under the hot tin roof and grieved.

The paintings, even those that were turned to the wall, were an affront to him, being inadequate now to what he had perceived. He slashed at them, tore them in strips. They lay in heaps on the floor.

Where, he asked himself, had he been all this time, while the horrors were preparing? How had he failed to see the rising of such a tide of red? Most of all, he brooded on the mystery of Edna Byrne, who might have been his sister; they came from such similar worlds and had grown so close. Hand in hand, like children, they had followed a lean back into deep woods, licking from their fingers, and smiling, the remains of purple-grey bread pudding, the sweet fat. And all the time her face had been turned in a quite different direction, attending to music that left him now in a thunderous silence across which no words of comfort could be shouted and no message would pass.

He drew his knees up on the narrow stretcher and writhed in an agony of cramped guts.

His lost sister. He wept for her, but no tears came. He wept for both of them and for Knack as well. He hugged a deeper loneliness in himself than he had ever known, some final lack that nothing could fill.

A death pact, that is what the newspapers called it: a lurid catch-phrase to cover love, pity, fury, terror – the unsolvable mysteries.

He thought of that couple in the lane, so lyrically, intensely involved in themselves and one another under the mizzling rain. Outside all weather and the chain of public events that had brought them together, and which their bodies, in passionate throes like the great coils and curves of the serpent, entirely threw off, they stood beyond words in their own occasion.

The image haunted him; and he was haunted too by the music, which she it seems had understood in one sense and he, if he understood at all, in another. As something equally compelling but which led to strength and sunlight – that is what his picture had proposed.

What music was it? Knack had never said. He had wrapped it up and taken it with him, and the police had shut and locked the piano, reducing it immediately, with all the rest of their furniture, to the same status as those sideboards, washstands and dressing tables in the shop outside, the debris of foundered, anonymous lives.

As for his own fate, that too was a mystery. He caught only the briefest glimpse of it in a half-heard shower of notes, or a feathered scrawl that would have dried now to the colour of old roofs or the side of that barn against which Milly Shoals, their neighbour at Glen Alpin, had chased white chickens inside under a coming storm; or of the earth at Childers.

And in another form, as in a bestiary, of that creature, nameless but neither terrible nor obscene, into which the couple in the lane had allowed themselves to be transformed, fine drops of moisture making brilliant all the hairs of its coat.

He did get up again. He took his things, walked out of the house without even locking the door and went back to the roads. When he was ready to face canvas again he found a place he could work in, the old Pier Pictures at Southport. It helped a little to hear warm tides washing round half-eaten piles and to smell clean, original salt.

He wrote to his sister-in-law:

Dear Hilda (if I may call you that)
I have read your letter many times. I agree we must accept, after being so long without word, that Jim, poor fellow, is among the missing who will not come back. You are very brave to have faced up to this at last after so many months of hoping against hope. I feel for your grief. After all this time, and other losses which I will not go into, I feel it too. Jim and I were very close as boys and I often thought of him in the years after. He and I, as you know, had the same mother – I never knew her – thought it never made any difference that the others were only half.

I have spent many years working and worrying for this family. We seem dogged with bad luck, or worse, I don't know what. My brother Pearsall is out of the army but has not found work and seems unable to settle. He was the youngest of us and I had great hopes for him, but he is already thirty – half his life gone and nothing started.

I am sorry to worry you with these thoughts. The fact is, I would like to do what I can for the boy, my nephew Gerald, and from what you say of him have good hopes he will turn out well. Above all, he must be given the best possible education. I get a little money from selling my work in the south – nothing much, but enough to help – and would be happy for his father's sake to pay for the boy's schooling. We could begin with that. I would suggest Toowoomba Grammar when the time comes. It is where his grandfather went.

None of the rest of us, except Pearsall, had any education to speak of and it is a great lack, though I know Jim educated himself and did well – and when Pearsall's time came we could only afford the State. Gerald must have more.

I realize it is a little time yet, and he is only ten, but I want to reassure you so that we can make plans. My friends in the south, who handle all money affairs, will keep in touch with you. Meanwhile, my best wishes to you in your sorrow – and to the boy.

Your affect. brother-in-law
    Frank Harland

NEPHEWS

[1]

Frank Harland's landscape, which my father had acquired for two pounds on the day of our first meeting, hung all the last year of my grandfather's life on the wall of my parents' bedroom. Its blues and greens dominated the room, and I thought of it as casting its own light when at five-thirty each afternoon I went in, quietly called my mother, and was allowed to lie with her for a minute or two on the high bed, before she told me regretfully but with firmness: 'Enough now Phil, I must go to your grandfather, poor love. He'll wonder what's happened to us.'

Later, in the storm that blew up round my grandfather's death, the picture got left behind.

'What about Frank Harland's picture?' I asked when Harland's name began to be known. 'Why don't we ask if we can have it back?'

My father looked doubtful. 'I think, son, that your Aunt Ollie's rather fond of that picture. She was fond of Frank, you know. I don't think we could ask for it now.'

So each year when I went to visit my grandmother on her birthday, travelling down on the motor-rail from South Brisbane and returning the following night, I would go at least once and stand before it, and though it bore no resemblance to the landscape of Southport itself, which was all flat water and liquid sky, would find there the exact emotional equivalent of the place as I had known it in the days of my grandfather's illness. The atmosphere of that time, which I felt for and regretted, was so strongly present that I might have gone out to the front bedroom expecting to find him restored and upright among his pillows, with his mouth open and his eyes shut, snoring, or passed my younger self on the back stairs, slipping out to relieve myself while I gazed through loquot leaves at the moon.

It was my grandmother who occupied the front bedroom now. Soon after Grandpa's death she had moved back – it was after all the main bedroom of the house, in which her various children had been conceived – and eventually she too came to spend most of her days there, no longer able to go downstairs but still dealing by telephone with even the most minor details of the business, on which she had never relinquished her hold. Once a week, on Fridays, my father drove down to consult with her over a working breakfast.

The room had been done up. The big altar-like dressing table with its silver-framed photographs of the family, the washstand and bedside cabinet, the wardrobe with its bevelled mirrors and scrolls and finials, had been cleared out and replaced with blondwood built-ins in the modern style. As if to dispel all shadows, and any secrets that might once have lurked in corners or at the back of shelves, the light was glaringly fluorescent. It made the room look as if it were lit to be photographed. The yellow tube-light cut its natural blue (which was the light off the sea as it passed the coarse, sharp whips of the bunyahs), draining the room so effectively of its heavy warmth that we might have been in another house altogether, with another aspect and view. Only the brass bed was the same. She had kept that. It was inconveniently high, it did not fit, but she lay in it.

I had been afraid of my grandmother in the old days. She had so much contempt for things and was herself such a straight stiff little person. Now, after so long, I saw a yielding in her. She had begun in that room, despite the difference of light and furniture and for all her strictness of gesture, to resemble my grandfather. The likeness was striking, almost shocking.

I had seen no resemblance between them when Grandpa was still living. They gave no sign, with their opposite and unaccommodating styles, of having shared a life. But they had, and my grandmother began to speak of him now as if they had indeed been a couple. Her stories were often cruel and showed lingering resentment, but there were others in which she and my grandfather appeared as young people with a passionate affinity, and it was out of these, as they softened her mouth in the telling, that the likeness emerged. Freed at last of the threat posed by his weakness she let her own appear, and began once again, but shyly, to approach him.

'He was the handsomest man I ever laid eyes on, your grandfather. And I was – goodness! – such a plain little thing. He was very gentle and had lovely manners but there was a spark. You could see he'd been a bit of a devil – back there in Gloucestershire. I liked that. But he'd had to work like a navvy down at the Ridge. You should have seen his poor hands! They were all cracked and swollen – no amount of scrubbing would get them clean. He tried to keep them out of sight. He was always pushing them into his pockets or tucking them away under his arms and refusing things so he wouldn't have to show them – he was ashamed. But I loved them, I really did! I used to look and look and want to touch them, and say to myself that I'd work my own hands to the bone if he was mine, I'd do anything for him. He'd never have to break his back or use his hands like that, ever again! What he couldn't see, poor dear, was that without them he'd have been *too* beautiful. I'd have felt – intimidated. Well, I was a silly schoolgirl, sixteen. I didn't know what I was saying, I didn't know what work was. And it all came true in the end, every bit of it. As you know.'

She lowered her eyes, smoothing the quilt with a ringed hand, and her mouth, which was unsteady these days, developed a shake. She brought her hand up to control it and the rings glittered.

'I wasn't always patient with him – towards the end. It all went on too long. Life does.'

The household was much changed. Della was gone – not as it happened with the iceman but to a niece at Mullimbimby where she had three grand-nephews to cook for. Aunt Connie too was gone; back to her husband. She was living in a cottage at Chelmer and putting up again with his going off three nights a week to 'choir practice' and coming back thick-tongued and amorous. All the lower part of the house was boarded up, and Aunt Ollie cooked now in a modern kitchenette, which was all she needed to prepare invalid meals for her mother and a steak and salad for Uncle Gil; there were no more visitors. She and Uncle Gil had grown closer, preparing I thought, like any old couple, for their last days together. Once a week, on Thursdays, he drove her to the supermarket to do the shopping, holding the big Super Snipe to a pace that allowed them to 'note every change', as Southport, that colonial version of an English watering place, was left behind by the spirit of progress that was sweeping south along the surf. Uncle Gil had slowed down. The something that had shaken loose in his head had settled back again, like a sheet of roofing-iron after a storm, or had lost connection. He lived on his pension and spent his days in a dinghy on the Broadwater or in the quieter reaches of the river. He had retired into his boyhood.

Only Aunt Roo had broken free. After a good deal of suspenseful hesitation she had married a stockbroker called Harry Price. Translated to

Brisbane and a showy mock-Tudor house on Hamilton Heights, she had redeemed her shameful untruths by making them real: her name was in the society pages, she was president of a little theatre group, Harry Price had twice taken her to England. It was perhaps because she had anticipated these events in the telling by a round ten years, and had already assimilated them long before they occurred, that they sat so lightly upon her. She continued to dress ten years younger than she was (and began to look it), gave up her bouts of hysteria, lost her sharp defiant look, and if she remained what people called theatrical it was the theatricality now of a once-famous actress in retirement, about whom there hung, in odd inflections of the voice or in the way she lifted her arms on occasion, an echo of the characters she had played: Hedda, Mrs Alving, Olga in *The Three Sisters*, Lady Macbeth, and before that, Juliet. Young people thought her wonderful. She could quote lines, strike attitudes that hit off great players to a tee, and had, it appeared, seen everybody: Pavlova and Oscar Asche, Dame Edith, Flora Robson and the Oliviers in London, Marie Bell in Paris, the Lunts in New York. Aunt Connie was astonished by the extent to which, in just a few years, her little sister had escaped her past (or recaptured it in a daring actuality) and exceeded now their most vivid notions of her. Occasionally, timidly, she accepted one of Aunt Roo's invitations. She would sit stunned and silent on the hot-pink upholstery, among the vases, between the celebrities, and stare. When I was old enough, I too was invited. I made no impression. Aunt Roo, whose confidant I had been in the old days, and who had thought of me then as a fellow spirit nourishing exotic dreams, was deeply disappointed.

'My nephew's a law student,' she told people the moment I appeared, as she said of Harry: 'my husband, the stockbroker.' But occasionally, to everyone's confusion, she would introduce me as 'our junior axeman'. Adding sweetly: 'We expect him to be State Champion one day, don't we, pet?'

They were very loose and informal, Aunt Roo's parties. Arranged on the spur of the moment after a dress-rehearsal or performance and open to all comers – including strangers who just happened to be passing and would drop in to see what was on – they took their tone from the actors, all amateurs who worked by day as secretaries or bank clerks. So one of these late-night festivities might have the languid air of a gathering at a French château, all muted endings and lyrical cynicism, since half the guests were still walking about in lives they had been allotted by Jean Anouilh, while another, though the same faces were to be seen there, had all the tenseness of a Puritan outpost at the edge of the forest, beset by real devils or menaced from within by darker forces than even the wilderness knew.

It was all very lively. There was a real snap in the air of restraints grown elastic and outrageously breaking, of creatures about to burst into a new form as an excitement worked through them that the more formal events of the theatre had failed to contain. The actors would not step down. Nor, now that the spell of change was on them, would they stick to their parts. A young fellow in invisible high-heels, who had played a chauffeur and was still sporting along with his makeup a leather cap and gauntlets, would suddenly assume the manner – the old-world refinements and studied hauteur – of the Countess he meant to be (in real life he was a window-dresser called Noël Clark); or a sensible librarian, typecast as a lady's companion, would tower up, grow craggy, and silence the company with a flood of mortal injuries – a born King Lear.

All this was just what Aunt Roo intended. Her parties were meant to make things *appear*. She herself appeared as a flamboyant ruler of the spirits, while Harry – impressed, but also, he would have confessed, just a wee bit intimidated – wondered and looked on. He was proud of her. She had so much verve. And she was always discovering people – she had discovered him. He found that he liked the smell of greasepaint and was sorry when people he approached were embarrassed by his suit or his solidity or by the trace of carmine on their cheeks. It made him feel like an intruder, whereas all he wanted, in his own house, was to be taken in.

He was a grave and courtly fellow of sixty, an ex-footballer, one of nature's bachelors.

'Harry's a brick,' Aunt Roo insisted, and he proved it by going the colour of one. But I guessed that there smouldered under his double-breasted jackets some obscure, un-Presbyterian dream that he caught just the tail of on Aunt Roo's theatre-nights, and that it was this he reached out for in the menagerie his house became on such occasions and in my Aunt's now sumptuous and commanding arms.

It was after midnight at one of the noisiest of these gatherings that I found myself sitting on a sofa next to a pale, intense girl with freckles, and a boy in uniform who slept drunkenly against her shoulder.

The girl was eating an apple and kept switching her pony-tail, which was red, in an angry way from side to side, till she said to no one in particular, though I took her exclamation as being addressed to me, 'Oh actors! They drive me up the wall. I could murder the lot of them!'

'Aren't you one?' I asked.

She rolled her eyes and bit the apple. 'Not me, I'm too *sensible*.'

She might have been quoting a remark she had heard made of herself, something her mother told visitors, and she gave me a sharp look now to see how I took it, whether as a recommendation or a profound lack. 'What about you?' she challenged.

'I'm a nephew,' I told her. 'Of Aunty – of Mrs Price. I'm Mrs Price's nephew. She's my aunty.'

She burst out laughing, showing all her teeth and with a bit of apple on her tongue, and when she had quietened down indicated the boy on the other side. He too was red-headed, but darker. He wore a bloused uniform with puttees, and was sleeping with his knees spread in the rough khaki and his hands hanging loose between them. I had taken him for another actor in costume. I saw now that he was in National Service.

'He's a nephew too,' she informed me. 'Of Frank Harland the painter – though I don't suppose you've ever heard of him.'

'Oh but I have,' I told her, astonished to have the name recur. 'As a matter of fact we used to know him. Quite well.'

She looked impressed, then checked herself; not much was said at these gatherings that you could take on trust. She flicked me a sideways glance that in no way committed her to belief and bit hard into the apple.

'Well *I've* never met him and Gerald won't take me there. I've asked him to, heaps of times, but he won't. I think he's ashamed. Here Gerald, wake up! There's a boy here who knows your uncle.' But Gerald did no more than murmur and settled back into sleep.

'Look,' the girl said, leaning across and setting their two faces side by side – his tanned one, sullen in sleep, with very white lids and a mouth that was too full, and her own all cheekbones, sharply alert – 'don't you think we're alike? Everyone says we are. People just assume we're brother and sister. Or twins. But Gerald's nineteen and we're not even related. We go in taxis sometimes and start carrying on in the back – you know, cuddling and breathing hard and talking about incest. You should see some of those drivers, they can't keep their eyes on the road. Gerald's a terrific actor, even your aunty says so. I just look dumb and breathe.'

Gerald Harland was one of my Aunt's 'discoveries' and it was she, some weeks later, who raised his case.

'Listen pet,' she began on an afternoon when we had reverted to the intimacy of a time at Southport when I was the only sharer of her illusions, 'I want you to be nice to him. Really, you must, I don't know why you've got it in for the boy. He's unfortunate. He lives with two awful uncles. One of them is that Frank Harland who used to come to the house at Southport, one of your father's lame ducks, a painter, though he's never got anywhere.' She meant by this that he was fifty and had never got to Sydney.

'Actually you'd be surprised,' I said. 'He's quite highly thought of.'

'Who is?'

'Harland – the painter.'

She made a mouth. 'Well Gerald says he's a horror, and I can believe it. He was a horror when I knew him. The place is a pigsty, and he never stops nagging the boy, worse even than the mother – oh, there's a mother as well! No pet, really, you must try and be nice to him. He's sensitive and has had a lot to put up with. All I'm asking you to do is to talk to him sometimes, or at least listen. No Phil, don't put that look on your face, it doesn't suit you. It isn't in your nature to be cynical. You're soft-hearted really like your father. If you don't watch out it'll grow to fit, you'll become a cypher.'

'Honestly Aunty, a cypher! Where do you get these ideas?'

'From listening. To clever men.'

'Fifth-rate actors you mean, pretending to be other people.'

'No kitten,' she said seriously, 'you're wrong about that. Actors don't pretend to be other people. They become themselves by finding other people inside them. A man who pretends to be someone he isn't is a cypher. Now promise me you'll give Gerald a hearing and don't try to be smart with me. I've known you too long. I'm not impressed.'

He was a year or two younger than I was, lean, athletic, defiantly careless;

indifferent to the impression he was making but with an eye for effects. He would confess with disarming simplicity that he was 'no great shakes as an actor, you know', or 'an absolute no-hoper at the office' (he was articled like me), but these deficiencies were so cheerfully asserted, and with so much boyish frankness and charm, that you felt bound to disagree, or to take them as failures in an area where he disdained to succeed. He had, I thought, a deep conviction of his own superiority. What his self-disparagement really said was 'By your lights I may be all these things, and shallow too, but those lights, you know, are too crude to catch my particular star. Still, I'm easy, I don't insist.' He carried his jackets hussar-fashion over one shoulder, rode a CZ two-stroke, and was good at games, especially tennis, which we played on a double court at my Aunt's, behind a fence weighed down with pink-flowering antignon. All energy on the court, and a most intense desire to win, he lounged off it as if competition were beneath him. He leaned against the wall of green with his legs crossed and a racquet in his arms, or sat between sets with his elbows on his knees, his flagrant hair dark from the tap and richly flopping. I refused to respond to his assumption that everything he felt and did was of interest.

'Listen,' he would say solemnly if you were drinking with him, 'I've got to go out now and take a leak.' Or quite out of the blue he would begin telling some happening from his childhood at Albury or Glen Innes, or from the time, at the end of the war, when he and his mother lived in eleven different boarding-houses in a single year.

'You know,' he would say gravely, 'we were very poor, we had no money at all – only what my mother could pick up by working in shops and places, where she was always being pestered – you know, by men. We would have to pack up and get away in the night, and there was always something we had to leave. We were always *abandoning* things. I remember some of those places best by what got left there. Well I wanted a watch, a real one that ticked – I had just started to tell the time – only we couldn't afford it so my mother bought me an egg-timer instead. It was filled with blue sand, and the sand sort of dimpled – I loved that – and all the grains rolled clockwise and drained away, then you turned it up and it happened all over again. I used to count the minutes off by it, especially at night when my mother was away. She was always having to go out and leave me – I used to be scared that one day *I* would be what got left – I used to watch the sand and hold my breath. Well, one day of course we left the egg-timer behind, and by the time I discovered it it was too late, we couldn't go back. I cried for a whole week. It was like losing a pet. It was just about the time my dad was reported missing – in the war you know – and my mother put adverts in the paper asking if any soldiers or anyone, POW's, had come across him or had news. Men used to reply, lots of them. I got several – you know – *uncles* that way. Not real ones of course. I just called them that.'

Gerald's stories were embarrassing. It was difficult to tell in what spirit they were offered or how you were to take them. They went too far. Beginning as self-conscious attempts to make himself interesting, they ended as dream-monologues that left the narrator isolated, withdrawn, in a silence it was not easy to break, unless he himself broke it with a kind of giggle. He would blush then and gulp his beer, looking at you sideways out of his bright round eyes. Then five minutes later would do it all over again.

Girls found it touching – his life, his embarrassments – especially those of them who were susceptible to a lean cheek and an adam's apple, and he soon learned to play up to them; but Jacky was the only one he was close to.

They were often together, and with their red hair and freckles might indeed have been twins. Even I saw it now. It wasn't so much their looks as the suggestion they gave of having deep secrets, shared jokes and affinities that were second nature to them and went back to a time even they might not recall. They leaned together, they whispered; or after sitting quite silent for long minutes would suddenly burst out laughing at the same instant. They had a language I could not fathom. It unnerved me.

Geraldn'Jacky.

I hated the ease with which their names, welded into a single breath, could be rolled off the tongue. As when they roared up on the CZ with Jacky riding pillion and people shouted: 'Here they are, it's Geraldn'Jacky!' Or when, glancing round the faces in a room, someone would look crestfallen and say 'But where are Geraldn'Jacky?' This glib linking of the two, this creation of a joint person with a single being, maddened me. It was as if the names were themselves powerful, and once linked must inevitably bring their owners together as well. Each time I heard it, that single breath of five syllables, I would wince and feel betrayed.

But this linking of names was only one of the conditions that made them one. They had a game they would play, and not just for taxi drivers, which involved the invention of a whole shared childhood of aunts, uncles, family anecdotes, illnesses. They vied bodly with one another in coming up with more and more outrageous memories, which they recounted with such mock-innocence and effrontery that even those who knew they were an invention were shocked; not by the events themselves, which after all had never really occurred, but by the power of their imagination. I was crazy with jealousy.

'Phil's jealous,' Jacky would tease. 'Just look at that face!'

'Is he? Are you, Phil?'

Gerald, his eyes set wide like a cat's, would assume an expression of utter innocence. 'But why? You don't need to be,' he would tell me, 'honest you don't.' And he would put his red head beside hers so that they really did look like creatures of a magical oneness.

Before such demonstrations of a relationship that was arcane, forbidden, and therefore, perhaps, doubly desirable, I would be torn once more between assurance and the sort of gloomy despair that could only justify Jacky's original complaint. What I feared was that in creating these fantasies of a passionate life together they would hit on the reality. How could they fail to? I watched them move closer each day in a past that had never existed, except as excited make-believe, and wondered when it would spring into existence at last as a future. How could they stay cool about such things? Was it pretence? Was it perversity? Were they subtler and more deceitful than I had dreamed?

'Listen,' Gerald said, 'I know what. Why don't you pretend to be Jacky's jealous boyfriend? You suspect, see, that she and I are – you know, and you're jealous.'

'Leave it Gerald, let's just not play at all,' Jacky advised.

'No, this is a good idea. We're brother and sister, see, like as usual and Phil can be –'

'Why not you?' I asked.

'Why not me *what*?'

'Why can't you be the jealous fiancé?'

'And you and Jacky the brother and sister?'

'Why not?'

'Is that what you want?' He seemed genuinely puzzled.

'No, but why not? Why do I have to be the *dill*?'

'You don't have to be a dill.'

'But I would be, wouldn't I?'

'Oh for heaven's sake,' Jacky exploded, 'let's just not play at all.'

'You don't have to be a dill. It's just that you're jealous.'

'Gerald, will you *stop*? You're such kids, both of you.'

'All right, then, we won't play. I just thought it'd be sort of a new twist.'
He sat and sulked. He was hurt, though it seemed to me that I, who was to
have been cast in the role of deceived lover, had the greater cause to feel
aggrieved.

'Oh, come on Gerald, stop sulking, anyone'd think you were a five-year-
old.' Jacky tugged at his arm. 'Come *on* now.' I didn't see why she was in
such a hurry always to humour him. 'Let's get a milkshake up at Con's. I'll
shout you if you can't afford it.'

'I can afford it.'

'Well for heaven's sake, let's go and get it then. Come on Phil. At least
you don't sulk. Honestly, Gerald, you're impossible sometimes. I don't
know why we put up with you.'

We, she had said *we*. The whole sky expanded and shone – it was better
than any game. But it was Gerald's arm she took. They struck out together
and I lagged behind, waiting for them to notice; for all the world like the
jealous fiancé I had refused to be.

I was always falling into such traps, many of which I myself had set. In
restaurants and at the pictures I made sure I was seated first and would be
driven to distraction if Jacky did not settle beside me. I did everything I
could, when we were all three together, to make Gerald reveal his worst
side, his tendency to whine or brag or get the sulks. I started arguments on
subjects he knew nothing about, and when he took the bait and showed off,
then got stuck and blustered, would sit back looking wonderfully cool. As
my aunt had suggested, I cultivated him in the hours after work, in the hope
that he might while we were alone, and under the influence of liquor, give
something away – something that would incriminate him and justify my
jealous suspicions or make Jacky entirely mine. What I failed to observe as
the months passed was how close we had grown, Gerald and I; how much
he had come to confide in me.

'Listen,' he said one night when we were alone at the Criterion, 'my uncle keeps on at me to bring you back. He remembers you from Southport.'

We were on our third or fourth beer and had been engaged till this moment in one of those wary discussions, all playful sparring, in which young men test one another, pushing a little, pushing further, retreating, pushing again, but making certain always to preserve the distance between them that the rituals of such places are designed to preserve. Gerald, with his half-shy insistence, was breaking the rules.

'Would you?' he urged. 'My uncle keeps on at me to bring you. I wish you would.'

He met my eye, smiled weakly, then looked away. For some reason it was important to him.

'You'd be doing me a big favour,' he said. Then darkly: 'It's something I don't want to talk about.'

He frowned, took a gulp of his beer.

'Anyway, you'll see for yourself,' he said, 'if you'll come. Will you?'

I put my finger under my collar and eased it. 'All right, yes. One of these nights.'

'No,' he insisted, 'I mean now, tonight. I know it sounds silly but I don't want to go home without you. Please say you'll come. It's true he asks about you. He never forgets anyone – anything – it's scary the way everything just sticks in his head. You think he's forgotten or hasn't seen or heard, and a week later it all comes out again, he's been stewing over it. I don't mean he talks all that much. He just broods and glares – it's worse than talk – and whatever you do you're never in the right. He torments people. That's what he likes. It makes me laugh reading that bullshit they write about him.' He gave a nervous laugh and stopped himself but couldn't stop talking. 'You know the sort of stuff the newspapers write. In the South, I mean, they never notice him here. It's all bullshit. He's ignorant as dirt. His head's full of maggots. He doesn't care about anyone really. All he knows is how to dole out some of his cash and then complain afterwards that people are bleeding him dry, and how he's sacrificed himself and had no thanks for it. Then he smothers you with –' He shook his head and took another quick gulp of beer. 'He disgusts me, I mean it! I'm not just trying to make myself interesting. I know that's what you think but it isn't true. You'll see for yourself.'

I knew, by this time, a good deal about Gerald's life, and might have seen earlier that his plunges from over-confidence into despondency and hopelessness were no new thing, and that his fears, irrational and childish as they sometimes appeared and as he dramatized and exploited them, went back to his childhood itself – to the years when he was being led up the steps of one boarding-house after another in Randwick or Petersham and had known many pretending uncles before any real one came on the scene. Not all of them can have been monsters, but they became so in the telling.

There was a Welsh carpenter with three fingers missing from his left hand who had a workshop at the back of a timberyard. He had taught Gerald at six to use a little plane.

The boy had never till then seen anything so beautiful as the almost transparent shavings he could coax from a plank; they made such a lovely sighing sound and such a heap of angelic curls on the floor, each with the grain in it that was really, the man explained, the years of the pine tree's life, whole winters and summers, many more than his own. He accepted that; but thought of them as falling just the same from the head of a secret child, his playmate, invisible to others but always there. Falling golden-blond, as his own fell red round the high chair at the barber's.

The Welshman was sentimental. He smelled of wood glue, had thick hair on his shoulders, sang loud hymns when he got drunk on Friday nights and had beaten Gerald once with a razor-strap for 'touching' himself. One of his successors, a young railway-worker of strict habits, a good-looking, fresh-faced youth who wore a serge waistcoat and hat and waved a stick with a flag on it to start the trains, had spared Gerald but beaten the woman; savagely, with his closed fists, for no other reason than that she was willing to go with him.

'Oh, uncles, they're a race apart,' Gerald told me. 'I know all about uncles.'

He did, he might do. I was prepared to believe in his desperation and to believe as well that there was some essential instability in things that he knew of and which I, till now, had failed to perceive. But I had my own view of Frank Harland.

'All right,' I said in a low voice, 'I'll come. But won't we be disturbing him?'

He laughed. 'Oh don't you worry, he'll let us know if we are. He's not slow at telling you off if you get in the way of his precious work. But you mustn't take too much notice of the house, you know, it's a pigsty, we live like pigs. There's only Uncle Tam to do anything – no woman – so nothing gets done properly. And he won't let anyone into the room *he* uses so nothing gets done there at all. But you'll see! I just don't want you to be put off, that's all.'

He set his glass down, half-finished. 'I'll take you pillion on the CZ.' He was already standing. 'Can we go?'

[2]

The house was in a street beyond the Dutton Park terminus, on a high ridge above the river, a single-storeyed weatherboard with a hallway straight through from the latticed verandah to a square yard of railed back-porch. The land sloped, so that the house, which you approached over a wooden footbridge, sat on stumps that were five feet high at the front and eighteen at the back, with a view to a low arc of mangroves on the bank opposite and a sweep of muddy, grey-brown river. Two planks of the footbridge were loose. They jumped under our boots. Paint had flaked from the verandah-lattice, showing the heads of rusty nails. The timber itself was split and weathered, the guttering sagged. Under the footbridge the ground fell away in a wilderness of morning-glory vines that in the late afternoon sunlight gave off a breath of steam, and faintly, drowsily hissed.

Gerald had paused before the open door. 'Look at this,' he said.

There was a gaping hole in the verandah boards. Someone, long ago, had nailed raw battens over it in an irregular cross. I knelt as he did and peered through. The open space of their under-the-house was cavernous. The slope fell away through the forest of blackened stumps from near darkness immediately below to the high-set lighted end.

Gerald was absorbed by something I couldn't see there.

'Isn't it scary,' he said. He meant it. When I clambered upright he continued to kneel with his eye to the gap.

I was beginning to be impatient with him, he took everything too far. But stepping into the hallway I felt its shakiness, a slight vibration of the whole structure on its supports, as uncanny, having still in my head that vision of the slope. Was that what Gerald meant? You were aware up here, as light struck through the floorboards, of the uncertain anchorage those stumps might have in the crumbling earth, but also of the furriness and palpable density of that wedge of dark. I had spent my whole life in houses like this, where under-the-house was another and always present dimension, a layer of air between lighted rooms and the damp earth: a place of early fears, secrets, childhood experiments, whispers, and where the thin covering over clay or sandy loam was of dustballs, rusty pins that had slipped through floorboards, peach stones, dog's fur, old nails and hinges and the handles of cups. I took it for granted. It was darkness domesticated, a part of local reality, the underside of things. But down in New England where Gerald came from, and in Sydney and Albury where his mother had taken him as a child, houses sat close to the ground and were of stone. For him that underworld was full of threat.

The shaky hallway and its creaking had drawn from the kitchen at the back a pale, soft barefooted figure with a frying-pan in his hand and a great deal of blond or greyish-blond hair. He might have been called up, armed with the blackened pan, out of a bed of straw. He blinked into the hallway, where the setting sun made us two dense indistinguishable silhouettes.

'Oh, it's you, love,' he sang in his tenor voice. I was reminded immediately, and disturbingly, of Della.

He was bulky, and might under other conditions have been tough, but there was something so comfortably domestic about him, he had such bleached wrists and forearms, and such an air about him of soapsuds and boiled milk with a skin on it and sour water in zinc pails, that I saw him as womanish when there was no physical reason for it. He had been scrubbing the pan with a ball of steel wool that gave off a strong odour of rust. When Gerald introduced me, he made a gesture – a helpless lifting of the elbows – that suggested he was too soapy-greasy to shake hands, and immediately afterwards a tilt of the head towards the other side of the hallway, which indicated, not altogether respectfully, that the man of the house was at work there and should not be disturbed.

'Stormy weather out there.' He made a face and giggled. 'Ol' Thunder's in one of 'is *moods*.'

He sounded like Della reporting on the weather in my grandmother's room after taking up a tray. There was the same air of solidarity, as between children against a tyrannous adult.

Across the hallway an open door led through a room piled with newspapers to what I had observed from the street was a long, closed-in verandah. There were odd bumps and crashes from out there of tins being battered or furniture shifted. 'That means a blow-up,' the man giggled. 'We know, don't we Jed? I hope you brought yer brolly!'

But when Frank Harland came out at last, in a short-sleeved shirt and dungarees, he was not at all the angry demiurge his brother had evoked. Abstracted at first and barely noticing any one of us, he stood with his back to the sink, where a line of ants was pouring out of a corner-hole, and stroked his moustache. Tam winked and lifted his chin. *You'll see.*

But I didn't. Frank Harland suddenly lighted up, producing the shy, rather boyish grin I remembered from Aunt Ollie's kitchen.

'By golly,' he said, 'I can hardly believe it. Those were the days, eh? That old picture-show? And your aunts. And Della and the iceman. And there was a terrible man with eyebrows, a friend. What was he called?'

'Uncle Haro.'

'Ah yes, Uncle Haro.' He repeated the sounds as if they were the formula for a bad smell. 'Oh, I remember it all, I've never forgotten any of it. You'll see! I'll show you!' He was dancing about on the linoleum, gaunt and awkward with his horny feet, in what Tam must have seen, with his mouth in a line of wary scepticism, as a new mood altogether, a transformation. *What's this, then,* Tam's look implied, *what's he up to now?* 'We must,' he was telling Tam, 'have a celebration.'

So while the brother Tam went out to buy sausages and beer, and Gerald, easier now, lounged on a windowsill where gold-and-white casements opened on to the green of mulberry leaves, Frank Harland, awkwardly amiable and eager to please, showed me where he worked and some of the pictures he had kept (out of affection, or because he had never got round to packing and sending them off) from the time ten years back when he was at Southport.

His work habits had not changed. There was the same low rough-wood table – the same, or another of similar design, its wooden slats all rainbow-puddled; the same crowd of peanut-paste jars with a fan of brushes; the chipped enamel mug, the rags stained and stiff with paint; and on the floor, a plate with dinner-scraps. Paper and cardboard sketches were fixed to a wall with drawing-pins or lay in heaps on the floor. Other larger works, on board or in frames, rested in stacks against the door of a half-open cupboard, its shelves already crammed. On the door of the cupboard, and at head-height all round the tongue-and-groove walls, were yellowed newspaper cuttings and pages from magazines, and on the floor along the skirting board, rows of books, of the kind that can be picked up from junk shops and auctions, their cloth fretted at the edges and blotched white where the cockroaches had been at them. In a corner, his stretcher bed. The lower crossbar had snapped out of its socket and was hanging loose. The pillow had no case. The blankets might have been the same greasy-grey army blankets of ten years ago.

I had the odd sensation, after so long, of being back on the stage of the Pier Pictures, with the great cavern of the empty theatre out front and the sea rising and falling around the piers below. The sunlit verandah, with its fleshy mulberry leaves and the gold and white reflection of its casements, might have been the magic-box of my childhood. It too was all up-in-the-air and shakily adrift, and the painter himself as custodian of it seemed entirely unchanged – hardly older at all; he had always looked old. Extraordinarily light on his feet and loose-limbed with excitement, he had pulled out a pile of paintings, and with muttered comments and chuckles and clicks of disgust was choosing some and rejecting others. He gave every indication of being unaware of us.

Gerald, at the window-sill, followed his uncle's movements with intense interest; as if he couldn't quite see what he was up to or guess the meaning of so much affability. He made me a series of gestures, not all of them convincing, that said *See? I told you.*

At last Frank Harland had found what he wanted. He rested three or four pictures against the wall and piled the remainder into the cupboard. 'Here,' he said, and turned one to the light. 'That's something I did then. A series, see?' And he drew out another and set them side by side.

They were studies, highly finished, of a boxer, a thin crouched half-caste youth. In one he was hugging the punching bag as if he were hanging on hard against forces that might tear him away. In the other, despairingly baffled but not yet defeated, he was shadow-boxing with it, lunging wildly at the shadow while the bag itself, slack and puffy with evil, solidly passive, simply hung there and half-obscured him, pushed him out to a corner of the frame. There was a naked globe. And all around stood the silent watchers, tree-trunks or house-stumps or transmogrified elders or wooden gods.

It was the hunch of the boy's body, its coiled energy turned in upon itself, already hopeless, and the savage light in his eyes, in the whites of his eyes, that struck me. Was it the same boy? It must have been. Somewhere out of frame there would be the dancing white man, the punchdrunk father, and further out again, my father and myself.

The painter had grown sober. The pictures had subdued him. They imposed themselves. Gerald let himself down from the sill and came closer. He too was impressed. The struggle was so uneven. The young half-caste brought his whole body to bear; he strained, he screwed himself up, he called on every last ounce of will and muscle, he drew his passions to a fist and bravely, despairingly struck out. But the enemy, just because it refused to declare itself, was always more powerful. He was done for before he began. But his courage somehow stood. It drew not only on itself but on what it was pitted against, and would be seen at full stretch only at the moment of inevitable defeat.

There was an odd stillness in the room, and I felt again what I had felt years ago at the occasion itself, the presence of a darkness that the naked globe on its cord was powerless to dispel.

'Yairs,' Frank Harland was saying. He reached out and touched the paint with a forefinger. 'They're – all right. They're all right.'

Slowly, shaking his head, he withdrew them and they were turned to the wall.

'Here,' he said, 'this is more like it! You'll recognize this.'

I fel the blood rise to the roots of my hair.

It was my Aunt Ollie and Della, I knew them at once, though there was no attempt at a likeness, except perhaps between the women themselves.

Their large bodies were entwined. The pattern of interlocking, inter-circling lines through which they emerged from the surface of the board, and which boldly contained their arms, breasts, shoulders, necks, heads, first caught the eye, then confused, then satisfied it. They floated but were anchored to the earth – it might have been by a million grains of flour on the arms of one of them that had once been seed-cells and before that sunlight and earth, or by the thickness of the paint itself that was metal and earth. They leaned together. They mirrored one another. They moved in and out of each other's forms but were always themselves. They communicated through a play of shared lines; presiding, in ordinary mystery, over a blue, ball-like, tunnel-like space that could have been simply an area of the picture that no line had had power to cross, but might also be an entrance into the further depths of it, or if palpable, a not-quite-rounded entity that the two women, by patting and pounding and passing it back and forth between them, were shaping into a fate.

I was astonished by the virtuosity and daring of the thing, but also by the delight it gave me, which had nothing to do with my recognizing the two figures, or with my believing I knew something about them which another viewer might miss, or with any affection I had had for Aunt Ollie, or my having been allowed to share at times the two women's affection for one another. It lay in something purer than recognition or even knowledge. In the painter's joy in what *he* had been at work on: his 'Two Fates', as the picture was called, of which the unmade space the women were presiding over was the inchoate Third.

'Yairs,' he said again in a long-drawn breath, considering the picture from his oblique, close view. 'That's the one!'

He sank into himself as he considered. After a time, without further comment, he set the Two Fates aside.

'Just one more, eh? I call this one – I call it "The Iceman" ' – he paused, producing the boyish grin – ' "as Heavenly – *Bridegroom*".'

Easy to see why he regarded it, in the presentation, with such wry humour. Though as before, as soon as it was fully displayed he turned solemn, he too was struck.

It was a self-portrait, the face all fragments. A force from 'out there' that was irresistible but might not, in the end, be destructive, had struck it to splinters that met the flat board at every angle, so that the figure emerged simultaneously in many planes. Turning one shoulder to the viewer out of ice or stone that had already disintegrated, and at the same time turning away, the figure was immediately recognizable. So was the pose. I would see it often in later years, in the reluctance he always showed to come in from his own distance. He would stand exactly like that: side on to the occcasion, only obliquely in view.

But there was something else, a more humorous reflection. It was of the iceman himself – Della's iceman, to whom my aunts in their jokey way had once likened him: the suitor who called but did not propose, who had never (as I could have told him in Della's case) popped the question. He saw himself in that comic light: as an imminent but un-annunciating angel.

'Well,' he growled now, no longer amused, 'that's about it, I reckon. Enough for one day.' He shot a quick glance in the direction of the sill, then set himself to returning the pictures to their stack, and seemed not to notice when Gerald, letting himself down like a gymnast, slipped quietly away.

But his eye missed nothing, I was sure of that. For all his absorption in the pictures he had been keenly aware of my reactions and keenly interested in them; there was an assured cunning in what he had shown. I was to be drawn into his world, though for what reason I couldn't yet tell; and Gerald, perched so lightly on the sill, looking so easy and pleased with himself but also puzzled – it was just the sort of expression that had put me off when I used to observe him at Aunt Roo's – had been playing the role of procurer. There was, between them, a clear understanding about why I had been brought here and the conditions under which I might be tempted back. Gerald had left on cue.

Frank Harland turned now and had something to say. He assumed, I was amused to see, the sidelong pose of the self-portrait, half-facing me but looking away. He coughed, shuffled, and indicating a portable record-player that had till then been hidden by the cupboard door, informed me, as if he felt a need to account for the thing, that it was a present. 'From an admirer. A lady from Melbourne sent it.'

He gave a grin, a mixture of embarrassment and almost childish vanity, and stood looking at the machine as if he couldn't fathom its use.

'I didn't see her, of course. Couldn't! I don't see people. But she heard I was fond of music and had it sent. From Chandlers. It was very nice of her. People can be kind, it's surprising.'

He continued to study it, clasping his hands behind his back, rocking a little on his heels, and began softly, tunelessly, to whistle: then said abruptly, without turning: 'I'd like you to come again. Now'n then I've got business to be done, you could help. I don't really understand these things. I need someone I can trust.'

He did look at me now, fixing me with his deep blue eyes. 'There's no one – no one I –. Here! Take a look at this f'r instance.'

Turning sharply away he took from his pocket a sheet of notepaper and thrust it towards me.

'No, no, I want you to *read* it! I want you to see the sort of thing –' He swallowed hard on what he saw as the perversity, the hard injustice of things.

It was a letter. It began in a small neat hand but degenerated almost immediately into passionate scrawl:

Dear Frank,

I am writing again because I can't help it, I've got no faith in your so-called *heart*, so don't expect this will do any good – no more than the others. I got the letter you asked that lawyer to send me. Why I wonder? Do you think I am a fool and don't know already what sort of a position I'm in? You are a coward not daring to face me yourself. This is a personal matter between us, not lawyer's business. I wasn't writing about what the law says but about what my heart says and what yours would say if you had one. I wrote as a *mother*! I'm talking about nature, Frank – not the law. Do you know the difference? Gerald is my son – my son and *Jim's* – nothing can change that. You had no part in it and never can have. Till the day I die it will make me closer to Gerald than you can ever be – and Jim too, a dead man, since he is the boy's natural father. I gave him up to you because I had no other way of keeping and educating the boy and you know that. Out of the kindness of your heart – what a joke! – you offered to adopt him and see he was sent to a decent school. In the state I was in, with no family to turn to and no means of support except hard work, who would blame me if I was tricked. After all you were family, Jim's own brother, and blood is thicker than water they say. What I didn't know was that you haven't got any blood in you, Frank, not a drop! You had to steal the boy from me, right from the start, and make of him what you can't make yourself – that's the real truth of it, that's why you had to steal and bring the law in and let lawyers make a son for you. Well I don't accept it. There's also nature Frank, you can't twist that. Thirty-two hours of labour – that's what Gerald cost me. You wouldn't know but it makes a difference. Let alone the nine months. You will never understand that, no matter how hard you try. It's beyond you and always will be, flesh is flesh. As for your so-called love – and what you want to *make* of him – the boy himself has told me what that means, if I didn't know it already. It means trying to twist him to the way you see things, because you think you own him. A man hardly sane! – that's the truth, I am a woman, Frank, you can't hide from me – with no love for anyone and no power to make the boy love you. I don't have to beg for love, Frank. That's a mother's power. Let your lawyers write what they like, with their high-falutin words no one can follow and their whereases and in due terms – I'll see you dead Frank, you vampire! Pretending to be a good brother and a helping hand in need. You're a monster. If no one else will tell you I will and it's the truth. If you knew the times I have sat here and the curses I've worked on you, you wouldn't sleep. I curse you now, at this minute. I hope you can feel it. I spit on your lawyer's letter and I spit on you . . .

There was more. The last page was almost indecipherable and gave way to obscenities. I guessed the letter had been started in a sober state and finished in a drunk one, but it might only have been overpowering emotion. It ended in a delirium of witch-like imprecations that had a weird and chilling power, as if words so rarely spoken retained in some mouths, and on some occasions, their original magic. I gave the letter back.

'Well, you c'n see what I've gotta put up with,' he said in a low voice. He had, I knew, been following every word as I read it. He knew the letter by heart. His chin was drawn down into his collar. He was stricken. He cringed under the woman's scorn.

'You c'n see what sort of –. I mean does a decent woman use words like that? Obscenities?'

His mouth was prim. He had narrow views of the proprieties, however daring he might be in imagination, and whatever 'savageries' he was capable of when it came to paint.

'Should I expose a boy I'm responsible for to the influence of a – of a mouth like that? I can't tell you what a scourge that woman's been. I adopted the boy. Ten years ago! Not a squeak out of 'er then. Only too glad to have him off of 'er hands. So she'd be free to see a bit of life as she called it – men! Now she accuses me of turning him against her, of alienating his affections, because I prefer him not to see a woman who's no better than a harlot.'

He half-swallowed the word, astonished perhaps that he had allowed himself to use it.

'She spoiled him silly as a kid. Taught him to expect things, as a right, that you have to work and struggle for. Made 'im believe he was all sorts of things. It's taken me years to put a bit of ordinary backbone into a boy who might have had character if his mother hadn't tried to buy his affection, or make up for her own foolishness and the desire to be out seeing a bit of life, by *indulging* him – by bribing him with sweets and toys and God knows what till he's come to think life is a sort of Christmas tree where gifts'll just keep falling at his feet. He resents me, I know that. He thinks I'm hard. It's because I want him to *be* something. To realize that life is serious. To make something of himself. Not to trade on – sensitivity and some belief he's got hold of that life is his for the asking and that he can miss out on the sweat and the grief. I know he sees her. I can tell the minute he walks in. He gets that smug look on his face – of being made special again by all that false love she ladles over him, all that sticky sweetness. Of course he goes to her! Who wouldn't? I can't give him that because it's a lie, it's the sort of unreal easy stuff he'll drown in. Our family,' – his voice rose in a long moan; he was speaking now out of an ancestral grief – 'is dogged by weakness or bad luck – I don't know what it is, but it's gotta be *fought*. One of us has to break out of it! I'd rather lose the boy than have that woman ruin him. He's the last of us.'

He closed his mouth hard now and his eyes were like flints. But he was beaten. His voice when it came was harsh with self-mockery.

'*He's mad that trusts in the tameness of a wolf, a horse's health, a boy's love or a whore's oath.* Do you recognize that? It's *Lear* – the Fool. I was as ignorant as a stone when I was a young man, all – sensitivity. But I educated myself. Not to know *Lear* is to be – unprepared for your own life. Up to this point I have been spared the wolves and the horses.'

[3]

Over the next months I got to know a little of what it was he had for me to do; but either he himself did not know the full extent of his resources, and of the purchases and exchanges of property he was committed to, or a natural secretiveness, allied to old fears of being betrayed or swindled, made it impossible for him to be open with me. He kept things back; then slowly, a little shamefaced at his own duplicity, revealed them. There was always something more. I came to know, from his shy looks and sly attempts at evasion, when he was keeping something from me that might be essential to what we had in hand, but real frankness was beyond him. He didn't consider himself untruthful; after all it was his business, he owed me nothing, and he had the highest regard for truth. It was a form of protection. I suspected him of hiding money in the house, no doubt in the most obvious places. He certainly had deals afoot that he had not declared, and there may have been others that he had lost all track of.

Since he had always dealt through agents, avoiding his own name if possible, it was difficult to determine what he owned and how much, over the years, he had paid for it. I was frequently exasperated. He would sit then twisting his knuckled hands, apologetic but unrepentant, only a little anxious as a child might be that he had gone too far. I was astonished at his innocence, his impracticality, mixed in as it was with native cunning and a tendency to cover his evasions either with a look of blue-eyed wide-eyed naivety, which really was false, or with little attempts to flatter or please me that I immediately saw through. I think he enjoyed our games.

'We get on well together, don't we?' he said once.

I laughed. It was one of those days when he had been most defiantly perverse. It had taken me a good hour to worm out of him the details of a land deal I knew he had made and which he was determined to deny.

'Frank, you're impossible,' I told him.

'Am I?'

He was delighted, but sweetened any bitterness I might have felt by presenting me, before I left, with a valuable and carefully chosen book.

He himself was never resentful of my victories. On the contrary, he seemed refreshed, relieved by them, as if I had cleansed him of a stubborn untruth. Or he was pleased with *me* for having demonstrated a strength of character and persistence that he genuinely admired and which proved his own wisdom in having chosen me.

There was, to all our dealings, this aspect of conflict and drama, of confessions wrought with difficulty, of a battle in which temperament was revealed and set at play in a struggle of wills; though why this should have been necessary when I was, after all, only a servant of his will, I could never fathom. Perhaps an engagement of this sort, over public and impersonal issues, was the only relationship he felt safe in. There was anyway, as I saw, a degree of real passion in it, in all meanings of the word, that gave to the practice of the law, which had not originally attracted me – it was my father's choice, not mine – a dimension that for the first time commanded the span of my interests and the whole of my being. I was variously puzzled, rewarded, exasperated, moved, amused; drawn deep into his world, then roughly pushed off again, dazzled by the largeness of his vision and brought up hard against some pettiness in him, some small-minded fear or superstition, that in no way fitted the boldness and scope of his thinking or the nobility of his dreams.

It was several months before I realized the extent of the thing: that though we never talked of anything but deeds, contracts, figures, all this was for him a matter of profound emotion that he could not otherwise express.

He would hum and ha, dancing about with supressed excitement, all hints but refusing to tell me what he was after, till he had got me to name some parcel of land – an acre here, ten acres there – that he pretended had slipped his mind.

'You mean Warlock's Spinney,' I would say at last. 'Is that it? Warlock's Spinney?'

'Ah, yairs, that's it.' And having got me to conjure up the place, he would sigh, give a shy smile, and step off into it.

It was always like this. What to me were mere names, dimensions, numbers – rolls in my deeds cabinet – were to him so present and real that in the mere syllables that identified them they would blaze up as paddocks where cattle grazed among stumps and ghostly water lay just below ground, or as patches of scrub he knew every inch of down to the last ant trail between stones.

He had it all clearly in mind, and the names were magic. Which is why, out of some old superstition, he would not pronounce them himself. Mackay's Bend, West Glen, Pint-Pot Creek Farm, Warlock's Spinney: 'Yairs, that one,' he would say, slowly expelling his breath.

It was always the same game between us. I got used to it. And in time I came to see that it wasn't at all random, this hunger he had for land. There was a plan. He was trusting me not only with commissions but with the knowledge, as it emerged, of a dream that could make him blush at times and lower his eyes before me – it was so large and boyish – or shrink back in wonder at what he had too nakedly revealed.

So there was, from the beginning, an intimacy in our dealings with one another that was not quite professional, or not merely so, and which drew us into a partnership that was too deep in the end to be broken, save by a breach of trust on my part or some final irrationality on his. He had given himself away. He had made me a sharer in his passion, an agent in the achieving of an ambition to which he had already devoted more than half his life.

Why me? I never did understand that. But his shyness, his gradual unveiling of himself to me as I was allowed to shake out of him the last details of what he wanted and what he was, the softness of the man under the scratchy exterior, his real innocence beyond the slyness and crude native wit, all this touched as well as exasperated, and without ever feeling sure of my ground I grew fond of him, as I believe he was of me. Perhaps he clung to some sentiment from his Southport days, or recalled an earlier secret, deeply shared though never spoken of, that already united us. More likely it was through Gerald that he was drawn to me. For it was understood that the real subject of all discourse between us, as he would in time be the recipient of all that we were piece by piece acquiring, the only inheritor of the dream, was Gerald. That too accounted for the emotion that was involved. Measurements, deed numbers, names were a form of code through which Frank Harland could express what he might otherwise admit to only in loving encounters with paint and canvas or in a rage of silence.

Still, there were aspects of all this that unnerved me. One was the letters from the woman, Gerald's mother – anguished cries to which, in Frank Harland's name, I wrote terse, businesslike replies. It disturbed me that when she and Gerald met, as they certainly did, she must show them to him as evidence of his uncle's hardness of heart and refusal to accept either her rights or her griefs, and that in so far as I had written them, she would name me as well. Though Gerald never referred to the matter, it cast a shadow between us.

It was Aunt Roo who openly attacked me.

'Phil love, I'm surprised at you. I know you're a law man and have no interest in anything but facts – facts will destroy the lot of us if we let them, and you know it, that's what's so shocking – but you could at least be loyal to friends.'

'But it was Gerald who took me to his uncle's. He knew what he was doing.'

'Did he? Did he? Oh, you've got no heart, Phil, I'm sorry to say that but it's true. The poor kid's boxed in on all sides and you're part of it. Can't you see that? He doesn't know which way to turn.'

I brazened it out with Aunt Roo. I was willing to let her think me cold and businesslike if it pleased her. But she was right about one thing. My relationship with Gerald had become increasingly confused.

In my dealings with Frank I did displace and betray him. But wasn't that what he wanted? Didn't it leave him free?

I was weaker than I seemed or could ever reveal. Playing on an affection he had aroused in me that had much to do with my longing not to be an only child, Gerald had made an elder brother of me, offering me up as the nephew Frank really wanted and ceding me, in the wake of our old rivalry, both his birthright and his girl. That is what disturbed me. Gerald and I had made a deal. Jacky was now, by unspoken agreement, mine. It was a deal I felt ashamed of – it wounded my manhood and it wounded her, but I was too weak to refuse. Which is why I kept my feelings closer than ever and remained as jealous, as uncertain as before.

Gerald had used me, I knew that; but I had agreed to be used as he had agreed to be displaced. And to give him his due, he had been caught as well, by a desire, not unlike my own, for the older brother I had become. I still resented his presence in our uneasy threesome, but my discomfort now took a darker form: as before a brother whose girl I had come to by trickery and low stealth – how could she ever forgive it? – or, since Gerald and Jacky still went on in their old way, as before a brother of the girl herself who had been there before me.

None of this could I have explained to Aunt Roo. She did me an injustice and I felt it, but I would not defend myself.

'You're all in it,' she insisted, 'and you'll all be responsible if the poor boy's driven to the edge. That awful Frank Harland on one side, the awful mother on the other, and now you! Playing the uncle's hand for him in cruel letters that take no account of feelings. The woman has *some* rights, I suppose.'

'I thought you disapproved of her.'

'I do, I disapprove of her way of life – so far as I've heard. She lives with an SP bookie, some sort of Syrian or Albanian, something like that. But a mother has *feelings* and they ought to be respected. Gerald's fond of her. He's torn, poor pet.'

'I do what I'm asked to do.'

'Ah yes, that's the let-out, you're not involved. But you *are*! The poor boy comes to me because he's got nobody else. He's in tears sometimes, pulled this way and that between the lot of you. If you saw him then, or if you took your eyes off your damned legal documents – I'm sorry to use such words, but you deserve it – and had to look that woman in the face, you wouldn't do it, I know you wouldn't. How can you let yourself?'

In fact I had already seen the woman. Dodging into the Astoria one afternoon out of a thunderstorm, and standing blind among the old-fashioned tables with their check cloths and cane-bottomed chairs, I had come face to face with Gerald and his mother in a corner, leaning together over a pot of tea and a tiered dish of pikelets and afternoon tea-cakes. The woman, I realized from her sharp look, knew me at once. Perhaps I had been pointed out to her on a previous occasion.

She was smartly dressed in a style that my mother would have called 'fast': a pillar-box hat with a checkered bow, a navy-blue suit, white plastic earrings. She was smoking, she wore too much make-up. No one could have predicted, from her air of brassy assurance, the intense, and in its own way guileless, passion of her letters, which rose immediately between us and made me blush.

As for Gerald, he might have been more embarrassed by the plate of cream cakes, one of which, half bitten, he held in his hand, and by the smear of icing-sugar on his mouth. I saw immediately (or thought I did) what it was that Frank feared from her influence. She brought out the pudgy child in him. But I saw too, in her, something Frank had warned me against and which I had failed perhaps to give full credit to. Gerald had her completely in his power. They looked more like lovers than mother and son – the spoiled young man and the older woman who pays.

'The boy's a fascinator,' Frank told me, 'he can't help it. It's a power or a weakness he's inherited. He uses it to make things easy for himself. He tries it on everyone. You too, I've seen it, you'd better watch out. He'll win you over in the end, he's bound to. Well I can't afford to be *won over*. He's won her already, but there's no depth to it because there's no depth to *her* – a woman who tells you every second week how much she loves, how much she suffers! Real love isn't talked about, not in those terms. Oh these people and their suffering! They can spin off whole yards of it at the drop of a hat!'

From Gerald I had another view.

I was wary now of the way he could work on me, or win me over as Frank put it, but I didn't think it was that – not this time. And it wasn't, either, mere resentment of Frank's acknowledged fame, though that too – a mixture of awe before the fact and a refusal to believe in the reality of it – was an element in his anger against the man; for Gerald really was, in his way, the more sensitive of the two, the more nervously responsive and aware, and had more obviously the fine, the 'artistic' temperament. What he failed to see was that this had nothing to do with it. Frank's understanding did not arise from his nerves. It was too broad and strong for that. It didn't glance or dash at things, wasn't at all quick. It worked by some slow process of absorption. What Gerald wanted was mystery, and what he had learned in his life with Frank was that there was none; only the question of how greatness – if that is what it was – might exist in a soul who was also petty, spiteful, selfish, ignorant and perverse. He despised Frank but could not get past him.

But there was something else now that put a chill upon the boy, and it was this that he tried to make me see.

We were, once again, in a corner of the Criterion. He was hunched over a glass of beer. His faced was pallid and blotched, his voice so low I could barely hear it.

'Listen,' he said, 'you've got no idea, no idea at all, what it's *really* like, how sordid and horrible, living in a house of old men. I know you think I'm spoiled and childish and grizzle about things. But you don't know! Uncle Tam's half crazy – don't you see that? He's spent his whole life as a kind of nursemaid to my grandfather, in one room up there at Killarney – he's like an old woman. Disgusting! – all that white flesh – the breasts! When he goes out shopping he stops in the park, I've seen him, to watch the schoolgirls playing netball. And at night – his bed's on the other side of the wall from mine. The walls in that place are like paper, you can hear every breath. I have to listen to him panting, moaning – you know what I mean. It's horrible. I can't do it myself because of what I have to hear *him* doing, it disgusts me, it's worse than boarding school. The whole house is just a shed really with partitions. At night all the boards creak and the rafters as well, it's the dew or the day's heat going out of them, but it sounds like people walking in the hallway or climbing over your head in the beams.

'I can hear *him* too – the other one. You'd be surprised how much noise old men make in a house like that – the phelgm in their throats, the farts, the things they mutter in their sleep, the sounds they make getting up in the morning – dressing, pissing in the bowl. You can't get away from it, you can't shut it out.

'He prowls round his room at night hugging himself – he's always doing that, have you noticed? Hugging his ribs and hissing through his teeth. I don't think he ever sleeps. I just lie there sometimes, listening to the boards creak and wondering where he is. And sometimes, when he thinks I'm asleep, he comes and stands in the door frame and stares. Then he creeps right up to the bed, and squats down with his face close to mine – I can feel his breath – and sort of moans. He doesn't actually touch me, it's worse than that. He – I can't explain it – he does it with his eyes. I turn my head away pretending to be asleep but I can feel it. He stares at the inside of my elbow where my arm's outside the sheet. I can feel it, it's like he was a dog – licking. I can feel his breath, I get goose pimples. It's like being licked by a mangy old dog. I lie as still as I can, trying to breathe normally – you know, deeply, as if I was asleep – but I want to scream. And sometimes, you know, I feel I'm going to choke. I could weep with – with shame! – can you understand that? I feel *ashamed!* I hate him because of what he wants. Oh, I know what he wants. He wants me to love him, that's what it is, and that's what disgusts me. It's a kind of love, all that hovering over me, all that licking – he think it's love, but it disgusts me. He thinks he's selfless and pure, and he is in a way, but to me it's – I can't say it! I feel I should get up and wash when he's crept out again but I have to lie there in the filth. I listen to him creeping away on his horrible bare feet – I can hear them sticking, and the sucking sound when he lifts them off the lino – and I haven't even been touched, that's the thing. I have to sleep in the *idea* of filth. And the worst is, he must come sometimes when I really am asleep. I can't bear the thought of it. I wake up half-dead from trying to be awake enough, while I'm sleeping, to know if he's been there, and what he's – Can you understand any of this? I feel sometimes that I'm getting just like them. I'll end up scratching my belly just the way Uncle Tam does, while he's *talking* to you, and stop combing my hair, and grow breasts, and sit perving on schoolgirls in the park. Or I'll be pure like *him*, absolutely eaten up with the need to love someone and with no way I can let myself show it. That's the worst thing, you know. Not knowing what I am, and being shit-scared of what I'm half way to becoming. Except that I can't be like him because I haven't got any talent and wouldn't be willing – don't worry, I know these things! – to pay the price.

'Poor Tam! He's so good-natured, and he's never had any sort of life at all. He suffers but can't break out. I'm fond of him. Only I can't bear to look at him sometimes, and I don't want us to be allies or conspirators or *mates*, I don't want to be *like* him. I can't bear it when he assumes, because I understand him, and because we're driven into a kind of alliance against *him*, that we're alike. We're not. We never will be, not ever! I'd rather –'

His cheeks were feverish, he no longer looked young. I felt for a moment, and the idea scared me, that I might not know him at all. There was a white light in his eyes, and an odd whiteness about the mouth that made me think he might be a fanatic. But of what faith?

'I want to be clean,' he said. 'Do you know what I mean by that?' There were angry tears in his eyes. 'I want to be straight and open and live a life that's – but everything around is so filthy. It's all lies and secrets and mean little plots, and I have to lie and plot as well. I hate it! How can I be clean or straight when it's all so filthy, and everything is so crooked and mean!'

I had no reason to doubt his sincerity in all this. The truth of it was too plainly, too painfully there in the hunch of his shoulders and the ugly pinched look of his mouth and jaw. But there was in everything Gerald did an element of exaggeration. He protected himself from the reality of what he felt by pushing it further – into play-acting. I believed him but found it impossible to react.

So I did not reach out as I might have done. I sat stolid, square, and gave no indication of the turmoil he had aroused in me, and after a moment he let out a kind of laugh. It was very loose and contemptuous and it convinced me more than anything he had said that he might be in real trouble.

But by then it was too late. He set his jaw at me. He defied me to offer consolation. If I had, I think, he would have hit me.

[4]

It happened that I was present in the house at West End on an extraordinary occasion; or perhaps Frank, for some reason of his own, had seen to it that I was there.

This was the visit, during a trip to a Brisbane eye-specialist, of the father, Clem Harland, and the wife whose advent in the old man's life, after nearly thirty years of being a widower, had disrupted the household and driven Tam Harland out.

When I got there the visitors had not yet arrived. Tam, in a highly nervous state, was in an apron, ducking his head in and out of the oven to see after scones. Gerald was at the kitchen table. He seemed amused. I guessed he had been teasing the older man.

'Tam's in such a *state*,' he announced in a sing-song voice. 'Aren't you Tam? Afraid of being shown up in front of the lady. Gunna show her what *real* scones are, aren't we Tam? Remind poor ol' dadda what he lost, what he's missing.'

'Shut up!' Tam told him, 'or I'll belt you one with the fuckin' iron.'

'Oh, playing tough! Gunna impress daddy, are we, with what a tough little boy we've become since we left home. Or is it the lady we're going to impress? Goodness me, what scones! Mr Harland – I mean – *Taaam*, where did you ever –?'

Tam swung around and made to hit him, but Gerald was already on his feet, fists up, dancing, while the older man, light on his toes but heavy-fisted and panting, swiped at him and Gerald darted his head to left and right, laughing.

'All right, Tam, all *right* you silly bugger! I know what a temper you've got. No need to impress *me*.'

'For God's sake!' Frank thundered from the doorway opposite. 'Will you two stop it! Tam! Lay off. Gerald, I would of expected you to have more sense. Your Uncle Tam's on edge.'

Gerald laughed.

'Tam,' the older brother said gently, 'I'm sorry all this had to be put on to you. It'd suit me a lot better too if they weren't –. The fact is,' he explained, turning to me, 'that my father treated Tam shabbily. He's a very remarkable man, on'y – Gerald, you'd oblige me if you did your hair and changed that shirt.' He reverted, with a frown, to the subject of the father. 'There are men, you know, whose power is – difficult to resist. It's a sign of greatness in some ways. But if it isn't harnessed and *used* it makes them – dangerous.'

He began, nervously, to beat at his thinning hair with an open palm. It was combed wet in a line across his skull, and his shirt, though tieless, was buttoned to the throat like a boy's. I couldn't have known it then, but in Frank Harland's mind this was a repetition of all those times, more than forty years back, when his father came to see him at Stanthorpe and his aunt had got him ready in just this way: hair watered and combed in a cowslick, a long-sleeved shirt all neatly done up.

Tam, fussing at the stove, barefoot, untidy, in a floral apron, was reliving other occasions.

It was Gerald who first heard the jumping of the two planks on the footbridge. Still tucking a clean shirt into his slacks, he stepped out into the hallway to greet them.

The old man – he must have been seventy – was magnificent. He had the look, but also the style, of a prosperous and influential squatter, the heir once, the ruler now, of a large and powerful estate. Standing at the threshold of the broken-down verandah in a Harris-tweed jacket and tie, powerful, smooth-cheeked, his thick grey hair all springy with vitality, he might have been paying a visit to a couple of scapegrace sons who were letting the family down by playing, for a spell, at being slum-dwellers. The sons in question appeared one behind the other at the end of the hallway, and looked so spare and shabby-neat the one, and so soft and dishevelled the other, that you rather admired the old man's tolerance in visiting a place whose every bare patch in the lino, and missing board and odour of unwashed clothes and scraps and old musty spots of damp, must deeply offend him.

'Frank!' he called softly, and opened his arms.

Frank Harland visibly shrank. But something at last moved him forward. His feet, in the floppy boots, scraped and were lifted. He was drawn down the hallway and allowed himself to be embraced.

'Well, well,' the man gurgled. 'Frank! I can hardly believe it.'

The two figures, locked together in the narrow passage, seemed unable to break. Frank Harland, once he had allowed himself to fall into his father's arms, was unwilling or unable to step away. The old man was making clucking sounds such as you might use to soothe a child, and patting his son's back, while Frank clutched at him and sobbed. Gerald, at the door of his room, was mesmerized. His face was dark with embarrassment and a kind of anguished disbelief.

'Well, well,' the old man snuffled, breaking away. 'Tam – son – come 'n give your old dad a hug. You're not sulking, I hope. You're not harbouring a grudge?'

Tam too moved forward as if entranced, shaking his head, clutching a dishcloth, and allowed himself to be enfolded. He looked as if he might be about to raise his head and howl.

'You know Elaine,' the old man said severely.

Tam nodded. He held out his hand.

'This is my wife, Elaine,' he told the rest of us, and the woman, who was shy and pretty, dressed in her best clothes for the city, stepped in over the threshold.

'Frank,' she said, 'Gerald,' as if getting the names off her tongue would deal with the large and unmanageable maleness of them all, bulking there in the hallway, this family she had acquired of three grown-up sons and a grandson; or would clear some of the emotion that had generated in the narrow passage with its view to a drop.

I felt for her. She was scared to death of Frank. Even when we sat down to Tam's scones and cups of scalding tea she seemed to find no room for manoeuvre in his rough household. Her bones were too brittle. Her little finger, when she raised it, looked as if it might snap off. She was afraid, if she touched anything, of acquiring a smear of dust and thus drawing attention to how much would have to be done here if the place was to be restored to decency and a measure of cosiness or grace. Not a doily in sight, and the teapot lid did not match. Neither did the cups. Not even as a broken set.

Tam watched fiercely for the least sign of condescension.

'Well,' said the old man, 'isn't this grand! A real family occasion.'

Tam poured, doing the honours. He relaxed a little once the comfortable old teapot was in his hand, and the scones, which were admired, had begun to impose their own shapes and consistency on such words as found their way round buttery fragments. When all was done he sat looking large and desolate on a footstool.

Frank, glowingly silent, had retired to the window.

The old man was reminiscing and his voice immediately charged the room with its own power; it had a wonderful softness. Tam's shoulders sagged. Frank cringed.

Clem Harland was speaking of the early days after the death of his second wife, when he and all five of his boys had lived together in the one-roomed shack at Killarney. Well, they wouldn't know the old place now. It had been renovated. New bathroom and lav – inside of course; a proper kitchen, a verandah with louvres. Not like the old days: the long lamplit evenings when they had sat together round the kitchen table while he told them stories or played a tune or two on the mouth organ. Frank was already doing his first bit of sketching by then. Yes, the first attempts of the artist belonged to those days, and who knows, maybe they owed something to the old place – Frank had always been fond of it. Certainly Killarney itself must have been an influence, couldn't help being. Early mornings when they had all got up together in winter fug and traipsed around half-asleep, bumping into one another in the dark. They all hated to wake up, those kids – well so did he! – they liked their warm beds – and most of all poor Jim. And the frost was terrible some days, the ground cracked under your boots, and the cows lumbering in out of the mist, which was half their warm breath and the warmth coming off their flanks, and your hands so stiff you couldn't hardly feel them till they warmed up a bit on the udders. Once you'd got the damned beasts into the stall, that is! Oh, and bath nights, the tin tub beside the sink. And how many was it, Frank? – six, seven lots of water in the old kettle? – the little ones, Tam and Pearsall together, last into the suds.

'The little ones!'

The old man, indicating large, uncomfortable Tam, and reminding his wife of Pearsall whom they had seen the night before, thought that a great joke.

'Well, time works changes, eh?'

But it had been wonderful, all that. Soaping their necks, giving their hair a good scrub and rinse – it was the days when kids got nits at school, you couldn't be too careful – while he told them some of the odd things that had happened to him. Odd things – very! Like a ghost-lady he had seen once, up at the ruins of the old homestead, who had looked right through him as if *he* was the ghost, because he was so desperate then, so young and poor and with so little hope in the world, that he had considered – *seriously* considered – doing away with himself. Well, they were hard times. And now look at him! Fifty years later – no, more, *more* – and he was still going strong, he had escaped that ghost-lady's melancholy predictions – and here they were all reunited again. Well, not quite all. Not Clyde, poor lad! Perhaps it was him the ghost lady had had her eye on. Could that be? Could it? Could she have had Clyde in mind, so many years before the boy was even thought of? *That* grief – Clyde's killing himself, though he couldn't have guessed it then, so many years ahead – was so much larger than the one he had been sitting in the dumps of when she'd looked at him, the gloom of a poor boy full of ambition and no prospects. Well, not Clyde, God rest him! And not Jim either, his eldest. Jim wasn't here either. To share in the –. Well, that was the Japs, no one could have predicted that. They'd never known, any of them, that they were in the shadow of another war. But Pearsall. What about him?

'You're wrong about Pearse, you know, Frank, you're too hard on him! I don't say myself that I *like* to see him earning his living as a – a race-course tout, not with the education he had. It's a disappointment to me too. But he gave us a real slap-up meal, didn't he love? Crabs! At a place at Sandgate. And his friend, Mrs Welles, is a real lady. Very refined and with a sense of humour, whatever they say of her. Anyway, we found her so, didn't we, love?'

Tam through all this had sat hunched on the footstool, visibly affected, both by his father's physical presence and by the whole world he was summoning up, which was still the only safety he had ever known; he looked now as if he might weep openly for his own exile from it, or for its having fallen in such ruins about him.

Frank was fidgety. He didn't interrupt to deny the old man's picture of things, even to defend himself over the matter of Pearsall, but he was not easy. He kept his head half-turned, as if he dared not meet the old man's eye, and in that way could hide the extent to which these old scenes, so painfully happy, grieved him, and the exasperation he felt at his father's easy sentimentality. He writhed. Once or twice he held his hand up as if to ward something off. Finally he sat just like Tam, hunched and defeated, while Clem Harland, in full flight, showed off a little now that he had made his point about Pearsall and established his ascendancy; not only for his new bride, who was clearly impressed, but for Gerald and myself.

What struck me, even more than the man's extraordinary vitalty and the seductiveness of his talk, was some missing term he provided, and not only physically, between the two brothers. I had seen no relationship till now between Tam's soft passivity and those qualities of austerity and bleak self-discipline that were in Frank the moral counterpart of his leathery toughness. But here was their common original.

What was sleek and plump in the old man, the result you felt of years of pampering and self-regard, had become in Tam a fatal laxness. The one quality he had failed to inherit was a belief in his own centrality. Tam did not have it because he had ceded that from the beginning to his father.

With Frank it was the opposite. He might have taken his father as a model for all he was not or would not be; or allowing for the large space in the world that his father occupied, and which he too conceded, sought qualities in himself that would make hard use of the rest. I had seen in Frank, on occasions when he wanted to make up to me for some deception or some imposition on my time or patience, a kind of charm that was very like what now appeared in the father. But it was shy in Frank's case; he distrusted it, it came too close to his vanity; which I also recognized the source of, and which he also distrusted. I thought I saw too what Frank had meant when he told me once: 'If you want to achieve anything in this world you've got to go against nature. Your *own* nature.'

Such a radical view of things was beyond Gerald, and it was for this reason perhaps that he missed Frank's powerful originality. As for his own, which had always been problematical, it seemed deeply compromised now by this garrulous old man, whose charm was his own charm raised to the highest pitch and shamelessly exploited. He blushed to see himself so nakedly exposed.

The old man, regardless, talked on. He was too pleased with himself and the occasion, too deeply in love with his own voice and the warmth of his feelings to be aware of the consternation he caused. Suddenly, without warning, Tam rose and fled, and Frank, with an abrupt gallantry I had never before seen in him, offered to show Elaine 'our bit of scrub'. Gerald and I were left alone with the man.

'Call me Grandpa,' he insisted with something like a whine. 'I *am* your grandpa, you know, an' you're the only one. I'd like to hear it. Grandpa. It's been too long, boy, too long.' He made to put a hand on Gerald's shoulder but Gerald ducked. 'You're like your father,' the old man said softly, 'when he was your age. My boy Jim.'

Frank had led the woman on to the back porch, where she stood for a time admiring the drop. When I picked them up again, minutes later, on the jungle slope that led down to the river, he was raising his hand to break a spider's web. He looked back grinning. Gallantly or with malice – I couldn't tell at that distance – he beckoned her in.

The old man meanwhile was engaged on yet another ghost story. I had missed the beginning.

'You jus' go an'get cleaned up, she says, an' it'll be on the table before you can say Jack Robinson, it's your favourite, steak 'n kidney. Well, I was astonished! You see, steak 'n kidney was my favourite, but how could the woman 'v known? She'd never seen me in 'er life before, an' I'd never seen her. I just stopped at that house because it looked clean, and cheap, an' because I'd been on the road all day an' thought, well I've had enough, I'll hole up for the night. So I step out of the kitchen, wash a bit – the bathroom was right across the hall – and when I come back it's already on the table. Steak 'n kidney – one of the best I've ever eaten.

'We sit on either side o' the table, tuck in, and don't say a blind word. Which is unusual for me – I like a bit of a talk when I'm eating, always have, it's more sociable. But she wasn't the type. She just watches me eat, and asks once or twice how it is and whether I'd like another helpin', and when we're finished she clears the table, puts all the dishes in the sink and says: You go on if you're tired, I won't be long. Righty-oh, I say. But when I go out into the hall I don't really know which way t' go, and when I glance back she's there at the kitchen door holdin' a tea-towel, keepin' an eye on me. As if she wants to see – you know, if I know the room.

'Well, there were only two rooms. Hers was on the right. The other one, on the left, must've belonged to 'er son – or 'er brother, I don't know. I stepped in, and I could feel she was still there in the light of the kitchen door, listening. I knew she hadn't come after me because I'd of heard the

boards creak. She was waiting but, listening. Weird, I think. I was beginnin'
t' get the creeps.

'I put the light on, and the room is very clean, which I knew it would be
from the outside of the house. Good bed, good springs to it. Only things
don't *feel* right. I don't know, I can't explain it. Perhaps it was the shoes. You
see, all round the walls, there were these pairs of shoes, all neatly set out
side by side and polished. A dead man's shoes! That's the thought that
come into me head. And straight away I saw what it was all about. The
woman thought I was someone else – a ghost of some brother or son who'd
got killed in the war. That's what it was. I'd eaten the steak 'n kidney and
now she wanted to see if I'd get into the bed.

'Well, I didn't! I tell you, I was so scared all of a sudden that when I went
down that hallway she might've thought I *was* a ghost, I was as white as one,
and shakin' so hard I could barely stay on me pins. I rushed right out of the
front door, and didn't stop till the next town.

'I did feel sorry but – for the woman I mean. There were lots of women
left like that, in those days, after the war. Maybe she'd never had any final
news an' had just gone on hoping. I don't know. Sometimes later I used to
think, well maybe I was a fool and missed an opportunity – you know – I'd
been hearin' too many jokes of the commercial traveller variety. But I don't
think it was that. She didn't try to stop me or anything. I went flying right
past her. She was still standin' there with the tea towel in her hands, she
didn't even call out. It was scary. I've often thought of it.'

Frank and the woman had come back – she was all smiles now, quite
charmed with him – and their appearance in the room broke a kind of spell.
It was something in the man's voice, some quality of low-keyed breathless-
ness and wonder in him at his own life, that mesmerized and drew you
in.

They left soon after, for the good hotel room Frank had provided. We
saw them to the gate, and Frank, a little anxious, asked me to go and find
Tam. When I went down to his favourite hiding-place under the house he
was sitting on the old wood-block in the half-dark, hunched up like a sulky
child and hugging a bottle of Fourex.

'Are they gone?' he asked. I told him they were waiting to say goodbye,
but he refused to budge. 'Well, you've seen 'im now,' he said tearfully, 'you
c'n see why I'm so upset. That woman's not the sort to look after him the

way I did. I loved that place! It was all I had. Nobody wants me here.' I tried
to reason with him but he would not come up, and in the end it was Frank
who went down to him.

Gerald, still gloomily subdued by all he had seen, came to the door with
me. He stopped at the hole in the verandah; peering down past the forest of
stumps to where Frank and Tam were seated side by side on the
wood-block.

'Look at them,' he said.

I looked. The two figures leaned together. Frank was clasping Tam in his
arms like a child, soothing the man's sobs with a low cooing that was so
gentle, so warm and feminine, that for a moment I shared Gerald's
surprise, though not the disgust or shame or sense of bewildered rage with
which he suddenly tore himself away, broke past me and plunged into his
room.

A week later, with a hundred pounds in banknotes that he had stolen out of
a tea-caddy, Gerald disappeared. He was traced to Sydney and brought
home. Frank refused to charge him and there was, Tam told me, no scene;
but when Tam went down next day to sit on the chopping-block under the
house, and comfort himself or sulk, there was something new there,
swinging feet-down from one of the beams.

'Honest t' God Phil, I'll never forget it, I'll never get over it. Nor will
Frank. I just looked up and –.' He closed his eyes, shook his head and drove
the terrible image off. 'I'll never go down there again, not ever. It gives me
the shivers just t' think of it. I couldn't! Not f' the life of me.'

I thought of Gerald's fascination with the place, the way he had set his
eye to the hole in the verandah boards and stared, but never went close;
already feeling perhaps the tug upon him of what was to happen there in its
forest of stumps but unable as yet to make out what it was. I remembered the shiver in his voice, 'Isn't it scary?', when he invited me to look
down and breathe its dust, asking me, I thought now, to make light of it,
to assure him it was all safe as houses down there, that it was his own too
lively imagination that made it a place he dared not approach. It was his
horror of it now, rather than the act itself, that haunted me. I could imagine
that. The rope business I could not. He would have had to crawl up through
its layer of dust till the drop from the beams was long enough and the ladder

he was dragging had purchase on the slope. Minutes! I could imagine that. When I thought of it the blood rose in me. I choked.

'I don't know, Phil,' my aunt told me when I appeared on her doorstep, 'whether I really want to see you. I don't want to see anybody just now. But especially you.'

I sat down in the big gloomy sitting-room. By daylight, and without its usual crowd, it seemed desolate, for all its objects interestingly placed. Aunt Roo strode about wearing a cashmere shawl. She was too distraught to sit.

'I didn't expect it,' I said. 'How could I have?'

I didn't mean simply that I had misunderstood Gerald or failed to take him seriously, but that self-destruction was so far from my own sense of things that it had never entered my head. Lack of imagination perhaps. But my grip on life was very strong at that time. I was shaken, and the shock had thrown me back on my youth.

'*I* expected it,' my aunt was saying, half to herself. 'Well, not that exactly – but I told you, Phil, I told you over and over that the boy was desperate. You wouldn't see it, you thought I was dramatizing. Well what do you think drama is all about? It's about the agonies people suffer, about what they *do*. Don't you believe that?'

'I didn't.'

'Well now you see, don't you? – Not that there's any satisfaction in it. Poor Gerald. I can't –' She stood wringing her hands a moment then came rapidly across the room. 'Listen,' she said, settling on a footstool so that our knees touched, 'I wouldn't try to see Jacky if I were you. Oh I know you'll want to, but it's the wrong time, pet. This has been a real blow to her, she's grief-stricken. She was so terribly fond of the boy.'

'Does she think I wasn't?'

Aunt Roo put her head on one side and regarded me. Something in my very appearance perhaps made her doubt it.

'Well I know you were, Phil, because I know *you*. But you put yourself on the other side, didn't you? That's how Jacky sees it. You were *his* man – the uncle's.'

'I thought,' I said bitterly, 'that I was my own man. I've told you that before.' I felt the injustice of being caught so many ways. There was too much to explain: my loyalty to Frank, the respect I had for his work but also for the man – he too had suffered; my affection for Gerald, which had been the wary affection of young men who must test themselves one against the other, an uneasy thing, but passionate in its way and painfully real; and more than all of that, my devotion to Jacky. 'Will she refuse to see me?'

My aunt shook her head. 'She says she will, but who knows? You'll have to settle that yourselves.'

I went to find Jacky one afternoon at the end of the week. I had never been to her house before. It was a windy day, not yet winter but with a westerly blowing that set all the palm-fronds streaming in one direction, like sea creatures swimming in from the Pacific. There was an odd electricity in the air that made things rasp, grow fretful and give off sparks.

Jacky's mother seemed suspicious of me. She showed me to a closed room off the verandah where Jacky was working at an old school-desk, deeply absorbed, like a child, with her paints. Outside, green things thrashed and tore themselves to pieces, snapping off twigs to litter a path; but the room was secure from all that. When I entered it even my excitement dropped and was stilled.

Jacky looked up briefly and then away.

'I knew you'd come.'

I sat with my back to the weather and she went on with her work.

She was colouring a set of costume designs for a play, her red hair falling in straight bands on either side of her face as she leaned close to the desk. Was she short-sighted? I'd never thought of that. I knew so little of her. I sat for a long time watching her dip the fine brush in water, which clouded blue; the clouds thinned out and dispersed through what might have been whole afternoons and great bright spaces of luminous sky. Once or twice she put the brush in her mouth and drew it slowly between her lips.

It was the first still time I had ever known with her. Until now I had been shy of our being alone together because there would have been nothing to say but what I felt for her, and she had not wanted to hear it. So there was always Gerald between us. He was still between us, but his death was so much larger for the moment than anything we might have to say to one another that I felt freed; we could be together without fear. The minutes opened out into what might have been hours and could be years. I lay my head back. I could have slept.

Suddenly she looked up and regarded me sideways past the fall of her hair.

'Why?' she demanded.

I must have looked particularly blank.

'Why did you let it happen? I thought you knew him!'

More minutes passed. She drew her cardigan round her shoulders and went back to her work.

'I wish you'd go,' she said after a bit.

But I continued to sit. I was in a dream, light-headed but leaden. Even with so much that was unresolved between us, and in the shadow of her questions, I felt easy, I was spell-bound by her presence and by my own; by our being at last so still and quiet together amid so much turmoil.

She made a gesture of impatience. 'I want you to *go*! Don't you understand *anything*?'

She pushed her work away and stared fiercely ahead.

'I don't want to see you again. Ever! Why are you so stupid always? You never *say* anything, you just sit in a dream as if it'd all been said already. Well it hasn't, it's time you woke up. You never see what's really happening because you're so full of yourself. I didn't love Gerald – not in that way. You knew the sort of trouble he was in, he trusted you, and you knew as well what that old horror was like – that Frank Harland – and you did nothing!'

She had got to her feet and stood turning her face from me, clenched and white. I went to her, though I did not wake up out of my dream. Not yet. I was too deeply lost in it. I touched her arm and she pushed me off.

'Leave me alone, don't touch me! You're such a *fool*. Don't you see I don't want you here?'

She went on for several minutes, berating me, blaming me, heaping accusations on my head while I continued to stand; then she broke down.

I took her in my arms then and she allowed it. I was utterly, foolishly happy. But it made no difference in the end. She pushed me off after a moment, refused to see me again, and rigorously kept her word. So there was no beginning after all.

HARLAND'S HALF ACRE

In a series of discontinuous dreams that were all voices, out of a delirium broken by days and sometimes weeks of mere existence, or spells in which he was engaged body and soul with a mess of paint and paper, he heard things.

The voices were of men spinning yarns beside an oildrum filled with coals, or at a siding waiting for the rattler. Or they came from the generations of men and women who were stacked up in him when he lay down to sleep and whose sleep he entered: Harlands and McQueens and before that Currys, and on the other side, Walkers and Ranleighs. They spoke of days of quiet reflection, a view across stones into the heart of midday or of the light off winter paddocks on empty afternoons, or of the lifetime it had taken one fellow to clear a hill; of ill-luck, loss, exultation, anger, endurance, and of small sights caught at sunset from the seat of a tractor – two spur-winged plovers, that was – or the glint of starlight out of pebbles under a stream.

Most of these voices he had not known. Others he could identify by what they told. It was what his father had told.

That Gem Harland, for instance, who in a card game lasting three nights had lost the last patch of cedar in the valley, along with a hundred and sixty acres of prime pasture, to a gimlet-eyed fellow from Warrnambool in Victoria, who had been an unsuccessful traveller till then, in kitchen goods, saucepans and that, but as Gem Harland laid down hand after hand saw his unconsidered off-spring – the Mackays they would be, and the Cramms and Salters – move in out of the dark.

—You've wiped me out, young fella. (He heard that clearly.) You've wiped me clean off the map.

The nervous giggle that followed must have been the youth's, astonished at what he had done. All that land! The weight of it fell heavily upon him and snuffed out laughter. He grew silent with the need to formulate out of his dull head some plan to meet his own life. His loins stirred; he would found a dynasty. The silence that claimed him was a grave one, it too was filled with voices. Some other cove, Frank told himself, will be listening to those. They're another story.

He set down what he heard the only way he knew. Not as a story.

   — I put my shirt on that mongrel, 'e was nipped at the post. Wattl I tell Milly? A man's a mug — Harland's luck! Look love, listen, it's like this . . . No, love, listen!

   — Beautiful she was, I used only the best. Silky-oak, six-be-threes. Just the sandpaperin' took me three nights. Then I give 'er a satin finish, three coats with sandpaperin' between. Finally I oiled 'er. She was beautiful, I could of sat and looked at 'er for a whole week. You can be in love with a thing, you know, as well as a person . . .

   — Jack? Is that you, Jack? Are you awake? Still listening?

   — Yairs . . . There was this light. I just caught it at the edge of the furrow as I brought the team round, outa the corner of me eye, an' when I looked up it was gone. Might'v been the whole earth uncoverin' itself to me, *I'm a beauty, I am*, in a flash . . .

   — Do you mean that, Tom? Do you really and truly? . . . Now let me, oh, what's the odds? I said it, didn' I? It's not the sayin' . . . Oh but it is, to me it is! . . .

   — That was the only possession, in the muddle and midst of things. Or of being possessed. And we did have ways of saying it. You don't need words. A tune for instance, knocked up on the fiddle and spoons, or from a squeezebox or comb; and in the moment when you stop to draw breath you hear it: a voice, *I'm a beauty, I am*. Or bees in a kerro tin, that sort of music, not yet honey. Or doves going hammer and tongs under the shingles of a weatherboard steeple. Or steps on gravel, then a rough fling of it against a moonlit pane — no, love, not rain not moonlight — that sort of music. We touch something then could be ours for ever. That's possession for you, the only sort there is. Only none of it can be passed on. Though it is of course, just the same, you're listening, aren't you?

There were silences he was drawn to from which no words emerged. They belonged to little girls in shabby frocks who sat on a stump in sunlight and regarded their feet. Scraggy kids of twelve or so who if they looked up saw no path, only familiar roofs being doused and a line of scurfy hills, while their bodies told them the world was enormous and time infinite just waiting to be filled. They couldn't get the two views together. The difficulty appeared as two sharp lines between their eyebrows that would not meet.

From the same source later – it seemed to him to be the same, but might not be – a little humming arose that was a tuneless lullaby. One of those girls, a woman now, rather slummocky in a nine-ply cardigan, was singing a two-year-old to sleep. She looked up frowning out of her freckles and the hills were still there, hadn't budged an inch, not in seven years. They hadn't stepped closer or moved off to give her room.

He felt sometimes that he came between such a woman and what she saw; and when she stopped looking through him and allowed him to become flesh and bone he felt the line of hills harden in her eyes, all burning at the edge, and saw things himself then all the clearer, because it was her view that came to him. If he met that woman later, at the counter of a store, among pails and brooms and harness-straps, or at the door of a shed, she might look up and words would pass between them. Not spoken of course.

– Well, so you seen it too. Doesn' help me but, does it?

– Doesn't it?

At times it was axefalls. He felt the hard blows knocking him off balance as some kid threw himself into it. There! An' anotheree! Fuckit! Fuckit! Fuck you! The sweat trickled down his brow, down from his armpits under the flannel vest, down the inside of his thighs, the only tears he would allow himself.

– It doesn' help me neither!

– Doesn't it?

He slapped the paint on just the same.

Once or twice, after so long, it was his aunt's voice. Hearing it he was a child again, pale, thin, sandy, sitting puzzled and goose-pimply with cold on the edge of his cousin's bed while she knelt to tie his boots.

She was unwilling to look up. She wanted it to be her own boy's boots she was lacing and him little and alive again, sixteen or seventeen – no, fifty years ago. But her voice was not resentful and she no longer accused him of tracing.

— So you saw that, Frank love, did you? Or did I tell it to you? Would I of?

And his uncle: 'Yes boy, that's it, that's the style. Match-talk, finger-talk. You got the hang of it now, I always knew you would. Bettern' maggin'.'

— And better than a galleon, Uncle Fred?

— Well son, diff'rent is what I'ud say. Not inferior though.

— Forgive me, I have not explained things well, not the way I would've wanted. The words in my head won't do it, only the paintings could tell the whole of it and they are in a language you don't read. What I leave you, my dear brothers — and you too father if you survive me — is only the smallest part of what I wanted to give you out of the great love I had for you, out of the —

That was his own voice. No less ghostly than the rest, he heard it out of the future, and covered it for the moment with the slap of paint and the scraping of a knifeblade through it, not daring to pause.

The breath of cattle came to him, the sound of a windmill creaking, a magpie's wing black-on-white, and its cry the colour of morning, smoke after flame. And there was a quilt, mostly green, that when darkness covered it like a second quilt showed its true colours. Hands had chosen them from a drawer full of remnants. The pads of his fingers felt for ridges. They were stitches where a needle had gone through with the force of a hand behind it, and behind that a body. He mimicked, as he brought his own colours into being, the movement of that hand.

The quilt was green beyond green, an island continent in the dark of his sleep. He had news of it and the news now must be spread. In colour, in colours. When all was done and the fragments gathered and laid side by side, he would have laid bare say half an acre. It wasn't much, no more than a glimpse. But as much as one man might catch sight of.

THE ISLAND

[1]

In the first hours after Gerald's death Frank Harland lay night and day on the camp-bed in his verandah studio and would speak to no one. He neither ate nor drank. He simply lay there on the grey blanket, unwashed, unshaven, in his clothes, and stared through the rafters.

During the first night a storm blew up: the mulberry tree knocked and thrashed at the sill, rain beat in, there were bangings, a sudden crash. I went in to latch the studio window, and hoping he might stir or speak, I sat for a time on an upturned case beside the bed.

It was like watching over a cadaver. The flesh had fallen away, leaving the sharply exposed cheekbones and jaw of a man of eighty. Veins were visible under the mottled skin, the eyes were icy. Smashed jars, sodden newspapers and sheets of cardboard were on the floor among runnels of red and blue watercolour, brushes, rags, warped books. Disorder was natural to any place where Frank was working but this was wreckage. I sat for half an hour, and felt when I got up that years had passed. It was only partly the man's skull-like mask and the immediate ruins made by the storm. It was something in myself as well, the beginnings of a process in which, my youth already gone, I put on the heaviness of decades. I had sat down in my twenties, and when I crossed the threshold of the spare room and looked out down the hallway towards the kitchen, it was as a man of forty that I saw Tam Harland standing, grey and flabby, at the head of the stairs. He raised his face towards me like a very old and helpless animal.

Poor Tam. It was painful to see the man wandering from room to room and finding nothing to do. He washed all the cups and saucers on the draining board, and the pots, pans and cullenders out of the cupboards, and when they were dry he took them off the draining board and washed them again. He gathered up armfuls of the yellowing, dusty, cobweb-trailed newspapers that for so long had stood in piles in the spare room and on the front verandah, and staggering through the hallway with them, and down

179

the back steps to the incinerator, sat with one bare foot tucked up under him and watched them burn; leaning forward occasionally to poke the ashes with a boiler-stick that was itself of an unnatural colour, bleached and softened with soapsuds and long years in the copper, till it too began to char. After that he scrubbed the floors, the bare boards of the front verandah, the front and back steps and the linoleum in the hall, sloshing about on his knees with a zinc pail and a wooden scrubbing brush and using an old-fashioned soap that left the whole house sharp with carbolic.

It might have been easier for him, I think, if there had been bloodstains. He could have scrubbed them away once and for all, and something would have been achieved. As it was, he dealt in every room of the house, on all its bare boards, and in cups, pans, cullenders, with invisible stains that could neither be located nor washed out. He did not go back into the darkness, which he had once found such a comfort, under the house.

I had agreed to stay for a day or two in the hope that Frank might stir, and to deal with the funeral arrangements and the police.

Putting aside old superstitions that I did not want to face, and trying not to think of my own part in what had been done, I slept in Gerald's room, listening as he had, and as he had evoked them for me, to the night-sounds of that house: the knuckle-like cracking and creaking of the ceiling joists, as after a day of tropical sunlight they gave up their heat, the plop of berries from the Moreton Bay fig whose fruit blocked all the southside guttering. Overhead small feet clawed at iron, and slithered and skid, ghostly steps in the hallway went on downstairs; on the other side of the wall, Tam's snufflings, and the groaning of bed-springs as he shifted his weight. Once – but I might have imagined this – I thought someone came to the open door and stood there, watching as I slept. A figure approached. It squatted, stared at my face, and I felt the eyes as palpable fingertips, feeling for the bones. I started awake.

There was nothing. Air flowed thickly from room to room through all the open door frames. Moonlight made bars on the floor and diagonals on the wall with its rough-wood bookshelves and the shirts, newly ironed, that hung one above the other from hooks.

What I was most aware of, because Gerald had been, was the great wedge of dark under the floorboards, that air-cushion on which the whole house floated, that layer of dust. It had the force of gravity, hauling every object, and my thoughts, strongly, irresistibly down.

Gerald had added the weight of his body to that darkness, feet pointing to the earth. I could still feel it, a counterweight to my own that was laid out lengthwise on his bed. I slept and woke, slept and woke unrefreshed, even in the coolness after the storm; and had the greatest difficulty holding my head upright, lifting my feet off the sticky-damp floor.

On the second night, about two o'clock, Tam whispered to me through the wall.

'You awake, Phil?'

'I am now.'

'Listen, I can't sleep. Could we have a game of cards?'

He made tea and we sat at the kitchen table playing euchre till the light came creeping in over the river and up the tangled slope; lighting the scrub that was aswarm with tiny, flickering wrens, climbing the trunks of trees, opening the bright dewy cups of the morning-glory. I was glad, after two nights, there being nothing more that I could do, to eat the bacon and eggs Tam cooked me, and leave.

The same day, while Tam was out doing the shopping, Frank went as well. He got up off his stretcher, walked out of the house taking nothing with him, and disappeared.

And now the time I had felt passing on the night I sat by Frank Harland's bed really did pass; not so fast as I had imagined, but fast enough.

My grandmother died after three years of a progressive illness. My father was in charge at last. People had assumed, since my grandmother was always there, that it was her energy that had kept the business alive; there was, about my father, something too fine and vague, not sufficiently aggressive or resilient, to suggest capacity in the affairs of men. His mother's going would reveal the truth.

It did. For whatever reason, either because she really had been the force behind the business, or because his own qualities, without the addition of hers, were not strong enough to endure, or because now that she was no longer there to be hurt by it, he could admit at last that the Markets had never suited him, had never been more than a duty undertaken that went clean against his nature – for whatever reason, the section began to decline and he was advised by friends to sell up while there was still a profit in it. The city markets were about to be demolished anyway to make way for a park; the whole enterprise would move to the suburbs. My father, who loved the noise and bustle of the old buildings, was unwilling to move. His style – the good grey suit and silk shirt – was not for the suburbs, or for anywhere nowadays. It belonged to an older style of imperial allegiance that had died with the war, in which gentlemen of a certain standing had kept up the pretence that Brisbane Queensland was on the same commuting terms with London as the Home Counties. He was out of place in the only place he had ever known. Some possibility he had seen in himself, and in the country, had died on him, leaving only a set of aspirations that were out of all proportion now to the realities of the day. He sold the business for a good price and he and my mother sailed for Europe.

In deciding that he should see England at last he was grasping for some vision of what it was in that place that had created this one, an actuality that would prove his view of things had been neither an affectation nor an empty dream. He had turned away from my grandmother to his father's world, and I was startled when I went down to the liner to get their luggage aboard to see how old he had grown. We seemed more than a generation apart.

When my grandfather was dying I had thought of him as approaching, day by day, a country that was more real to him than the one the rest of us lived in. I had called it England. Now my father was on the way there. I watched the liner pull away from the wharf, saw the gap of brown water widen, heard the band strike up 'Auld Lang Syne', felt the taut streamers snap and flutter while we smiled and kept waving.

He died off Capetown. My mother saw him buried, spent two lonely weeks in that place, of which she would never speak, and sailed home again. England – whatever it was – had not been her dream. We sold the house and moved together into a unit on Hamilton Heights.

It was in all ways the end of an era. I noticed, now that he was gone, that my father had been almost the last of his kind. You no longer saw round the city, in bars, or in trams, those formally-attired old men who had in their time stood for so much in the way of a firmer world and a sterner set of values; reading in the men's section of the tram their well-thumbed leather-bound copies of the classics, with the tram-ticket folded thin under a ring; raising their hats to ladies; under no circumstances, even on the hottest days in February, appearing in public without a jacket and tie.

They lived, the men of that generation, in a world of their own strict choice, defying climate and place. Manners and morals were inseparable and both derived from some reality that stood over and above the actual. There was some foolishness in it but a good deal of courage as well. I had enough of my grandfather in me to regret the passing of the old ways. It was, as my Aunt Roo would have said, another aspect of my classicism; by which she meant, as usual, that side of me that was incurably romantic.

As for Frank Harland, he had simply gone back on the road. It was nearly a year before I had word of him. He was at Cooktown. Then later at Magnetic Island, then at Yeppoon. He had already given instructions that the house should be settled on Tam, who stayed on, took in half a dozen students, for companionship and because he had to have someone to fuss over, and was soon drawn into a new life among the young.

'That house was a mistake,' Frank wrote. 'Houses are not for me. They never were. I won't make that blue again.'

The notes began at last to come regularly; he was moving in. From Childers, Tin Can Bay, Noosa. Finally, after another long period of silence, I had a letter from Worawun. He was back in the Bay, almost on the doorstep; had been settled there, in his own patch of scrub between the Passage and the surf, for almost a year; in a fettler's tent, with an open-sided pole-and-bark studio behind it of his own making. He was at work. He named a day when I should come down to the island and find him, and gave me a list of the things he wanted me to bring: tins of Nu-Plastic paint.

He was in better shape than I expected, stringy but toughened, and chirpy as a cricket. He was living the life that suited him, the life he had always lived, even in the house at West End – he had knocked a few walls out, that's all; the inner view was always like this. I saw, too, that this wasn't, as I had thought when I drove down, one of his makeshift camps. It was permanent. He would be here now for the rest of his life. That was, I think, absolutely understood between us from the first day.

His tent was of a kind I had often seen in my childhood, a tarpaulin drawn tight over an A-frame of raw saplings, the cross-poles and supports still with their covering of tattered bark and the ropes pegged with wooden spikes. You saw such tents from the slow-moving trains of those days, often with railway-workers beside them in flannel singlets and braces, who would step away from a cookpot or billy for a moment to call out greetings and ask for papers, which you rolled up and threw on to the frosty grass.

He had strung up a hammock for sleeping, and at the back, under a canopy of bark-slabs upheld by poles, had his work bench, knocked up as usual from whatever was to hand. The scrub, its trunks all spotted and pealed with grey, lime, mushroom, ochre, came right up to where he worked; and Frank, himself all spotted brown and pealing white or pink, in a straw hat and frayed army-shirt, was as much part of it as any straight trunk or gnarled and papery limb. He was not so much painting it as painting out of it; out of a mode of being in which one of these misshapen but entirely natural forms might have found a way of restating itself as liquid, or had developed a system for spreading its own light and colour in dense strokes on a surface, of playing in and out of itself in vivid self-mutation.

He kept his distance at first, and I saw that it would always be like this. We had each time to go back to beginnings.

Standing defensively at the entrance to the tent, side-on and stoop-shouldered, he would fix me with a look that immediately brought me to a halt. We would stand facing one another thus for long seconds, sometimes minutes. Then he would smile, turn his back, and I was free to move in.

But the space he had established between us would impose itself for a time, even after I had crossed it. It might be half an hour before we were fully at ease. We stood, slowly circling one another, while he considered what I had to say, what he had summoned me to discuss. He was uneasy; we might have been meeting as conspirators on a bit of waste-land at the edge of a city or in an empty square. But at last, grounding himself in familiar objects, he would take up a brush and begin to clean it or shift a bottle from one side of his table to the other – bringing himself home. Or he would go and stare at the piece of work he was engaged on, standing for a long time silent before it; then examining it closer, reach for a brush, and leaning over his work bench, try something, try something more, till he was immersed.

I was free to settle then, I could talk. And he would listen, laugh, make his own monosyllabic explosions of disagreement or assent. Or I could sit in silence and watch.

The silence was deep but never absolute. There was always the slight hushing sound of a breeze high up in the leaves, even when all below was still, the clatter of banksia cones, a low ground-bass of tickings and fumblings and brittle rustling, as straws or small bones were lifted, egg-shells cracked, twigs tapped and fretted, tiny wings flapped, and a grasshopper's saw-foot rasped across bark. Each sound was infinitesimal, but multiplied they made a continuous burring note, so low and unchanging that the ear could ignore it and the mind might take its ceaseless buzz for silence.

I went when he sent for me and stayed for as long as he was content to have me there: sometimes twice in the same month, more often once in six. He had his own seasons.

He had grown hard, and was, so far as I could see, quite immune to all changes of weather and to heat or cold. I thought of him often, out there in the dark, as a parent might think of an errant child. We had moved to opposite poles of it, that relationship that had opened up, by the merest accident, all those years ago at Southport; as he had moved in time from one end of the Bay (the southern end, closed in by the low sandy pit of South Stradbroke) to the island, his island, that closes the Bay to the north. His island – with the wide still waters of the Bay on one hand, the Pacific on the other, and the tattered grey gum-forest and banksia scrub between.

Comfortably installed at my desk above the river, working late on a set of draft documents, or fretting over a few terse phrases of Tacitus that could make alive for a moment, in the unsettled present, a world that was two thousand years gone, all its endings settled and known, I would turn aside to watch the tide of moonlight go sweeping down the last of the city reaches before it broke up in channels at the mouth.

Out there, the Bay and its wrecks as I knew them from Thomas Welsby: the *Sovereign*, wrecked on the South Passage Bar on 11 March 1847, the *Countess of Derby*, 1853, the *Phoebe Dunbar* gone ashore at Amity, 5 May 1856, the *Young Australia* broken up off Cape Moreton, 1872; the Bay with its shoals of whiting, bream, perch, tailor, the big fish – sailfish and marlin, and the rays like the shadow, thrown small on the sandy bottom, of giant, delta-shaped space-ships. I thought of Frank out there; especially on nights of storm or in the cyclone season after the turn of the year when the river would be swollen and the fig trees and palms in suburban gardens clattered and churned. The Bay then was all pitched black tents. Rain-lashed, wind-rocked in his flimsy white one, he was always in my thoughts. Down on his island: on his island, one of the many, each with its history of vanished tribes – the Nooghies and Noonunckle – of convicts, lepers, whalemen, and those old ladies at Dunwich whom my mother would go once a year to see dance for pennies, laughing and tossing up their skirts. And in our time, Frank Harland.

Slowly, over months then years he revealed it to me, all the details of his world: the scribbles under bark that might have been the most ancient indecipherable writing; the lemon and lime-green of new flesh where the rust-red roughened skin had shucked from a trunk; a hive where he got honey; cranes on a lagoon that suddenly broke skyward, as if the pale water had taken on flesh from their reflections and was flocking away past the vine-hung and orchid-sprouting treetops; the procession, at dusk, of board-riders and their girls, like the ghosts of the Nooghies and Noonunckle whose middens he had shown me, trooping back on Sunday evening on old, deep-worn tracks past the edge of his camp.

I came to see his life here as the only one I could imagine for him. He had settled at last among his works, found a way of making them stand up around him as rust-red, powdery blood, as tatters of buff-coloured flesh, as scribbles under the skin that were the record of another existence, as the wandering crimson of ant-lines, companionable trickles. I came to see how time might pass here, and the grainy days and deepening nights become weeks, months, a decade, half a lifetime . . .

He would live and work for the rest of his life now in a state of almost complete isolation; connected to the city across the Bay only by the glow its lights made over the treetops on starless nights and the passage of suburban board-riders past his patch of scrub, and to the disruptive decade we had broken into by the piles of newspaper he collected each fortnight from the local store, on which he puddled thick house-paint and from which, on occasion, a headline might start up and catch his eye, or a whole paragraph or column emerge for a moment because framed by vivid strokes: some corner of a corrupted dream, a clash in this city or that between demonstrators and police, or a private killing – one single shocking death – out in the suburbs. He laid his paint thickly over these events and made his own news. Forms emerged from the forest about him and the forests from which these sheets of newsprint, by a long process, had themselves emerged. Fresh occasions and immanent, uncarnate creatures swam to the surface of the paper as to the surface of his mind, pushing their way through street happenings and accidents, the rhetoric of public men, the columns of chanting students and of closing prices on the exchange, the horse's mouths and the mouths of murderers and their victims in great sweeps and slashes, as his hand obscured the regular smeared newsprint and restored to it the colours of earth.

Only occasionally now were there human figures in this world. They had to be detached from the other shapes here of trunk and wing, or from the great vertical masses that were blue-green, blue-purple, purple-red water. The spirit that moved back and forth in him was like the breeze that swung between land and sea, or the tides to which his sandfly bites responded with itch and quiet; or as his eye conceived of the world either horizontally in bars of sand-light, sea-light, sky-light, each a kingdom of creatures, or vertically in the up-thrust of rocks, tree trunks, foam.

When he admitted the human to this world it was on nature's terms. Picnickers raising smoke out of flat water, crouched surf-board riders, lone walkers by the sea with a dog or a solid shadow at their heels, gave up their separateness and the hard lines of a species, and as they moved on into the landscape resumed earlier connections, between bough and bone, and hand or foot-print and leaf. Celebratory or destructive forces caught them up, poured on through them.

Each new work as I saw it in that place, with the man's clawed and blotched hand steadying it at the edge, was a newly emergent form out of the island itself, roughly torn away like bark from a tree; as if there were continuity in essence, but also in the movement of a real hand over paper, between all the individual parts of this world, and each made object had to be judged first against the natural objects it rose from and among which he now set it down.

The newspapers responded by creating their own version of all this. On to the popular figure of the artist in the garret, the misfit and man apart, they grafted a local image; that of the bush hatter, the old-timer still panning for gold in exhausted creeks or pursuing a vision so unique to the ragged, head-shaking, nickering, half-animal bagman as to put him permanently, but sentimentally, beyond the company of men.

I used to take him clippings. He would ask me to read them aloud to him, not wanting to show too much interest; but I suspected he had come across some of these pieces already, on pages he had smeared with earth or rust or shit-colours – I could imagine with how much vengeful glee. Since the hermit painter was a public figure intended for general enjoyment, Frank had decided to get his own entertainment from him.

'Well, c'n y' beat that!' he'd say, as if he were hearing about someone else, 'it takes all sorts! Sounds interesting, eh, this Bottlebrush Man? Wouldn' want t' meet 'im in the dark but – waddaya reckon? Sounds as mad as a meat-axe. An' I'm not sure I'd want t' see anything he akcherly paints. I mean, what would 'e paint, what would 'e see, down *there*? Even worse if what 'e painted just come out of 'is head. You wouldn' want what comes off the edge of a meat-axe, would you? Nobody would.'

Or deserting this vein of easy parody, he would stomp about and turn grumpy. 'Silly ol' coot! What does he think he's up to? Who's he tryin' t' fool? I'm sick of hearing about 'im!'

His growing fame, if that is what it could be called that was so trivial, so much on the level of what was accorded as well to pop-stars, rippers and prisoners on the run, was a genuine astonishment to him. Whatever vanities he was capable of, I don't think he had considered it as a real possibility.

'What about the sand-fly bites,' he'd complain. 'I notice they never mention sand-flies. And they never mention me back-ache, either. Oh well, it's my back. Can't expect the general public to take an interest in that, I s'pose. And sand-flies are bad for business – the tourist business.'

Or again: 'What's 'e up to in the papers, that artist bloke you know? I bet that last cyclone did 'im a bit of damage. Knocked the old bugger flat, I'd reckon, serves 'im right! Any news about that in the *Coo-rier Mail*? Wouldn' want t' miss the latest episode. Not f' quids!'

When there really was nothing he became playfully or half-seriously concerned.

'That artist friend of yours – you know, the hermit. Must've kicked the bucket. Not a word about 'im in the papers these days. Must've given up the ghost. No wonder, that sort of life!'

His position as public bagman, poor bugger and self-created outcast was all the more ironic in that the works he produced, in the new affluence and scramble for 'hedges against inflation', were worth several thousand dollars apiece. He was the real thing, everyone knew it now (crazy, of course, but what can you expect? – even in Australia) and I was the lawyer who for some unfathomable reason had been made custodian and doorkeeper to it all: to a storehouse of fragile, unpredictable, spasmodically brilliant occasions at which traffic accidents, small wars, marriages, deaths, perverse gropings and slashings and assaults were so thickly covered with earth and blood that they became desirable backdrops to suburban dinner parties and inter-national conference halls in multi-storeyed office blocks. Sheets of card-board that had once been the sides of cartons containing condensed milk or corned beef, or mixing-machines or refrigerators, had come now to contain forests or the sea. Collectors everywhere were hungry to acquire them. Museum directors dreamed of hauling them into houses of culture in all the capital cities of the land. Frank Harland's lone encounters with himself, with newspaper events, and with house-paints that might equally have gone on to a migrant's terrace or the feature-wall of a unit, could be seen now to proclaim a people's newly-discovered identity in a place it scarcely knew existed, and whose actual presence, like the old coot who had created it, might in the natural state have evoked a fastidious pooh!

Only rarely was I instructed to bring visitors – people who had been recommended by his gallery in the south, some of them distinguished, nearly all of them from Overseas.

They were difficult occasions. The visitors, always too formally attired for an excursion into the scrub across a swamp that after the lightest rain could be soft and mucky under foot, were invariably exasperated long before we arrived at the slope below the camp; by heat, by sweat, by swarms of tiny insects. The business of first calling to Frank across a buffering space in which flies danced and bigger insects zigged and zoomed, while with eyes averted, a sticklike figure, he stood side-on to the occasion, unwilling to emerge, was not always made up for by the talk that followed and the impatience he showed at having people poke about among his 'things'.

He would assume a resentful stance, audibly whinging, and in an attempt to divert them from what they had plainly come for would offer wonders of the most banal sort, an ant-trail, a chrysalis, in the hope they would believe it was 'significant'. Or he would lead them off Indian-file to look at 'views', bits of nondescript scrub that might have been anywhere, all sticks and tatters, that they studied with puzzled frowns and wondered about later – they were so *drab*.

He would make tea, in a billy of course, and the visitors drank it in the open, perched on rocks under the blackboys and shifting as the sun shifted or when attacked by ants.

Worst of all were the times when he was unable, at the last moment, to emerge at all. He would stand at first sighting with a pained expression, grim, tormented; then with a vague gesture of apology he would take to his heels and go rabbiting barefoot through the scrub; or abandoning the camp before we even reached it, would be holed up somewhere watching, all impatience for us to quit.

Once, with a flare of his old humour, or out of malice (the visitor was a Melbourne art critic), he left as the only remnant of his presence a large and shakily printed notice: DIG.

If the distinguished critic had been alone he might have spread a handkerchief I think and got down on his knees. He was never quite convinced that by insisting it was a joke, a Frank Harland special, I hadn't deprived him of a unique and private gift. He settled in the end for the notice itself; which the artist had raised from worthlessness with a flamboyant signature.

Frank Harland had at last, as my Aunt Roo would have put it, got somewhere. He had gone to earth.

[2]

Whenever I had a commission from Frank, but also occasionally when I simply wanted to relax over a good cup of tea, and more and more often over the years as the free and easy atmosphere of the place drew me, I would call in on the household at Dutton Park, Tam's house of students.

Tam was a natural home-maker and the changes in the place, and in Tam himself, delighted me. His kitchen with its battered pots and pans, and its recipe books all dog-eared on a shelf, was a pleasant place to sit for an hour or two in the late afternoon.

Students drifted in and out, calling down the hallway or coming in barefoot to get mugs of tea, and Tam made faces behind them that said, 'Tell you later – more strife!' These youths and their girls were his family. He nagged, spoiled, bullied them; he subjected them to bouts of the sulks and fits of temper, then later, to make amends, made them special treats; he cleaned, cooked, listened to their complaints, took up their causes, followed them on demos. Once when I was there they were engaged in preparing banners for a march. The yard below, which a previous generation had cleared and planted with sunflowers, was draped with huge monosyllabic directives, OUT NOW, and Frank's verandah, where Tam's Maoists slept, was vivid again with dribbles of paint.

'It's goin' great,' Tam told me as he shuffled backwards and forwards bearing tea. 'It'll be big, this one, I hope you're all set to bail us out. Y'know,' he said reflectively, 'I didn' think I would at first, but I really *love* demos! On'y right now I got a pudding to make, you can help me.' He took out his mixing bowls. 'D' you realize Phil, some a' these kids had never even heard of Golden Syrup pudding till I made it for them? All they know, most of 'em, is hamburgers and Smiths Crisps, with you-know-what to follow – I won't say it in case the place is bugged.' He held a thumb and forefinger close to his lips and sucked. 'I dunno sometimes what I've got myself mixed up in, except that I am.

'On'y I never go down you-know-where – under the house. It's funny that, it used to be where I went to – you know, sulk. It was so womblike.' He gave me a shy look and giggled. He had picked up from his young friends their habit of easy self-analysis. 'Well, I don't need that any more, I've grown out of it. An' t' tell the real truth, I'd be scared. It was a terrible, terrible thing that. Terrible! I'll never get over it. If it wasn't for these youngsters taking up so much of my time, making such *demands*, and making the house – you know, so noisy, I couldn' stand it, I'd get out.'

I also visited Tam, since the household was often in trouble, when either he or one of his friends had need of the law.

Tam had begun to be a well-known figure at marches. Soft, fattish, furious, he rejected with contempt the chiacking of the pot-bellied loungers round the doors of pubs and the taunts of women shoppers with umbrellas, who told him he ought to be ashamed of himself at his age, making a disturbance and being part of a rabble.

'They're the ones who ought to be ashamed,' he would tell me passionately. 'What difference does it make how old I am? Right is right. I give it to 'em, don't you worry. Old bludgers! Silly old bags! I can give as good as I get. I'm not so soft!'

Several times, on these marches, he was arrested, and it was during one of his spells in the watch-house, among a group of students, that he found his brother Pearsall, in an adjoining cell full of derelicts, drunks and half-caste youths in boxer-shorts and torn and bloodied singlets.

'It was a shock, Phil, I can't tell you. I couldn' believe it at first. My heart – it just dropped right into me boots. There I was on one side of the bars, with my lot, and there was poor Pearse. He pretended not to know who I was at first – as if *I* was the one who'd changed. Then he cried like a baby. Terrible! It was terrible! Thank heavens it wasn't Frank who found him like that. He'd been sleeping rough, in building sites and bus shelters an' that, he looked awful. You know – hair all down over his shoulders and nails like – like animal claws. He was sick as well. These derros injure themselves and don't even know they've done it. He was all raw scabs. He looked so old. And you know he was the youngest of us, Pearse. Can't hardly be fifty. I kept saying to myself, thank heavens Frank can't see him! You mustn't tell him, Phil. I can look after Pearse, I always could, I know how to *handle* him. Frank's had enough.'

So for a time, as well as his 'youngsters', Tam had his brother Pearsall to care for, a terrible man. Violent, unpredictable, he scrounged money from the students and stole and sold their books, he moped, raged, attacked people, and had once a fortnight at least to be bailed out of the watch-house after being picked up in one of the parks. Tam was infinitely patient with him. But at last, on one of these drinking bouts, he disappeared altogether and could not be traced. For three nights Tam and I roamed the railway-yards with their abandoned carriages, and all the dark places of the city, searching for him and making enquiries of foul-mouthed, foul-smelling bundles who might have seen him somewhere or been with him earlier that night or the day or night before, and who looked at us, when they did not start up all claws, out of a distance like the gap between species.

It was a grim business, that progress from Albert Park, round the swamplands along Gilcrist Avenue and the golf links, through bare dark churchyards in the Valley, across the river to South Brisbane. There were vagrants everywhere, either alone or in groups under the trees.

'People don't know about this, Phil, or they wouldn' let it happen. You've got to have one of your own, and see him go down, or you don't even know it's there. You just walk past. You don't know it exists.'

Tam stood on the pavement in his worn overcoat and moaned.

'And there's so many! The place is full of them. Why doesn't somebody do something? It makes me so wild I could just *punch* someone, *anyone*! How does it happen?'

He shivered, folded his arms, clasped himself.

'No I shouldn' say that. I *know* how it happens. It's so easy. Take me home, Phil, it's no good looking any more. We won't find him now. He's gone somewhere right under.'

He raised his head and looked at me.

'You won't believe this, Phil, because you only saw him in his bad days, when he wasn't himself, but he was that – sweet-natured, Pearse, when he was a little kid. He had the nicest nature of any of us, you ask Frank. No, you mustn't do that! But it's true. An' he was clever as well, when he was little. It'd kill Frank to see this.'

So it was that my Aunt Roo had occasion to challenge me, one evening, about my reputation.

'I believe you act for radicals,' she complained. 'Like that Tam Harland. I told you ages ago, pet, those people are no good. Even if he is so famous, that other one!'

'Oh, for Heaven's sake Auntie! Tam Harland isn't a radical.'

'Well he acts like one, I've seen his name in the papers. Resisting arrest! I don't know how you can do it, knowing what your poor father would think. Those people are concerned with nothing but pulling the world down, they're never satisfied. And in a country like this, where we have *everything!* I don't know what's got into you, Phil. Don't you believe in order? It doesn't make sense. Everything's crazy. I've lived too long.'

This light-hearted conversation, for my aunt had no real concern with public issues, took place not in her mock-Tudor house on Hamilton Heights but on the lawn of a genuine Georgian house in Sydney, under a pole where every morning at eight a flag was run up by a boy in a white jacket, and a jetty with a capstan at the end, and a clean white railing, carried the rights of private ownership far out into the bay.

A rose light was touching the scrub of the headlands opposite – it might have been original, and air still warm from the day's heat danced in across garden-beds planted thick with day-lilies in every colour of rust. We were in deck-chairs drinking tea. Quick, red-breasted bulbuls were in the trees, bobbing their crested heads and squabbling or trilling. On the terrace, beyond, two girls from a hire-service agency were laying a buffet-table. I had turned my chair out of the sun to watch them. They shook out, one after the other, four damask cloths, very stiff and shiny, smoothed them at the corners so that they fell in rounded folds, then laid out plates and cutlery. They were engaged while they did it in some sort of argument that demanded pauses in the work in which one of them, several times over, was led to stop, consider, and lift her shoulders in a shrug. At last the darker and more vocal of the two carried out through the French doors a table-decoration, an epergne with green lily-shaped trumpets. When it was settled dead centre (which the blonde girl judged) and all the little baskets had been hung, the trumpets were filled with delphiniums, and the baskets with pink and white rose-buds.

The blonde girl, in a kind of dream, stood admiring it. With her hands clasped before her and her blonde head tilted she had the look of a solemn votary. The other, flinging some word across her shoulder that made the blonde girl protest, stepped boldly to the terrace balustrade, and stretching her body in an easy, athletic way that made her uniform the flimsiest disguise, took a breath of the view – that is how I saw it: the harbour, the virgin shore, the far-off suntouched towers – entirely fabulous at that distance – of the first city, and the iron arc of the Bridge.

Aunt Roo too had got somewhere. She had got to Vaucluse.

In the mineral boom of '70, when the whole country was on a spree, setting down vast sums or little stock-piled savings against the promise, in parts of the country that no one till then had heard of and few men except abos had ever seen, of deep, invaluable riches – a late, it might even be last revival, in the breasts of shopkeepers, widows, retired schoolteachers, bank clerks, young marrieds and professors of literature, of a belief that the land was more even than they had imagined, and was preparing now, on cash payment and to men filled with the spirit of adventure, to reveal its final and most precious secrets – in those days that brought overnight fortunes to some and ruin to others, Harry Price, Aunt Roo's quiet stockbroker, made a killing: his Poseidon shares went to two hundred and seventy six dollars on the London Exchange.

He had had tips of course, from people in the know. The deep gods had smiled on him, but a government geologist had smiled first.

This stroke of good fortune was followed, a week later, by a stroke of the commoner sort of which he received no notice of all. The deep gods, fickle as ever, had turned away.

Aunt Roo had been fond of the man, though he had had no talent save for the making of money; she mourned him. But finding herself a widow with an income too large to express itself in a mere country town like Brisbane, she decided to risk all and make a change. She settled at Darling Point, and after a decent period during which there was no unseemly gossip, married a newly-bereaved media baron and became the second Lady Ashburn.

Sir Charles, or Ashes as I was encouraged to call him, was a cultivated man, a collector of fine arts from Asia and a foundation member of Musica Viva. He was Hungarian. His family had had the milk-run at Eisenstadt, seat of the Esterhazys and birthplace of Joseph Haydn. Arriving in Australia at the start of the war, penniless and without education, he had begun in the hardware business, moved on to agricultural machinery, bought up cheap (in lieu of a bad debt) a couple of dying country papers and a seed-catalogue, captured one and then two city dailies, got a television franchise, supported and then withdrew his support from a government, and was one of the most powerful men of the day.

He himself had only the simplest tastes – he never drank anything but Carlsberg, but his new lady (unlike the last, a timid and intimidating woman who for as long as anyone had known her had been deaf in five languages) turned out to be a proper hostess. 'Runnymede', under Aunt Roo's management, became the centre of a noisy social scene.

Aunt Roo's gatherings were popular because they were open, up-to-date and wonderfully 'mixed'. Too late into the field to compete with the established hostesses, the Black and White Gang as she called them, who were all anyway the most ferocious snobs, she asked everyone: from High

Court judges and the Anglican Archbishop to the young fellows in leather and jeans who worked for American Boys (they were mostly from Whale Beach in fact, or Swan Hill or Moruya, but affected trans-Pacific accents and were butch and crew-cut in the Californian style), along with big names in medical research, models, molls, Iron Men who were into alchemy, gay activists, black activists, builders' labourers, followers of the Ananda Marg, standover men for the bosses who ran the video games and the Oxford Street gay bars and suburban massage-parlours, left-wing Laborites from Victoria, red-necked Nationalists from the north, poets who had done time for car theft, former opera tenors who had made a fortune out of the health food racket or trained greyhounds.

Style was the thing at these random gatherings, and the high level of display that gave everything here immediate visibility and a hard edge allowed for the widest possible variety of it and the most rapid and radical change. Transformation was commonplace.

So a young surfing-star who read Herman Hesse, a deep-eyed, mild-mannered boy, too self-contained, might catch suddenly in a line of mouth the natural shark-like grimace of a grazier with his eye on office, and perceive something surprising about himself; or in a toss of his blond curls, the empty-headed coquettishness of a media starlet, and perceive something more surprising still. Or a High Court judge might see himself for a moment as an American Boy, and after chatting up various members of that blond, blue-eyed team of nicely set-up young fellows, alarm the wife of a colleague with the twang he had acquired, and an odd thrusting-forward of his crotch in the loose-fitting evening trousers that suggested jockeys and jeans. Mouths, noses, jaws, ears, breasts had a way here of travelling and transposing themselves. It was part of the new openness, a breakdown in the structure of things that made them relative, flexible. Reality was just as it appeared to be. I recalled what Aunt Roo had once told me: 'Actors don't pretend to be other people; they become themselves by finding other people inside them.' Her genius was for creating occasions where actors, as she defined them, were given scope. I was astonished how clearly, and how early, she had grasped a principle that was at work everywhere now. We had just caught up with her.

Long years ago, when my life had not yet declared itself to me, I had thought of devoting myself to Latin and Greek. I liked the idea (or thought I did) of a language that had stopped growing and was past change. I thought it might be safe. (I had an odd idea of the classics, being essentially a romantic, and an odd idea as well of what might constitute safety.)

Now, so much later, in Sydney, I was offered another chance, and it amused me that it should appear in what seemed to me to be a Roman form – except that Rome was not the finished dream of a provincial youth in love with his own lateness, but what it must always have been, an utterly unsafe and slippery world of cheap deals, ruthless blood-lettings, shabby betrayals; of flesh, knives, pillows, costumes, cash – I mean my Aunt Roo's world, with Ashes, broken nose and accent and all, as an emperor from the provinces and my Aunt Roo, with her frizzled Afro and her flat-chested diaphanous gowns, as his scheming consort.

'Listen pet,' she told me, 'your Uncle Ashes wants to do something for you. He's soft-hearted really, whatever they say of him. He respects you, he appreciates your abilities, he thinks of you as a son. His own sons, poor pet, are monsters. They've done everything they can to hurt him – it's not just that they're Hungarians.'

(One of these sons had started up a rival transport business that had driven his father's company to the wall. I had a Brisbane client, a friend of Ashes, who had gone bankrupt over the affair. The other worked for a libertarian newspaper and regularly pilloried his father and all he stood for.)

'Why don't you let Ashes help you, Phil? He'd do it because he's fond of you, and because he's a little bit fond of me as well and you're my nephew, the only one I have.' She smiled weakly, and laying her hand over mine she pressed it. 'I feel, Phil – it's difficult to say this – I feel we'd be doing something for your father. But also, you know,' and she began to weep, 'for your poor grandfather. I loved him and I treated him so badly, I really did! I'm sorry now and it's too late to tell him. Can you understand any of this? Can you, pet? I feel so alone sometimes. Except for you and poor Connie there's no one left, no one who's actual *family*.' She began to weep passionately now.

'Aunt Roo,' I said firmly.

'Yes kitten, I know. But sometimes I can't help it. Will you let Ashes speak to you? Will you let him help you?'

'I'll listen, I always do, don't I? But, you know, I'm doing quite well already.'

'In Brisbane?'

'Why not?'

'Defending radicals and riff-raff?'

'Aunty, we've been through all that. But I promise, if Ashes has anything to say, to *offer*, I'll consider it, I really will.'

He was a shy man, and I wondered sometimes, hearing my radical friends describe him, how he had come to be a monster. I never heard him say a bad word of anyone. They were all good fellows really, even his enemies, 'Zough not so clever, you know, ass zey sink.' He would tap his skull with a forefinger and show his gapped teeth in a grin.

He liked each morning to stand at the breakfast-room window (he would consult his watch and get up from the table) to see his flag raised on the lawn. Standing very solemnly with his shoulders back he would watch the colourful rag creep up the pole, like the servant of some far-flung empire, renewing himself at the source.

Some mornings, in his shabby silk gown, he would look quite bowed and defeated. Perhaps he had woken in the night and heard his god deserting him, creeping away over the Axminster carpet. He had a wounded look: no longer the emperor but the emperor's statue, even its godlike power in dispute and the broken nose even further mutilated by irreverent hands. Shuffling to the window he would watch the flag go up, and it was as if the uniformed attendant was the merest sop to reality – the flag climbed by the force of his attention upon it in an act of heroic will. When he turned he looked younger, fresher, fully restored to his own being. He rubbed his hands, grinned, descended on the world again, where it sat in the shape of an egg in a china cup, and tapped and cracked it.

Watching him spoon coddled white into his mouth, I thought that the mysteries of power might be greater even than the mysteries of love.

And the man really was fond of me. He would take my hand sometimes in his hairy fist and shake it so that I too felt the animal power; but was too shy to say anything or to make a clear offer. Perhaps he feared to let me see into his affairs. He wanted me to play the ideal son, and the facts of how he exercised authority would not bear scrutiny. (His own sons had done just what he expected of them: shown themselves true offspring of the wolf.) He tended to avoid my eye when the table-talk turned to business. What he preferred was to call me into his den when he had a record on, settle me with a glass, pour himself a Carlsberg, and with his sleeves rolled up share with me, beyond the actualities of ordinary discourse, the triumphs of that other boy from Eisenstadt who had also made good, his beloved Haydn.

'He iss ze real master, you know' he would tell me with passion. 'He iss half a peasant, you can hear zat – hear? – zat drone? – and half a prince, but superior absolutely to hiss own princes. No fuss, no fuss, zat iss ze master for you.' He would draw his great head down to his shoulders and make little percussive noises with his lips. 'Zat drone he would have heard ass a boy – oh, any Sunday, from a village band. And he takes it into ze halls of princes!'

'So what do you sink of all zis?' he asked me once as we wandered glass in hand through the throng. His gesture suggested that he had just conjured the whole show up.

I shrugged my shoulders and began, with a preliminary 'Oh,' what was never meant to be a reply. He laughed and slapped me lightly on the back, and I was reminded, in a ghostly way, of Uncle Haro; I wondered if Aunt Roo had ever seen the resemblance. One of his secrets, I saw, was to make no judgments of people, and no demand either except that they obey his will.

'Look,' he said with a grin. 'It's Hector.'

Close by, in a group of over-dressed women, a man was standing on one foot, holding the other, which was obscenely naked and white, in the air before him. Hanging from the ends of his fingers, and retaining the shape of the foot like a black skin he had slipped off, was a transparent sock.

He was a Scotsman called Hector McPhail, a handsome man of sixty with a crest of silver hair, an unmistakable figure. I had seen a woman swim up to him once at one of these promiscuous affairs and say breathlessly: 'It's you, I know it is! You're Hector McPhail.' 'Oh my dear woman,' he told her grandly, sweeping a hand over his shining hair, 'I wish I were. But you do me too much honour, to take me for that extraordinary genius!'

He was a painter, very much admired and not at all a fake; but a talent for play-acting, his infallible touch, and the success it had brought him, made him fear that he was. He drank too much and was a great performer for ladies.

'You see,' he was explaining now, 'we all have a totem just like the abos, but a secret one, though our bodies sometimes betray it. I've got these webbed feet for instance. See?' He displayed one, standing firm on the other like a dancer, and did not wobble. He lifted his head on the rather scraggy neck and showed his crest. The naked foot, which looked as if it had never seen sunlight, was indeed webbed.

The ladies looked at it askance; as if it might stand for something other than itself, or as if a great man's feet, if they were not of clay, ought to remain discreetly hidden. Or maybe they feared that his penetrating eye had discerned their own totem: the mushroom, the butcher-bird, the red-necked paddymelon.

He glanced up, caught my eye, gave a half-shy grin and said: 'Hello, Phil, how's the old Frank?'

The ladies turned to see who it was but saw no one they recognized.

Hector's enquiry was ritual. He admired Frank and had often asked me with real solicitude if there was anything he could send him, anything he might need. But this public question, the result usually of my surprising him in a performance he was not quite proud of, was a spell to ward off an alien and uneasy spirit.

'Now Sir Charles there, Ashes,' he announced, 'is a kind of giant panda, see?'

Uncle Ashes beamed.

In her old way of deep loyalty to 'causes', Aunt Roo introduced me once again to Jacky, since she too had 'got somewhere'. She had made a name for herself (it wasn't her own of course) as a designer of trim custom-made clothes for the boutiques. She was married, separated and had two small boys.

'Poor Jacky. He was a brute that Bailey Gayle, I can't tell you the life he led her. She's so brave! But she always was, Jacky, she's got grit. She stuck to him when any other woman would have –. Oh, I could have predicted the sort of hopeless type she'd go for! Smooth as cream. But he beat her up on the quiet, she was always having to lie and hide the bruises. Soft but brutal, you know the sort, they're always like that. Blond, puffy. He had lovely white hands that looked as if they wouldn't know how to make a fist – no visible bones. But he broke the poor girl's arm once, then went to all his friends – his women friends as well as the men – and whined for sympathy because she'd made him violent. Well, that was *his* line – expecting people to take pity on him because he was a brute. She needs a break at last, she's been unfortunate. And she's got a soft spot for you, Phil, deep down, she always did have. You were the type she should have gone for.'

'What type's that?' I asked ironically.

Aunt Roo gave me one of her looks. She had no use for irony. 'Well not a brute, anyway. Because you know, pet, you're quite tough in the end. It's the soft men go for violence.'

'Is this another of your theories, Auntie?'

'No, it's observation. I've been around long enough, you know, to do some observing of my own.'

Just the same, Jacky, when we finally got round to speaking of it, had a different story to tell.

'It's true what Bailey says, though he does himself no good going round confessing to people. It's disgusting in fact. He ought to have more pride. But we were happy enough for a while.' Her brow creased. Always utterly honest with herself she made an amendment. 'No that's not true either – it was blissful. Only I frustrated him, I was too dissatisfied with things, too restless, he had to hit out to save himself. Then he found he got more satisfaction out of that than –. Well, maybe it was what I wanted as well, the bruises were proof of something. But Roo's wrong, I didn't hide them. I went round showing them off like medals! People bring out the worst in one another.' She gave a nervous laugh. 'Actually, I look at him sometimes, great soppy blond thing that he is, when he comes round to take the boys, and I think he's still the most *delicious* man I ever saw. That'd shock Roo. She'd think I was crazy. But there it is.'

It came to be a custom that on afternoons when I was free I would go out in the green van she drove to help Jacky make deliveries. We would sit sipping flagon white in little partitioned spaces at the back of boutiques, among the new creations on hangers, while Jacky and her friends, easy self-confident girls who were mostly separated as she was, laughed, joked, teased and drew me in. I felt like a schoolboy, raw and provincial. I had no talent for slipping in and out of skins; it required a kind of wit I entirely lacked. I felt the weight of my seriousness. Though they were not unkind. Just quietly amused that people elsewhere, it seemed, lived differently.

It was more than a difference of style, which was the word they used over and over. It was, I thought, a question of character – an old fashioned word that nobody used at all. It had to do with pasts, with futures. To justify myself to them I would have had to produce my whole life, my father with his small-town dandyism and extravagance, my grandfather, Aunt Ollie, Aunt Roo as she had been in the old days and was now. It would have been the history of a place more coherent than this, more settled, and for all its tropical realities of heat and storm, more English – all terms that had no currency here. Most of all, I would have had to produce Frank; not as the Bottlebrush Man of the newspaper headlines but as he was.

It was my devotion to Frank that I might have found it hardest to account for. What had begun casually, almost by accident, had become a vocation – that was how I saw it; and not just a vocation either; a fate. When I looked back to the beginning (but where had it begun? At the Pier Pictures, in my father's interest in prodigies and lame ducks?), and puzzled over *myself*, over a temperament and all that had shaped it, Frank was central, I could see that now. Everything had conspired to make him so. I had developed, I guessed, some of his oddness – that too was a matter of character declaring itself at last.

In my relationship with Jacky it was Frank now, not Gerald who stood between us. Years back, when we had parted and gone our ways, seeking lives to replace the one we might have shared, it was Frank who had become my responsibility. For Jacky it was her boys.

Two small insistent bodies, very different from one another and too stubborn in their demands to be ignored, they were called Errol and Mark. I was fond of them but would not let them call me uncle, though they would have preferred it; it would have made things easier with their friends.

In the end, with that flair for the truth that rhymes sometimes reveal, especially as children hear them, they found their own name for me: Phil the Dill.

[3]

The island always had something new for him. He spent long hours poking about in bits of scrub, among sandy patches where blackboys grew among shimmering, sunlight-silvered grasstops, always with an eye for the detail that was essential and repeated, small-scale and large: the coiled shell-shape of fern buds or the line of regular knobs along the backbone of a frond.

Each morning, just after dawn, he took a solitary walk along the shore. From far off I would see him splashing through channels where the beach was scored with light, stooping in his old hat to examine a ghost-crab frozen on the sand and waiting to scuttle off down a pinhole, the three-toed print of an oyster-catcher, or the bird itself holding its profile against the sea, its scissor-beak shut but its eye, sharper than the beak, alert to pounce. Gulls scattered before him, lifting their legs out of the wet, and took off yelping, clappering. When he came back it would be with new additions to the hoard of beach finds that lay in piles on table tops and rickety shelves or in heaps outside the entrance to the tent: land things the sea had taken that came back shaped by the sea, the shucking of forests, transparent crab or cicada-shapes where a creature had slipped out of itself, twists of frayed rope, horned driftwood, moulded plastic, lumps of pumice, cuttlefish bones. One afternoon, turning over all this evidence of the island's life, and of the life around it, I found something unlikely.

'What's this, Frank?'

He was taken off-guard for a moment. As always when first challenged he closed himself tight against scrutiny, then with a shy grin opened up, let me into a secret.

'It's a present,' he told me. 'From a young lady.'

It was a little gold-and-black-striped tiger in nylon fur, of the kind that bobs about over dashboards or in the rear window of cars.

'There are these young people. They come over to surf. They've been coming – oh, for ages. They drop in sometimes for a cuppa. Jeff and Darren are the boys and the girl's Katie. They don't read the newspapers so they don't know I'm a *misfit*. They seem – well they've sort of adopted me, they call me –' He gave a chuckle and would have swallowed the word, but at last got it out. 'Pop! They call me Pop.' He glanced up to see how I took it. 'They're not just being kind, you know. They treat me – well you'll see how. The boys are very beautiful. It's frightening.'

He sat very still, grown serious again, and shook his head over whatever vision it was he had called up; he was not easy with it. He turned away to his work, and we sat on in silence while bees stumbled about on their rounds, flies bubbled or whizzed, and the long downward-pointing gum-leaves turned from pink to grey as the sun shifted.

I did see them at last. One Sunday afternoon when we were seated together in the deepening light, Frank hunched over his work, I on that occasion reading to him from a new book, there was a shout from below. Frank, brush in hand, went to the edge of the workshop. A barefoot, half-naked figure had appeared about fifty yards off on the white-sand path.

'Hi Pop, seeyah!'

'Hi Jeff. Aren't you coming up?'

'Nah, you got visitors, we'll seeyah next week. Just wanted to make sure you were O.K.'

'I'm O.K.'

'Good then. Seeyah Sunday arvo.'

Frank lifted his hand and stood for a moment watching the figure move off in silhouette through the line of trees.

'That was Jeff,' he told me when he had come back and settled. 'He's a panel-beater at Barnes Auto. He's the one that does the talking. Darren's a house-painter. All *he* ever says is un*reeel*.' He chuckled and repeated it in something like the boy's voice: 'Un*reel*! Katie says hiya, then she starts cleaning up. She reckons I'm a bit of a mess – can't see why, can you?' He glanced round at the shambles that was his camp. I had seldom seen him in a better humour. 'She's doing a diploma in Human Movements whatever that is. I'd rather not think.'

I met them, all three, when they appeared one Saturday afternoon on their way to the surf. They had left their boards and a bag full of provisions at the entrance to the clearing, and came, light-footed, half-clothed, along the narrow path between the banksias, and were disconcerted at first to find he was not alone. They held back, like shy natives, and it was only Frank's obvious disappointment I think that made them agree at last to come on to the camp.

The two boys shook hands, rough but formal, then fell back. They were used to having him to themselves.

Very contained and serious, they were not much more than schoolboys, sixteen at the most. They wore board-shorts, nothing else, but their nakedness was a uniform that covered them like armour, they were unconscious of it; physical perfection was accidental like any other attribute. It was this, I guessed, that had made Frank qualify his declaration of beauty. You had to look close to see, behind identical muscles and leathery tan, blond sun-bleached hair and faces patched raw pink, how different they were.

The bolder of the two stood warily alert. Not hostile exactly but on the lookout. This was Jeff, the one who did the talking, though he said nothing at all now; he narrowed his green eyes, watching me. The effort of standing tall gave him an air of childish concentration, as if he were focusing on a difficult mental problem.

The other was all looseness. He kept his eye on the first, ready to support or follow, and affected the same half-tough stance, but could not manage it.

It was Katie who was really at ease. In no way challenged, and not in the least intimidated by my clothes or the way I talked, or by any suggestion I might have given of a previous claim, she weighed me up. She had reserves of irony, I guessed, that her companions knew nothing of.

Frank meanwhile was dancing about preparing tea; delighted both by the arrival of his young friends and by the slight embarrassment we caused one another.

Katie came and stood beside me at the table. With a half-hearted flick of her hand she shooed off half a dozen wasps. They had found the remains of some cold chops and were tearing, with persistence, at gobbets of fat.

'Pop,' she said, giving me one of her sharp looks. 'Is he somebody, then? Is he a millionaire or something?'

I laughed. 'Whatever made you think that? He's a painter.'

'Oh I know *that*. I saw a programme on TV, that's all. This old bloke was a millionaire.'

'That's different,' I said, 'that's American. Frank is just – Frank.'

She grinned and seemed pleased. 'That's what Jeff says!'

Frank by now had drawn the two boys out. They were engaged in conversation, exchanging words that were mostly ritual. The boys sat on up-turned fruit-cases, Frank on the edge of his work-bench, hugging his knees.

'You been all right then, have you?' Jeff asked. 'That spotta rain Wednesday. Djuget any a' that?'

'A few drops. Nothing to write home about.'

'Rained like buggery out Jindalee, eh Darren?'

'Unreal! It was unreal.'

Jeff lifted his chin and jerked it westward. 'Waddabout that rope on the hammock? Needs changin'.'

'Yairs. I already thought.'

'We'll bring some Saturday, eh Darren? You remind me.'

'He's terrific, isn't he?' Katie was saying. Her eye was on Frank. He was, I saw, their very own discovery, a kind of wonder the island had thrown up. She didn't resent me as Jeff did, but she could not see how I might be fitted to an idea of Frank that was already complete, entirely of this place and no other.

'He's very fond of you all,' I told her. 'You mean a lot to him.'

'Do we?' She grinned. Then, accepting a responsibility, she creased her brow and regarded the pile of dirty plates with their scraps of charred fat, and the clutter in which they had been set down, as if forever.

'I keep telling myself I'll get down and clean this place up,' she said, 'but look at it! You wouldn' know where to start.'

She began gingerly to shift a plate from one part of the table to another. But this too was ritual. When Jeff called, 'Hey Katie, we're off,' she gave the plates another shove, made a face at me, and let it go till next time.

'Right then, we'll be off,' Jeff announced, getting up and standing squarely at the entrance to the tent. 'Seeyah Saturday, Pop, we'll bring that rope. Anythink else you can think of?'

Darren too had risen. They bulked in the doorway, and Jeff, still wary but more confident now, stepped forward and put out his hand. Very formally, we shook.

'Right then, seeyah Pop. Take care a'yerself.'

Frank stood at the tentpole and watched them move off lightly over the leaves. He raised his hand. They had stopped at the edge of the clearing to resume their things, and all three looked back now and were waving. Then the boys took up their surf-boards, Katie her armful of packages, and they moved on.

So it happened that two or three times each year, when something unusual came up, I would hear from Jeff, either at home or at the office. He was always very formal and constrained, aware of a difference between us, but over the years we came to admit to ourselves, and tacitly to one another, that Frank was a shared responsibility. We might have been brothers, with nothing in common but a loved and difficult parent.

'I been tryin' t' get 'im to close in the hut,' Jeff would tell me, 'but you know what 'e's like. S'like takin' to a brick wall. Offered t' come down with Darren an' do it for 'im, but 'e's that stubborn, Frank, I got nowhere. D'y' reckon you could talk 'im into it? Katie's worried 'e'll get pneumonia. Gets bloody cold these nights. We worry, both of us.'

On one occasion he was wiped out by a fire. A great wall of flame came sweeping through his camp. He lay in a hollow in the ground and let it roar over him. His hut and tent were burned and the forest all round was blackened and strewn with small furred animals turned to balls of char, but Frank got up without even a scorchmark, tore the last black tatters off his tent-frame, salvaged what he could of his saucepans, mugs, bottles, and began all over again.

'It was the smell I didn' care for,' he told us. 'The heat was nothing much, it was too quick. Good practice, I reckon, for you-know-where. But the smell was horrible. And it'd break your heart to see those echidnas curled up on themselves and turned to ash. And the paddymelons. An' birds even! They must of fallen straight out of the sky. All the heat goes up, y' see, so I went down.'

On yet another occasion when a cyclone blew up lashing the whole coast, carrying away beaches in great king-tides, shredding forests, flattening the flimsy wooden settlements along the shore, leaving a trail of smashed timber and sheet-iron and soaked bags in its wake and flooding all the low-lying suburbs of the city, I had a quick call from Jeff at six o'clock on the Saturday night. He was ringing from the public phone box at the parking-place.

'He's O.K.,' Jeff told me. 'Got a walloping but! Lost the roof off the hut and half 'is stuff is down the beach. It's not too bad, considering. Darren's with us. We'll help 'im get a roof on and 'e'll do the rest 'imself. Oh yes, *he's* in good shape, never better. Cyclone was a bit of entertainment. You should see 'im! Jumpin' round like a two-year-old.'

I went down myself next morning. In the damp wreckage of his camp, amid torn leaves and twigs and whole branches that had been scattered about the clearing, he was working away stripped to the waist, still humming with the energy and excitement of it all.

'You should of been here, Phil. It was –. You could hear the sea buzzing like a great swarm, that was the first thing. Then it roared like it was going to break right over the island. Just the wind at first. All the trees they rose up, you'd of thought they were going to lift themselves right out of the earth. They rose up –' He himself rose on tiptoe and stretched his arms skyward – 'the whole forest! It was extraordinary. An' I reckon they'd of done it too if the rain hadn't come on. It was the rain that held it all down, bashed it back into the ground again, it was that heavy. You couldn't stand up in it. I tried to and it kept beatin' me back into the mud. I thought I'd drown. I reckon that's why the trees didn't make it, not this time. My hut did but. It shook and shook, then it lifted itself right up, turned a coupla sommersaults as it went, and sailed right away over the tops of the trees like a kiddy's kite. I'd of been scared of following it if the rain hadn't come. I just slithered about then, holding on to the tentpole, and the rain was like bloody fists, beating me into the ground, and my nose and mouth were so full of it I thought this is it Frank, you're goin' t' be buried standing up, or drowned an' buried both at the same time. What an experience! But look, no damage at all. Or hardly.'

He indicated the tentpole, the clearing, which was smashed and faintly steaming in the sunlight, and himself with only minor scratches.

'Of course I lost a few things. They just went sailing off after the roof. I was holding on to the tentpole with one hand and tryin' t' grab 'em out of the air with the other as they went whippin' past. They were bein' sort of sucked down a plughole – only *up* if you know what I mean. That old army blanket a' mine – you know the one. Had it since the army. Well, that went. An' me army sweater! Oh, and heaps a' things! Still, it could of been worse. The boys 'v been and we're building a new studio. A proper one. It'll last this time. It'll last me out, any rate.'

He was happier, I think, than I had ever seen him. Some of the storm's electric violence had got into him as he lay huddled under his tent, holding fast to a raw pole of it and feeling the vibrations go down through him, the strokes of power. Out of a black sky a palpable force had hauled and tugged at the pole, trying to wrench it from his grip and out of the earth; and only the earth had held steady in the black din that was the sea and in the twisting and turning of the sky, as the forest drove its roots down but gave up leaves and limbs. He had held on to the pole for seven hours. First in the sick light, then in darkness. Till just before dawn the wind simply dropped into the middle of the island like a stone, and when he struggled to his feet and went out it was morning, the first light of creation; astonishingly pale and clear with the slick of new birth on everything, on mud, leaves, branches, and all things wet with colour.

'It was what Hopkins was tryin' t' show me,' he said dreamily. 'I see that now. I thought I'd seen it already but I hadn't. You need blackness, a card covered with black, and then all the colours leap out for the first time. I was staggering about drunk with it. Shouting. It wasn't just that I was knocked silly by the storm. And that's when the boys come, Jeff and Darren.' He looked anew at some further vision: two half-naked figures coming in under a wash of rainbow-coloured air. 'They must of – well, it was good of them really. They must of left before it was even over.'

The boys' coming, and their part in the rebuilding of the hut, confirmed a relationship that was already one of the supports of his life. It was for him the vivid physical quality of what he had experienced, the long ordeal of holding for so long to that shuddering pole, of feeling through his wrists and chest and thorax the rhythms of the island itself as it hung on against sea and sky, that had endowed with such force the image of the two boys, who were now in fact young men, stepping up without fuss and calling to him from the path: 'You there, Pop? You oright? – the extraordinary at that point brought down to earth and losing none of its beauty or power.

Recalling the moment, Frank drew his chin down. His expression was childlike and vulnerable. 'I been very fortunate, Phil. At this stage of my life. You don't expect it. It's –'

He made a gesture that took in the hut, the tent, what remained of his possessions, all laid out to dry and faintly steaming in the sun.

'I can't wait to get going again! Maybe it's what I needed, a good shaking up, a good duckin'.' He laughed. 'Well – it was a bit more than I needed in fact, but you can't bargain, can yer? Here, help me with this. I want to get a roof back on. You never know when the buggers 'll start beatin' you flat again.'

I stripped and we worked all afternoon. When I left it was with the satisfaction of knowing that he had, once again, a precarious roof over his head.

It was about this time that I was woken late one night by a telephone call. It was not all that rare an occurrence but rare enough to bring my mother to the door. I made a little sign that was part of the language we had developed, indicating that it was not a family matter but that I would have to go out. I heard her pass through to the kitchen and begin making tea. A few minutes later I was sitting at the bench with her.

It was an odd hour, two-thirty, and I would remember it afterwards by the way the kitchen looked at that time of night.

It was a kitchen of the new kind where everything is out of sight, pots, pans, dishes; no hooks for cups, no spoons or ladles or cannisters; a machine for eating up garbage locked away under the sink. It was all clean white plastic and natural wood, polished and glazed to show the grain. Even the handles by which you opened drawers or cupboards were integrated into the beading, with just a smooth finger-grip underneath. Every surface was unbroken and might have been impenetrable.

It was still hot. Close against the windowpane were the upper branches of a Moreton Bay fig, an old giant going back decades, whose roots were in the cliff. It went down three storeys like the unit block itself and had been saved and included in the plan. Its leaves too looked plastic, glossy-green and tough; but the flying-foxes that had been congregating in its darkness for as long as it had stood there, going back longer perhaps than any of us, still flocked in at dusk to gorge on its seed-filled berries and kept up a continuous disturbance of small furry lives in the cave of its boughs.

Silent by day, when the unit-block was at its most lively, the tree came alive at nightfall as the building was darkened and slept. It was as if life flowed back and forth between the two with the regularity of light and dark. I could hear it rustling now in the strange night-silence, and could hear as well, from down river, the regular thug thug, like a heartbeat, of a dredger, keeping the river-mouth clear of mud.

'Tam thinks he's found Pearsall,' I told my mother at last. 'He wants me to go and try to bring him in.' I looked quickly away.

She saw immediately what it was.

'That – timber yard?'

I nodded.

It was a story that had been all over the evening papers. Early that day, two seven-year-olds wagging school had climbed through a fence into a suburban gully and found a slave camp – that is what the newspapers called it. It was a four-acre timber yard, six miles from the GPO, as all distances are measured in this city, on one of the old tramlines.

Nearly a hundred men had been found in chains there, derelicts, drunks, vagrants, men without home or family. They had been forced to work by day and had slept at night, many of them roped to their cots, in a rat-infested bunk-house. Some had had their bail paid by benefactors at the city watch-house, only to find themselves in a new sort of captivity. Others had been picked up in parks or off the streets. Many were pensioners; their captors had collected their pension money and used it for their keep. But most, having no means of support, were kept by their own labour. They were all men whose passage from a backlane shed or building site, from wagons on the shunting lines at South Brisbane, or from under the fig trees in Musgrave Park, into the slave camp or timber yard had gone quite unnoticed. They had never been missed.

Those who had been there long enough were kept unfettered because they had no will to leave; not even through an open gate. Whatever the horrors (reporters spoke of beatings with lengths of hosepipe, of cots with maggoty sacks for mattress and blanket), the city of regular bus-services and clean citizens and police cars had no temptation for them. No one had ever broken out.

All night the police, with dogs and searchlights set up on wagons, had been hunting down absconders; in the timber yard itself with its great thirty-foot towers of planks and in the dense scrub of the neighbouring gully. Large crowds had gathered from surrounding streets, to watch the men, bearded, barefoot, dirty, many of them wild-eyed with terror, being herded into police vans or ambulances and carried off.

I had seen only a few moments of it, on the news. It had sickened me. The cowed and desperate men, young or old it made no difference, had been driven to resistance at last. They punched out wildly at their deliverers, swearing, shouting, struggling in the arms of the law. One of them, with his head turned away from the cameras for shame, had been forced to show, as a policeman gripped and held up his wrist, the raw mark of chains. And on the other side of a barrier, the spectators: housewives with small round-eyed children in their arms, men in shorts and singlets, boys on bicycles, all staring at what had for so long been going on in their midst. With compassion, some of them, others with distaste or with frank hostility, but all with puzzlement at the appearance in this flat, quiet suburb where everyone minded his business, of a monstrosity, and most of all with wonder at the way these men fought to stay, their unwillingness to come out and join their shocked, uncomprehending neighbours. Backyards ran down into the gully where these men had been chained and beaten. No one had heard or seen anything. Nothing had been reported.

It was a hot night, and people's faces under the lamps were greasy with passion. Episodes of swift, indiscriminate violence kept breaking across the crowd – between police and spectators, police and reporters, or among the spectators themselves. Some spirit of disruption that we had failed to take account of was in the open at last and running loose among us. As the cameras caught them, barefoot spectators, derelicts in their rags, officers of the law who with buttons torn from their shirts lashed out with boots, belts, already-bloodied fists, were thrown savagely together in frame after frame. We were all involved, there was no escape from it.

In the end my mother had got up, turned the set off and walked out of the room, and it was in the light of the last image as it faded from the screen and the obscene shouting died into silence that we felt it difficult now to meet one another's gaze. The kitchen was too still, its surfaces too bare and clean.

My mother leaned across the bench and folded her hands over mine. 'Ring me as soon as you can,' she said. 'Tell Tam I'll come over if – if it's what he thinks. But I hope it isn't.'

Tam was waiting in the dark of the verandah. He was just sitting there on a cane-bottomed chair, hugging himself, his mouth grim and his hair, now that he had let it grow, a tangled mane. The moment he saw me he was on his feet, his mouth working and the spit flying round a jabber of words I could barely comprehend. He took a deep breath, and it so filled him that tears ran down the floury cheeks. I had to hold him and let him gasp himself still.

'I'm all right now,' he assured me, snuffling into a dirty handkerchief. 'Let's get going.'

He marched off on his small feet, determined, unsteady, over the loose planks of the footbridge.

'One of my Maoists wanted to come,' he told me. 'It was good of him, but no, I told him, it's not the time.'

We were on our way to the watch-house, where the more violent of the prisoners were being held. If Pearsall was not there, we would go on to the hospital where they had taken those who were ill. The rest, the worst lot, were in mental wards.

Tam sat hunched in upon himself as we drove and said nothing. Perhaps he too was remembering, at this chill hour of morning, when the streets were blue and only an odd sheet of newspaper lifted and turned under the lamps, those nights, two years ago, when we had gone out like this to examine bundles on the seats of bus-shelters and under a litter of cardboard cartons in empty doorways, and been driven off – on one occasion by a figure, all teeth and hair, that had started up shrieking out of a mound of rags like some kind of crazed animal, while a whole row of men, and a few women, laughed, catcalled, taunted us out of a blurred radiance of metho or cheap port.

The watch-house, when we arrived, was worse than any of that. Dozens of shocked, subdued women, who might have been wives, mothers, sisters, and their sons or sons-in-law, had ignored the police-calls that asked them to wait till an indentification had been made and were packed into the foyer.

Those who had arrived first had fallen back against the walls and were quiet. The recent arrivals were all shouting. The young policeman at the desk had lost control. He too was shouting. He seemed about to burst into tears. Behind him others were taking down names and letting people through, two at a time, to where the men were held.

Tonight, out in the parks, under bridges, in the bus shelters and round building sites, the derelicts would sleep unmolested. There was no more room in here and no forces to go out and bring them in.

A woman was led through the crowd, hysterically weeping. It parted before her.

Difficult to say what she had found in there. It was this consideration, which of the two might be worse, disappointment or discovery, that made the crowd pause and grow still. But almost immediately the shouting resumed, and the shoving to get to the door.

And now, from inside, an eerie howling made itself heard, was added to, and rose in the new silence to a din. It was as if a whole kennel of dogs had been let loose. There was nothing human in it.

The doors were blown open as by an explosion or a sudden gust of wind and a young policeman fell into the crowd. He was howling and holding his hands over his face; they were covered with blood. He was followed immediately by two pale-faced visitors who were hurled out bodily. From inside, amid the howling, shrieks were heard, low grunts and thuds; then the doors again slammed shut. The howling rose to a frenzy, and in a moment the crowd in the waiting room too had begun to howl. The effect was contagious and terrible.

'Tam, this is impossible,' I shouted. 'Come away.'

Tam's face was set. 'No. You needn't stay if you don't want to, but I will. I want to see – the whole of it.'

At last quiet was restored and three or four policemen, very red-faced and dishevelled, one with his shirt ripped all down his back, shouldered their way through a hostile crowd. They were tense, resentful, and one of them still burned with a visible anger; the others were trying to calm him. The air that flowed out with them was like the breath from a sty. Suddenly the angry policeman broke and turned back, the others struggled with him. He struck out wildly and two of his fellow-officers, after a brief scuffle, pinioned his arms and led him off. The crowd fell still.

At last, after what seemed an age, there was a place on one of the benches along the wall and Tam slid into it. Later I too found a place, lay my head back on the cool wall and must have slept.

'Phil?'

Tam was standing before me. The room was almost deserted.

'We can go in now.'

I knew the place well, and Tam knew it too – it was where he had found Pearsall that first time, two years ago; but I had never seen it like this.

Forty or fifty men, long-haired and bearded so that it was difficult to tell the old from the merely worn and ill-used, their faces streaked with grime and sweat or caked with blood, barefoot some, others in broken shoes without socks or boots with the soles flapping, lay sprawled on the floors of the cell or stood trancelike at the bars. They seemed utterly cowed now, but the violence was not gone; it was in abeyance. One felt it in the tense voices of the policemen, who were very tired, and in their bodies, a barely suppressed rage – not, strangely enough, at the condition of these men and those who were responsible for it, but at the men themselves, who continued to give trouble and whose very abjectness, when they did not, aroused disgust. Whatever it was that had allowed them to be chained and beaten provoked others now to beat them again.

My own reaction, in the foul, stinking, breathing presence of them, was not compassion, as I expected, but shame, panic, a sense of deep unclean-ness that made me want to rush out and plunge into salt water – only the clean salt of the ocean would do. What I wanted to re-establish was my own cleanliness, and I felt ashamed of that too.

Tam was made of sterner stuff. He was approaching the men and asking, quietly, if they knew Pearsall or had lately or at any time heard of him. He moved from man to man and was insistent, having understood that it would be impossible to recognize his brother in this crowd – all the men were alike in their filth – and that if he called Pearsall's name he would deny himself, he would crawl for cover among the ragged, indistinguishable bodies and make himself safe.

When he was satisfied at last that the men knew nothing, or if they did, were determined not to tell, he was for going on to the hospital, and from there, if we found no sign of him, to the mental wards. But a policeman told him firmly, though not ungently, that it would not be allowed. The men there would be treated first and nursed back to some sort of normality. All this – he indicated the cells and the waiting room – had been a kind of midnight madness. There would be no more of it.

'I don't know,' Tam told me as we walked away, 'whether I'm glad or sorry. I had a dread of it – of finding him, I mean. That he should have let them – do *that* to him. But if he isn't one of these men, Phil, where is he?'

We had come out into a busy street. Early traffic was on the move. The first buses, the six-five, the six-eleven, were bringing workers into the city, men in overalls with leather kit-bags, boys with duffle-bags, girls in little groups who laughed over their shoulders, their blonde hair freshly rinsed. The morning papers were stacked up on the pavement, being loaded into vans. A thin, grey-headed woman in a smock was setting out cut flowers in pails, tight-packed bunches of stocks, paper cornets of yellow, pink and red rosebuds. The early pubs were open, with all the sash-windows up and the first drinkers setting their glasses along the sill.

But Pearsall was not among the sick or even the mad. He had simply gone lost. He was moving about somewhere by night or day in this city and was invisible.

'I can't believe it, it's all happened so fast,' Tam whispered. 'It seems no time ago that there were five of us. Now there's just me and Frank.'

'And your father,' I reminded.

He looked alarmed for an instant, then recovered some of his wry humour.

'I'll tell you something, Phil. I reckon he'll outlast the lot of us. An' you know what? He knows it, he's always known it, the old bugger! He's up there counting us off!'

[4]

There was to be a Harland retrospective, and slowly, over the months, it began to be put together. I went back and forth between Brisbane and Sydney to consult with trustees, negotiate with owners and to carry messages and apologies from the painter himself. He had decided to stick, as he put it, to the sandflies.

'Too busy,' he snapped, when invited to look over a batch of drawings. 'I don't want t' be lumbered with all that, I'd be put off! Too much back there I don't want t' know about. All those *things*. They'll have t' look after themselves, I got something else t' do. I'm short of time. I'm starting to fall t' bits.' He grinned, showing the gaps in his teeth. 'It's not such a bad way t' go, actually, once you get used to it. They give you time for that. You'd think but,' he added, 'after you'd shucked off so much, that you'd feel – I dunno, freer or lighter or something, or you'd see clearer what it was all about. Well *I* don't. It's just more and more of a *mess!*'

So as the artist himself fell to bits, a catalogue *raisonné* of his works was being assembled, by experts; led by that art-critic who had sweated uphill with me one day at the island and got nothing for it but a placard and the message DIG. He had finally got down to it, he was on his knees; digging up facts, theories, interpretations, influences; re-assembling groups of drawings that had been scattered, deciding on dates and titles. Everyone now wanted to know all there was to know. Real facts, apocryphal stories, letters, they were all relevant; including a scratchy tape from the National Library in Canberra on which a pair of anonymous honey-eaters could be heard filling the silence between Frank's crabbed refusals of speech.

'Yairs,' he told me when I played it to him to see if there was something he wanted to add, 'I remember that lady. Hazel Someone. Hazel. She was nice. A bit dizzy but. I had nothing to say, I'd already said it all, but the birds had a good time. Just listen to 'em! They were after some cake she brought. They really appreciated it. You can hear.'

The paintings began to surface now in great numbers. Some of them hadn't been heard of for nearly forty years.

'My God,' Frank said, looking at the slides. His glasses sat on the end of his nose, his mouth was drawn almost to his chin. 'Did I do that. I ought to've been shot! Some of this stuff I don't even recognize. Y' reckon there could be a Harland *forger*?' He gave a humorous snort. 'I suppose not, I'm not *famous* enough.'

But the sight of so many lost products of his hand produced a profound gloom in him. It was, I suppose, for all the variety and colour, a proof of limits. He was driven back to his work. 'Nah!' he said, refusing to look at any more. 'I'll leave that to the professors, let them decide, I'm too pushed. I'm falling to bits fast now. A good sou'easter and there'd be nothing left of me but the pong!'

It was true. He was suddenly a lot less steady on his feet; he had head-pains, dizzy spells, his sight was failing. It had taken several months before he would see the eye-specialist in Brisbane who got him to throw away at last the glasses he had been using, picked up years ago in a junk shop in Cairns. Twice in the last year he had fallen and been a whole day unable to move.

'I did call out a fair bit,' he admitted. 'I reckon the ants heard. They turned up from everywhere, little buggers! I must be sweeter than I think.'

But when we tried to get him to move to the city, where one or other of us could see he was properly looked after, he wouldn't hear of it. 'What for?' he snapped. 'Why should *I* move? If they want me the buggers can find me *here*.'

There were days, I suspected, when he forgot to eat. Milk sat about in cartons and went sour or was set in saucers for the cats, half-wild blacks and tabbies that had gone feral and haunted the banksia scrub in packs. Food rotted and the rats moved in, till the cats drove them off again. There was a winter when I expected at any moment to hear the phone ring and have to go down and bring him back.

Some of the locals kept an eye on him, and Jeff's surfing friends from the beach. The CIA he called them. 'I can't hardly budge these days,' he complained, 'before the CIA is out. Snooping! They're behind every bloody tree. Some a' the buggers get themselves up as animals I reckon – birds! As if I wouldn't recognize a six-foot budgie when I see one – I'm not that far gone – wearing thongs! Jeff's mates they are, or maybe they're yours. That Mrs Footsy or whatever she's called, down at the shop. She's one. I'm not senile you know, I still got some of me faculties.'

At weekends Jeff and Katie watched him. The call when it came was from Jeff.

You wait for these things; you know they are on the way but when they come they are always a shock. One of the surfies had found Frank on the path to the beach. He had been there a long time, impossible to say how long, but he was sun-burned right through the shirt. He was all scractches and heavily bruised, as if he had been in a fight or had been mauled and clawed at by beasts. His hip was broken. I called the medical helicopter and set off through the early-morning traffic.

Jeff was with him when I arrived, squatting on one heel beside the makeshift stretcher they had used to bring him up from the beach. A steady, serious young man of twenty-three or four, he knew me well enough now to have no defences. He glanced up and his eyes were hopeless.

'Frank?' I whispered.

He lay very still under a blanket, his eyes open but glassy, and stared at the sky. He was so frail I was startled. They had set the stretcher down in a shady place outside the tent and his body scarcely broke the ground.

'Frank?'

He did not move, but the ball of his eye rolled and acknowledged me: there was a slight compression of the lips, not quite a smile. Jeff, who had been calm till now, suddenly broke away, and Frank's gaze followed him. A crease appeared on the brow, the lips moved. *Sorry* he was saying, or trying to say. *Sorry to be such a trouble. To be causing pain.* I shook my head and brushed an ant from his cheek. I think he understood. Once again his eye went to where Jeff stood supporting himself with one arm against the trunk of a bloodwood, the other across his face.

Minutes passed. None of us moved. Frank met my gaze, held it a moment, and I nodded. Silence had never been a burden between us. We had sat for hours sometimes in just such an easy absence of speech while the island spoke for us with its medley of sound, layer on layer of small lives fretting or ticking or whirring above or below us; letting our minds free on the long waves of it. So it was a little time before I identified now, in the familiar hum and click of the place, a new note that was regular, insistent. Rotor blades. Jeff too had heard it. He came and stood at my shoulder, making a shade with his hand.

It was far off over the low shoreline, slipping in sideways out of the blue. It turned, hovered, the big blades swung; the pilot was trying to judge how much room he had. Now it was right above us. Solid sound was clamped over our ears.

Frank too had seen it and heard the low buzzing grow out of the sea.

'It's all right Frank,' I told him. 'It's the helicopter.'

He frowned. In the roar of the engines, perhaps, he had failed to hear me. All round us the trees were stirring. They rose up. They swayed and rustled, they lifted their boughs. Strips flared off tree-trunks, the side of the tent bellied. The ground sprang up and was alive as ants were flicked out of their path, dead leaves flipped over, then bits of solid bark went tumbling and scattering, then stones. In the tent a dozen jam-jars clashed and fell, but soundlessly, with a thud that was lost in the great roaring and whooshing as a hundred feet above us a hole in the sky was opened and everything, turning on its own centre, slowly at first, then with speed, rose up.

'Aaargh.'

Frank gave a long sigh, a sound with no voice behind it, only breath and bones. And now stillness dropped on the clearing, things fell back into their real weight and silence.

'Listen,' Jeff whispered, drawing me back a moment. Frank had already been got ready and the two stretcher-men were carrying him across to the helicopter. 'I've never been up.' He was tense and sweating.

'It's nothing,' I told him. 'Ten minutes.'

He nodded but was deathly pale.

Minutes later we were being lifted over the treetops. Jeff, crouching opposite, his chin drawn up to his knees, watched us fall away sideways from the land, and when he caught my eye gave a sheepish grin, but was still clenching and unclenching his jaw. We were drifting out over the limpid, green-blue waters of the Passage with its channels of a deeper colour, cobalt, and the forests of seaweed lifting and blowing under the surface.

Now the surf-side swings into view: the long beach, tilted, then whitecaps, then endless blue. Southward the Bay and its islands, stretching sixty miles to where the long narrow arm of South Stradbroke touches – or almost touches – the northward-pointing spit of the Broadwater, the air so clear I could see all the way to Southport, twenty-five years back – no, more.

This high free feeling is what it is like to float in time, I tell myself; *beyond the limits, beyond flesh*. I reach out and my fingers find a papery dryness. It has the texture of bark and my fingertips see through it into the earth; so that when, quite casually, my grandfather lays his hand on my head and says 'Thank you boy', I feel the occasion open to include vast stretches of time, the future as well as the past, in which we in our generations are very small, though not unimportant, and a deep contentment comes over me, as of being and belonging just where I am. It is final. It is also a beginning. I am seated once again at the end of Grandpa's bed, curled up hard against the rails. I do not look up from my book, but his breath fills the spaces of it, and I hear him, very softly, call my name; hear it quite distinctly in his still-familiar voice – the moment is open again. It is as if it had taken all this time – thirty years – for the sound to travel the length of the bed and reach me; as you hear a word spoken sometimes and fail to catch its sense, and then later, thirty years later, you hear it clearer and do. I looked up. There were tears on my cheeks.

'Phil. Phil!'

It was Jeff.

It had happened while I was looking away, back or ahead – anyway out across the Bay from a great height.

What is it, Jeff's eyes were asking. What's happened?

I shook my head. He sank back on his haunches.

So it had come at last and would be in all the afternoon papers, a small national event. Harland. You didn't need to add the Christian name; that was for friends. Harland. A household word, evoking the whole story of his having set himself apart, of his choosing to live rough, 'down there', at the very moment when the rest of the continent, the lucky island, was moving deeper in behind a wall of thirty-storey tower blocks and the columns of figures they stood for, into the dazzling light of bathroom-tiles and stainless steel towel-racks, Waterford glass, Christofle tableware. 'Look, that painter bloke –' His death would be commented on, and the works, now that they were complete, would move into a new price-range, a new constellation.

I had been there when it happened – or almost there. So had Jeff. *Yes I was there. No there was nothing, the usual mess. What else would you expect?*

I heard Frank's laughter. 'So now there's nothing left of me but the pong.'

And the pictures, the marvellous pictures.

Our shadow was dancing in over the river-mouth, its intricate system of channels and islands dense with mangroves, all their gothic roots exposed by the tide. Pelicans crowded the mud-banks. Small ships, each with its tumbling sea-wake and an airy wake of gulls, were making their way, not blindly as you could see from so high up, through the maze of narrow openings into the Bay.

We sat one on each side of him, as I had sat the night Gerald died, and when I got up had felt, as my body moved on ahead, that twenty years had passed.

And now they really had passed and I was just where I thought I'd been.

[5]

The Harland retrospective was to be a national festival, something more now than one man's life works, so many stations on the way of Frank Harland's progress from a remote hamlet in Southern Queensland, all sunstruck roofs and stumps in burnt paddocks, to wherever he had at last got to; so many occasions of stooping over a bench, always of the same kind and knocked up by his own hands out of firewood or fruit cases, in the Pier Pictures at Southport, in a boat shed at Cooktown, in the corner of someone's verandah at Yeppoon, an abandoned greenkeeper's cottage at Maryborough, a verandah studio at West End. More too than the visions behind eyes rubbed red after sandgrits or salt had got in them that insisted on the particulate graininess of things.

Seeing the pictures unpacked from their cases and hung at last in the big white-walled rooms, I was astonished by their number, by how much space he had covered in the fifty years of his working life, how many square-yards of canvas, sheets of newsprint, sides of cartons and strips of board; and what sweeps of the imagination he had made that had carried his intense encounters with a few square inches of the world into a dimension that could no longer be named or fixed at a particular latitude, Cooktown or Yeppoon or Dornoch Terrace, or in any decade.

He had never been anywhere much. It didn't matter. It wasn't a question of geography. He had been where the event took him. The pictures were stepping stones. You could set them side by side and they might stretch all the way back to the house at Killarney. You could follow them and find there the lean, intense youth I had so often imagined from his recollection of those early years and from the child I had sometimes glimpsed in Frank himself – a skinny, sandy-headed kid with freckles, hunched over a kitchen table among his sleeping brothers, sketching a head or the play of lamplight on cloth while his father's voice led him out across paddocks in the dark.

But that would get you no further in the end than any other view of him, since the pictures, however you laid them out and whatever allowance you made for gaps (for many of the pictures were still missing) made a line that could not be followed to any known place of beginning or any known beginner.

I had seen as much of Frank over the years as anyone, and might have claimed to have been present at the real occasion of some of his most powerful achievements. The 'Two Fates', when I saw it unpacked, made such a deep impression on me that I could barely speak. It seemed to me to express now just what I had most understood and loved in my Aunt Ollie, and in Della. It was a coincidence of feeling I had known before – on those occasions when, standing before the little landscape in my parents' bedroom at Southport, I had wondered how it was that a picture made by another man in another time and place, and of another landscape, could speak so deeply for my feelings in this one.

I knew enough now to expect no explanation. The thing was a mystery. I paid this much respect to the Frank I knew: I recognized a faculty in him that nothing in the way of intelligence or observation or even sympathy on my part, however deep, would reveal to me. To admit that was to acknowledge the man's uniqueness; but also my own. I had sat in the same light with him in which some of these works came into being and had watched the action of his hand. But all that did was increase the mystery. *I was there. It was not like this. Now it is.*

But if I had been a privileged witness to so much of the work, and a sharer in some of his secrets, there was still more to surprise me on these walls than I expected, and nothing to confirm a cosy familiarity. Some of the early pictures were like nothing I had ever seen him do.

In one a spare, priest-like figure, in what looked like a Ned Kelly helmet made of gauze, was officiating at an altar among golden trunks; out of which he conjured up clouds (was it?) that were made up of a million tiny molecules, a syllabary of living breath. His hands made motions in space: the clouds rose out of the earth. They rose through the branches of trees. They sat on the skyline like a becalmed flat-bottomed fleet.

It was called 'Prospero I', though the painter himself had not named it, and was used to prefigure a series of pictures that I did recognize because I had seen Frank do them: abstracts for which he had had only numbers. I associated them with his wild bees, since I first saw the pictures on the day he took me to see the swarm. We lugged home a kerosene-tin of dark bush-honey, and then he took out the first of the set, showed me what he had been doing, and lay down the preliminary strokes of 'Prospero III'.

So much of it was like that. Impossible to imagine from outside where any of these images had been before he found and set them down – the made things among the things of natural or accidental growth. They were part of another nature, not only his: rock samples or chunks of mineral torn up from the floors of dried-up seas, branches of a hitherto unrecorded flora or skeletons of its fauna, great chipped tablets that told, in an unknown language, of struggles, triumphs, defeats, rites of passage, common loss; the history of a different star. I could have wept. Not only for the power of individual pictures and the joy of seeing again paintings that recalled to me odd moments in Frank's company and the echo, distinctly caught, of his voice; but for the immense distance I felt between the man I had known and the dweller on that star, whose loneliness I had barely touched and had understood only as I translated it into my own terms. The distance was immeasurable.

Their gathering now in a clean, well-lighted place made the paintings even harder to read. Carefully arranged by experts to illustrate a line of development, a phase, or the variation over decades of a theme, they falsified the truth by creating a pattern that was too orderly, too whole. Mess, that was what was missing, and it was essential – the mess that was continuous, beyond the edge of cardboard or paper, with a clawlike hand gripping the raw edge; with frayed and grubby cuffs, untidy scrub stripping in tatters or being torn at by beaks or carted off in parcels by ants; with newsprint still wet with events – all that he had sopped up out of tins and out of his own head once the lid was off, and smeared on with a finger or knife blade or allowed to drip and puddle as he dealt at arm's length with the spurt and flow of things.

I turned away. I did not want, in this public place, to stand back and observe that picture from the Kunsthalle in Wiesbaden, his 'Untitled 14', that had been Frank's tribute in red to Knack and Edna, his sharing of their fate.

I made quickly for the far-off exit, but was arrested by a group of early pictures that was, the experts told us, of only documentary interest: apprentice work from the artist's youth. It was the fragmentary set of landscapes to which our own picture belonged, a dozen variations, alike but sharply different, in blue and green.

They were evocations of Killarney. I saw that now. Not perhaps of the place itself but of some idea of it, some ideal, that might have been the same idea that was in the head of the original Harlands, Frank's forebears, when they named it for a place in Ireland they had never set eyes on but felt for because their parents had. Could any of them be identified, I wondered, as a parcel of actual land, a potato field or cow paddock, Pint Pot Creek Farm or Warlock's Spinney, for which I held the deeds in my Brisbane office? – part of the achievement, over long years, of a dream that Frank himself had seen the folly of before he even stopped buying up the last piece of it, and which would be inherited now, as his will directed, by Tam, by Pearsall if he could be found, by his father.

I thought of my own landscape with its break of light on the horizon (it would be mine if it ever turned up again, I too stood at the end of a line) and decided I had seen enough. I would take the rest on trust: all those fragments of blue-green, green-gold forest, and the skyscrapers of the Pacific climbing up, up, them tumbling in a wreck of stars.

[6]

The party, by Aunt Roo's standards, was a small one, got up like those late-night affairs of so many years ago on the spur of the moment, out of a reluctance she always felt, when she saw people kissing goodbye or lingering around cloakrooms, to let an occasion end. When I heard them arriving and went out to see what it was a line of a dozen cars was winding up the drive, slowed to funeral pace by Aunt Roo's Daimler. She was bringing a couple of art dealers from Melbourne and a girl in castoffs from Tempe Tip, who had dived into the back seat at the last moment and was Hector McPhail's girlfriend or step-daughter or niece; Hector was so pissed, she told them, that she wouldn't drive with him. 'Hullo, Phil,' he said, stumbling up the long steps in a crumpled white suit. He stopped dead before me, and the rest of the formula hung unspoken between us; he giggled at the gap. Then he said very soberly: 'Hullo, mate. We're the party for Frank's wake.'

Below, on the gravel, people were climbing out of cars, the women lifting the hems of their skirts and looking dazzled as they came up the steps to the lighted facade, the men calling from car to car with parking-instructions. Doors slammed. One man in a dinner-suit stood against a cypress to piss.

'Sorry pet,' Aunt Roo whispered as she hurried on into the house, 'it just happened. You know how it is.'

Within minutes she had summoned up drinks, music, a grumpy maid, and had us gathered in the back sitting-room. A former conservatory, it opened on to the terrace, and was bare save for a Steinway and some lifesized woollen sculptures, four of which, drunkenly asprawl, sat at a nursery-table drinking from knitted cups while two more, passionately entangled, stared at one another's eyeballs on the floor.

The couple from Melbourne were called the Munts. Arthur Munt, a big man, wore a blue boiler-suit, his wife pigtails, a pinafore, a blouse with leg o' mutton sleeves and banded red-and-white stockings.

Suddenly there was a commotion in the hall, more arrivals. It was Jim Dalton the television interviewer. People crowded forward to see him lead in an old fellow who had caused a sensation at the Gallery and whom everyone now wanted to meet.

'That man,' Mrs Munt informed me, 'is extraordinary, I saw him at the Gallery. He's Frank Harland's father and he's eighty-six years old. You should hear him talk! I've never heard anything like it – that sort of eloquence, these days. And that old fake Frank used to pretend he was a boy from the sticks! That man is magnificent.'

The magnificent Clem Harland, in a new suit and with a big spotted handkerchief in his breast pocket, looked very pleased with himself. It was more than twenty years since I had last seen him. He didn't look a day older. He had the sort of smooth, babylike features that life does not touch, and stood now – vacant, expectant, his grey hair tingling you felt with electricity – ready to make the most of everything – the eats, the drink – and already casting about for a receptive ear.

'He talked on TV,' Mrs Munt told me in a whisper, 'and afterwards as well. Someone, thank God, had the foresight to get it down on tape. We should be recording all these old people. Look,' she said even lower, 'there's that Hector McPhail. He looks dreadful. If he keeps on jigging about like that he'll have a heart attack. Serve him right!'

Jacky slipped in from the garden, nodded briskly to Mrs Munt, and turning aside, whispered: 'Have you seen Frank Harland's father? He was at the Gallery. He told us how Harland liked his bread pudding – on the wet side – then burst into tears. He's a stunner. They're all crazy about him.'

It was at this point, when the party was already in full swing, that a disturbance occurred out on the terrace and everyone's attention was drawn. A woman in a flannel nightie had appeared there and was in vigorous argument with others. Observing a couple who were out admiring the view, she had stepped through the French windows and challenged them, demanding who they were, how they had got into the house, and what, at that time of the night, they thought they were doing.

'This is the residence of Lady Ashburn,' she told them grandly, 'you're trespassing – if not worse! I'm in charge here. Lady Ashburn's out. You'd better leave before she gets back or I'll be in the pooh.'

But seeing, when she followed their gaze, that her sister was there after all and that some sort of party was in progress, she changed her tack.

'Good evening,' she told Arthur Munt, since despite the boiler-suit he appeared not to be a burglar, 'I'm Lady Ashburn's sister. From Brisbane. Do you happen to have seen my husband Jack? He's a very tall man. He's wearing –'

Her memory got hooked on the word. Looking down at her own state of undress she frowned and acknowledged a second error. 'Fools!' she muttered and stalked off.

She came to a halt in the very centre of the room, and finding herself surrounded by strangers, she clasped her nightie to her in a clenched fist and screwing her eyes shut, simply stood, in the belief perhaps that when she opened them again all these people would have vanished and she would be back in her own bed. She stood quite still on the rug and wished us away.

I touched her elbow.

'Aunt Connie.'

The eyes snapped open.

'Oh, Phil dear, it's you. I'm so relieved! I was asleep, but I woke up feeling peckish so I went out to the kitchen – you know your Aunt Roo always has such delicious things in the fridge – only tit-bits, nothing really substantial, but the very best. Then I heard the voices. Is it a celebration?'

'It's people who've been to an exhibition, Auntie. Frank Harland.'

'What?'

She was deaf. I had to repeat the name so loud that it must have sounded, in the silence, like the announcement of his imminent return.

'Oh *him*,' she said with disgust. 'Is *he* here? One of your father's lame ducks, Phil,' and with a little laugh she turned to explain it to Mrs Munt. 'My mother couldn't stand the sight of him. We used to call him the iceman, Roo and I, because of Ollie. There was this iceman who courted – well it's complicated, you wouldn't understand. I can't be bothered with it. Huh,' she said, 'Frank Harland! I wonder what happened to *him*?'

It was for her a name from thirty years back at Southport, not the happiest time of her life. She was astonished after so long, and here in Sydney, to have it crop up again. A bad sign, bad! Perhaps it was because she had, for the last year or so, been so deeply lost in her own life, and often rose up out of one time or place to find herself in quite another, that he had recurred in this way. She'd better shut up and say nothing, give nothing away. She clamped her jaw shut.

'Oh but go on,' Mrs Munt was urging, 'this is fascinating! It's just what I was saying a moment ago. These old people –'

But Aunt Roo had come up, unflustered, solicitous. 'Connie pet, are you all right?'

'Yes Roo, thank you, I was hungry that's all. I got up to see what was in the fridge. I found – well, I don't remember what, but it was very nice. Is that all right?'

'Of course pet. I'll get them to bring you something more.'

'No thank you. But I *am* glad I found Phil. I don't know any of these other people. I was a bit –. You didn't tell me there would be a party. I thought I was in the wrong house.'

'Sorry sweet, I would have if I'd known. But it was – you know – spur of the moment.'

'Did you know Frank Harland too?' Mrs Munt demanded.

But Aunt Roo had already moved away, and Aunt Connie, taking my elbow and drawing me down toward her, whispered aloud: 'Who *is* that woman, Phil?' She glanced quickly at the grey pigtails, the pinafore; it might have been some bigger girl who had tormented her at school. 'Why does she keep talking about that awful man? Is she *senile*?'

Jacky covered her face with her hands and began to laugh.

'Here Auntie,' I said, 'we'll take you into the other room. You remember Jacky, don't you?'

'Of course I do,' she said brightly. 'How are you keeping, dear?' Then with a moan: 'We don't have to have that other one, do we Phil – the Wizard of Oz? Some of these people are such freaks you wouldn't know what to make of them, nobody would.'

We went through into the larger and more formal sitting room and sat at the far end of it under a standard-lamp. The voices of the others seemed far off. There was a view through Norfolk pines to the wide, glittering floor of the harbour where ships were at anchor, solid black, and a late ferry moved, visible only as lopsided windows in the dark. Aunt Connie, looking very frail when she sat, with the flannel nighty drawn about her and her feet in fluffy slip-ons, fell asleep, her head lolling, her jaw shakily ajar.

Widowed now for nearly seven years she lived in a nursing home at New Farm, but every six months or so Aunt Roo brought her to Sydney, just for a change.

Suddenly, waking, she jerked upright, glanced about quickly to see if anyone had noticed her lapse and said: 'What did you say, dear? Did you say something?' She regarded us both as if we were about to provide her, like a child, with some special treat; she sat back, waiting for us to explain why we had brought her here in the middle of the night and were standing before her so solemn and intent.

It occurred to me then that I had never in my life actually sat down and talked to her. She was the one in the family to whom no one ever listened. It had always been so. What impressed me was how little she had changed in all the years I had known her – how under the deep changes she had always been, as she was now, entirely herself, entirely uninteresting. It was, in its way, a kind of triumph. I leaned forward and lay my hand on hers.

'Are you all right, Auntie?'

She smiled sweetly.

Outside, the rest of the party were crowding into the television-room for the late-night news, which would include a replay of the opening of Frank's exhibition, and of course the interview with Frank Harland's father. The old man had been settled in a leather armchair to see himself on TV. The rest stood respectfully about him or leaned in corners against the walls. He would see himself break down and cry, this time in front of thousands.

'Phil dear.'

'Yes Aunt Connie?'

'I'm a little bit worried about your Uncle Jack. He won't know where I've got to, I wasn't expecting all this, it's a surprise party. Could you just slip into the bedroom and tell him – tell him –'

She frowned, and looking at the deep hollow of the nightgown between her knees, its trough of shadow, drew back and began plucking angrily at the fluff of her sleeve.

'Phil,' she said severely as if we had out-stayed a welcome in her house, 'I think I'd like to have a rest now. Could you and Miss – could you put the light out and leave me? I want to think something over. Something has come up. I have to think about it.'

'Are you sure you'll be all right?'

'Yes, of course. You just go on to bed dear and I'll bring you in a nice cup of –'

She looked startled and clamped her jaw shut, pressing her lips together so that all their vertical lines showed. She sewed her mouth up.

I put out the light and she sat then slumped in her chair against the velvet dark, great swathes of moonlit water with the green light of the ferry far out chugging in to the shore. Behind us, the voices of the telecast. Seen through an open door, its metallic light fell on a tabletop and the arm of a leather chair where Clem Harland, that grand old man, was watching himself weep on TV, and wept.

Suddenly Aunt Connie called to us from the other side of the room. She sounded alarmed. But when I stepped towards her she was smiling, her wispy hair lit up against the glass.

'I just wanted to say, dear, isn't this a lovely party? I'm glad they asked me, aren't you?'

And in that moment something remarkable happened. The depression that had been over me all day, which I had first felt in the gallery, in front of Frank's pictures, all their raw edges squared off behind frames, fell from me. I too felt light-headed, light-hearted. And it had to do I thought with the small lost person at the window, so unsure of herself and which house she was in, which life, but happy for a moment to be there, and offering, out of long years, nothing more than this – a bundle of bones and nerve in a flannel nightie under a cloud of hair. I would have gone to her then and tried to show something of what I felt, how important at this moment, and after so long, her ordinary presence was to me, but she had already slipped into some other dream.

'You go to bed, love, I'll be with you in a minute. I've got this –'

She frowned. Then the small duty she had felt pressing, some minor untidiness she had meant to clear up, or rite that had still to be enacted, was forgotten. Her brow cleared. She looked up and laughed.

'Go on and enjoy yourself, you two, I'm happy just sitting. It's such a lovely party. I'm glad they asked me, aren't you?'

Also available in Vintage

David Malouf

THE CONVERSATIONS AT CURLOW CREEK

Winner of the 1996 International IMPAC Dublin Literary Award

'A strange, beautiful novel...The writing is poetic, precise, meditative...It represents a deepening of Malouf's style, offering the reader greater intensity and confirming Malouf's position as one of the most exciting and uncompromising writers now producing novels in English'
Colm Toibín, *Punch*

'In New South Wales in the 1820s, an escaped convict-turning-bushranger and the officer who is to oversee his execution talk, sleep fitfully and talk again all through the night which is to end with the former's death at dawn...The novel opens onto enchanted vistas – memories, dreams, intimations of tenderness and of transcendence'
Lucy Hughes-Hallett, *Sunday Times*

'A compelling and richly rewarding novel'
Helen Dunmore, *The Times*

'Exquisite and intriguing'
Kate Figes, *Elle*

VINTAGE

David Malouf

FLY AWAY PETER

For three very different people brought together by their love for birds, life on the Queensland coast in 1914 is the timeless and idyllic world of sandpipers, ibises and kingfishers. In another hemisphere civilisation rushes headlong into a brutal conflict. Life there is lived from moment to moment.

Inevitably, the two young men – sanctuary owner and employee – are drawn to the war, and into the mud and horror of the trenches of Armentières. Alone on the beach, their friend Imogen, the middle-aged wildlife photographer, must acknowledge for all three of them that the past cannot be held.

'Simply, brilliantly and naturalistically told'
Guardian

'The continuities of nature are set against the obscenities of war...to construct a memorable book'
Sunday Telegraph

'The novel of a poet without a single trace of overwriting'
Daily Telegraph

VINTAGE

David Malouf

AN IMAGINARY LIFE

'Elegant and resonant narrative...an exhilarating
use of language'
Observer

'A brilliantly inventive novel...Malouf puts on a dazzling
literary display in this arresting, original, lyrical work'
Wall Street Journal

'David Malouf, a spare and delicate writer, presents here the
first-person story of the Roman poet Ovid's exile in the distant, frosty wastes...hypnotic in its gripping accumulation
of detail, its gradual unwrapping of human reality amid
what at first seems a barbarian and unknowable environ-
ment. At the centre of this meticulously well-told tale is
Ovid's encounter with a wild boy, brought up among the
deer in the snow'
Sunday Times

'A work of unusual intelligence and imagination, full of
surprising images and insights...One of those rare books you
end up underlining and copying out into notebooks and
reading out loud to friends'
New York Times Book Review

VINTAGE